Prais

"The world of art is ᴜʟᴏᴡɴ ᴡɪᴅᴇ ᴏᴘᴇɴ ɪɴ ᴊᴀʀᴀɴ ᴊᴏꜱᴛ's *The Estate*, as her protagonist's gift for literally entering works of art unlocks a mystery and the truth in a novel that is at once fantastic, romantic, and always exciting."

> —Jonathan Santlofer, author of *The Last Mona Lisa* and *The Lost Van Gogh*

"Sarah Jost has crafted a story that shimmers with intrigue. This is a haunting, twisting plot fueled by obsession, magic, and above all, the extraordinary power and beauty of art."

> —Michael Thompson, author of *How to Be Remembered*

"A thought-provoking meditation on the dubious world of art investment that also delves into the spiritual sphere as sculpture specialist Camille Leray's hidden talent—an ability to tap into the thoughts of a deceased artist—pulls her into a dark and dangerous past. I adored it."

> —Jo Leevers, author of *Tell Me How This Ends*

"Sarah Jost takes an irresistible concept and imbues it with tenderness and introspection. *Five First Chances* is a touching time-loop story that explores the nuances of love, family, friendship, and the beauty of life's imperfections."

> —Margarita Montimore, *USA Today* bestselling author of *Oona Out of Order*

"Jost's brilliant debut is a fascinating exploration of how the choices we make affect our relationships and ultimately our ability to feel good about our lives. Full of hope and heart, this book is a compassionate ode to the beautiful messiness of being human."

—Glendy Vanderah, bestselling author
of *Where the Forest Meets the Stars*

"What rules of physics wouldn't you bend to bring back someone you loved? Sarah Jost's inventive debut is a heart-wrenching emotional roller coaster that asks big questions about how to be at peace with our all-too-short mortal lives. A tender love story tucked inside a larger tale of a woman coming into her own, this lightly magical fable of love won and lost is perfect for fans of Rebecca Serle and Josie Silver."

—Ashley Winstead, author of *The Boyfriend
Candidate* and *The Last Housewife*

"Captivating and poignant, *Five First Chances* is a reminder that every risk we take can bring us closer to the life we were meant to lead. Jost will break your heart but hold on to the pieces with care."

—Annette Christie, author of *The Rehearsals*
and *For Twice in My Life*

"A clever, thoughtful exploration of what could have been— and what might still be if only we had the chance to try again.

In *First Five Chances*, Sarah Jost expertly weaves a compelling time-loop concept with profound themes of friendship, family, loss, and love."

—Shauna Robinson, author of *The Banned Bookshop of Maggie Banks*

"An engaging debut with a time-travel element that allows thoughtful character development and structure. This novel will be popular with romance and domestic-fiction readers and is reminiscent of Matt Haig's *The Midnight Library* and Rebecca Serle's *In Five Years*."

—*Booklist*

"Jost tugs at the heartstrings in her tearjerker debut... Anyone who has ever wished for a do-over will see themselves in Jost's poignant tale of love lost and found."

—*Publishers Weekly*

The
Estate

SARAH JOST

sourcebooks
landmark

Copyright © 2024 by Sarah Jost
Cover and internal design © 2024 by Sourcebooks
Cover design by Sarah Brody/Sourcebooks
Cover photographs © Thammanoon Khamchalee/Shutterstock, Hilda Weges/Arcangel

Published by Sourcebooks Landmark, an imprint of Sourcebooks
P.O. Box 4410, Naperville, Illinois 60567-4410
(630) 961-3900
sourcebooks.com

Cataloging-in-Publication Data is on file with the Library of Congress.

Printed and bound in the United States of America.
VP 10 9 8 7 6 5 4 3 2 1

To my mother, who has always loved Brittany

**Il y a toujours quelque chose
d'absent qui me tourmente.**

There is always something
missing that torments me.

—CAMILLE CLAUDEL,
letter to Rodin, 1886

Prologue

SWIMMING TO THE LIGHT

REDISCOVERY OF A LONG-LOST MASTERPIECE.

THE TIMES, 24 APRIL 2018

A sculpture kept for nearly one hundred years in a private collection has been authenticated as the lost masterpiece of the nineteenth-century French sculptor Constance Sorel.

There are times when reality meets, and surpasses, our wildest dreams. Rob Burton, head of sales at Courtenay has just announced, in an exclusive press conference, that *Night Swimming* has been found. The sculpture was acquired by Mary Pelham's great-grandfather in Paris in the late 1920s and stayed on the family property in Buckinghamshire until the death of her mother last year when Courtenay was asked to value the estate for probate. "We had no idea what we had," Mrs. Pelham said. "I don't think my mother liked the sculpture very much and my father used it as a doorstop."

Constance Sorel was the lover and muse to the uncontested master of late nineteenth-century French sculpture Edmond Boisseau and learned to sculpt under his guidance. After the fallout of their romantic and working relationships, she retired to her cousin's estate in Brittany, D'Arvor Castle. It is there that she allegedly created what she herself called her "masterpiece": *Night Swimming*, the later neglected doorstop of Buckinghamshire.

The excitement of this discovery is linked to the last years of Sorel's life and the mystery surrounding them. The recognition she gained during her lifetime was mainly due to her close association with Boisseau, and after their separation she seems to have slipped quietly into oblivion; her death was recorded by a private doctor in Rennes, in 1923, and the location of her burial was only identified a few years ago. To this day, nobody knows how she went from a confident, assured artist living in a castle to an anonymous body in a pauper's grave. More importantly, there is no record of what happened to her in the last ten years of her life. Of *Night Swimming* there were no sketches, no copies. The only, now famous, mention by Sorel herself is in her last known letter to Anne Foucault, sent during a short stay in Paris in 1913. But it is Boisseau, once more, who laid the groundwork to propel

Night Swimming to fame. In a letter to his art dealer in June 1913, he describes it as such:

Little Constance came to me on her short visit from the country, and to my surprise she brought me some work, like in the golden days—I thought she had made it quite clear that she would not have me help, but here she was. She stood in my workshop with pink cheeks, her wild hair she still doesn't know how to make pretty, in short that fieriness in her that is both her greatest gift and her downfall. There wasn't much in terms of work—she had a few sketches of Arthurian matter, which were quite good but not very far on, but she also brought with her a small sculpture she called Night Swimming. *It was, my dear friend, the best work I have ever laid eyes on by someone who isn't me.*

Night Swimming disappeared without a trace after that, along with its maker. Was it destroyed or stolen? The wildest rumors had it that Boisseau stole it and passed it off as one of his own works, which added to the sensationalism of the story.

Sorel's body of work was rediscovered for itself in the 1990s among a global resurgence of interest in women artists, culminating in 2015 when another Courtenay auctioneer, Camille Leray, published an article about her, "L'oubliée," whose publication alongside the emergence of the Me Too movement finally propelled the forgotten artist into the spotlight. Sorel became a romantic, oppressed, repressed symbol of all women suffering for their love and their art, and *Night Swimming* the holy grail of all the masterpieces that history lost or destroyed. Ms. Leray has since found and sold several of Sorel's sculptures at Courtenay. It is certainly humble success compared to the works of Sorel's famous lover (*read our latest article here: Boisseau's The Yearning sold at Sotheby's New York, for a record-breaking twenty million dollars*) but the rediscovery of *Night Swimming* could set Sorel firmly on the map of the most sought-after artists out there.

Curators and private collectors have fought tooth and nail to be invited to the exclusive showcase of the sculpture at Courtenay's London showrooms ahead of the sale at the end of next month.

We contacted Camille Leray for interview, but she declined to comment.

1

THE TRICK IS to walk in and present yourself as if you belong, as if you are a step ahead of everyone else. As I enter the Courtenay's showrooms on Bury Street, a stone's throw away from Christie's and St. James's Park, I nod to Tabitha, Rob's assistant, in the lobby. She is greeting guests and checking their names off the narrow list, flanked by a security guard and a photographer. I'm not on her list, but of course she knows me; she startles, then nods as I breeze past her. She's checking in a couple—I recognize one of our top clients, who inherited a family fortune made in biscuits that crumble perfectly in your tea. On his arm is a young woman in an Audrey Hepburn black dress, so eager to be here that her face looks about to melt with excitement.

"Congratulations. What a coup." The man accosts me as I brush past.

I ignore him. I'm not here for networking tonight. I'm

trying hard to contain my anxiety, to fake it until I make it, as they say. *Act like nothing's wrong. You are in control,* I repeat to myself, like a mantra. As I ascend to the showcase on the upper floor, I try to make my feet fall with authority. My steps echo hard against the marble, veined with gray like the skin of the dying.

How long before someone tells me I shouldn't be here? *Focus, Camille.* The iPad case tucked under one arm surely would fool most into thinking that I'm here for work, as does the well-cut suit—navy, today, my reliable favorite. My hair was trimmed expensively this morning, its cut just above the shoulders designed to highlight a briskness in its swaying. I know people assume that its copper-redness is intentional, signifying some kind of power and coldheartedness that I let them think I possess. Maybe today my genetics are finally going to come in handy.

Camille Leray—French sculpture specialist, my badge says. *Specialist.* I'm bloody good at this, or I was; I can read it in most eyes as I emerge into the room, all taking a beat to appreciate that the expert has arrived. The one that found *Night Swimming.*

I haven't found it. I'm not doing fine. I look great.

I have barely left the threshold when Rob blocks my way.

"Leray. I didn't think you were coming."

His lips are a tight bar of steel across his face disguised as a polite smile. I recognize it. We've worked together long enough that I should fear it.

Rob is ex-army, if you'd believe it. Well, he briefly "lost his way" (his words) in his early twenties; then military school helped "put his head back together." He trained in business, then found himself in the art world where his true passion had always lain. Though it was thirty years ago, he still looks ready to fight: broad-shouldered, silver buzz cut, a towering six foot five to my five foot three. He also happens to be my boss, and he forbid me to come.

"I'm not one to miss free champagne," I tell him, grabbing a flute from a passing waiter.

"I meant I didn't think you were *invited*."

He stares at me, and to my relief my hand doesn't shake as I take a sip. He wants to say more, but he can't. There are so few people here and the atmosphere is reverential. This is Courtenay's most publicized sale, and our dear clients can't catch a whiff that anything might not be first-rate. I shake my elbow out of Rob's hand, smiling sweetly at him, and walk toward what I'm here to see.

The sculpture.

They're all huddled around it. Biscuit Man is explaining something to his companion about Sorel's signature style: how fluid her women are, always caught in such expressive movements that they seem about to fall, the materials to collapse. He describes Sorel as Boisseau's muse, a "stunningly beautiful" woman, "too gifted for her own good—such a shame she gave up on art, that she couldn't hack it in the end. Must have been hard for a woman then, I suppose." His partner in the Hepburn dress stares at it through the glass case; I cast her a sideways look of solidarity, because he is so awful, but she is enthralled.

He's wrong on many counts, but I have had to accept, in my line of work, that many of those who can afford to buy art are.

Man being wrong, reason one: Sorel was so much more than Boisseau's muse.

Man being wrong, reason two: her signature style isn't just the visuals of her sculptures. It's the *emotion* she makes you feel. She draws you in, and there's a rich, addictive world underneath her works. She speaks to you so directly, from her heart—her art is so personal. There is no other artist like her, and that's why I'm so unprofessionally, personally, obsessed with her. We go back a long way, Constance and I. I've always felt we were tied by so much more than the world of fine art and sales.

Man being wrong, reason three: that sculpture, in the case— the one everybody is looking at—that's not *Night Swimming*.

"Pretty, isn't she?"

Rob is back at my side. He likes being crass about art-works, talking them down to provoke me. I always thought, in the ten years we worked together, that he didn't mean it, but today there's doubt. Things have started to feel cartoon-ish lately, as if I've been losing my grasp on reality. Perhaps Rob doesn't really value art. Perhaps none of them truly appreciate it and I have been deluded all along.

I nod. "Oh, yes."

"So, what is she *telling* you today? Hopefully that she can't wait to be admired by the whole wide world."

He pretends he is joking but there's an edge of threat to his voice. *Don't do anything you might regret, Camille.*

The biggest argument we had about the sculpture was just before the press release. I can still picture the scene; my frustration is still very much alive. Rob was sat very still at his desk, and I stood in front of him, increasingly tense at his refusal to listen to me. "Fuck me, Leray," he said. "The provenance is perfect. You found the photo of it in Boisseau's workshop, you found the note, by his own hand. *Women swimming at night,* C. Sorel, on loan. At the back of a soap order, in his archives—bloody hell, that was a masterstroke, and I wouldn't have expected less from you." He stopped, lowered his voice. "I'm about to press send, and our careers are about to go through the roof. And now you're telling me it's not right? Because of your *hunch*? You need to stop pissing about and accept that we're both bloody geniuses about to roll in gold."

I slammed my hands flat on the surface of his desk, mahogany polished to such a shine that I could see the reflection of my face in it. I hadn't slept for days; shadows had been creeping under my eyes, dulling the gray of their irises. I didn't like my body betraying my interiority, when I had made it my life's work to cover it up. *Reliable, professional, of sharp mind and even temper,* read every single one of my references.

But the statue was wrong, it was dangerous, and nobody was listening. I looked up at Rob, pressing down hard on the desk so my fingers wouldn't tremble. "Something's not right. I'm the leading expert in her work. We've worked together for a long time, Rob. You of all people should believe me." That was an understatement, but I couldn't tell him what had really happened when I tried to access the sculpture the first time. That I had been avoiding it and the toll it had taken, resisting its broken, cursed, and dangerous call ever since.

Rob looked at me with concern rather than anger, and that's when I knew he had stopped taking me seriously. To be fair to him, all the evidence I had found in days and nights of frantic research had, in fact, pointed the attribution to Sorel. "You *don't* know it, Leray, because it *is Night Swimming*. And *that* is the end of your 'doubts,' you hear me?" He banged his desk with every word he emphasized, like a military drum. As I left, he reached for a cloth to wipe off our fingerprints.

But I couldn't let it go. I had worked with Constance's art for years and it had never felt like that. This couldn't possibly be *Night Swimming*, I couldn't bear to see it displayed as such for everyone to see; if I didn't do something, I was allowing them to betray her. For weeks, while things ran their course and the showcase and sale were being organized, my doubts made me spiral slowly into hell. I stopped eating, I stopped sleeping, I barely left the office, going over the facts again and again, trapped.

It all came to a head three days ago: when I came into the office, trying to plead with Rob once more to take the sculpture off the sale.

"I know you don't believe me, but it's—dangerous, Rob. We can't have that out there. And she wouldn't make anything like that." To my shame, I started sobbing. I didn't even know what day it was, when I last slept. All I could think of was what had happened that first time I tried to tap into the sculpture. Rob took one look at my crumpled shirt, my hair sticking out in all sorts of places, my clammy skin. He handled me calmly, almost kindly, which was worse. He said I had been working too hard and told me he was signing me off for a month on "gardening leave." That he didn't expect me to come to the showcase today. He meant that he forbid me to come. Like some of those terrible, awkward fakes we sometimes are asked to look at, I was best locked up inside a shameful cupboard.

"What's the name of your friend again?" I flinched at his (accurate) use of *friend*, singular. "The baker?"

"Lowen."

"Is it Cornwall that he lives in now? Why don't you go and spend a few days with him, you know, get some sea air, blow the cobwebs away."

I nodded, too stunned to really listen to him.

"And, Leray?" His voice caught me again as I slipped out of his office, feeling like I'd just been punched in the gut so hard that there soon would be nothing left of me for the internal bleeding. "You *are* good at this. Maybe a bit too good. Sometimes we can get cocky, and our hunches start to betray us."

———

Rob doesn't know what he's talking about when he mentions my "hunch." None of them have ever known what I can do, and why I appear to be so good at my job.

Fine art is more than the sum of its parts. It's more than catalogues raisonnés, dates that fit the story, gallery archives, sales records, materials and pigments, even skills. Art comes to life in those flashes of human connection; it is a mini-portal from the viewer's soul into an artist's world. To connect with art, to allow it to speak to you deeply, is a spiritual, if not supernatural, experience.

And for me, it is even more so.

Since I was little, I have been able to enter the world of art. As if by magic. When I *tap* into a piece, I'm able to visit the world of the artist's mind when they created it. For a little while, I can walk into their internal, to me very physical, landscape, made of the memories and feelings they poured into that specific piece. Their experiences play out for me on a loop, their emotions imbue everything I walk through. It is something I have come to realize only I can do. A glitch, a wonderful gift once bestowed upon an emotionally starved child.

My gift, and my way of working it, took me years to refine. The first time it happened was with a classmate's drawing in preschool. We had all spent the afternoon drawing clumsy lines barely identifiable as objects from the real world. I wanted the girl next to me, Hannah, to be my friend. I didn't have any friends. I didn't know how to get her to notice me—I yearned for her and her friendship so much that, one afternoon, when everybody else was playing, I crept up to the desk and stared at her drawing. I think I intended to steal it, but as I stared at it, something else happened. It was like my own feelings, my straining to connect with her through what she had made, opened a door that sucked me in. It was mild then, unrefined, but I saw it in my mind's eye: her mother's golden hair and the warmth of her hand on Hannah's head, her doting father, who had just repaired her Barbie, and her ginger cat, Tiffin. I saw that Hannah had intended to draw them as they ate the vanilla-strawberry birthday cake with sprinkles that her mother had made for her. This was so different from my own home life. I would have happily stayed in that loop all afternoon, but our teacher gently nudged me out of it. *Go and play with the others, Camille; it's no good staying by yourself all the time. Everybody needs friends.* I blinked, then approached Hannah and told her how I loved ginger cats and strawberry cakes. We were friends for a whole week after that.

At the beginning I used my gift to do precisely this: try to connect with people, but also enrich my own life with their feelings. The humble, everyday drawings and paintings and bits of arts and crafts became a way for me to escape the drabness of my own family life, its loneliness. It brought color to my existence, taught me feelings my parents weren't sharing: joy, compassion, love.

Until, age nine, I found fine art. Paintings and sculptures that artists had made, whose only function was to be beautiful, to sublimize an aspect of the human experience. That changed everything, opened up a new world whose sensations went much deeper than the love a grandma poured into some cinnamon biscuits in her grandchild's lunch box. The hit was extraordinary—like nothing I had ever experienced. From that point on, I sought the company of the finest works of art. I strained to refine the use of my gift to explore the depths and vivid, detailed worlds of real artists, geniuses whose every breath spurred them to create. Whose raison d'être was to pick up a brush or dig their fingertips into clay, make their vivid internal worlds come to life. Those worlds were limitless, dizzying, addictive.

And it was all thanks to Maxime Foucault, who introduced me to it.

Now, in my midthirties, I have refined my gift, learned to be selective of what I use it for. I've been lucky to carve my way into a career in fine art, and my gift informs my work. My process is controlled, and I work through the steps methodically, like you would put on gloves, open a toolbox, and take the sharp implements out one by one.

First, I must attune to the sculpture. I prefer to be alone; I work best intensely, with no distractions. I start by spending time with the work, observing it, measuring it, starting from the outside until I know it well enough to pierce the surface, and everything else melts away.

As I attune to it, water rises and my real surroundings fade as well as the work itself. I find I'm standing at the edge of a pond at night, full of voices and echoes. When I dive in, I must swim to follow the light at the bottom, emerging into the artist's reality, a symbolic upside-down land of the artist's mind when they made it. It can be a beach, it can be a house, a field, or a dreamlike checkerboard. Over the years, I have managed to attune so precisely that I can conjure the artist, just the way you can will things to life in a lucid dream. Sometimes they say and do things that make part of their memories, the fabric of the piece, but I can't respond. Everything in the landscape is feeling, meaning, and I inhabit it completely, as a witness. I absorb it, understand the piece and its significance to the artist's life.

I call this world "Avalon," no matter what form it takes, the name of the mythical island where King Arthur was taken to rest between life and death. That's the name I chose when trying to make sense of my gift as a young teenager, when I realized this wasn't normal. It took me a while to come to terms with the fact that nobody else seemed to have the same experience. All I could find was Stendhal syndrome, which has never been medically proven, but is rumored to

come on when people are overly affected by artwork, leading
to fainting, confusion, even hallucinations. It wasn't the same
for me, I knew. My experience was too real.

To return to my reality I must swim back, and I regain
awareness with a new understanding of the art. Time works
differently in Avalon; whereas I feel that I spent hours there,
and I come back exhausted and buzzing, on a high nothing
else can come close to. To an external observer, it looks like
I've had a small seizure, some kind of absence lasting only
a few seconds. I know this because Lowen is the only one I
have ever allowed to see the process. I still don't know if he
believed me, even though he said he did.

So I hide my gift, using it secretly for the art I'm in charge
of selling: my ambling in Avalon feeds the story I present to
buyers, allowing me to make the piece come alive with meaning, with emotional relevance. I make sure the art I sell is
personal. I see myself as a conduit, in charge of telling people
the truth about a piece, why it mattered so much to the artist
and why it should matter to anyone who buys it. I'm no different from any other outstanding auctioneer who works
with integrity and cares deeply about the human experience.
Except I always know the truth for sure. Well, until recently.

If anybody in the art world found out about my gift, they
would think I'm mad, some kind of hippiesque charlatan,
and I would lose all credibility as an expert, no matter how
good my knowledge actually is and how many hours of
actual research and labor I've put into building my career.

Over the years, to compensate and hide my insider knowledge, I've made sure to work twice as hard as anybody else to earn my reputation and their respect. At Courtenay, I'm the one everyone jokes about keeping a sleeping bag and hair straighteners in the office. My life is art, appraising and selling. My whole life.

I never thought it would be taken away from me, until this wrong *Night Swimming* landed on my desk. Now I can't look at it without fear, but I can't let it be sold as Constance Sorel's; that sculpture feels like nothing she's ever made, and the night I tried to tap into it left me scarred and terrified. I know I need to try once more to tell them the truth. Even if it has to be desperate and public.

So here I am today, forcing my way to the presale showcase, looking professional on the outside and, on the inside, in a state of disarray. I care about her so much, and what will be labeled as hers. And also…I need them to believe me—the buyers, the experts, the journalists, Rob. I need to know they respect my judgment enough to *listen*. I clutch my hands into fists to stifle their shaking. I know I must resist the pull of the sculpture, keep my head on straight and speak clearly, but I can't stop looking at it.

"Leray. Go home. Remember what we talked about yesterday."

I don't turn to Rob, who is still at my elbow like a bouncer ready to whisk me out of the room any minute.

"This is wrong." I only intended to speak to him, but the

words come out of my mouth loud enough that conversations around us quieten.

"Camille." The warning hisses through his tense jaw.

"What is going on?" Biscuit Man asks behind me, addressing Rob. The man in charge. Rob's hand grips my upper arm.

Murmurs rise behind me, but much harder to ignore, the sculpture is trying to pull me in and I'm fighting to resist it. Sorel's works have always been my comfort zone. Since I found her, I've always felt I understood her. That our lives were connected across time and space. But this—this is something else, so deep and full of destruction, like a black hole trying to suck me in. Normally I can choose when to go, I can control it, but the water is here, risen to my ankles, heavy and wet and empty all at once. I don't want to go in again. I can't—

"That's not right. There's something wrong with it." I aim for a strong, calm professional statement but it comes out as a desperate plea. Rob is escorting me out now and I can only use all the fight in me to stay in this reality, to shut out the dark pond taking shape around me, crawling all over the parquet—rising, rising…

"Wait. Leray, are you OK?" Rob stops. Among the spreading night, a glimpse of his furious yet concerned eyes reach me.

"Please help, I don't want to go in," I whisper to him, trying to cling on to him, but, as if someone has pulled a giant plug or exploded a dam, the water engulfs me.

Oh, God. I'm back in.

It is dark, like it always is, but somehow burning. I have to swim, I know I need to find the bottom, but there is no light—this water is thick like tar, filling my eyes, my lungs. Screams ambush me, distorted sonars through the substance. *Useless. Never good enough. Better off if you died;* hands wrestling me in place while others slap me, hard. It's like sleep apnea, like drowning. It is relentless: the anguish, the violence, the terror, the deepest, darkest kind of primal fear. I am small, and terrified, and vulnerable; I am ten years old, cowering, too scared even to sob. I resist swimming deeper with all my might. *She stole you. She took you away. I miss you. You drowned him. Stay here with me, at the bottom. Let us die together.* Keys locking me in, irons on my ankles, my wrists. My reality smashed into smithereens, the hammer cracking my skull. They're holding me down. I'm going to die, to suffocate, and people want me to—

And suddenly I see her, floating across from me, and her face is terrified, screaming for help. The woman in the Hepburn dress.

Jesus. How is she here? How—her eyes are bulging, she is gasping for air, her hand trying to clutch mine, but she is too far—*No, oh my God, no…* This kicks some life into me, and I fight with everything I have to get close enough to grab her, and my mind wins, in the nick of time; the water recedes, the parquet rises hard to meet my body. I'm prone, feeling like I've landed from a great height, my body burning with the absence of oxygen. Rob is splashing cold water in my face. It gets into my nose—the idiot used sparkling water—I gasp, pushing him away, scrambling on my hands and knees to find enough air.

What happened? It was like the first time I went in, except—except I tried to resist it and couldn't. Did I really pull that woman in with me? That's impossible. I've tried before to show Lowen but it never worked. My ears are buzzing, blood leaving my brain and extremities. Am I going to faint again? Or throw up? I still feel the sludge of darkness on my skin, inside my ears and nose. I feel sticky, heavy, like a bird caught in an oil slick. I look for the woman. I need to ask her...

"Someone fainted!" The shrill call of an emergency helps to bring me back. Rob and I turn at once. The first thing I see are her silver stilettos. She is lying on the floor, motionless, while her useless companion attempts to revive her.

"Camille, what the fuck?" Rob hisses, letting me go as we both rush to her.

"Could this be Stendhal syndrome?" Biscuit Man asks the onlookers, while the security guard props her legs up on someone's bag. I crouch on the floor next to her. Is he right, or have I...done this to her? How did she follow me? I take her hand, patting it gently, praying she just had a funny turn.

"That's fucking made up, mate." I know Rob is beyond crisis mode because he's never sworn in front of a client before.

Finally, she resurfaces. Everybody breathes a sigh of relief, but her first words are not words. She screams. It ripples across the small crowd, scrambling like an army of spiders under our skins. Then she looks straight at me, snatches her hand out of mine. "Get away from me!" I'm sure her eyes aren't the same as they were before. They're bigger, swallowed somehow. She points to the sculpture. The room is silent, the worst kind of silence, as she starts sobbing.

"Get me out of here," she tells her companion, who helps her up. Her legs are jelly and he has to prop her up. "Away from that thing. And away from her!"

Nobody else moves as he walks her out. I turn to Rob, then to the potential buyers. They're all looking at the sculpture, and I swear I see in them a glimpse of that terror, making them back away, slowly, toward the exit. Then Rob shakes his head and springs back to life. "I need to deal with this. Leray, get out. *Now*."

This time, I do. My head is buzzing, nausea rolling through me. I need air. I need—as I exit the room, I turn around, trying one last time to make sense of what happened. It's like the aftermath of a disaster; people seeking each other's support, tending to their unease. Did I do this? Did I bring it all out somehow, whatever wrongness is inside that sculpture?

And that's when I notice him. He's standing at the back but, unlike everyone else, isn't cowering away, or gulping champagne as if to build up courage. He is looking straight at me, and I can't believe I didn't notice him before. When did he arrive? How could I have missed him?

Maxime Foucault.

I can't help it; for a second, despite the urgency of getting out of that room, I turn to him like a sunflower drawn to his features, to the warmth of his utter charisma and the desperate way I have missed him. He's not smiling at me. His eyes are probing, clever, calm.

I don't see him in fifteen years, and he finally turns up to see me crash our biggest sale?

Shame breaks the spell and I stumble down the stairs. I hurry away as if I am leaving a burning building, the walls melting around me, threatening to close me in. I run to try and escape the mental image of the woman floating in the dark pond, her mouth opened in a silent scream.

My power has never been dangerous before. To me, or to others.

But now, it might be.

2

ROB'S EMAIL COMES a week later, the day after the auction, at the same time as the news article. The masterpiece nobody wants—can Night Swimming be cursed? I've been on my sofa for days.

"It's not *Night Swimming,*" I mutter as I close the browser tab, revealing my open mailbox and allowing Rob's words to hit me full in the head.

Subject: end of contract.

I click to read the message. He must be joking. This must be a tantrum. With immediate effect due to gross misconduct. He copied HR in. When I close my laptop, I know I have to let the realization sink in.

I don't work at Courtenay anymore. Before worrying about the mortgage on my extortionate London one-bedroom flat, "merely a hop away from Kensington High Street and Hyde Park," a thought comes, clear and pure as rain on a hot evening: my career is over. All the late nights studying, all that time spent looking for rare articles and visiting obscure collections, weekends spent doing the jobs nobody wanted, wading through hoarders' houses to evaluate their contents, working my way up in the auction house to my dream job were all for nothing.

My whole life has gone.

It was going to go wrong sooner or later. They were going to realize you're unstable, away with the fairies. I don't know why they gave you the job in the first place. Maman's voice in my head. My least favorite of the voices. She spoke every time something went wrong. When she found out I had been awarded a full scholarship for the boarding school they had wanted me to get into (no way would my parents have been able to afford school fees, but they wanted me out of the way), she acted as if she was disappointed by the school's poor standards. Then she waited for the first report I didn't get one hundred percent on to prove that she had been right.

And now it is the same again. Although Maman died ten years ago, I can always count on her in these moments.

Here in my living room, the sound of passing cars reaching me through the open window, I am once more swimming in the dark—but in a darkness of my own making. I replay what happened at Courtenay once again. Did they all recoil because of me, not my gift? Because of how unhinged I acted? Did it all just—*get* to me, like Rob said? The pressure of tight deadlines when millions of pounds are at stake isn't for the weak. It finally leaked out of me—my fear, my brokenness—and I thought I had it all under control. Maybe what I saw in the sculpture were my own issues, my own weaknesses, my own wrongness. I projected them onto the first thing that I couldn't understand because I just wasn't good enough. *They should have never hired you, never trusted you. They finally saw the truth about you.* I was never worthy of my gift.

———

I don't have to go to work anymore, so there goes my perception of time. I leave my email open on my laptop, hoping for some kind of ping to bring me back to reality—Rob begging me to come back as Courtenay simply can't function without me. But it lies there quietly for days until I notice it's disconnected. I type my name and password again. *Unknown username.* They didn't waste time kicking me out of the system. More time passes as I cry on the sofa, then on the floor.

I fall into a routine. I wake up in my bed around 7:30 a.m., then remember in a pang why my alarm did not go off. I stare at the ceiling awhile, until I'm too stressed by its blank canvas. What's next? How can there be a *next* when I'm feeling this bad? Then I get up, put on a robe (if I'm feeling fancy), and walk to the sofa, turning on Netflix and pressing "watch again" on BBC's *Pride and Prejudice*. Sometimes (if I'm feeling *really* fancy) I might spend an hour or two rewinding and rewatching the pond scene over and over again. I don't really feel hunger, but when I know, rationally, that I ought to eat, I go scavenge in the cupboards. I'm not a cook—never had time to make anything when I was working—so the offerings are meager. I soon run out of peanut butter.

It must have been two weeks or a bit more, I think. I have allowed my phone's battery to run out completely. No point without the work emails or calls about an exciting piece brought in for valuation... When I quickly scan myself, like in that mindfulness class Courtenay made us all take during our lunch breaks a couple of years ago, I realize my overriding emotion is fear. I don't even know what of; it's a sticky kind of dread, something clinging to me and clouding every thought I have, every action I propose to take. My nervous system is in overdrive, my heart beating that bit too fast, my body both too cold and too hot.

I'm trapped in it, and thinking about the fear only seems to make it worse.

I try to conjure my happy place: D'Arvor's grounds and turrets, the lake glistening in the sunlight. But I can't conjure it without thinking of Maxime Foucault, its owner, and remembering that he too had witnessed my demise, so the fear sparks up all over again.

Perhaps I should text Lowen. Perhaps Rob was right when he mentioned him. Lowen has been my best friend since the start of secondary school. *Was.* Is? He wouldn't have tried to get in touch because of what he said to me last time we met, and how I received it. It's not been the same between us since then, but I didn't expect it to be. I knew we both needed some distance, and him moving back home to Cornwall provided that. But perhaps this counts as an emergency?

Lowen and I always wanted our lives to be such wildly different shapes and colors, we might as well have been painting, he a Dutch still life of fruit, and I a Botticelli. And there's this way he used to look at me every time I talked about work, as if he was readying the dust brush and pan to come and pick up the pieces. He is the best person I know, the best I have ever known, the only person I've ever bared my soul to, but he can be a patronizing twit.

No, I need to sort out my mess by myself. Like always. So I take a deep breath, grab my laptop, shake my arms, which have fallen asleep for lack of use, and open my personal email.

The fifty unread messages make my heart skid, my palms sweat. I don't look at them. I know nobody uses my personal address and all I receive is special offers, beribboned in we've missed you, targeted at lonely single women in their thirties. As if I was going to buy a mop just to feel like someone is happy with me. I open a blank message to Rob.

I can't believe you've done this to me, I type with one hand, the other plunging a spoon into a jar of Nutella. I had been saving the Nutella for a special occasion and this is it. Call it anger fuel.

The response pings almost immediately. I shouldn't be talking to you, Leray. But I hope you're OK.

When can I come back from my "gardening leave"? The leaves are gardened to the max and I am suitably contrite. Surely I can help fix things? We can have another go at the sale? I'm fully on side, I promise.

The thought of ever working with that sculpture again covers me in a cold sweat, but I'm desperate. I need to be back, working with art; I'll have to figure the rest out later.

Rob's answer is not the one I was hoping for. Again, I'm not supposed to communicate with you. But I think you need to know. That woman, the one who fainted? She's in a psychiatric hospital. A proper breakdown. And her partner is blaming us—he's in a right state, throwing threats and demanding compensation all about the place. So I would lie low if I were you. You're the last person who can fix this whole mess.

I stare at the email, the semblance of a grip I had managed to gather dissipating once more.

It wasn't in my head, then. It was real—it hurt her. *I* have hurt someone.

A few minutes pass, which I spend groaning into a sofa cushion, feral like a cat. I imagine Rob must have felt bad for me, because another email comes.

Listen, I'll write you a decent reference. That's the best I can do for you. I hope it's enough. Please go through HR next time.

I whimper with anger and am about to shut my laptop

when my eyes catch sight of an unread email a few lines down, sent three days ago, more precisely the subject of the message.

On behalf of Maxime Foucault.

The effect is so instant that I sit up straight, forgetting the slump my back has now adopted as its natural curve. I brush some crumbs off my pajamas, straighten my hair, run my fingers under my eyes as if suddenly Maxime can see me here, on my sofa. I press pause on *Pride and Prejudice*.

Maxime Foucault's hair might be lighter than Mister Darcy's (though equally tousled); he might have a bit more of a sense of humor, be more *agreeable*, as Jane Austen might have put it. But deep down, he is just as broody, charismatic, and kind. Plus he owns the most impressive castle in Brittany. His family is rich, of course, but also fascinating, and private, and down-to-earth, in a "we escaped the French Revolution with our heads on our shoulders and managed to live our lives in a preserved and respected French aristocracy because nobody would ever mess with us" kind of way.

He is, in short, something else. Tossed together by the randomness of fate, we have met before on a few occasions I will never forget. He was at Courtenay, and now this?

I feel warmth spread across my cheeks and I bring the back of my hand to them. My hands are too hot; my childhood eczema has started to flare up again. *He can't see you, Camille. And why would he remember you? It is likely to be a coincidence.* I go back to the sofa to open the email.

Dear Ms. Leray,

I am writing on behalf of Maxime Foucault. He wishes to invite you to his residence, le château D'Arvor, in order to appraise some artworks from the estate. Mr. Foucault would much appreciate consulting your expertise in this matter and about the sculptures themselves, which have only very recently come to light and he suspects to be by Constance Sorel. As you most likely know, she was a distant relative of the Foucault family and lived some years in the castle. It is Mr. Foucault's understanding that you might have some availability in the coming weeks. All expenses will of course be covered.

Sincerely,

Anaïs Garnier, assistante

I don't waste any more time, typing with fingers made erratic by adrenaline:

Apologies for the delayed response. I would love to come and discuss appraising the estate. Would Thursday next week be suitable? A first appraisal can take up to a day, depending on the number of works. Happy to share my initial thoughts with Mr. Foucault, then communicate any further findings via email.

I press send, then throw myself back against the cushions. All these years, and even through email, even indirectly, he still undoes me. *It's work, Camille. Like any other request.* I try to rationalize, but I can't. It's him, but not only him—it is D'Arvor as well, and Constance. The one estate on earth that has held my heart for nearly thirty years, keeping it going by pumping it quietly with longing. How long have I been hoping for this exact email—how many articles or mentions of my name in prestigious sales did I hope he would notice? And he chooses now.

I'm about to close the laptop when a response pings through.

Camille,

So professional of you, but I'll need you for more than half a day. Can you spare a week? I'll make it worth your while, I promise.

M.

That's him. That's come directly from his personal email address. A *week*? What does he want to talk to me about that would justify a whole week spent in his castle in a professional capacity?

And "some artworks" by Constance Sorel, plural? There it is—a hint of aliveness in me again, finally.

I don't know if Maxime and I have *history*. That might be too small a word for me and much too big a word for him, if he were to be asked. I don't know if he remembers meeting me at all or if he's simply reaching out to the leading expert on the artist he is appraising. But there are coincidences in life that, when you pay attention, have to be more than that, *have* to be fate, some kind of design that makes perfect sense, even if you don't know what sense yet. He might easily have forgotten our meetings, but every one of them has been formative to me.

A month ago, I would have been over the moon to receive his invitation. I would be straight out the door, gone shopping for castle-compatible outfits, thinking my life had finally given me the opportunity I deserved. I would be prepped to meet him again and show him the woman I have become: a bloody hardworking, tough heroine who takes no crap. Someone who has managed to engineer her career so well, it has culminated in her long-term dream man—begging for her expertise.

But now I'm broken, out of the game, and worse: I am afraid. What I felt when I tried to tap into *Wrong Night Swimming* hasn't dissipated. How I struggled to get out of it and back to reality is lingering in me. In some ways, that first night, working alone with it, was worse than the showcase. I couldn't find the light. I had sunk deep into that horrible lake of death, unable to breathe. It was like being a child locked up in a closet again, with no air. I was trapped, my lungs burning, tears streaming from my eyes, the voices telling me how disgusting, pathetic I was. I woke up on the office floor and realized I had passed out for hours. It was the first time I'd been "absent" for more than a few seconds, and the first time I hadn't been able to control my entry and return.

Get a grip, Camille. I go to reread the emails, startling at this seemingly innocent statement I glossed over before: *It is Mr. Foucault's understanding that you might have some availability in the coming weeks.*

His most recent face flashes in my mind again, his calm, perceptive demeanor as I ran from the showcase. His elegant silhouette framed by the window, his head of burnt-caramel curls, determined jaw, and those eyes—almost supernatural, sharp like the edges of an emerald. If he found some potential Sorels in his castle, it makes sense that he would have come to check out the sale, to see how it might affect the value of his pieces. Perhaps he came in at the very end. Perhaps he didn't see me act unhinged, disruptive, and he thinks it's all a terrible mistake. He must have given me the benefit of the doubt—he wouldn't have contacted me otherwise. But how can I face him right now, when my gift is suddenly out of my control? When there is a real possibility that I could be a danger to myself and others when in the presence of art? The memories of being trapped, drowning in *Wrong Night Swimming,* are so physical that I find myself gasping for air. That woman's horrified face, her black dress tight like a rope around her neck. I think we could have died in there. I think… What if I don't get out next time? What if I hurt him or his family?

Him wanting to meet with me, inviting me to D'Arvor, has been my dream for years. And now it's happened—it's the worst possible timing.

I can't go right now; I'll ask for more time. I'll find some treatment—there must be some pills out there that can stabilize me, take the edge off my dread, perhaps even dull my gift or impede it temporarily. I'll tell Maxime that I'm under the weather and I'll go when I'm back to normal, able to handle whatever curveball he is going to throw at me, because this visit could never be straightforward. Not for me, anyway.

For now, I decide it is best to try my new strategy of rolling into a little ball and pretending the world beyond my flat doesn't exist. That I can stay here forever, as long as I want, and that I haven't counted that I have exactly five months of mortgage payments until my savings are wiped out. I feel around for the remote, press play on Mr. Darcy again, whispering my question at him: *What am I going to do?*

The answer doesn't come from Regency England, but from the doorbell.

3

FOR THE SECOND time today, I scramble to sit up straight, taking in my surroundings in a panic. The flat is a mess. I sniff the air, trying to figure out if the visitors are my neighbors alerted by some kind of smell, but I remember that I did have a shower this morning (I was feeling combative), and that my flat gets so hot from April to September that I leave the windows permanently cracked open.

I gingerly approach the door to peer through the spyhole; then my hesitation melts away. I open the door and fling myself at him.

"Bloody hell, Cam," Lowen says, and he sounds angry but holds me nonetheless. The contact of another human body startles me after days of seeing, let alone touching, no one. The contact with *him* startles me after months of living a five-hour drive away from each other. Startling in a way that makes me want to stay like that, being hugged tight by him, until the end of time. Lowen always brings me back to an earth I don't mind living on.

We stay like this a few moments until he holds me out at arm's length.

"Good to know you're alive."

"Why are you angry with me?" I ask.

"I'm not angry."

That's not true. I know him like I know, when I'm outside, if it's sunny or raining.

"You didn't tell me you were coming."

He sighs. "I rang you. I texted you. Many times over. Where's your phone?"

I nod to the sofa, the most likely place it might be. Dropped between the cushions, perhaps? I can't remember the last time I charged it. "Ah."

"Will you let me in?"

"Not if you've come to tell me off."

He ruffles his brown hair with one hand, a familiar gesture that gives his mane its tendency of sticking out a bit. Alongside his hazelnut eyes, lined with thick eyelashes I'm rather jealous of, the hair gives him, even in his midthirties, a perpetually boyish vibe. I take him in fondly, even the things I normally tease him about: the old band T-shirt and those nonsensical tattoos that started to creep down his forearms as soon as he left the corporate world for the wonderfully hipster universe of wheat. He's still a bit gruff. "I've come to make you dinner." And then, when he sees the light in my eyes, he fights to stifle a smile. "You still like food, then."

"You know what?" I finally step aside to invite him in, my stomach grumbling. "I think I do."

He kicks his trainers off outside the door. He's always been respectful like that—something his mum taught him. His whole family is amazing. I wonder why I haven't visited them more often in recent years. I sit at the tiny kitchen table as he opens a plastic bag that I somehow managed to miss entirely, sighing at the lack of kitchen equipment in my cupboards.

"I'm glad you're here," I tell him as he sets up a chopping board and a wok. "But remind me why you're here?"

He produces alien offerings like mushrooms, a piece of meat, noodles crackling in a packet. I watch him grab a knife and slice a pepper, the tattoos undulating on his forearms as his muscles move. He is precise, fast. I love to eat; he loves to cook. In that respect, we're an excellent team.

"I was worried about you."

Lowen and I go back a long way. We found each other in boarding school, the only two kids in our year on full scholarships, both clever and studious and from families who couldn't afford the school, feeling utterly out of our depth. I can't even remember how our friendship started; it just *appeared*, the way care packages of Harrods truffles and branded trainers materialized for our dorm-mates, and it lasted. Perhaps our backgrounds had glued us together, as if the two of us, united, could better weather all the comments about second homes in Barbados and how tedious it was looking after a horse. We weren't bullied, but we didn't fit. Lowen was taller than the other boys, I was colder and more bookish than the girls, and that granted us some kind of distant respect that also kept us from being properly adopted by the rest.

Lowen's home in St. Ives, a stone's throw from his father's tiny bakery on Loe Street, was a bit too small for his family, which somehow made it perfect and homey in every way. His Sundays were spent surfing on Porthmeor Beach and eating corned beef sandwiches; his dad ran the bakery, but it was his mum who made the Saturday afternoon scones. They would be gobbled up hot from the oven as soon as Lowen and his three brothers tumbled back in, a gaggle of sturdy boys, brown hair sticking out and matted with salt. When he invited me to spend the summers with them, I stumbled into the exact opposite of my own universe and kept looking at his childhood with the amazement of a kid in a sweetshop.

"I wish we could go back to being teenagers," I tell him now.

His back is turned, but I can tell he's smiling. "Not for me, thanks."

"But…your mum's scones?"

"I see. My stir-fry not good enough for you?"

His tone is lighthearted, but his gaze falls on my little

cemetery of empty jars—the tombstones of my dinners for the past week or so.

"Seriously, Cam, you need to start taking better care of yourself."

He's right, but it also annoys me that he says it. There it is—our familiar dynamic. "I've been doing perfectly fine, thanks."

"That's not what your boss seems to think."

At that, the lightness slips out of the conversation. "Rob called you?"

"I'm still your emergency contact, apparently."

He's tossing vegetables into the pan, to a great sizzling sound and even greater aromas of toasted sesame and caramelized chicken. My mouth waters though I'm appalled.

"Well, he's not my boss anymore—he had no right to send me a babysitter."

"I saw the article about the sale and figured—I called you but your phone was off. I tried to call you at work, and he said you're not working for them anymore. Then he said I better check on you."

"As you can see, I'm OK." I close my eyes as flashes of the showdown in Courtenay fight their way into my brain. The woman next to me, screaming. Levels of blood-mud rising in me, choking me, making a mark that can't be erased.

I shiver. A change of subject is needed. "How is it going back home?"

"Good. I mean Dad is living up to his title of bread tyrant.

He bosses me about in that tiny back room like I'm twelve again." He smiles. After the stroke that could have taken his dad, we both know being bossed about is a good thing.

"Do you ever… think about doing your own thing?" I ask, tentatively.

He shrugs. "Not a chance. It is *James's and Son*."

He places a steaming plate of noodles in front of me. I swear he is a magician—it looks exquisite, and I'm hungry but also ashamed. Lowen is the person who knows me best in the world, but I still don't like being vulnerable in front of him. I don't like him knowing that I've messed up so massively, that after all the years of arguing with him about my job, I got fired. The *I told you so* is looming, as large as my appetite for his cooking.

Lowen always says that he doesn't get art. But it isn't that he hates it; if you put him in front of the right piece at the right time, it will speak to him too. I know because I saw him suddenly develop a burst of violent "hay fever" in front of Delacroix's *Orphan Girl at the Cemetery*. It's the art world that he hates. He hates the poshness of it, the astronomical sums of money, the power games. In art, Lowen mainly appreciates craft, dedication, skill. A strong message. We used to argue about this a lot, when I defended my job and he maintained that I was a cog in a big heartless machine.

He's not eating. He's watching me through those damn eyelashes. "You're trying to change the subject. I know you're not OK," he finally says. "That job is your whole life."

Does it sound like a jibe? "So is yours," I say. "You dropped everything for it." I immediately regret saying it, but I hold his gaze through the steam, until the appetizing smell wins and I plunge my fork into my noodles.

"Not the same," he says quietly.

I'm so glad he is here. I want to avoid our old quarrels.

"You might be right," I concede. "I don't think I'm *that* OK."

The mood shifts to something a bit more open, a bit more honest, and I start wondering how long I haven't been doing fine for, actually. If it's just since *Wrong Night Swimming* that I've started to struggle, or if it all started before. Seeing Lowen properly for the first time in three years makes me realize the gulf that has grown between us, because we've let it. *I* have let it. Him moving away gave me another reason to plunge myself into work. Weekends stopped being an opportunity to rest and socialize, and became a good time to go to the office because it was quieter. There was so much to do that my working week needed to stretch to evenings, then six, seven days. And so my life continued to slip quietly into a world of clay and bronze and might have petrified itself.

Maybe Lowen did help keep some other parts of me alive. I can feel the words start bubbling up, all the things I should have told him, that I want to tell him now.

"I've missed you," I say.

His lips lift, but there's a touch of something else in his eyes. Resignation? Nostalgia? It makes me want to brush over that version of his self-portrait with a different color.

"Same, Cam."

We look at each other and I know both of us are thinking about the night when he told me he was moving away, in this very flat. The night of my thirty-second birthday... It makes me wonder about all the doors I've shut because of my job and the life I thought I wanted.

Lowen abruptly gets up and goes to the sink, starts filling it with hot water, steam soon creeping up his forearms.

"I have a dishwasher," I tell him.

"I know." He grabs a sponge and starts scrubbing. After a while, he asks: "So, are you going to tell me what happened?"

It feels good to talk to him again, so I tell him about Courtenay's *Night Swimming*, about knowing it couldn't be a Sorel when I tried to tap into it. I gloss over the showcase, tell him I lost my job because I disagreed with Rob on the attribution. I don't tell him that I couldn't resist the sculpture's call, that I feel I nearly died in it. I don't tell him about the woman in the Hepburn dress, her companion threatening to sue. I keep to myself that I'm terrified I'll never again be able to look at art without hurting myself or someone else.

His voice is drowned in the splashing of water and the rattle of cutlery. "Has it never happened to you before?"

"What? Losing my job? You know it hasn't." I can still feel the dread pulsing in me. I hide my shaking hands under the table.

Lowen is the only person on earth who knows about my gift. I loved my summers in Cornwall with him and his family. They filled my heart with love and warmth, and I didn't know how to repay them. One stormy night, I told him about a sketch his grandfather had made that was hanging above the fireplace. It was a humble pencil drawing of a fishing boat. I told Lowen about his grandfather's PTSD from the war, and how he found peace watching the boats in St. Ives Harbour. How much he loved sitting there with his son, Lowen's dad, holding his hand in the sun, wind, and rain, eating hevva cake. How those were the times he felt peace, stitching his heart together thread by thread. Lowen never knew his granddad, but he immediately believed me. He was the one who told me it was a gift, not something that marked me as weird, deficient. I don't think he still feels the same now. He certainly wouldn't if I told him the whole truth about what happened at the showcase.

It's taking up so much space, Cam. I don't know what emotions are yours; I don't even know if you're allowing yourself to have any. I feel like I'm losing you.

"No—coming across a fake. That would mess you up, wouldn't it, with your—*way* of getting into the art?"

Though I hate that he can't bring himself to mention my gift openly, the fact he believes me so completely derails me.

"I guess it would," I say, tears prickling out of nowhere.

"I'm sorry. I know how much finding *Night Swimming* meant to you."

"Lowen...I just don't want to feel like that ever again."

I want to feel safe. I want to put everything that's just

happened in a little box and forget about it. Lowen leaves the sink and comes around to my side of the table, puts his arms around my shoulders. He is standing, I am sitting, and I bury my face against his T-shirt and cry.

Last time I cried like that was here, on my birthday, three years ago. With him.

—

"I have to go, Cam," he said. We were sitting on my sofa, the TV playing softly. He'd made me a birthday cake that neither of us had an appetite for. I remember it was raining and steam was rising inside the windows, shutting out the world.

"But you'll be back?" I asked. I was in shock. His dad had had a stroke six months prior and Lowen had, understandably, spent a lot more time in St. Ives. But his dad was doing so well that he was almost fully recovered, and Lowen had been back at work, in London, spending my free Friday nights at mine, watching the silliest action movies we could find, the only genre where our tastes overlapped.

He shook his head. "They need me," he said.

"I know, but...for how long? I thought your dad was doing much better."

Not my finest moment, I knew even then, but I was petrified at the thought of losing him. We had been inseparable in school, then only apart briefly when going to uni—and still, we would call each other all the time and spend most holidays together, either with his family or in my house when my parents were away. (I didn't want to subject Lowen to my family life when we were all under the same roof. Also, knowing him, he would have stood up for me, but it would only make things worse.) Then, as soon as possible, we had moved to London.

"He needs help with the bakery."

"And you're the only one who can do it?"

"*Cam.*" He was right to put his foot down.

"Sorry."

"The thing is…" He brought up his hand, absent-mindedly, to his hair. I'd never seen him so nervous, looking almost harassed. As if he hadn't slept for a week. He didn't have the tattoos then, and I could trace one long blue vein on his forearm. "I think that's what I want to do. Bread, pastries, the lot. I think I would be good at it."

"You'd be amazing." I spoke with the fervor I knew he deserved. He'd always loved cooking, had spent most of his life helping his dad in the bakery and his mum in the kitchen. "That's not the question."

"Thanks," he half smiled. "But what is it?"

The cake. I wasn't in the habit of doing this, but his news had shocked me. I stared at the beautiful opera cake he'd made—the thin, precise layers of chocolate, coffee, and genoise—and something took shape. What he had felt as he worked on it. I was shaking, so I bent forward to set my drink back on the coffee table. As soon as I did, Lowen caught my hand in his, and I startled at the contact of my cold fingers, which had just held a glass full of melting ice, against his warm, dry palm. "Cam," he repeated. "What's the question?"

We didn't hold hands; we had never been tactile friends. It felt weird. It felt like he was changing something. I tried to back off from what I'd sensed about the cake. I wasn't ready for that.

"I don't know," I said. "I'll just miss you, I guess."

"I'll ask *you* a question then," he said, and I shifted, unsure, my hand still in his. My first impulse was to shrink away. Something rose in me that I was pretty sure was apprehension, the urge to stop the conveyor belt we sat on. I knew what he would say would change everything we had. "Will you come with me?"

"What?"

He was sitting next to me, knees open, his elbows on his thighs, his head bent, gently prying my fingers apart and examining my hand as if it was a precious object he had just dug out of the ground. He wasn't looking at me, but I knew how he felt, because he had written it in a delicate creation of chocolate and eggs.

This is why you stick to fine art, I reminded myself.

"I think I love you," he said.

———

Right now, three years later, I realize Lowen is the only person who has ever made me feel safe. My whole world has shattered, but he used to be my rock, and now he is here.

He is still holding me, drawing slow circles on my back. My eyes shut tight against his chest; I bring a hand up to the nape of his neck.

He stills.

"Cam?" His voice is muffled but he doesn't pull back.

I don't think. I just—I open my eyes, use my hand to coax his head down, his lips toward mine. I want to drink him in as an antidote, I want to perform some kind of magic, restore me and us to what we used to be, bring myself back to when my life was brimming with success and possibilities.

Our lips merely graze; then he comes to life. That is, he throws himself away from me, as if a spring has propelled him to the other end of the room. He presses one hand on the table between us, holding the other one out as if to stop whatever dangerous move I might make next.

I stand there, heart beating in my throat, cheeks burning.

"No." His response is hoarse and strangled.

I can't bear this silence, and I know I should explain myself, so I say the stupidest of all things. "You said you loved me."

I see his eyes widen with confusion, and I want the upstairs flat to flood and the ceiling to burst and to be washed away into the street, down into the sewers, to the sea—*gone*.

He doesn't say, *That was three years ago.* He says something kinder, something worse. "You've been through a lot, and you're not yourself."

And I can only agree. As he fills the kettle, the humiliation takes hold, spreading like the aftermath of banging your funny bone, but I know. I know that in a day or a week, or more likely, about ten years, I'll feel grateful that he turned me down. That it was the kind thing to do.

We don't say anything while he makes the tea, tutting at the absence of milk in the fridge, then opening the small bottle he's brought. I'm so caught up in what has just happened that I don't realize he's only filled one mug until he places it in front of me.

"You're not having any?" I'm relieved there is a simple question I can ask, with a straightforward answer. *Yes* or *no*. Something concrete. Not like, *Why did we never try to save our friendship after I turned you down three years ago? You were an idiot back then. I was an idiot just now. Can we just call it even and go back to the way it was? Put a Jason Bourne on and I'll make up the sofa bed for you?*

He shakes his head. "I have to go back."

I nod. Lowen works six days a week, with a 4 a.m. start, but I feel sick at the thought of my flat returning to what it was this morning: bare, only filled with my own thoughts. I didn't used to be scared of being alone, because I could always conjure the company of the artists I was working on to keep me focused. I miss that feeling of always being able to escape into other worlds, other people's problems.

"I'll be off, then."

I follow him to the front door, watch him bend to put his trainers on. I know there was more food in his bag and that he has left it behind on purpose. Besides that, he's come with nothing. He really wasn't planning on staying, and that makes me sadder than anything else.

"Lowen?"

His hand is poised on the latch. He turns around.

"Yeah?"

I don't want to cry again. I've cried more in the past two weeks than I have in my whole life and it is highly unsettling. I look away because seeing his face fall with that kind of resigned worry is more than I can bear. I don't want to think about the years that have carved that precise expression without me even realizing until now.

"I mean it. I'm sorry for everything."

"Ah, don't trouble yourself. Take care, OK?"

He hesitates, then his hand presses my shoulder, fast and hot, and in a metallic click, he opens the door, and I hear his footsteps rattle on the stairs, taking him out of the building, long after he must have gotten to Paddington Station.

I stay like that, my forehead on the door, for a long while. I wonder what my life would be like right now if I had gone with him to Cornwall. Could we have gone as friends? I know me trying to kiss him wasn't some kind of epiphany, the unveiling of long-dormant lust, but a manic blind rush toward that feeling of being loved, being safe, along with the burning need for something to happen. I was extremely unfair to Lowen. I don't know how he puts up with me. But he didn't; he left.

What should I do now? What *can* I do?

Then, as I tap my head softly against the door hoping this might reset me somehow, I remember Maxime's email. The invitation.

Some artworks from the estate...which have only very recently come to light.

I'll make it worth your while, I promise.

Right now, at my lowest, it hits me. Why he might have emailed me exactly now, just after the failed sale.

Oh my God... has Maxime got the real *Night Swimming*?

Even if there is the smallest chance that he thinks he has found it, he might see me as the only one who would believe him and put things right.

This might be the reset I need. If I were to find Constance's authentic masterpiece, everything would be restored. My reputation would soar to even greater heights. I would be back on track, and more.

And also, a promise from Maxime... His green eyes, his hands pulling me up. *Thank you for saving me.* A shiver climbs up my spine.

Right. I peel myself off the front door and set out to pack my bags.

4

LATE-AFTERNOON LIGHT MOTTLES the carriage as the train glides through the Breton countryside. The Paris-Rennes fast train is busy; it is the summer holidays here, and families with sun hats and baguettes have invaded all nooks and crannies of the carriage. I'm sharing my four-seater with a mother and her toddler, who is pressing his face against the window and running a commentary on everything he sees—*cows, woods, trees, fields, tractors.* His mother speaks quietly into the phone, a glossy magazine splayed open on her lap.

"*Oui,*" she says in her native French, "we're arriving at sixteen fifty-three. Yes, in front of the station. See you soon, Dad. I can't wait for you to meet Lucas."

She can't be older than midtwenties, makeup free. She glances at her son, peeling some stray curls off his forehead. I wonder what their story is—why her father wouldn't have met her child until now. She feels my gaze, cocks her head, and looks me straight in the eyes, defiant. I turn back to the window, thinking of the loving, yet absent-minded way she stroked her son's hair.

Maman wouldn't have stroked my hair; I heard her explain many a time to her friends, even to strangers, that French children were less spoiled than British ones, less pandered to, and turned out better for it. She certainly set out to apply that rule to her dealings with me. I was a surprise, she told me. I don't think my parents hadn't wanted me; I just think they hadn't considered that children might take up some space in their relationship.

As a family, we spent every summer in Brittany. Rennes, where I'm headed now, would often be our base. The biggest city in Brittany, with a lively center, ideally connected to all the Breton places of interest by bus or train, it was also where my mother's family was from.

I haven't been back since I became old enough for my parents to leave me behind, and I didn't expect the train journey to conjure our trips so strongly—the small station platforms, the fields blurring into one another. These holidays always felt sad, but necessary, and as a child I never quite understood why on either count. Maman's emotions were as opaque to me as sea glass; I could see their colors but not their original shape or provenance. Maman's grandfather, who had brought her up, had been a gardener at D'Arvor. I remember Dad holding her hand as she wept, staring at the deep carpet of ferns under the oak trees of Brocéliande, then turning around to catch a glimpse of the castle's roofs. She was even more brittle here—emotions would get the better of her at unexpected times—yet she kept bringing us back. As a child, she would have only ever watched the castle from the grounds, knowing there was more than one invisible barrier separating her from them. But somehow she couldn't let the place go, even though she had no family left there. We were supposed to be her family now, or at least Dad was; they dragged me along with them out of necessity, just like another suitcase.

On every single one of our trips, we visited D'Arvor, but of course we could only roam the public part of the estate. The footpaths darting in and out of the forest, outside of the river, offered tantalizing glimpses of the stunning castle in the distance. I think Maman's longing would sometimes make us creep a bit off-path, but we wouldn't cross the line of the water.

Except that one time.

You could never know what mood Maman was going to be in when around the castle. When she wasn't crying, she would say strange things, allude to the supernatural, which, with no particular explanation or context given, made a great impression on me as a child. I thought D'Arvor's estate was teeming with fairies, korrigans, and ghosts. They would gather in and around the lake at the edge of the private grounds, a silvery mirror gleaming between the trees. "There," Maman would say, pointing to the dazzling reflections of the sky on the water. "Can you see the turrets? The palace down below?" Then, knocking the jar of pâté out of my hands and replacing it with a carrot stick. "Not that, Camille—have *this*."

I would find out later that D'Arvor was rumored to be the true home of the fairy Viviane, a palace of crystal Merlin had built her and protected under the illusion of a lake, a magical sunken home where she brought up Lancelot. I always believed Maman. I believed her so hard that I thought I was the only one who couldn't see it.

So one afternoon, when I was seven, I slipped away from the picnic blanket. As I approached the lake, I remember a voice beckoning me closer, some kind of soft chanting. My heart beat loudly and I thought, *The fairy knows I'm here.* I got closer, looking so hard for those white turrets. I reckoned the fairy would give me the macarons Maman had just snatched away. The whispers grew stronger the closer I progressed to the castle; supernatural fingers tickled my toes and soothed me into a trance. There were things in that castle, souls in that place that I yearned for. Everything around me was brimming with beauty, ready to feed my hunger, and I wanted to *absorb* that place, to disappear in it and never be found.

The long reeds must have obscured exactly where the shore stopped and the lake started, because I fell in.

Afterward, my parents swore the water wasn't that deep, that it had been a fright more than anything else. But I remember the struggle to survive. Nobody had taught me to swim; I was trapped between the bottom and the surface, my feet and hands flapping in slow motion as if restrained, held too still by the mass of deep green darkness that wanted to keep me. I can still remember the panic, the thought that this surely couldn't be how it all ended. Where was the fairy— why wasn't she rescuing me?

I don't know how I got out. I must have managed to drag myself out before collapsing onto the shore, the commotion finally alerting my dad, who carried me to the closest building: the castle. I remember Maman, vivid with embarrassment, knocking on the imposing door. It opened immediately, as if we'd been expected, and she humbly, with a kind of new stutter, requested to use their phone to order a taxi.

The way the Foucaults sprung to life and I found myself at the heart of their solicitude was like nothing I had experienced before. I was brought into a grand pale-yellow sitting room, allowed to lie, even in my soaked clothes, on a sofa covered in silk, the likes of which I had only ever seen in the period dramas Maman liked to watch. Maxime's mother wrapped me in two blankets, and a kindly older lady with bright red hair—I'm assuming his grandmother—brought me a hot chocolate and a caramel wrapped in golden foil.

"Poor dear. The same happened to him," she said, eyes full of sympathy and tears, but I wasn't sure who "him" was. "Poor mouse."

Who needed fairies, when you could have this? After my

near death, I was high on adrenaline and pain and sugar, in all kinds of shock. The living room was grander than anything I had ever known; surely all of our own house could have fit in it. The wallpaper and the intricate moldings channeled the perfection of a buttery sponge cake with icing. And the people living here were *nice*?

I was playing a game of closing and opening my eyes to see when I would wake up at home, in my own sad bedroom, when a boy materialized in front of me. "I'm sorry," he said, looking like he was on the verge of tears. I stared at him. He was very pretty, with his messy blond locks, a couple of freckles on his nose. "I didn't mean for you to fall in." He placed a daisy, long-stemmed and perfect, on my lap. "Sometimes I pretend I'm Viviane. It's just a game." My fingers grasped the flower; the petals were softer than skin. I knew I should thank him, but I said: "Who's Viviane?"

The boy smiled. He was missing one of his front teeth. I felt something strong—longing. Then he did something extraordinary. "Come," he said, taking my hand. "I'll show you." He turned to his grandmother who was sitting on one of the chairs, absorbed in a plate of sugary butter cake. "You won't tell on us, Annie, will you?"

She shook her head. "Just so long as you don't go too far. She might come back for you, you know."

My father and Maxime's mother were chatting just outside of the open french windows. I assumed Maman was waiting for the taxi outside, stoking the anger and resentment she would deal me later. I wanted the boy to take me as far away as possible so we'd get lost. I would stay in the castle indefinitely, living like a mouse between its walls, tapping into its beauty for my meals. I scrambled to extricate myself from the blankets without letting go of the boy's hand.

I don't remember the route we took but there were a lot of stairs as we climbed to the eaves, a long room used for storage. My jaw dropped as I discovered another whole house in furniture and trinkets and old bikes up there. All those objects I could tap into—I was shaking with excitement, with need, not knowing where to start, my head pulsing. But the boy stopped in front of a small bronze sculpture standing on a mahogany side table.

"That's Viviane, the lady of the lake," he said. "Someone who stayed in the castle a long time ago made this."

As I looked at the sculpture, the fairy peering into the pond while, slowly, her garment and body turned into water, her hand so close to grasping a key fastened in reeds, I heard her call for me again. The boy's green eyes were on me. Steady, clever. His hand tightened on mine. I felt safe, in the way you would if suddenly your old life didn't matter anymore, and there was a whole new existence ahead of you. When I felt dark water lap at my ankles, I recoiled at the fresh memory of my near-drowning in the lake.

"I think she's calling me to her palace, the one below the lake," I whispered. This was much stronger than my experience with other objects, and the pond was new.

"I thought you were very brave," the boy said. His hand made me feel like I would never drown again because he held me. Perhaps the upside-down world wasn't out there but right here. Perhaps I could hide from my parents in there and never have to leave this place. I closed my eyes, wanting to meet Viviane, following her voice, and I jumped in.

That was the first time I connected with art—fine art. It was more exhilarating than scary—I was propelled by the call of this new world, the prospect of an escape, the thrill of the boy's hand in mine. I swam and swam to the crystal glow below, emerging into Avalon for the first time. It was eerily familiar—so familiar I thought I'd traveled back in time, or just come to and it was the same afternoon. The pond was there, and the forest too, and D'Arvor's white turrets in the distance. I looked around for my parents, but when my heart quieted and I really paid attention, I understood this wasn't my world. Everything around me was imbued with emotion, the shapes and colors glowing too bright for human eyes. Every stone was a jewel, every carpet of moss a soft bed. The water was transparent and pure. I didn't have a word, then, for what inhabiting that world made me feel; now I know it was *safe*. I tried a few steps. The grass felt real like it does when you don't know yet you're dreaming.

There was a lady there. I missed her at first because she was sprawled on her back in the long grass, her hands on her tummy, watching the sky. I approached her, but she didn't move; she didn't seem to notice me at all. She was wearing a stripy gray dress, an apron tied around her waist. The apron was very dirty, and I thought of how much trouble I'd be in if I had made the same mess.

Then she turned away from me, propping herself up on her elbow. There was another lady emerging from the lake. Her wet hair, long, thick, was a dark shade of copper, sticking to her arms, down to her waist. She was wearing a red dress, soaked and clinging to her.

Have you found it? the lady in gray called out to her, her brown eyes sparkling.

What?

The sunken palace, Viviane.

They both laughed as Viviane started drying her hair. Everything glowed and they were just…so happy. I basked in it. I yearned to lie between them in the grass, our arms intertwined. Whoever the lady in gray was, she was friends with a fairy. The lady in red. She had found the magic in this place and she was *happy*.

You're here.

Viviane's eyes were on me—I thought she was smiling at me—but it couldn't be. Not with so much kindness. Tears prickled at my throat, as I anticipated this to be a cruel joke. I turned around, but I was the only one there.

You're here, my love.

I am? I asked, but she continued, as if she hadn't heard me:

Come join us.

Their feelings washed over me. They loved me. They welcomed me here, wanted me, cherished me. Tears started rolling down my cheeks, as I experienced unconditional love for the first time.

Mesmerized, yearning, I approached them, but even as I stood right in front of them, they continued to wave and beckon. The lady in gray...her hands. Red and sore, with the skin breaking on the knuckles. I'd never seen anyone with the same hands as mine.

Here's my Lancelot. Come, you must be hungry.

I turned around once more, catching the edge of a giggle and a mop of unruly blond curls disappearing between the trees at the edge of the lake.

The boy? The one in the castle? Was he here too?

I was going to run after him when I heard my name, felt my hand being tugged. It was dark now, I was cold. I didn't want to leave, but even then, so young, I understood that I shouldn't stay too long. I walked back to the water. I wasn't scared of the pond anymore.

I swam back the way I came, even though, in the real world, I couldn't swim. I emerged into my own body standing in the attic like in the aftermath of a missed breath, vibrating.

"What happened? You were, like, gone." The boy nudged me.

"What? For how long?" I asked, trying to get my bearings.

"I counted to thirty," he said.

It had felt to me like thirty minutes or more. "You're so lucky to have this sculpture," I said.

He shrugged. "It's just an old thing. You wanted to know who she was, so..."

"She exists! She is real, she lives in there." My words tumbled as I struggled to catch my breath and tell him everything.

"Wow," the boy said, when I was finished. "Do you think I could have a go too?"

I nodded. Hadn't he been there? My head was spinning and I felt very sleepy. He stared at the sculpture for a while. To keep the dizziness at bay, I curled up in an armchair covered in a dust sheet, my eyelids heavy, trying to get my head around what had happened. This felt like nothing I had experienced before, not when tapping into classmates' clay pots or their home-knitted scarves. I knew I *needed* more of that lady's world. More of those feelings.

"I might ask to keep the sculpture in my room," the boy said after a little while. "So I can keep trying."

"What's your name?" I asked. The excitement had settled a little, so I could really take him in now. *He* had opened this to me. He had led me to her. He lived in this place full of magical things.

"Max," he said.

I giggled.

"What?" He asked.

"Your name is too short for such a big place."

His mouth lifted in a toothless smile. "All right. Maximilien Philippe Erwan Foucault. Better?"

I nodded, trying to commit his name to memory. He laughed.

"What's funny?" I asked.

"You're supposed to tell me your name."

"Camille Leray," I said, regretting the plainness of my own identity.

He bowed. He was going to say something when his mother barged in and scolded him for my disappearance.

In the taxi taking us back to the *gîte*, Maman seethed next to me while Dad blabbed aimlessly about D'Arvor's exquisite gardens in one of his typical monologues designed to defuse a *situation*. I felt fizzy with the day, untouchable. My life had opened to reveal a whole other dimension: being loved. Being wanted, in a new world I felt the ache to go back to and explore. My heart ached at the thought of never being inside the castle or seeing Maxime Foucault again. The place and the boy that, together, had introduced me to fine art. I promised myself I would go back one day. And in the meantime, I knew the world was full of galleries and museums brimming with sculptures and paintings, beautiful objects that *mattered*. I would make it my task to explore them all.

It would be a few years before I could find out who had made *Viviane*, the artist whose imaginary meeting with the fairy had led to the exquisite sculpture in D'Arvor's attic. There was very little published about Constance Sorel, and when I was old enough, I chased her sculptures in obscure collections and her name in the footnotes of Boisseau's biographies. Slowly, work by work, emotion by emotion, and source by source, I traced most of her history, collecting notes about her life and unearthing her works alongside my full-time job as my "passion project." The truth is I found refuge in her universe. As I matured, I was able to understand a wider palette of her emotions, but after that first time it always felt like home. In many ways, I found connection with her that I could not dream of in the real world. Whenever I felt unloved, disappointed, failing, I would go to her.

As I explored, I discovered Constance's childhood, then her Parisian years, her relationship with Boisseau and the impact it had on her, how she sought refuge from their breakup and her tainted reputation at D'Arvor. But I knew, from my experience with *Viviane*, that parts were missing. There were some works from her time at D'Arvor in Rennes, but nothing from after 1913. I searched and searched for what had happened to her after D'Arvor, where she had gone next, and when I found her name and death recorded in Rennes, with no further information, and managed to track her to a pauper's grave, the shock sent me spiraling. What had happened to her? *Viviane* was so full of love and hope for a better future—how did she end up there? It haunted me. There were only a few of her letters surviving, in the archives of the Boisseau Museum. Some of his letters were addressed to her, or mentioned her to others. I pored over those, and found her last known letter, the last reference she and he made to a work of hers: *Night Swimming*. It was 1913; she wrote that she was in Paris to show the sculpture to Boisseau, which a letter of his confirmed. Why was she back there, with him? *You know how much* Night Swimming *means,* she wrote, *it is the key to the sunken palace. Our upside-down world. I have, in short, poured into it everything I have.*

I knew I had to find it. Constance didn't deserve to die anonymously. The world needed to know her and what had happened to her. It felt like only I could fulfill this mission.

5

CONSTANCE'S LIFE CAN be split roughly into two different periods: Paris, and D'Arvor. In Paris, Boisseau's influence was strong; she was young, and he was her mentor, already a legend. When they broke up and she moved to D'Arvor to stay with her cousins, her style changed. It became freer, more personal, anchored in her direct experiences. It was a way to find her own voice, I suppose, away from *his* influence. I like to imagine her now, on a much slower train but on the same route, our eyes watching the same landscape unroll.

Brittany is made of coast and forests, fields and rocks; a land of beauty and revenge, in the constant push and pull of sweetness and violence. It brims with Arthurian legends, and Constance must have felt their influence too. As the train takes me to Rennes, I press my temple against the window, to hear the hoofs of Arthur's horse stamping through the gorse of the Val Sans Retour, the whispers of magic brooks bubbling under the canopy of Brocéliande. Merlin wanders in his prison of air; Morgane entraps disloyal lovers and turns them into stone. *Fairies are so vengeful,* Maman used to say. *You mustn't cross them.* She was good at telling those stories; they are still etched into my core.

The French train company's jingle announces Rennes, the four notes and their rise awakening my memories of past travels. Now I'm returning, my own person, a functioning adult. Well, I hope that's what I still am, that my breakdown over the last few weeks will soon dissipate in this new landscape.

I get up, alongside most of the people in the carriage, to retrieve my suitcase from the overhead locker.

"What happened to your hands?"

The little boy opposite me, standing up on the seat, is staring.

"It's eczema," I tell him, glancing down where red cracks spread over my knuckles like stars.

"Ugh," he says, stretching out his little hand toward mine.

"Matthieu, *non.*" His mother snatches him back. "Leave the lady alone." She grabs her bag and gives me an angry look, before pulling him through the train carriage to the door at the far end. As they trundle off, their suitcase clashing with the armrests, I hear her tell him, "You don't want to catch it."

"It's not contagious," I call out to her, making a few people startle.

She has left her *Paris Match* magazine behind. The

respectable kind of celeb magazine. Only curated interviews, pictures of ex-Olympians and foreign royal families posing in manicured interiors. *At home with the Foucaults at Château D'Arvor*, the cover says. I flick it open for the photos, anticipation rising as if Maxime is about to jump out of the page. A premeeting of some kind, on glossy paper, much better than the swift, dreamlike glance of him I caught at Courtenay. The Foucaults aren't paparazzi bait; they live a quiet life— their wealth and respectability act like a heavy curtain drawn between them and the crassness of the world. They have enough money, but not enough scandal, I suppose.

A quiet life in Brittany—I lap up the photos and text avidly as the train slows. Here they are, normal people doing normal tasks in their château. Marie-Laure, the matriarch, poking at rosemary in the herb garden, in immaculate stone-blue trousers but well-used gardening gloves; Dominique, the father, half-obscured in the chiaroscuro of the wine cellar; and finally, Maxime and his brother, Frédéric, walking in the grounds, caught sharing companionable laughter.

They're clearly opposites. Frédéric has dark hair and his shape is solid, compact, his hands resting awkwardly at his sides. Here, I can take my time studying recent Maxime— the whole of him. It seems the photographer caught him off guard; his features are relaxed, with sexy crinkling at the corners of his green eyes. His face has weathered from the sleek twentysomething student that he was. He is now, it sounds weird to say, an actual man in his midthirties, with the same curly butterscotch hair but some stubble, almost like an afterthought, proof that he's worked through the night; his shirt is open at the collar, golden chest hair visible. He is real, and impossible to look away from. The article doesn't mention a wife. He is the kind of man the world holds its breath for, so if he had gotten married, I would know.

That family, their lives, are what Maman craved. Her claim to it was some ancestors who had been robbed of their titles and lands during the French Revolution, or so her family legend went. Nothing but struggle had ensued for the surviving descendants, but they had kept alive a strong sense of their greatness. Maman had expected a prince, someone to sweep her off her feet and restore her to the status she had been robbed of. Alas, she had fallen in love with a humble, salt-of-the-earth French student from Reading on his year abroad. She followed him to England, and as her paintings never sold for more than the cost of her materials, she started teaching art in a comprehensive school she hated. Maman despised every single thing about her life. She never blamed Dad, because she genuinely loved him. She blamed me: childcare costs, education costs, emotional labor.

If she could see me now, she would be pleased. I'm about to walk into D'Arvor not as the recipient of charity, not as an intruding visitor, but someone whose expertise they're seeking. Someone who handles and appraises the finest art there is. It makes me happy that I might still make her proud of me.

When I walk out of the station, zigzagging my suitcase

between scooters and smeared dog mess, I can't see Maxime anywhere. I look for the mother and her little boy, a grandfather hugging them both, but they're already gone.

As a few pickups happen, cars driving in and off into the distance, I battle a feeling of abandonment in my chest. Before, I would have been annoyed about my time being wasted. Now I fear that I must have got something wrong. Did I dream all of this?

After about fifteen minutes of wondering at what point I should call a taxi, an ancient Clio pulls over, coming to a squeaking halt in front of me. A woman who looks like she is in her late twenties, with olive skin, striking eyebrows, and an air of being hurried, jumps out, fumbles on the passenger's side for a piece of cardboard. I think it might have my name on it; it stays under her arm as she approaches me.

"Madame Leray?" she asks.

"Yes, that's me. Hi." I try not to sound surprised, or disappointed. She has appeared out of nowhere and all I can imagine is that she must be Maxime's assistant, Anaïs, who organized the trip.

She nods politely and takes my bag. I expected Maxime in the newest four-by-four smelling of leather and spruces, or a chauffeur in one of those sleek black cabs. I open the trunk of the Clio—my fingers leave prints in the dust. I throw my suitcase in and go to open the door.

"Wrong side," the woman says, as she squeezes past me and drops into the driver's seat.

"Of course." Everything is on the other side here. I too feel off-kilter. In the hot and muggy air, this urban landscape doesn't feel like the France of my childhood. The car is a mess, and I have to wipe some chewing gum wrappers off the seat. Empty water bottles crunch under my soles. The carpet is peeling off; I wouldn't be surprised if her feet get damp when it rains.

Maxime should pay his assistants more.

I struggle with the stubborn seat belt while she waits, her hand on the gear stick.

"How long is the journey?" I ask her.

"About forty minutes."

We glide without a word out of the city, the motorway turning into small roads cutting through fields, or the occasional sleepy villages. All around, the wild dense forest competes for space with fields of corn and wheat. The two faces of Brittany, like Viviane and Morgane. Nurturing and wild, dangerous and loving.

"Maxime is busy, then?" I try to ask casually, probing for more information, checking that I haven't been kidnapped.

Anaïs nods, rummaging in the glove box in front of me to find a pair of sunglasses. Her hand is slender, her movements fast and accurate. She is dressed the opposite of her car. Simple and immaculate, fuss-free, in a white T-shirt and gray jeans.

"He was delayed at the gallery, but he should be on his way."

Good—he hasn't forgotten about me. Anaïs doesn't make

further attempts at conversation, but her silence isn't hostile. She opens a packet of chewing gum, unwraps two of them— they're the long bendy bars Maman used to give me to chew on when I was hungry, the silver wrappers light and powdery between my fingers. Chlorophyll, its minty essence spreads fast through the car. She scrunches the wrappers and drops them on the floor, then offers me the packet. I shake my head, silently begging her to keep both hands on the wheel.

"So, can you tell me more?" I ask.

"About what?"

She's not a very good assistant. I would have expected her to thrust a heavy dossier into my hands, some reading for the journey, to brief me about what is to come and what will be expected of me.

"About why I'm here? What exactly Maxime needs me to help with?"

Her side-eye catches me. "You're on first-name terms with him?"

I shrug. "We met briefly when we were studying at St. Andrews."

"I see. I'm afraid I don't know. Some sculptures. I'm not really in the confidence. I don't particularly like art."

But she works with Maxime at the gallery, right? So that must be a lie, but why? I would have expected her to ask me questions, try to endear herself to me in an attempt to secure her next work experience. I try another tactic. "What is it like, working for him?"

"For who?"

"Well, Maxime."

Her laughter surprises me. It bursts out of her, childish and giddy and pure. "I like you. You've barely arrived, and you've already got the hang of it all."

She slows for a junction, then brakes a little harshly. The seat belt tenses on my chest as I'm yanked forward. We watch a Ford Ka drive past us, someone with purple hair at its wheel. At first glance, I think it's a teenager; when she drives closer, I realize she must be in her seventies. *You can't even see things right anymore, Camille.* It's ridiculous, but it upsets me.

"What do you mean?" What if nothing I find in D'Arvor is as I expect? What if my childhood memories are all illusions, or worse: projections? What have I just walked into?

She shrugs. "Those great families. I think everyone around them plies to them a bit. Some kind of innate deference, you know?"

I nod, unsettled by the fact she found it so funny, and glance around the car; the piece of cardboard lies discarded on the back seat, bearing my misspelled name in huge hasty letters. **CAMILLE LEROY**. Perhaps that is the one they expect, a different version of me who exists more perfectly, glitch-free. The unflappable expert they wanted, not this skittish woman so easily derailed by inside jokes.

The expert better be back before we meet with Maxime. I straighten in my seat and smooth some pleats from my skirt, trying to summon her.

6

THE WEATHER, OF course, has taken a turn for the atmospheric when we turn onto the private drive guarded by spiky golden gates. Clouds hang so low and heavy that they make the last stretch of the journey feel claustrophobic, as if we are being pressed into the earth, squeezed into our smallest selves in preparation for the castle.

At first hidden by ancient woods, D'Arvor reveals itself all at once like a jump scare. It is both familiar and awesome to me, a breathtaking sight, and at once I am seven again and drenched in pond water and half-drowned, the castle luring me in.

Camille, you're an expert. You are returned a grown, professional woman. To focus, I tell myself the history of the building, a medieval fortress with moat "modernized" in the fifteenth century as a hunting lodge, then extended in the mid-1800s, with new wings and elegant white turrets wrapped around its fortified, austere core. The moat was filled in and the river artificially diverted to loop around the castle at some distance, pouring into the lake at the edge of the woods.

France is littered with castles, but D'Arvor is different. It has always been lived in, always hidden from the public; its heart has not been diluted or lost. It is alive, arrogant, magnificent, violent, and in love, and its turrets impale the sky like the thorny tails of dragons. The chain of its echoes is unbroken: the steps of the knights who defended it, the horns of hunting parties, the cries of the revolution, the balls that the Foucaults still sometimes host. And its grounds are perfect, ever-changing depending on where your eyes land, like the castle itself, moving seamlessly from sweet summer meadows to the dark thorny woods of Brocéliande.

Now that I'm an adult, I realize it is no more a princess castle to me, but something darker. Perhaps it is all the years I have spent refining my gift; this castle is full of the hands who made it, twitching and scratching; I trained myself to ignore those, to be more selective about what I tap into— only the finest. But here, the finest is everywhere, it was built on suffering, and I am porous to it.

You're tired from the journey. It's only a headache.

Anaïs drives the car almost right up to the front door, then turns, the gravel crunching under the wheels, to park around the side of the building. Her driving is more timid here: crawling, as if trying to stay silent. I half expect her to cover the car in hay to hide it.

"We're here."

Neither of us move.

I've seen hundreds of castles in my time. I've been in many houses that most would consider the height of luxury. Always a stranger, like here. Always someone who comes in wearing silent shoes, picking up trinket after trinket, replacing them exactly where they were found. D'Arvor is different. Firstly, its history has been preserved; I know I will find no hyper-modern renovations inside, no chrome kitchens or walk-in showers. The bare layers of its age are its unsurpassed luxury.

Secondly, it knows me. It speaks to me. As I take it in, I know my love for this soul of stone started that day it nearly took me, deep into my childhood; and now, finally back, finally grown up, I am begging for it to love me.

Anaïs springs to life first. "Are you coming?" She unbuckles and gets out to open the trunk.

I grab my suitcase and follow her around the castle, fighting hard to keep out the cries and aches of the chiseling masons. I have to stay in control.

We walk up the steps leading to the entrance, resplendent in white mortar and stained glass, and with what feels like an intake of breath, it swallows us into the cool darkness of the castle. The floor is laid with striking black and white checkerboard marble tiles; it is grand, yet a glimpse into the turret on the side reveals it as a mudroom, wellies and coats piling through the door ajar. This castle is a lived-in beast.

"The family is not yet available. Would you like some

refreshments?" Anaïs asks, indicating that I should leave my suitcase in the hall.

I want to be alone—being back almost thirty years later is more overwhelming than I thought. I want some time to reset my weariness into the giddiness I yearn for, to plead with the chorus of past voices to leave me alone. "I'd love a cup of tea."

"Of course," she says, with the hint of a knowing smile. "Please take a seat in the yellow salon—second door on the left."

When Constance walked in battered and bruised by Paris, this entrance hall might have smelled of fresh plaster and paint. *Channel Constance. She'll make you feel right where you belong.* I place my hand on the banister, searching for the remnants of her touch, as she walked in single, filled with a renewed confidence in her own creation, taking the reins of her own fate away from Boisseau.

The castle belonged to some remote cousins, Raymond Foucault and his much younger wife, Anne. Raymond's grandfather had bought it after it was seized during the revolution. What I know of Raymond was that he was harsh, sullen, respected, and feared. Anne was more progressive than her husband; we still have her letter inviting Constance to stay, despite her bruised reputation. Constance had had an affair with one of the most famous married men in France. A very public affair—her sculptures disclosed her unapologetic passion for him to the world. When the relationship broke down, he was unscathed, and she lost every bit of respect and reputation she had worked so hard to build. When she stormed into D'Arvor and immediately set out to order kilos of clay, it must have been a shock to its inhabitants.

Constance's feet walked on the stones I'm standing on. She came in, doused with rain, on a moody August day, defiant, faking the confidence I am trying to tap into now. I set off down the corridor, admiring the decor as I go, following her ghost. She became happy here. I hear her boots knocking off droplets of rain on the marble. I caress the wallpaper, faded like a dry rose, reach for the tips of her fingers probing mine at the edges of the walls. Here she was free from the expectations bestowed on women in their late twenties. D'Arvor was remote; she barely had to engage with anything except her own inner world. The castle held her like a live-in secret.

Then what happened to her here? The thought that I'm closer to finding out, that she might tell me, makes me hold my breath as I continue walking, entirely absorbed in my search for her. Then there's a noise suddenly—something at the corner of my perception. It is piercing, an animalistic wail, just out of reach...

The kitchen at the end of the corridor takes me by surprise. It is a big homely space, the appliances old-fashioned and low to the ground. A Persian rug is thrown on the flagstone floor. Orchids stand in the window. I remember a letter where Constance mentioned stealing poached pears...

"Wrong room."

I startle as it isn't Constance that is half-bent into the gaping fridge, but Anaïs. She doesn't look best pleased with my interruption, a spoon in hand, a hint of chocolate at the corner of her lips. I consider for a moment that we might all be reduced to little girls here, breaking into forbidden spaces. Some longing beats in my chest, then settles into a headache. I've been getting headaches a lot recently.

"Do you have a cat?" I ask, thinking about the noise, but it is gone now.

She stares at me like I'm mad. "Are you all right?" She asks eventually, putting the spoon down.

I nod. "Can I please have some water?"

The clink of a glass, while the tap goes, glugs, then stops.

"Thank you."

"There was water in the salon. I even went to the trouble of cutting cucumber and lemon. Quite refreshing." She appraises me, her arms folded, eyes sharp between smoky eyelids. "Hmm. I don't think water is going to cut it." She beckons me to the fridge. "Over here."

I do as I'm told, fearing that she'll brandish some kind of extortionate champagne, but also dying to get a rare glimpse into the domesticity of the Foucaults. There's nothing better to reveal a human's true nature than the contents of their fridge. We both peer into the old appliance, which starts buzzing and rumbling raucously. The light makes Anaïs's cheeks glow gold, scatters glitter in her eyes. She's also excited, I notice, and only half managing to hide it.

"They always keep the leftovers here and, of course, the cheese." She gestures to the dairy treasures within: a big terracotta bowl of chocolate mousse on the middle shelf, into which serving spoons, including hers, have already carved round hollows; a small plate of profiteroles, cut in half to reveal an ooze of crème anglaise; some fromage blanc in a family-sized plastic tub; slabs of butter. And cheeses on the shelf below, individually wrapped in gingham wax paper, all in distinctive shapes like a child's wooden block puzzle. The fridge smells like a cheesemonger's, like Maman's fridge just before Christmas.

Anaïs follows my eyes, takes the plate of profiteroles. "Go on," she says, just the way Maxime's grandmother encouraged me twenty-five years ago with her caramels.

No, Camille. We don't take charity. I shake my head, sipping water.

"Up to you." Her eyes close as she savors the pastry. "Delicious." I envy her boldness to take what she wants. "A definite perk of being here," she says. "I'll never take it for granted."

Noticing for the first time the expensive cut and materials of her clothes, how her white T-shirt hugs her slender hips, silky and uncreased, her Chanel ballerina flats absorbing the sound of her steps, I think that her own fridge can't have lacked any of those treats. I'm not naive; I know that being

Maxime's assistant would only be accessible to someone from a privileged background, someone whose parents are paying the rent while you're gaining experience for prestige and a fraction of the price of your skills. The art world is full of people like that.

But there's something different about Anaïs. I want to know more about the contrast between her clothes and her car, her guardedness on the journey and spontaneity in the presence of food, but she speaks first: "They all have their favorites. Marie-Laure likes hard cheeses, crumbly, made with alpine milk. This is Maxime's."

I peer at the wheel she's pointing at, pink like a skin and rimmed in thin wood. "Vacherin Mont-D'Or. Divisive," I say.

It's the strongest cheese I remember having. Thick and oozy with a taste of dark cellar and musty barrels. Not for the fainthearted, even French.

"Yes," Anaïs says. "Not a fan myself. I told him I'm not going anywhere near him after he's had some. I can tolerate a lot, but not Vacherin."

What she is alluding to sounds so intimate—*going near him*, yet it is so deliberately ambiguous. I feel like she means to confuse me; she definitely meant for it to sound territorial. "I'm sorry—what do you mean?" I stammer as she slams the fridge's door shut. But she's walking out of the kitchen and I run after her, looking at her from head to toe, for clues that I've missed. What is the nature of her relationship with Maxime, exactly?

"Come on," she beckons. "If you're going to snoop around, I might as well show you your room before dinner."

———

As I follow her up the grand staircase, I try to push my questions about the present to the side. *Who cares about Maxime, when you get to be so close to Constance?* The weight of history is real, a thick blanket on my shoulders, weaved with the threads of those who lived and died within these walls. I try to shake it off, admire all its grandeur objectively, but I feel more porous, less able to shut them out, as if what happened at Courtenay left me with an open wound. Or it's just down to the particular makeup of this place, the way it whispers directly to my heart. I'm still shaken and scared at the prospect of the dark pond opening in my mind, the water lapping at my ankles and running down the steps in a murky waterfall, taking with it my grip on reality, my self-control. What will happen when Maxime needs me to engage with the works and it all goes wrong? If I collapse, or worse—if I damage something, someone? My suitcase catches on the stairs as we ascend; in a blink, I lose my balance, fall backward. Anaïs catches me.

False alarm. *You're fine. You're absolutely fine.*

"All good." I snap, snatching my arm away from her.

We continue down the corridor. I expected to be tucked under the eaves, in an old nursery, but the door she opens is right in the middle.

"Here," she says. "This is the room she stayed in."

"Hmm?"

As soon as I walk in, it starts pulling me in. Something calling my subconscious. I'm trying to stay grounded, to focus on what makes the room so charming, the concrete beats of its architecture and furniture: huge windows from floor to ceiling flanked with silver brocade curtains, opening onto the beautiful French garden. The headboard is an ancient gilded wooden frame. A pattern of twisting ferns, not so much drawn as textured, creeps up the wallpaper, catching the late sunlight. The Versailles parquet glows like a pool of honey. A door at the far end of the room reveals an old-fashioned en suite with a roll-top bath.

"Constance Sorel." Anaïs stands in the doorway watching me as I come to a halt in the middle of the room. If I progress any further, I'll be gone. Many of these objects she has touched, handled. "This was her room here."

"Has it changed much?"

"I'm not sure. I think they had been decorating when she came. Legend has it she made some of the finishing touches." She waves her hand around vaguely.

Constance's presence floods into me as if through a cracked dam. She is in the room, examining it as I did, her striped travel dress shuffling around her; she pats, like I do, the heavy silkiness of the curtains, imagining what sculpture would best adorn the gardens; then she throws her hat off onto the Louis XV desk and falls onto the bed backward, and she feels...

When I open my eyes, it is Anaïs who is lying on the bed, grinning, her eyes closed. An expression that I haven't seen on her face before, of complete and utter relief, of excitement...

"I'm in love," she says.

I stare at her, brought back to this reality by this sudden change, by the brazenness and familiarity of her move; her eyes fling open and she darts off the bed as if she has been stung. "I'm so sorry. I was—I don't know what I—"

What is happening? Is this some kind of joke? Then I catch some unease on her face, a flicker of the woman in the Hepburn dress.

Oh no. Have Constance's emotions I was feeling...*leaked* out of me again? Impossible. I wasn't even in Avalon. Anaïs must be messing with me. I clinch my fists tight, close my eyes, try to reset. "It's fine," I tell her, forcing my voice to be light. *Nothing to see here. I won't be playing your game, whatever it is.* "I understand the feeling. It's an amazing room."

"Yes. Well, it's an amazing place." Her face slides shut. "Careful though. It's near-impossible to leave."

I don't want to ever leave it. Why would I? Whether at my parents' house in Reading, my flat in London, Lowen's family home, or our halls of residence, I've been a guest, willing or unwilling, wanted or unwanted, all my life. D'Arvor is the place I've been desperately saving my heart for. I want it to adopt me and never let me go.

"You won't tell Max, will you?" Anaïs's voice asks behind me, bringing me back.

"Tell him what?"

She's in the doorway, her long black hair falling in curls along her bare arms, crossed on her chest more in protection than defiance. After her childish move of throwing herself onto the bed, she seems much younger and unsure. "That I was late picking you up from the station. That I took my crappy car. That I just acted like I was an eight-year-old at a sleepover."

I can't help but smile. "We're in France. Beds are comfortable and lateness is fashionable."

She smiles too. "Thank you. Dinner is at eight. I'll see you then."

"What should I expect? I haven't got a clue about how to behave here." I'm surprised I've come out and admitted it—especially to her. But there's something vulnerable about her right now that invites confidence.

"Don't worry. You'll soon learn the rules," she says before shutting the bedroom door.

7

WHEN EIGHT O'CLOCK comes and I take myself downstairs, I'm not sure where to go and I'm not brave enough to start opening all the doors. It's an unsettling feeling, a little bit like being on a French exchange, worried that I will set a foot wrong and cause offense. I can't see or hear anyone around, so I decide to bet on the familiarity of the yellow salon.

The door is open. I walk in gingerly, hardly more confident than the soaked child I once was. It all looks the same: the fine furniture, the icing-white moldings, lit upward by gold fixtures... I know I'm trespassing, but I can't help it.

Let me call a doctor. The poor darling girl.

Thank you, but she'll be quite all right. We shouldn't—we can't barge in on you like this. The clumsy, useless child. We'll go back to the gîte and she'll be just fine... Please, don't. She dwells on the attention.

A man is standing in front of the tall arched windows, a smaller but by no means lesser version of those in Versailles's gallery of mirrors. I remember one of them at least serves as a door opening onto the garden. That's not Maxime; he is shorter, stockier, and his hair is dark and straight, combed back. I relax a fraction, clearing my throat to signal my presence.

"Oh, hello." He turns to face me.

"I'm sorry, I'm afraid I'm a bit lost. I'm Camille Leray."

He approaches me, his hand catching awkwardly in his pocket before he can shake mine. "Nice to meet you, Ms. Leray—welcome."

I wait for him to introduce himself, although I saw him in Paris Match this afternoon.

"This is Frédéric Foucault," Anaïs's voice says behind me. "Maxime's brother."

"Ah," he says, with some kind of apologetic shrug. "Yes. That's me, the brother."

Thrust into real life, he appears reassuringly clumsy, like a young Labrador that hasn't quite taken the measure of his stockiness.

"I see you finally found the yellow salon," Anaïs says to me. I look for a smirk, the trace of a shared joke, but find none. Then: "Shall we go and eat? Marie-Laure is waiting for us."

I notice how Frédéric seems to follow her too. She leads us to a room across the hall where a waiflike woman with shoulder-length hair is setting silver cutlery on the table. She straightens and shakes my hand.

"Frédéric, have you not fetched our guest a drink? You must excuse him."

Her red lipstick brings out the milkiness of her skin, making the whole of her seem almost translucent.

"You must forgive me, Maman." Frédéric addresses her using the formal *vous*. Even my own mother never requested this—in French, the *vous* is usually reserved for strangers or adults whom familiarity will never be in reach. Yet in Frédéric's mouth, it is full of adoration.

In the way she looks at me, ready to envelop me in her attention and warmth, I know immediately that Marie-Laure Foucault is the kind of mother everyone would dream of. Her very presence in the room triggers a yearning in me that I always kept simmering. When we shake hands, the contrast between her soft, cool skin and mine, itchy and on fire, is that of a mother's palm on a feverish forehead.

It reminds me of what I felt when I first met Constance. The love she radiated back at child-me.

"Nice to meet you," I say. "Thank you for having me."

"Oh, thank you for agreeing to come, and sorry we weren't able to meet you when you first arrived. I trust Lila showed you around?"

She gestures, as she speaks, for us to take our seats around the table.

"I don't think I've met Lila yet," I say, and the room stops. What is going on? Frédéric stares at me across the table. Marie-Laure turns to the woman who picked me up, the one person who has spent time with me since I arrived, and who clearly isn't Anaïs. "Lila, have you not introduced yourself?"

The woman cocks her head; she's filling everyone's glass with water. "I'm sorry, there must have been some confusion."

Marie-Laure looks at her, then at me. I can tell she disapproves, but I don't know of which one of us. "This is Lila Madani. Maxime's girlfriend."

My eyes meet Lila's—under her contrived look of embarrassment, there's a spark of mischief. She has enjoyed my mistake and that's why she allowed it. I recoil at the thought that I asked her what it was like to be working for Maxime.

He has a girlfriend.

"*Enchantée*," I tell her coldly.

She is even more stunning when there's chaos in her eyes, something burning low under her outward deference to the place and the family. *So, this is the competition*, says a voice I'm not proud of. *And what a competition it is.*

Marie-Laure sits down and we all finally follow suit. She leaves me no time to wallow in the news, and that's probably for the best. She goes on to apologize for receiving me in the "little" dining room, used by the family on a daily basis, rather than the formal one in the oldest part of the castle. "It is cozier here," she says. "Much more practical as it is so close to the kitchen." I enthuse about the perfect proportions of the room, my eyes darting to the soft green wall panels, the high vases on the mantelpiece brimming with real roses. The table can seat ten, is laid for six, with two empty places.

Marie-Laure nods to Frédéric, then to the wine.

"In the absence of real men, you defer to me," he smiles.

"Yes, I suppose you'll do, darling."

I love their quiet teasing, the clear affection between them. A proper family dinner. I lean into it until my unease at Lila's antics recedes.

"Is Maxime joining us?" I ask, as we pass around dishes of chicken, green beans, and new potatoes. Simple, perfect cooking, infused with garlic and garden herbs, which is a relief. *I know how to eat chicken and beans.* Despite his general aura of clumsiness, Frédéric uses the corkscrew with the precision of someone who was trained in the cradle, for whom it is nothing but daily habit. He tops my glass up high with golden wine.

"I'm afraid he's been delayed," Marie-Laure says, echoing Lila. "He might join us in time for dessert."

I catch some flicker on Frédéric's face, brotherly annoyance perhaps, that makes me wonder how often Maxime misses these family dinners. It seems to me that the height of indulgence might not be the expensive wine or the gilded clock chiming along, but to have such a family and not turn up for them, knowing they'll always be there, eating their dark, sliced, and soft beans in the glow of the firelight. If I belonged here, you'd have to peel me off this room like stubborn wallpaper.

I might understand Maman better now. How inadequate it can make you feel to sit among them, yet be unable to *be* them. How it can make you wrestle with contradictions. I thought dining with them would be some kind of achievement, a milestone, but it is stoking my fire of yearning and aspiration.

I cannot be better looked after during dinner. My glass is always full, and Marie-Laure's conversation is warm and attentive. We talk about my job and my family ties to the area. She regales me with more facts about the estate, the gardens mainly, which she seems particularly fond of. The fact that I understand the history and architectural importance of the castle seems to earn me her respect. She even asks how I think the kitchen should be refurbished to maintain the spirit of the house. A glow spreads in me, fueled not only by the wine, but the way she looks at me, the way she and Frédéric seem to hang on my words. Lila stays mostly silent and I wonder if she is contrite, or if she is always like this around the family. When we were alone, self-effacement didn't seem her thing.

"Have you ever seen Viviane's sunken palace? In the lake," I ask when the conversation has turned to the gardens once more.

Marie-Laure smiles as she offers the last few potatoes to the table, receiving polite nods of rejection. "I can't say I have. I must not be in the fairy's graces."

"That's hard to believe," I say.

"Aren't you a darling?" My cheeks flush at her warmth.

"Max was adamant we saw it when we were little," Frédéric says. "That was the day a girl almost drowned in the lake, do you remember, Maman? Whose mother was so awful."

My knife slips out of my hand and clatters onto my plate. The yellow salon, Marie-Laure's blankets, Maxime pulling me up to the attic. Maman slapping caramels out of my hands. *Viviane.* I can see it all dancing in the shadows around the fireplace. I didn't think they'd remember. Somehow, it doesn't feel right to tell them it was me. I don't want them to think that I'm a weird stalker, and I don't want them to associate me with my parents. That desperate part of me throwing herself into the water because she was hearing voices is best kept hidden.

"Lila, please be a dear and go get the cheese from the kitchen?" Marie-Laure asks.

Lila gets up wordlessly, gathering empty dishes.

"Do you need help?" I go to pull back my chair, but Marie-Laure gestures for me to stay as Lila walks out of the room.

"They were desperate for it to be special," Frédéric says, apropos of nothing.

"What, darling?"

"D'Arvor."

"I'm not sure who 'they' are," Marie-Laure says with an air of benevolence, "but it *is* special. Very special and our privilege to be its guardians. It has known many triumphs and tragedies."

"Like Constance Sorel?" I ask.

"Yes," Frédéric says at the same time as Marie-Laure says, "No." Then she seems to think about it. "I was thinking more along the lines of...political troubles."

"She was an incredibly gifted artist and D'Arvor played a big part in her life," I say, my heart beating so hard I worry they might hear it. They must know more here. Perhaps even what happened to her in the end. If they trust me enough, if they like me enough, they might be willing to share.

"Ah, so this is what you meant. I'm sorry to say I do not quite agree with you on this matter, Ms. Leray. And with Maxime being so thrilled about the sculptures, I'm clearly in the minority here, so you best ignore me." She's addressing me directly, her voice soft and intelligent, and our eyes meet over the tablecloth.

"If you have any insights into her life here," I say, carefully, lightly, "I—"

"The past isn't always good to tamper with, Ms. Leray. I hope you will bear this in mind when you help us."

My brain frazzles at the way she shuts me down and I decide it's best not to push it. Yet.

As Lila reappears with a basket of sliced baguette and a cheese platter bejeweled with grapes, I notice the Mont-D'Or isn't there. Maxime isn't expected, after all. Why is he not here, when he asked for me?

Marie-Laure, a great hostess, moves the conversation on. The cheeses are crumbly and nutty and salty, and the baguette light as a cloud. My wine has turned to red under the watchful care of Frédéric. Nine, then ten o'clock chime as we talk about architecture and topiary, a moment I would love to bottle up if I could.

Then it's time for dessert. "Lila, will you please fetch—" Marie-Laure stops when we all notice that Lila is gone. I marvel at her escape, her soundless Chanel pumps on the well-trodden floors. Like me, she knows how to skulk, erase her presence in these great houses.

"Probably out back smoking," Frédéric says.

"I'll get it," I offer. I could do with stretching my legs, and the cold white light of the fridge has its appeal right now. A haze has spread at the edges of the room. I thought I was enjoying myself, but my jaw is clenched.

"Don't be silly. You're a guest. Frédéric…"

"Please, allow me."

Marie-Laure nods. "There's fromage blanc and berries in the fridge." I pick up the cheese platter.

I'm tipsy, at the edge of drunk, suddenly aware of how many times they've refilled my glass, how many times I sipped to steady myself. The lamps struggle to reach into all the corners of the corridor as I sway my way through. The walk seems to last an eternity, long shadows coming alive, reaching for my wrists and ankles from their places of rest. I realize with a jolt I've gone the wrong way, suddenly unsure where the kitchen was—is?—and the platter sways in my hands; a couple of grapes fall and roll into the darkness. The yellow salon appears, lit up and golden and welcoming, and I duck in to escape the whispers that are trying to take hold of my brain.

The french door has been left open. It is now dark outside and the water of the fountains has stilled. I leave the platter on a table and go stand behind the curtains to breathe in the night, clear my head. The windows project squares of gold on the gravel of the terrace, a stark frontier into unknown darkness. The night air seeps with mist. There is no moon; the only source of light is behind me, and I feel the need to stay hidden from the creatures taking over the gardens at night, perhaps the ghostly washerwomen Maman used to mention, scrubbing and wringing shrouds in the river. The steps on the gravel must be them coming to get me, singling me out as the impostor; they will drag me out and throw me into the lake. I beg the castle to keep me, to protect me—

"I told you to take my car."

I duck further behind the curtains, holding my breath.

"How do you know I didn't?"

"You might as well be driving a tin box at high speed."

It's Lila. And I think she's talking to Maxime. The burning in me doesn't subside. But at least they are people of flesh and reality.

"But I like my car."

"You're impossible."

"Max, are you sure about all of this?"

A silence. The crunch of their steps stops.

"Why do you ask?"

"It's not *that*; it's..."

She sounds so unsure, whereas his voice is smooth and deep like honey. It is so strange and wonderful to hear that voice again, mere paces away from me, that I forget the rather precarious position I'm in.

"You better tell me."

"It's such a risk. A huge gamble."

"It's my risk to take. You don't need to worry about it."

Another silence, then Lila says: "I'm not sure she's the right choice. I don't know if she'll fit. That's all."

Is she talking about me? To Maxime?

"She is. You have to trust me."

The right choice for what? To help with authenticating the sculptures? Selling them?

How would Lila know that I'm struggling? How can she see inside my head, how much I fear that she is right, and that I'm not up to this environment, these people, this—life?

"Max, there was a moment, earlier, when I was showing her around—"

The headache intensifies. Is she referring to when I was overwhelmed with Constance's presence in my room? Is my gift really leaking out of me so easily that I'm unable to control it even when walking around the castle? This could be bad. And here, where everything is magnified, where my emotions run untethered, it could get much worse.

What does this mean for the sculptures? Will I be able to work with them? The fear is so strong, so sudden, like a bucket of ice tipped over. I don't know what Constance has experienced here. Marie-Laure's voice echoes in my head. *The past isn't always good to tamper with.* She seemed so dismissive of Constance, almost—scared. Was she? Am I about to walk into another twisted and dark Avalon, totally unprepared?

But it's Constance. I know her. I *know* her. She was happy here.

Lila's voice. "I thought we could both escape dessert. It would be such a shame if, say, you were delayed further."

"You look like you've seen a ghost, Lila. Come here."

I imagine Maxime pressing her against his chest in the silence. My fingers draw his shape silently against the curtains, the brocade merging with the fabric of his shirt. He is a knight, returned from some kind of quest. I am his lady-in-waiting. I allow myself to indulge just for a second that I'm the one who gets to tangle my fingers in the locks on his neck, stroke the stubble on his jaw.

Then I hear his voice, muffled: "My love. What would I do without you?"

8

I DREAM OF Lowen. We are standing side by side in front of D'Arvor's lake. It is so dark that I can't see its contours, but I can smell it: fresh water and pure night. In the castle, a masquerade ball is in full swing. Distorted violins reach us; they sound like someone crying. *Just swim*, Lowen tells me. *It's not hard. Come on, Cam.* I'm reluctant to; I don't know what lurks in the water, but I know it's terrible. I know something is about to snatch me any second. I dip a toe in and brace myself, until the fear spreads fast into my mind and I run to the castle. *Cam!* I know Lowen is running behind me—I get to the door of the yellow salon; then I turn back to him. But he's vanished. I turn to the ball, the pyramids of éclairs and mountains of fromage blanc streaked with coulis, red and thick and coagulated. I remember Maxime. *Find Maxime. He will help.* I move from guest to guest, pleading with them to take off their masks, but when they do, every single one is Constance, laughing at me.

I open my eyes and the gorgeous bedroom comes into view. The sun is already pouring onto the parquet and blackbirds are singing. It takes a while for my heart to stop pounding and the unease to lift from my chest. *What a stupid dream. Stupid brain.*

I'd say it's 8 a.m. I'm amazed I fell asleep so quickly last night. After catching Lila and Maxime's conversation, I tiptoed back to the kitchen and brought in the dessert, which was eaten among yet more pleasant conversation. I felt jittery, however—uncomfortable in my own skin. I refused Marie-Laure's offer of coffee and turned in early. However I *did* find my room and did *not* get lost, and did *not* meet any ghosts, and the bed cocooned me without creaking ominously, as if the castle was taking me under its wing, reassuring me that Lila was wrong and I am welcome here.

Noises of life echo in the corridor, footsteps on the runner carpet, doors opening and closing—I can't identify whether people are coming or going, or if there's a fixed time for breakfast, when and where I would be expected to turn up, what awaits me. I wish I knew. I wish the codes of this place were instinctive to me.

And also…the headache lingers as I start to really take in my surroundings. The pieces of furniture, trying to grab me by the hands that made them. Constance choosing the shade of these very curtains—

I want you to make this yours. You belong here.

The pond is opening at my feet, threatening to wash away the room and take me, with the bed, into its depths. I've worked so hard to get my gift under control, and now I'm constantly fighting it. I should have thought that, in my weakened state, it would be a struggle to resist D'Arvor's voices, when I'm not ready for them.

I'm not sure she's the right choice. I don't know if she'll fit. I groan and pull the bedsheet over my head.

The universe turns peach, fragrant with softener. That's fine—I can stay here all day, right? I carefully stretch an arm out, pat the bedside cabinet and retrieve my phone to check the time.

8:13 a.m., and I have a text from Lowen.

Cam, sorry about buggering off last week. Can we talk about it? How about I pop by at the weekend? Make you some scones?

I reply immediately, relieved.

I'm not about, sorry. I'm actually in France, if you can believe it.

Ah, good for you. What for? You finally taking a holiday?

I wish. I type this as a reflex, but I don't wish. I haven't taken a holiday in years and wouldn't know what to do with myself if I did, especially right now. I don't really feel like telling Lowen about D'Arvor. There's nothing to say—I don't know what the job is yet.

I add: I should be back in a week or so—talk then?

I'm on a course then. Abroad as well.

Oh, what kind of course? Good for you too

This is fine. Talking to him like this. Casual, friendly conversation, lighthearted emojis.

A pastry course. It's in Rennes actually

I type, erase… I'm aware he must be seeing my three dots.

Rennes? In Brittany? That Rennes?

You were the one who recommended it to me. Months ago. Maybe years, even? Anyway they've had a cancellation and I was on the waiting list.

I remember that conversation. Going through our old motions, the arguing we always seemed to fall back on since he'd left London. I had once again canceled a visit to Cornwall, and on FaceTime he took a jab at the fact that I worked too hard. I then told him about a prestigious pastry course my mother had always raved about, threw it into the conversation like a grenade, like something he would never have the guts to do, when I was actually doing the unkind, defensive thing of turning the attention away from the fact that I'd flaked on him. I can't believe he actually went and signed up.

You didn't tell me

It's quite competitive. I never thought I'd get in. Applied on a whim and only found out about a month ago—a fluke.

I know we're both thinking that he could have told me in London and about the conversation that was cut short.

Not a fluke!! Congratulations

So where are you exactly? Anywhere near-ish?

I have to tell him now, don't I? I take the coward's way, staying vague. In Brittany too. About an hour's drive away

You'll be gone by the time I arrive though.

Yeah, I don't really know but it's likely. I hope you have a great time.

A beat, then I type: I'm proud of you.

The ticks turn blue, and Lowen's online status disappears after a few seconds. I imagine him staring at my text, then putting the phone back in his pocket. I have no idea what he felt.

Things are good in this bed cave, I tell myself, as the ache of Lowen's theoretical proximity and the current mess of our friendship flood over me. *Things are safer under the bedsheet.*

For the longest time, Lowen was my only anchor. At boarding school we would escape the common rooms and pad along the corridors to the library, where we would read on a beanbag each, for hours—he, comics, and I, Gombrich's *The Story of Art*. When we grew older and more defiant, he'd sneak into my dorm and we'd sit side by side on my creaky single bed, me hugging my knees as he bent to turn the volume of his Discman up and up, the Foo Fighters blaring in our ears, the teachers on duty threatening us with detention if they caught Lowen there again.

Our real intimacy started because of my failure; it was the only time failure brought me anything good. I hadn't told anyone at school I couldn't swim; Lowen figured it out in our first year after I got a detention for the third PE swimming lesson I skipped. "You can't have your period three times in a month," the PE teacher told me, loud and humiliating, when she found me hiding at the back of the library. Lowen invited me to come and spend some time with his family for the holidays. He said he could teach me, and I hated being out of my depth. That first summer was the best of my life, full of scones, fish and chips, sand, and laughter.

After that, I stayed with him every summer of secondary school. Lowen taught me how to become a competent swimmer, how to tackle the mental and physical fatigue. He knew where and when it was safe to go and I trusted him. We'd spend the summers on Porthmeor Beach eating his mother's ham sandwiches or walking up and down the coastal path to Carbis Bay. He never judged me for what I didn't know—he understood my parents hadn't bothered teaching me things like swimming or riding a bike. He still jokes sometimes that learning to swim unlocked that will of iron he thinks I have; that conviction I had until recently that working harder and harder was the key to conquering my feelings of inadequacy.

I miss that certainty now. And the cramped Cornish cottage, the smell of wood burning and fresh bread in the living room, the mismatched sofas, the handmade blankets piled on every surface. As I conjure it, D'Arvor seems to expand. It stretches so vast, it is so full, it might swallow me. But as much as I would rather stay under my bedsheet right now, I can't. I have to go face them all.

You have to meet Maxime.

To give myself courage, I conjure the memory of the first time I met Maxime Foucault as an adult. The memory that has fed my fantasies over the years. This Camille Leray was twenty-one years old, quiet and solemn in a packed, tipsy, and loud university bar in St. Andrews. I had red hair down to my hips that was not yet straightened, wore glasses not contacts, and was still short (*Say* petite, *Camille, it makes it sound prettier*, Maman used to say). I was a master's student studying art history; it was December, the stuffiness of the bar and the heat of all the bodies a stark contrast to the bitter cold of pre-Christmas up North. At all social occasions, my friends and I were the corner gang, hovering in the shadows of the walls, talking about Böcklin, drinking neat spirits that we hated, and watching the party from the corner of our eyes. As art historians, we were cursed with too much attention to detail and historical context to fool ourselves that we were a cool crew. Plus the actual cool crew all had something in common: they were posh.

That night, the last Thursday before we broke up for Christmas, I had been tasked to go to the bar to get another round. The pub was packed, and I felt the disadvantage of my lack of height as I fought my way among blond and pink-cheeked boys built like rugby players, and tall equestrian girls, their bare shoulders sparkling with glitter. I was the nerd in dungarees and knockoff Doc Martens, *'scusing* herself slowly and painfully toward the bar.

It got worse when "Mr. Brightside" started playing, very loudly, and they *all* started to move. In a blink, the floor space turned into a mosh pit, heavy bodies jumping up and down and, because they were drunk, sideways, erratically. Panicked, I tried to retreat to my safe corner, but an elbow slammed into my chest, knocking the air out of my lungs, and I found myself on the ground. *It's only a bar. This is not a stampede. Don't panic, Camille.* I tried to get up, but nobody had noticed me. Feet stomped on my hands, and legs pressed around me so closely that I couldn't move.

Until two strong hands caught me and pulled me up. "Are you all right?" I hung on to impossibly green eyes and a tall body shielding me from the surrounding madness. The smell of pine trees and spring water, conjuring the clearing of an enchanted wood, a place of rest. I had seen those eyes before, but that was impossible. Why would he be here? He was supposed to be in France within the thick walls of his castle. That's where my mind had placed him, all these years, with the thought that I could always find him if I wanted to. "I don't know," I said, fighting for my voice. He shook his head. "Let's get you out of here."

And he did. We slammed the door on the bar, shutting out the Killers, and found ourselves shivering on the snowy pavement.

"That was really dangerous," he said with irritation, raking his fingers through his hair. "Are you sure you're quite all right?"

I realized I'd been staring at him. I needed to be sure it was him. "Yes, I am. Sorry, but... are you French?"

He spoke English with a heavy accent he clearly wasn't bothered to work on. "Yes," he said. "I'm from Brittany. I'm on my year abroad here."

"Me too," I replied, in French. "Well, I'm only half-French, so this is not my year abroad, but..."

I realized his eyes never left mine, not even when a loud scooter nearly skid on the ice mere meters away from us. "Which half?"

"Pardon?"

"Which one of your parents is French?"

"Oh. My mother." *Brittany.* My thoughts were a whirlpool of excitement and confusion. His presence was intoxicating. It was like being back there again. D'Arvor and his magical lake, digging its roots in Brocéliande. I did seriously consider that, because of my ordeal, I might be completely making him up. Any minute, I might snap out of it and realize I was speaking to a spotty first-year engineer called Bryan. "She was from Brittany too. Whereabouts are you from, exactly?" I had to be absolutely sure.

"West of Rennes. At the edge of the Paimpont Forest."

He had used its official name. Not its storied name, marked forever by the legends of King Arthur and his knights. "Brocéliande," I whispered.

"Yes," he smiled in recognition, then the smile melted into something more intense. "Have we met before? I'm Maxime

Foucault." He was stooping slightly to talk to me, like he aimed to shield me from the cold. He was, of course, younger and more fresh-faced than the man who stared at me in Courtenay; he has been, at every age, the most handsome version of himself.

I felt too shy to mention that we had indeed met before, when we were seven. Surely he wouldn't remember. "Camille Leray," I said.

"Camille Leray," he repeated, as his face opened with a wide smile, his eyes flickered, and he started to say something else—

The door of the bar had slammed opened and Tallulah Something, the most attractive girl in my course, was calling out to him. Maxime shot me a look of apology. "Shall we go back in?"

I shook my head, putting on the cardigan that I had, really elegantly, kept tied around my waist. Compared to Tallulah I was a right mess, like some kind of small farm boy time-traveling from the 1950s. "I better be off."

"I'll walk you home," he said, as Tallulah scowled.

I smiled, trying to be cool. "I think you're needed here. I'm just five minutes away." I could see he was conflicted. *Please choose to stay with me,* I begged him silently.

"All right, if you're sure. I'll see you later, I suppose."

"Thank you for rescuing me," I told him in French as I walked away.

I found out we were on the same course; I don't think

he had bothered turning up for lectures much in the first term. I would love to say that we became friends, but he was popular, permanently surrounded. Tallulah made sure nobody else would dream of going near him, not with the motives I had. I wanted to smell him again. I wanted to imagine how he would touch me, even the first movement of pulling me toward him; I wanted to know the heat signature of his hands and exactly where he would choose to place them—my shoulder blades, like wings unfolding just before takeoff, or perhaps my neck. From the onset, he was a deeply physical, obsessive crush. I dreamt and dreamt of him on my sunken mattress that had seen too many students' bodies.

We didn't speak again properly until the Victoria and Albert Museum, the summer after the course, when I managed to make a fool of myself and spoil anything we could have had.

———

After a slow, frustrating wash under the treacle of water provided by the old-fashioned bath, wrapped in a towel, I tiptoe to the window to take in the view. The sun is up now, but the morning still bears the rags of dawn, mist clinging over the water basins like Merlin's potions. Sparrows and blue tits are shaking in the sand of the paths. As I survey the hard, precise beauty of the garden, the night and thoughts of inadequacy disperse and I fall in love with it all over again. I become aware of my body breathing under the soft towel, of my feet stroking the parquet, of the intense physicality of the kind of lust running through me.

In my studies as well as my work, I thrived on adrenaline, always pinging toward the next task—it felt like being in love. That need for the next gratification—stumbling across a masterpiece, tapping into its world, the excitement when audiences realized they wanted it, *had* to have it, then hearing the hammer fall on a record-breaking sale. I miss it more than I can say.

I think D'Arvor is the only place that could create that buzz again. Something that reconnects me, from a single point in my lower belly, to hunger for fine things, for touching and being touched. I push the window wide-open, letting the morning cool my skin, and that place I always forget to dry, the hollow between my collarbones. There are still droplets trapped there and I spread them with one finger, imagining it as the place where beads of sweat would pool, where a lover would be able to taste the salt of my skin—

He's here. He walks right out of the woods and, of course, because this is the height of ridiculousness, because I was thinking about a dress of misty tulle and thorny flowers in my hair, he is shirtless, wearing only black jogging bottoms, loose trainers, and a white towel thrown around his neck. If he wasn't speaking on the phone, he'd be the most clichéd chapter of a Regency erotica novel. Maxime. I don't think I'd guessed the triangular shape of his torso right, the lines of the lean muscles of his chest—not like someone who drinks protein shakes and works out four hours a day, but like someone who swims on the regular. His wet locks are flattened and stick to his forehead. He darts through the lawn like a stag toward me at the window. I should close it, draw back the curtain, but I'm caught up in my most feverish dream. A bit closer and I'll be able to hear what he's saying on the phone—

He's right under my window when he looks up—startles, frowns. His eyes say, *Were you spying on me?* The charm is broken. I wave in lieu of an apology, skittish and awkward, at the same time trying to retreat and close the window. The towel is slipping—I can feel its corner coming loose at my armpit—and as I hurry backward, it gets stuck on the window latch and I find myself naked, scampering away to the depths of the darkened bedroom. I don't know whether Maxime saw this. I wrap myself in my dressing gown and drop on the bed, my head in my hands. It's so ridiculous that I burst out laughing. My laughter sounds mad, like it isn't my own. I look up, half expecting to see Constance standing over me, holding her mask, but I'm alone.

9

MAXIME IS SITTING at the breakfast table when I finally enter the dining room. It's just him, and both of us are dressed appropriately this time. I opted for my "expert" attire of a strict black trouser suit to arm myself against my wobbliness. A few weeks without wearing it has been enough to make it feel like slipping on someone else's skin, someone I am trying to impersonate, which is exactly the point. I walked through a cloud of perfume, hoping for it to work some Merlin kind of magic, make Maxime forget about the balcony and the towel. *New Beginnings Mist.* I'd buy that. A whole vat of it, please.

He is leaning back in his chair, wearing a white shirt and chinos, his long legs stretched under the table. He is so relaxed, almost reclined, like a Roman emperor, reading a newspaper. As he spots me, he stands up.

"Camille Leray. Delighted to meet you." He addresses

me in English, his French accent transporting me back at once to a snowy pavement in St. Andrews. After Courtenay, I expected him more sullen, broody, rather than this relaxed demeanor I'm immediately wrapped in, this knowing smile. He's always had a way of taking you in, as if you are the only person on earth.

I take a quiet breath and step forward to shake the hand he's offered. "Hello, Maxime. We've met before," I say in French. Luckily I'm also an expert at sounding confident— years of practice.

"Did you mean just now, when you were hanging out of my window half naked, or when we studied together?"

Despite dying inside, I hold his gaze. "Really pleased to see you again."

"Likewise. Thank you for coming."

So, he remembers St. Andrews, but does he remember the following summer, in London, at the Victoria and Albert Museum, when we almost—

He gestures for me to sit in front of a lush farmhouse-style breakfast: a pile of fresh croissants, golden butter in a ceramic dish, and homemade apple jam. I sink into my seat, realizing, after the relief of Maxime's friendly demeanor, that I'm ravenous.

"I see you've met Ms. Leray." Marie-Laure is coming in with a pot of coffee.

We thank her as she fills both our mugs, wide-brimmed like bowls, duck egg blue and old-fashioned.

"You will show her the sculptures today, then?" She seems tired, much more so than yesterday, with a deep wrinkle between her brows, as if the strings connecting her features are a little too short.

"Milk?" Maxime asks me. I nod and reach out for the jug. "Allow me." His hand brushes mine as he pours.

Calm down, Camille. For goodness' sake.

"I can't wait to take a look at the sculptures," I say, "and to find out exactly what you need me for."

"After breakfast," he says.

Marie-Laure nods. "I'll be in the garden."

Maxime puts a hand on her arm as she goes to leave. "How about you sit down? Just for a minute, and have some coffee?"

She shakes her head, smiles at him. "I have to tend to my roses. They're very demanding children."

I sip my coffee as she leaves the room (milky, hot, delicious), watching Maxime's brow furrow as he checks his phone.

"Is she all right?" I ask.

"Who? My mother? She's always worried about something."

"Really? What about?" Then I realize it might sound ignorant, as if I'm implying that rich people can't have worries. (*They don't, really. Not real worries, when they can have anything they ever wanted;* that's what Lowen would say when drama would erupt at boarding school. I bat the thought away.)

Maxime half shrugs. "Me, mainly." His smile has a hint of wickedness that vanishes so quickly I wonder if I dreamt it. "So." He throws his napkin on the table. "Shall we get to it?"

———

It soon transpires that by *getting to it* he means an extensive tour of the castle, starting with the grounds. I'm in his hands, following him as he talks about the history of the estate and rare spruces. The dew soaks the leather of my brogues as we draw a wide circle around the castle, to more water basins, square and mirror-like in the morning. I half expect to see Maxime's reflection appear on them alone, without mine. This can't possibly be real—*a tour of D'Arvor with him.* I've studied archives and old maps of the estate until I knew its layout by heart, but it is so much better to see it all in person. The air smells of damp grass, of the rosebushes we walk past, at which Marie-Laure is already working with huge shears, a wide-brimmed straw hat obscuring her face. The sun presses on us, fighting the cooler breeze coming from the sea. Everywhere I look, my eyes are met with the silver loops of the river. I follow them to catch a glimpse of the lake. Viviane's voice echoes in my head. *Je t'attends. I am waiting for you.* Or is it Constance's?

"Is it true that Louis XV snogged Madame de Pompadour in your orangery?" I ask, knowing full well it's rubbish trivia, but trying to trick my brain into staying in the present.

Maxime still hasn't told me why I'm here, and I know I'm going to face Constance's sculptures soon. I'm scared. What if my gift is tainted, turned against me and my sanity? What if I can't do whatever Maxime needs me to do to help him? Or what if I find myself pulled in and incapable of returning to reality? This estate is the source of my gift, the key to understanding Constance's fate. I feel jittery, sensitive, raw, and that's no good.

Maxime's lips lift slightly. "There are many rumors about D'Arvor. But that one isn't true, I'm afraid."

"Ah," I say, half my brain still distracted by the worrying, "I imagine it must have been very difficult to fumble when wearing eighteenth-century dress anyway. The corsets, the endless ribbons…"

"Another legend is that Louis XV came up with the idea of his famous topiary costume here, while visiting the gardens."

"Is that also inaccurate?"

"Probably. Though my great-grandmother used to swear that his ghost would visit her. She said she connected with a lot of—people."

He looks away and I glance at his face, which has tensed inexplicably. "Were you close?"

"Yes. She lived until the incredible age of a hundred and five. She never looked or acted older than seventy either. A bit of a local celebrity, a wonder of nature, with a notorious sweet tooth. But she had her demons."

We walk a bit farther, the silence filled by blackbird

calls. I wonder why Maxime chose to show me the outside of D'Arvor rather than the inside. I'm aware I've not been shown the most ancient part of the castle yet, which I'm so excited about. Then it dawns on me.

"Are we going to Constance's workshop?" I ask. "I thought it was in the old barns? By the river?"

"I think you're mistaken," Maxime says. "She always worked in her room. Anyway, I'm afraid many of the outbuildings are rather derelict. It takes much time and love to maintain these great places. There hasn't been much time recently."

But love, he implies, *that* runs deep.

"I understand."

It takes some more silence before he speaks again. He must be thinking about the nature of love, perhaps, or heritage. "Can you imagine trying to undress somebody disguised as a hedge, though? You'd prick yourself."

I nearly choke, but he is already on his way back to the house, darting with his long elastic steps across the lawn, when I put my hand on his arm to stop him.

"Maxime?"

"Yes?"

"The tour was great, but... why do you need me here?"

He smiles. "You're about to find out."

10

I HURRY BACK inside after Maxime, and when I come to stand next to him at the bottom of the stairs, I'm acutely conscious of my quick breathing. I know he can hear it too. I remove my suit jacket. He steps a little closer to me, close enough that my naked arm feels his warmth.

"I trust Lila has shown you around the house?"

Only he can call D'Arvor a *house*. "Only the recent part," I tell him. "I would love to—"

But he interrupts me, deep in thought. "Very well. So you have your bearings."

I nod, willing myself to settle. He is so *here*, so alive, all muscles and flesh against the backdrop of cold polished stone. *He's not yours, Camille.* "Lila seems lovely."

The corners of his mouth lift. "Lila is many things, but I wouldn't say *lovely*, exactly." I want to ask what he means, but he continues: "Well, to the attic we go, then. The sculptures are still where we found them."

It is a repeat of that day when we were seven, except that he doesn't hold my hand. I follow him upstairs, then up another hidden and smaller service staircase. The servant quarters under the eaves, he tells me, started serving as storage around the time of Constance's stay. "Raymond Foucault didn't need many staff. He didn't want anyone around. He wasn't a socialite," Maxime says as he opens the door.

"He sounds like an interesting character."

"Raymond was a formidable man. His grandfather acquired the estate after the revolution; he had made a fortune in trade, hosted lavish parties, and put the Foucaults on the map. Raymond was very different, but he focused on what really mattered: preserving the estate and securing our family's heritage."

"I couldn't find much about his wife, Anne," I say.

"You've been researching her?" Maxime stops on the threshold, blocking me out.

"She's the one who invited Constance. Of course I've researched her."

I may be considered an expert in my field, I may have spent countless hours studying French art and history, but in Maxime's presence, I feel all I know is a thick curtain veiling a truth only accessible to the initiated. I am back to being the child he led, who didn't know what she was looking at. No matter how hard I work, I can never be like the Foucaults, with that innate firsthand knowledge they inherited.

"She was much younger than him when they married.

She would have looked forward to having some company here. I have a feeling that, when she invited Constance over, she went a bit rogue." He smiles.

"What do you mean?"

"Only that Raymond wouldn't have been one for supporting struggling artists."

"I'm glad Constance had D'Arvor," I say. "She really fell in love with the place." I have to work so hard to concentrate on the present moment, on what he is saying. I want to—but the past is calling to me through all the objects behind Maxime, the walls seeping with history. *Keep your cool, Camille.*

Maxime's eyes dart to me, two pins of green in the darkness. "You do know her well, don't you?"

At once, the voices recede and I find myself basking in his praise, but he has already turned away, beckoning me in.

As soon as I step into the attic, I know this is all at once the best and the worst room I could be in. The whispers are strong, dissonant, and the headache increases tenfold. The space is packed full of old objects and furniture covered in dust sheets that might as well be ghosts ready to pounce. Behind me, Maxime flips a switch and a single bare light bulb turns on, much farther down the room, barely managing to illuminate where we stand. I wince and he seems to assume it's because of the light. "Sorry," he says. "This space hasn't been given much thought over the years. It's just family junk. Or so I thought."

I shake my head. "That's OK." I can barely breathe, let

alone speak. I must shut out all the random objects trying to grab and pull me in, competing for attention. So many people have made them, used them. They felt so much. *It's never been like this. I was always good at being selective. I taught myself to be in control. Where's this control now?* Panic unfolds—I must be broken. My experience in *Wrong Night Swimming* has derailed my gift. I conjure child-Maxime's hand in mine, and *Viviane*. I desperately call for the peace I felt, the love and safety I accessed in Constance's world. Except *Viviane* is not here, among the four plasters Maxime leads me to, set up hastily on a trestle table.

"I was tidying up over there," Maxime points to the very far end of the room, then he sees my doubtful face at the word *tidying* and chuckles. "Believe it or not, it used to be much worse—we had a roof leak and had to have some repairs done—and I came across those. Nobody in my family knew they were there. Luckily, they were spared by the leak. I cleaned them up as best I could, but they were in excellent condition."

I'm dying to look at the sculptures, but I'm also terrified. There's something pulsing in this attic, something strong and desperate. I swear I catch a glimpse of a child jumping up and down in the darkened space, giggling. A crown of blond curls at the corner of my eye. Is this the memory of seven-year-old me following Maxime? The sweetness, but also something darker. Marie-Laure's words come to mind— *It has known many triumphs and tragedies.* Is this the sound of swords clicking? Of broken violins? A baby's cries—that latches onto me, a drill into my head.

I was really hoping I'd walk in here and be able to calmly use my process. But now I'm like an addict who overdosed looking at a new drug, knowing it will end me. I reach for my iPad, but my hands are shaking. *There would have been plenty of babies here, Camille. So many generations. Please, focus on the task at hand.*

These sculptures do look like hers. It is so exciting. *It's the best thing that has happened to you in years*, I reason. I should be desperate to throw myself into Constance's world, to explore the new experiences of hers that have been opened to me. Perhaps some secrets of her past, some answers as to what happened to her. But the dark pond taking shape at my feet, uninvited, is tar, not water. It's threatening to engulf me, while everything screams at me not to go in.

Oh no. It wasn't supposed to be like that. Not with Constance's work. Her work has always been safe. But not this.

I can't go in. I won't. I must resist, or it will all go wrong again.

"Are you all right?"

I didn't realize I'd shut my eyes, that my hand is gripping the table to try and stabilize me, that I've been swaying. I can barely nod because I'm hanging on as hard as I can, but at once Maxime's hands are on my upper arms, guiding me to the safety of a chair covered in a dust sheet. I shiver, remembering the snowy pavement in St. Andrews.

"These sculptures are strong. Loud." This thought should have remained in my head.

"You look unwell." He pulls out his phone and types something on it. What a poor show I'm making; what a laughable "expert" I'm turning out to be, half fainting as soon as priceless works come into view. What if Maxime tells me not to bother after all, sends me back to London? *She's unstable. A liability. It all gets to her.*

"I'm fine," I say. "It's just…"

I'm going to lie to him, tell him I'm claustrophobic, when I feel his hand on my wrist and he's dropping down on his heels, leveling with me. He's so incredibly close that the smell of spring water and pinewood reaches me. He still wears the same aftershave, then, or is that just his natural scent, Brocéliande on his skin? Anyhow, it helps calm everything; the dark pond recedes. We stay like this for a few moments, some kind of threads holding us exactly the right amount of close and apart…

Finally, he speaks. "Camille, were you…?" He stops, rubbing his palm on his stubble. "This is going to sound so wild—there was a child here, a little girl, once…"

My heart stops. My eyes shoot up to his. I find my voice: "She was brought in after she nearly drowned in the lake. Then you showed her *Viviane.*"

In the dark, his eyes widen, and I swear they start glowing low.

"Fuck," he whispers uncharacteristically. "Really? You're not messing with me?"

"That was me. I remember it too."

"That's—but then we met again later. What are the chances?"

"Very slim." I had no idea we would end up on the same course, or bump into each other that summer in London, but somehow it feels like he might believe that I stalked him. I need to change the subject. "Maxime, where is *Viviane* now? I can't see her."

"My parents donated it to the Beaux Arts Museum in Rennes twenty years ago. I'm still angry about it. Lucky I was the one who found the others, as an adult." He sounds distracted. "Camille, I remember vividly being here with you as a child, and I remember St. Andrews, and the V&A. I've always known—suspected—felt—"

His hand finds mine, and I know he feels me shaking, but we're interrupted.

"Max?" Lila's voice snips the thread, from the threshold, and Maxime jumps up. "You asked for some water?"

"Thank you."

"What's going on?" she asks, picking her way swiftly and silently between cumbersome furniture to take a look at me. She looks worried, her eyes darting from me to the sculptures, my silent judges, and back.

"It's a bit claustrophobic and dusty in here," Maxime says, moving the glass of water from Lila's hand to mine. I drink grateful long gulps. I still can't believe he remembers. I can't believe he… What was he going to say—what exactly— about what he felt?

"I'll be all right in a minute," I say. "Thank you so much, Lila."

"I'll move them," Maxime says, as if to himself.

"What?" Lila asks.

"You can't work in here." This time, he addresses me directly. "I can hardly see my own hands. I was so excited to show them to you—I should have thought to move them to a better place."

"I can use a flashlight. Or even just a desk lamp would do the trick."

He waves me off. "There's an old nursery across the corridor. It's clean, dry, and bright with no direct sunlight. I'll have Frédéric set up a desk and some better lighting. Is there anything else you would need? I could—"

"Maxime." I stop him. Both he and Lila look at me with some trepidation. I'm starting to feel better. The water helped, but also…he's not sending me back. He seems to believe in me. "You still haven't told me what you need, exactly? Do you want these plasters authenticated? Valued? Do you want me to study them and tell you when Constance made them, what they meant? I can do all of that; I just need to know why exactly I'm here."

"All of the above. I want to know what we have. I've literally just found them and, even as an art dealer, I'm not the living expert on Constance Sorel. It would be great to know what they're worth in the current market—for information." He glances at Lila, but she seems to be studying a pair of ancient ice skates in a cardboard box. "Of course you'll invoice me for your time. Whatever you need, that's not a problem."

"Are you thinking of selling them?" I ask him, unprepared to believe it. "That's what my services are normally used for. In that case you need to know..." I'm about to tell him that I don't work for Courtenay anymore, but he stops me.

"We'll talk about the details later. For now, I just want your expert opinion. On everything." He takes the empty glass off me and nudges Lila to take it, and I have the distinct impression he's holding something back. That he's feeling awkward because she's here. "Do you think we might have something good here? Or have I just got it completely wrong and those are the results of Auntie Flo going crazy in a car boot sale in the nineteen eighties? It would not be the first time D'Arvor's 'treasure trove' disappointed."

Now I'm feeling better, I can look at the sculptures. All plaster, fragile, and patinated, in extremely good condition. They are beautiful and moving, and my heart flutters at the thought of what I may uncover in them, if I manage to get a grip. Certainly not amateurish, clumsy, or fake. They radiate Constance's vision, of that I am certain.

"I don't think you should worry about that. I think you definitely have something good here."

11

OF COURSE, MY main thought is to be alone with
Maxime again so we can continue our conversation, but he
has to go to Rennes for a meeting. He promises that Frédéric
will set up my "office" for tomorrow morning and leaves me
alone in D'Arvor's dining room, where someone (I assume
Marie-Laure, or perhaps the servants of the Beast) has left
an inviting spread of salad, cold meat, and cheeses. I help
myself and eat lunch alone, wondering where they all are, but
grateful for a bit of quiet.

Maxime is absent at dinner again. After observing them
for twenty-four hours, I'm feeling a little more involved in
the routine of the family; I get up every time Lila is asked
to fetch something in the kitchen and Marie-Laure is starting to let me help, as if I am another surrogate daughter, or
maybe the poor cousin invited to stay. Lila is watching me
somewhat warily and I wonder what she saw of the scene

with Maxime earlier. It's a moment my heart keeps returning to, sending small electric jolts through me. I'm both galvanized and absent-minded in my conversations with Marie-Laure and Frédéric.

"I'll set up the little room for you after dinner," Frédéric says.

"What for, dear?" Marie-Laure asks.

"Maxime wants me to move the sculptures to where Ms. Leray can have a better look at them. What kind of lighting do you need?"

"To be honest, anything would be better than the attic's," I say.

"We have some kind of pedestal lamp somewhere. Do you remember, Maman? Maxime and I used to use it for our pretend plays."

"Pretend plays?" Lila asks, looking up from her new potatoes.

"That would do the trick," he continues. "If I can find it."

"That's nice," I say. "Playing together as boys."

He snorts.

"Frédéric," Marie-Laure scolds him.

He turns to me and smiles. "Maxime takes pretending very seriously. Playing with him wasn't always much fun."

Then I see his eyes meet Marie-Laure's; there's an awkward silence. I look to Lila, but she is busy stacking up our empty plates. In my book, she is the one who plays tricks. I wonder what she made of finding Maxime and me in the attic earlier. I can't read her, and she unsettles me. All I know is she doesn't like having me here.

As I toss and turn in bed this second night, I know there's no way on earth that I'm going to fall asleep. My brain is restless, one moment wondering what Maxime was about to say about the girl he showed *Viviane* to—about *me* (I'm thrilled he remembers, hardly dare to let myself consider it might have meant something to him too), then my brain dips into fear again remembering how unwell I became just from being near the sculptures and how unable I was to control what spoke to me.

I just want to know what we have.

Was the authentic *Night Swimming* among the sculptures? I didn't think so—but I looked so quickly, my brain distracted by fighting the dread... I need to find it—it would save my career—but I also need to know what happened to Constance. However, will I be able to do this now that the grip I have on reality is starting to escape me?

The room is dark, holding its breath. I'm not going mad. My gift is real, but I have built everything else on research, on being rational, knowledgeable. It was so stressful in the attic earlier, with Maxime watching me, that years of my accumulated emotions got the better of me. It must have been stage fright. I need to be alone with the sculptures, try to read them again. I need to delve in, really focus, away from personal distractions. That will reassure me that I can still do it.

I get up, throw my dressing gown on, and grab my phone to use as a light. I hope Frédéric has moved the sculptures like he said he would; skulking about the attic at night would be too eerie for my liking. I open my door and pad down the carpeted corridor as quietly as possible, to the service staircase.

It's 3:00 a.m. The quietest time of night, too late for night owls and too early for early risers. Except the castle never sleeps. I thought it was a cliché, because the two-bed council house in Reading I grew up in was porous and silent as if it was made of cardboard, but it's true. Cracks and thumps accompany me every step of the way. The staircase is narrow and pitch-black. To reassure myself, I think of bakers. I think of all of the ones who are up already, cutting and shaping the dough. I think of Lowen in the warmth of his dad's bakery on Fore Street, the steamed windows, the golden light of the back room, where he is shaping bread rolls. It makes the ominous night of the castle feel kinder.

When I get to the old nursery's door, my future office, it is ajar. A long table resting on skinny trestles stands bare in the moonlight. I jump out of my skin when I catch a glimpse of someone in the room, a thin silhouette with a drooped head in the corner...but it's the lamp Frédéric was talking about at dinner.

The sculptures are still in the attic, then. Damn. I breathe in and make my way to the door, considering briefly whether turning the light bulb on will make it more or less scary altogether. I decide it is better to know what I'm facing and put off anything that would relish skulking in the darkness. The light doesn't make a big difference to my part of the room, but at least reveals there are no demons sitting in a circle, nothing hanging from the ceiling. I take some time to remind myself I'm here for Constance, and nobody else. I just need to shut all the other voices out. It's not perfect, but it does feel a little easier this time. I keep my jaw clenched, my eyes focused, ignore the soldiers, the hunters, and the babies. I turn my phone flashlight up and approach the sculptures standing on the table in a semicircle.

They really are stunning, about thirty centimeters high, all representing couples. Constance had that way of capturing intense *life*, bottling it up in her compositions. They are electric, their hands reaching out, their bodies perched precariously on the tipping point of gravity. She loved merging human flesh with landscape: rocks weighing down the skirts of her women, preventing them from taking flight; the sensual curve of long hair meeting a wave, pulled back. I come closer to the sculptures, trying to focus on their stylistic qualities, whereas their emotions, like the volume of a stereo turned up, up, up, scream me in.

You can do this, Camille. You're in charge.

I don't want to go in. Not yet. And it's a tiny bit easier now, at 3 a.m., to fight it. It's quieter, I feel more prepared having been here earlier today. And also…

She's *here*. Excitement takes over as I realize I know

these sculptures from research, that I had presumed them lost. Sorel mentioned them in the rare letters she sent to her former Parisian benefactors, when she was trying to obtain commissions to cast her plasters in bronze. She was still hoping to make it, to become a respected sculptor in her own right. Although a few other works did get cast, now mostly tucked away in the Boisseau Museum's storage room, I wasn't aware that these plasters had survived. I know them by heart, being described or sketched in her letters, and now they're real. In front of me.

I can't believe they've been sleeping here all this time; that the Foucaults have literally been sitting under them, drinking champagne.

The four couples in front of me all come from Arthurian legend. *Merlin and Morgane*, as well as *Uther and Igerna*, and *Yvain and Laudine*, but the one that immediately stands out to me is *Guinevere and Lancelot*.

Sorel joined Boisseau's workshop in Paris because she wanted to work with him. She knew his genius and admired him deeply; in his fifties, he had risen to unprecedented notoriety. He was much older, widely acclaimed; his craft and productivity were unsurpassed. A rock star of clay and bronze, physically imposing, handsome, tormented by genius but charmingly shy when it came to romance.

His creations were selling so fast he had a whole team working for him. He also took on students, some women traveling from abroad, who'd come to Paris for the thrill of a couple of lessons from the master. Sculpture is physical work—it requires heavy lifting, twisting wires and creating armatures, and mixing plaster and ferrying heavy lumps of clay. It was an art that was deemed manly and that women, at the time, were frowned upon for tackling in any serious manner. They had better stick to watercolor or embroidery, and keep their delicate fingers clean and their arms weak.

But Sorel was always contrary. Sure of her own talent, driven by her passion for sculptures, she demanded Boisseau's time and attention. *Whenever I looked around,* he wrote much later, *Mademoiselle Sorel was there, that gaze of hers so intense it made my hands burn. She was no amateur. She was an apprentice.* After a while, he tasked her with some work on the hands and feet of his sculptures and allowed her to use his models when he was done with them. She stayed late, after everybody else had left, and brought in her own candles so she could practice her craft.

Boisseau kept returning to classical mythology, and during her time in Paris, Sorel explored Ovid's *Metamorphoses* in her own works; she always chose to represent couples. I know why; with Boisseau, she was changing, too. Under his guidance, she was sharpening her skills and mind, becoming a powerful artist. Under his hands, she was turning into a woman who knew desire, whose body plied to yearning and whose mind to obsession. He breathed air into her life. Around him, she was dizzy with new possibilities. It was exhilarating.

In her works, I have felt her skin cracking and splitting

when she broke the ice that had formed, overnight, on top of the water buckets. The hindrance of her skirts, that she would fasten up at her waist when she was alone. The burning muscles of her arms, her back, the sweat pooling between her collarbones. I have felt how she used men's condescension as fuel for her ambitions. It spoke to the way my own skin cracked in the cold of unheated old houses, the nights spent at the computer until every muscle of my back and neck ached. The way I had to earn every single bit of respect I ever received, ten times over. We both worked tirelessly to break our ceilings. Constance's faith in herself, her hunger for living every experience to the full, her total commitment to her vision, gave me a rush every time I tapped into it. With her, I felt I could bust my own limitations, that she offered layers and experiences and emotions I soon could not do without. I needed more and more.

I have also experienced the warmth that spread through her when Boisseau beckoned her to the fire, one night when he stayed late, and wrapped her shoulders in a shawl, their first kiss, as she was trembling with cold, then suddenly hot all over. She was deeply infatuated, and so was he. Their story was complex, doomed, and formative. His teaching and resources unlocked the love of her life: sculpture. Neither could exist without the other.

Until her association with him became her downfall. Parisian society eventually got wind of their affair and, with relief, found a familiar box to put her in: the muse, the mistress of a Great Man. He wanted her to stay and continue working with him, but she left. After their breakup, she tried to make it work in the Parisian art world, but without his name and protection, everything dwindled. She was not only a woman, but a tainted one. She was a wild thing with strong arms wearing men's clothes for ease of working. They didn't know what to do with her.

I am done with Paris, she wrote back to Anne Foucault, *therefore I am very tempted to accept your invitation. I need D'Arvor to wrap me up in its wings. I need to believe in fairies and magic again—the vengeful ones who trap untrue lovers in stone, I mean. The kind of magic that repairs a broken heart.*

PS I am also quite handy with a saw and a hammer, if that is of any use to your castle.

In Brittany, she immersed herself in local Arthurian legend. Anne would tell stories at night by the fire in the dining room. Constance revisited the places of her childhood that tourism had just started to exploit: the Val Sans Retour, Brocéliande, where she searched for Merlin's tomb. She worked hard to develop her own style, which soon moved away from the Arthurian cycle to scenes of ordinary life. Until now, I only knew *Viviane* as an example of the earlier. Other works of her time at D'Arvor I saw a few years back in an exhibition in Rennes's Beaux-Arts Museum: a set of scenes and portraits of ordinary rural life. All exquisite, but very different, in her attempt to sublimize the humble happiness of everyday tasks. I remember tapping into these and finding them too quiet for her. I only went to see them once.

These sculptures in front of me right now, these four Arthurian couples in the attic, are a missing piece of the puzzle of her life, the link between Paris and Brittany. Heartbroken on more than one count, Constance would have initially brought the remnants of her tumultuous love story to D'Arvor. She would have continued to seek inspiration in dramatic legends of magic and broken hearts.

I've been telling myself all of this, going over her life, as a way to stay here. The sculptures are calling, the pond rising, and I'm scared. I don't trust myself and my gift anymore. I know I'm going to have to relent, but I'm trying hard to stick to my process and, first, observe. I've been staring at *Guinevere and Lancelot* a while now, the lovers who could never be together, trying hard to analyze it from the outside. Sorel portrayed the push and pull so clearly in their movements, their arms intertwining without ever touching. Guinevere's dress looks so heavy it almost tips her backward into Lancelot's arms, yet she pulls away.

Her composition draws you in, and you keep looking for the place of connection, going round and round them without ever quite finding it.

They want me in… Not yet.

Not yet, not yet. I take a step back, trying to hang on to this reality. *You can do this. You are in charge.*

This is the find of a lifetime, something that very few

experts get to experience: access to a whole new chapter of the life of the artist they have devoted their life to. D'Arvor has lovingly preserved and provided me with this opportunity.

Yet, I try to stifle a tiny touch of disappointment that *Night Swimming* isn't here. I take a look around the attic, in a daze, wondering if it could be hidden here somewhere, still undiscovered. I'm not bold enough to start ripping dust sheets off the Foucaults' family heirlooms.

Yet.

The pull intensifies, water rising to my knees. It vibrates with echoes, monsters down below. Will I ever get used to this new fear that permeates my process now? The loss of control, the new prospect of spiraling, the danger?

I should take measurements, write detailed descriptions of them. I squeeze my tape measure in my hand, allowing the sharp edge to cut my skin. A flash again. Maxime's eyes, as they landed on me earlier today in this very space.

But then we met again later. What are the chances?

All around me there are threads linking us all—the castle, Constance, Maxime, and me—alive and organic and here I am, a spider at the center of the web. Or am I a fly, struggling to break free?

I've always known—suspected—felt—

I swear Lancelot's eyes flash green at me—I gasp as my grip on reality snaps and the flash flood takes me.

I prepare for the struggle, the fight for my life, but once inside the pond, things still, except for my heart beating in my ears, the headache of my clenched jaw. It is cold, dark, and I start trying to focus on what is beyond the fear. Where the light should be all the way down, in Avalon, I hear blackbirds, glimpse a pond in the sunset, golden branches of gorse.

That below is Constance's world. My heart soars—*that* is the way it's always been. Perhaps just a little more muted, tainted by my own fears, but I think it is safe.

I swim through into an Avalon that glows gold and green, and straightaway I look for her. I want her to tell me I'm going to be OK, impart some of her wisdom, reassurance. My legs shake as I survey it all. It is pretty, with such giddiness in the air—but Constance isn't here. Instead, Lancelot and Guinevere stand by the pond, their hands intertwined, their words reaching me.

My love, what would I do without you?

That's unusual. Where is she? I stare at them as they loop and loop in their loving charades, a distortion in the air. There it is again—the crippling feeling that something isn't right.

I put my faith in you.

You are my better half; you are the key to unlocking it all.

They embrace, the warmth of infatuation and devotion pouring into the landscape, liquid gold in the pond. I watch them, feeling like a voyeur, unsettled at Constance's absence. Is this more proof that my gift is broken? Or was our connection severed somehow?

I walk and walk, trying to find her. The cracks of dry branches make me jump. A hooded figure scampers away from me. A branch falls—the whole tree. It is two-dimensional like the decor of a theater.

It's all going wrong; it's uncanny, as if my doubts are attacking the substance of this world.

Oh, God—the pond. I need the pond to be real. What if I can't go back? I run, but the water keeps receding ahead of my feet—

There's someone else in here, someone who shouldn't be. I catch her eyes, terrified, at the edge of the water.

Lila.

She immediately dives in and I race after her, heart beating in my temples. I swim through as fast as I can but can't quite catch up with her. The shock of the fast return, of reality hitting me in the face makes me stumble as I get my bearings.

"Lila?" I run out of the attic to the sound of her scampering down the stairs. "Wait!" I whisper-shout as we tumble down after each other through the dark house, a shock after the golden sun in *Lancelot*. To my surprise, instead of ducking off into her bedroom, she continues down the main staircase, stepping into a land of marble and echoes like you do in a different dimension.

She's clumsy, like she's drunk, and I catch her halfway down, stopping her with my hand on her shoulder.

"Lila, wait." She struggles free and I realize I shouldn't be holding her. "Sorry, I'm so sorry, but please hear me out—"

"How did you do this?" We're in the darkness, suspended between two floors. Her eyes are two pools of shadows.

I take a breath, rub my hand on my forehead. "What? Lila, please, we're going to wake—" I stretch out my hand, not touching her this time, but in what I hope is an appeasing gesture.

"You were there, standing like a ghost, and then...and then, you..."

"I what?" I need to hear it. I realize I never got to speak to the lady in the Hepburn dress and find out what she experienced. *How* she got in there. I hide my hands deep in the pockets of my robe to hide their shaking.

"You put things in my head," Lila says.

"What things?"

I need to know exactly what it was like for her. How much I can affect others. She shakes her head. "I saw... I felt it, that...the Val Sans Retour, I was there."

Creaking floorboards upstairs make both of us jump. We wait, but no one comes. I wonder how many ghosts are eavesdropping on us.

"How did you know?" Lila asks again. "The Miroir aux Fées. The pond, in Brocéliande. What did you do?" She regains some defiance as she crosses her arms on her chest.

This hardens me to her. "What did *you* do, Lila?"

"I didn't do anything."

"You were following me, though?"

"What?"

Now I'm crossing my arms too, mirroring her on the stairs.

"Since I arrived you've been playing tricks, then watching me like you can't wait for me to trip on one of your silent wires. I know you don't want me here, but please, leave me alone to get on with it. It's clearly going to be best for both of us."

"You think I don't want you here?"

"You said I didn't belong here. That you thought I would do a bad job of it. I overheard you on the first night, talking to Maxime."

A long silence. In a stray pool of moonlight, her face falls. "What exactly did you hear?"

We're interrupted by the front door below us opening and closing.

"Max!" Lila is gone in a flash, rushing down. I follow. Is she going to tell him that I was snooping? Or worse, that I've hurt her? She doesn't seem hurt, just spooked.

At the bottom of the stairs, Maxime turns on a lamp on a Louis XV sideboard. He is shaking a fine pellicle of rain off his coat. The light makes his hair glow like gold thread. Lila throws herself into his arms and he receives her, surprised. I freeze on the last step.

"What's going on? It's so late," he says, his hands on her waist. "Or early." Then he sees me. "Camille? Is there a problem?"

I look at my hand, gripping the banister, on fire. The cracked knuckles. The warmth of a woolen blanket in an icy room. The sun pouring onto the water's silvery surface, as the lovers embrace, Constance and Boisseau, and Maxime and

Lila. Despite everything that happened, I find a trace of the love of Lancelot and Guinevere in me still, as they embraced in an Avalon of gilded ferns.

"I just had a nightmare. I woke Ms. Leray up in the process. Sorry." Against his chest, Lila's voice is small. He closes his arms around her protectively. One of her legs has hooked itself around his knee as if she is hoping to merge with him.

That's what I want. For the first time in years, it hits me. That kind of love. Someone to save you, scoop you up, be the guiding light you need. Not in the past, not by surrogacy, but for real. In *this* world. Feeding on rays from Constance's mind, unspoiled by my own doubts and demons, I allow myself to want it.

I should turn around and go back to my room, but I can't take my eyes off Lila and Maxime. When he brings his hand up to stroke her hair away from her face, smoothing long dark locks between his fingers, I notice her hair is wet. Did I really take her into the pond with me? Or did she *choose* to swim in to follow me? Is she going to tell him?

Maxime's eyes meet mine over her shoulder. In a blink we're back in the attic, and I know he feels our connection too. If I could tap into this—hang on to this for a bit longer—would my fear and brokenness melt away?

I just want to know what we have.

My heart beats as the water falls from Lila, and from Maxime's coat, hitting the marble.

You are my better half; you are the key to unlocking it all.

12

THE NEXT DAY, I do what I do best and retreat to the safety of work. I settle into my new office and spend more time studying *Guinevere and Lancelot*, which has now been safely moved. I decide it's best if I do everything I can to resist going back in. I could be interrupted and sweep someone in with me again. The thought makes me shudder.

I didn't see Lila, or Maxime for that matter, at breakfast. I will have to deal with this job as any normal expert would: from the outside. I throw a clean dust sheet over the rest of the sculptures, leaving them for later, take a painkiller to fight the headache, put headphones on, play distracting music. I harden myself against my gift as much as possible. Slowly my old habits of taking measurements, making notes, and doing research take over.

Still, the sculpture glows with filigrees of infatuation, devotion, danger. That's enough for me to know, I reason with myself, staying safely ashore. I can infer from the subject and the context that Sorel loved Boisseau despite breaking off their relationship and removing herself from his entourage. That his influence was more lasting than I had believed. I wonder if he visited her here. Lila identified this Avalon as the Miroir aux Fées, the fairies' mirror, a pond in Brocéliande, not far from here. While Avalon can take me to different places, that's one I haven't visited yet in Constance's work. It would make sense that she would have been there—but was Boisseau with her? I pour my excitement into research, hoping to find evidence of a visit, some hints I might have missed of their affair continuing beyond Paris.

She did bring *Night Swimming* to him, much later. Like Lancelot, did she never stop loving him? Was he the reason why she disappeared in the end? Can her love for him have been her downfall?

But then, why didn't he help? Why did he let her be buried unknown, unloved? He was still alive when she died.

If only I had *Night Swimming*.

I'm poring over copies of Boisseau's letters from his museum's archives when Maxime appears. Something comes alive in the room. I swear the sculptures turn to watch him.

You are the key to unlocking it all.

I look up, hastily removing my glasses, straightening my hair. He keeps his distance, leaning against the doorframe. I notice how tired he looks, though the shadows under his eyes add something to his presence. *God, Camille.* I know instinctively, from his hurried demeanor, that this won't be the time to resume our aborted conversation.

He confirms he wants me to put together a thorough dossier on the sculptures, including valuations, recommendations for which auction house to handle the sale, and prospective buyers I can think of. So he knows I'm not with Courtenay anymore—it's a relief that I don't have to revisit the "why" with him. It is a shock, however, that he's so clearly considering selling the sculptures.

"I'm off to Rennes for business," he says, indicating that now is not the time to ask why. "Will you be all right here? Do you have everything you need?"

No, I don't, I want to tell him. *I want more time with you, real answers, and...* I glance at *Guinevere and Lancelot*, lust and giddiness bubbling in me still. But I'm here to do a job.

"I'll guard your sculptures with my life," I tell him.

The corners of his mouth lift. "That won't be necessary. I hope."

He's about to leave when he turns back, like an afterthought. "Lila will look after you. Anything you need."

"That's kind, but I'm fine."

He is hovering, still. Gosh he is dreamy, in a dark-blue suit cut to highlight every line of him, with that slightly harassed tinge, yet that intense, undivided attention set on me. "Lila was quite shaken last night, and she doesn't have nightmares," he says.

I look down at my laptop, where I have typed basic notes,

pretending to click on something. "I don't think she likes me very much."

"Might that be because she doesn't understand you?"

I swallow. "What do you mean?"

You are my better half. He's smiling at me knowingly, sharp and soft at the same time.

"You are hard to understand. What you do with—art—*that* makes you extraordinary. Some might say scary."

What does he mean? I hear the sculptures whisper under their veil, but I laugh it off. "Thank you very much. But I don't think anyone has ever been scared of a laptop and a tape measure."

He smiles. "I've followed your career. Nobody can sell art as well as you. For the prices you get. I have always taken a keen interest in what you were doing. And the truth is, I think you could do even better. I think you have been holding back."

The room tilts on its axis and the world is at once upside-down. I thought I had been the one watching him from a distance.

"When did you start checking in on me?" I ask.

"Since the V&A," he says, then goes to leave.

"Maxime!" He's already halfway down the stairs. "We need to talk about this…"

He stops, looks up at me. I dominate him from the threshold above, so why does it feel that he holds all the keys? *Someone to be the guiding light you need.* Every fiber of my body stretches toward him as he smiles up at me. He's not angry; he's not calling me a witch, or an impostor. I hold his gaze, all at once beset by that need to be loved for the whole of who I am, to grow and to blossom, rather than contain myself. It is so intense it is threatening to bleed me out. "Please," I finally say.

"I really need to be off, Camille. But we will talk about this. Don't you worry. In the meantime, keep up the good work. There's no need to be afraid of who you are here."

I can't hold him back any longer, but when he's disappeared further down the staircase, his voice echoes to the eaves, disembodied, as if I've dreamt it. "For what it's worth, I have always thought you were rather likable."

I stifle a groan, sliding my back against the wall until I'm sitting on my heels in the corridor. I slam the office's door shut on the sculptures to muffle them.

Since the V&A. That afternoon we spent together that became the best date I have ever been on. And all these years since, I assumed Maxime must have thought me deranged.

Our master's program was over. The chance of getting closer to him had not materialized, and I had been too awkward, too self-conscious, to make it happen. It was July, and I was back living at my parents' while they were in France. I hated being in their house, so I spent most of my days in central London, before doing evening shifts waitressing in a French restaurant in Kensington. Lowen had gone home to Cornwall and we had planned for me to visit for a week;

I had already pushed it back a couple of times, telling him that most of my earnings were eaten up by my commute, so I had to save up more. That was true, but I had also given myself homework: before the September start of my internship at Courtenay, I would know all the eighteenth-through-twentieth century works of London's biggest museums. I roamed the galleries endlessly, studying until I could picture their treasures with my eyes closed. On the phone, Lowen disapproved: "You've just handed in your dissertation. Why can't you just relax for a bit?"

I was learning as much as I could because I also worried that, once I started at Courtenay's, they would realize I was a fraud. That I didn't have rich parents, had never visited the Met, or traveled farther than France. I already knew nobody could ever know about my gift, and that I would have to work five times harder than everybody else to make sure I never relied on it too much. I knew I would be entering a world that revolved around provenance and market value, knowledge and authority, and that's what I would be judged on.

Mainly, I wanted to earn my place among them, their respect. That summer I filled page after page of cheap notebooks, practicing dating any work I came across within ten years of its making, attributing it to the right movement, then specific artist. I had a rigorous schedule: I would do this for three hours; then, as a reward, I would find a piece I really liked and allow myself to enter it.

In truth, that's all I wanted to do. I was nervous, scared, not feeling up to the task, and in my most frustrating moments, using my gift reminded me of why I was there in the first place. During my breaks, I looked for those pieces exuding everything I felt I lacked, and spent time wandering in landscapes built in hope, love, determination, optimism, confidence. I sought to overcome my own inadequacy through the muttered words of artists whose feet I sat at, reliving their moments of epiphany. But nothing was quite doing it, and I kept looking for the next hit, hoping it would give me the boost I needed—that something in me would unlock.

Until I stumbled upon the only sculpture by Sorel in a London public collection. Her *Young Woman in the Tide* was at the V&A, in their sculpture collection, tucked in a shadowy corner.

She was an oasis in a room full of Boisseau's overdeveloped muscles, the stench of his sweat and pipes, the sound of his hands clapping against his models' buttocks. In contrast, *The Tide* was perfect. It cooled me right down, against the stuffiness of London at the heart of summer. It was a later piece that she had made at D'Arvor, dated 1911.

I could have so easily missed it, but once I found it, I kept returning to it. She embodied the passion and determination I needed—the idea that you could reinvent yourself thoroughly, for the better. I needed this like a daily injection; it kept me going.

A young woman was disappearing into the calf-height

sea, searching for something in the opaque layer of bronze, one hand held back, at the edge of losing balance, in that familiar movement of trying to push yourself to safety, but there was nothing there to meet her. Yet she was smiling, knowing the sea would absorb her fall. Every time I swam through, I emerged from the pond in D'Arvor, the familiarity of the dreamscape hitting me like the rush of an almost-too-hot bath. I watched Constance throw herself into the shimmering water and float on her back as it slowly turned into a beach eaten by a shallow, stormy tide. Her epiphany was a simple moment of perfect solitude. The hope of new beginnings.

"Will I ever be good enough?" I asked her, because I knew what she would say next, to herself. But it was good to act it out as a conversation, and with every visit, I timed my question better, until I really felt she was responding.

I believe in you. You can do it all.

"But what if I can't? What if I've been fooling myself that I can make it in that world?" My dreams, shimmering through the water, on some days seemed destined to wash away. But Constance was my friend, my guardian angel, and she floated and smiled.

Perhaps he was right. Perhaps you are *extraordinary.*

"Camille? It's Camille, right?"

That time I stayed a tad too long. I was starting to feel tingly, lightheaded. My feet dragged on the sand. Then a voice came, like a sonar through layers of water, from the world above, and I almost missed it. Almost, but it was a voice I had sharpened my ears to search for in the university's corridors.

I managed to drag my body through the return swim. "Hello?" A hand was shaking my shoulder and I realized that my absence had been long enough to be noticed this time. I gasped as I came to.

Last time I had seen Maxime had been from afar, at a leaving party. Now he was standing right in front of me, miles away from Scotland or France.

"Uh, hi," I said. I was weak, but still riding on a high, less self-conscious than usual. "You're still here."

His eyes searched me with the intensity of someone who thinks they might have a crisis on their hands before one corner of his mouth lifted. "What do you mean?"

"I thought you'd be back in Brittany by now."

"I wanted to make the most of it."

"Make the most of…?"

"The UK. I've done a kind of grand tour. Picked my way down from Scotland at my leisure."

The way his mouth slowed on the word *leisure*, deliberately, made the soft space behind my sternum flutter. I'd seen that vibe on him at parties, when he leaned backward, nursing red wine in a plastic cup, all angles and teeth gleaming, listening deeply to his partners as if he already knew everything about them. He intimidated me; I can only explain my boldness then, at that precise moment in the museum, as remnants of *The Tide*'s feelings in me. Constance's confidence in what I could achieve.

"I'm glad you're still here."

"It's good to see you too. I kept meaning to talk to you some more, up there, but…"

"You were busy." I knew he had not turned up for most of the compulsory lectures; he searched my face for a few seconds before saying: "I wasn't busy—*you* were. Mind if I sit down?"

"Be my guest."

The bench wasn't very wide and I could feel the heat of his bare arm on my skin. We chatted easily, as people came and went between us and the sculptures. He told me he had decided to steal the summer for himself before returning to "*les choses sérieuses*," serious life. I conjured a different self that was flirty, light, relaxed, and conversation flowed between us like seaweed in the shallows.

"So, what were you looking at?" Maxime asked eventually. I nodded toward *The Tide*.

"How strange," he said. "That's the one I came to see. I'm related to the sculptor, in a way."

"That's incredible." I feigned astonishment, part of me disappointed still that he didn't remember us meeting at D'Arvor as children. "Do you like her work, then?"

Instead of responding, he got up to get closer to the sculpture. His presence made the figurine look so much smaller. He kept one hand in his pocket, rubbed his chin. He didn't have stubble to speak of then. My own hair was longer, down to my waist, held back by a handkerchief, and I hadn't yet developed those annoying wrinkles that come when you arch your eyebrows too much. We were both fresh-faced and oblivious.

"Perhaps I shouldn't admit this, given my connection to Sorel, but I'm not enthralled," he said.

"How can you not be 'enthralled,'" I said vehemently, "when her art is *everything.*"

He turned to me, an eyebrow cocked.

"Everything…? Nothing, nobody, is *everything*, Camille. That's simply impossible."

"It may be small, it may be overlooked. Perhaps it doesn't do a huge song and dance like *The Thinker* or *The Gates of Whatnot.*"

"*Whatnot?* I'm unfamiliar with that one."

I didn't let his amusement deter me. "But it's what she poured into it."

"Molten bronze. At the end of the day, it's just matter, isn't it?"

And he had a master's in the history of art? He was in dire need of a true education. "No. *Look.*"

The rest is a blur, as I threw myself into delivering my Sorel 101 lecture, detailing what she had meant for us to find in her art and why it was so much more valuable than any other painting in pride of place at the Louvres.

I don't know for sure—I've gone over that afternoon so many times since—but I think I got carried away and went back into *The Tide*. I was so keen for Maxime to see it; I felt so bold that I forgot myself. I allowed myself to lose control over my gift and let it take me back; I had spent too long there already, and the boundaries of the below and the above started to blur. The only feeling that stands out now when I think back is that he was *with me*. His presence so stark, the smell of pine and rain had started to imbue Avalon. I floated between the two worlds, overwhelmed by Constance and Maxime, not knowing whom I most longed for.

Maxime was sitting so close I felt he was propping me up. The museum's bench kept melting under me, my mind washing over from one world into the next. I tried to regain my control. Constance, Maxime. The pond, the gallery. Over, and over—I searched for an anchor, finding none.

"Wow." Was it Constance or Maxime?

"That was… You make me feel…"

"What?" I whispered, the room darkening around me once more as the sun faded and the lighting dimmed. My cheeks were burning and I brought the back of my hand against them to cool them down. My hand was cold as if it had actually been dipped in water. I felt algae brush my shins.

"Embarrassed," he said.

"What? I—" He was there. We were still in the museum.

"I used to like her work, as a child. We had one of her sculptures at home. But then, I—I guess I lost sight of it. I dismissed her like everybody else." He wasn't taking his eyes off me. They followed me in the ebb and flow of the tide.

"You're staring at me," I said, as the room grew warm, or was it the sea? A stray ray of hot sun on my skin?

He bent forward; my heart slowed; I thought he was going to stroke my hair, but he picked something out of it. We both stared at it. It looked like a tiny piece of seaweed.

"Because you are quite extraordinary, Camille."

I tipped over. Backward, into the water. Because when Maxime's hand found my neck under the heavy curtain of my hair and cupped it, gently holding it in place as he bent forward to kiss me, his eyes a whirlpool into a completely different Avalon, I felt my grip loosen, the water rush in like a tsunami, and everything went dark.

13

THE LIGHT DIMS as I sit in the corridor, brimming with the intensity of our moment in the V&A, the way my infatuation with Maxime swallowed me whole. The way, now that I think about it, that my gift felt stronger, more active when he was coaxing me. Exactly what does he know? More importantly: What does he want from me, and is there anything I would be able to refuse him? I nearly lost myself then, blurring my bearings between Avalon and reality. Would I do it again, for him? What if I go too far this time, hit the point of no return?

I thought D'Arvor would be a safe way to regain my reputation, to get back in the saddle of appraising and authenticating, but everything feels more exciting and dangerous here, with him.

On the other side of the door, the sculptures pulse and sing. I think of Lancelot's intense devotion for a woman he could never have. Of Morgane, learning from Merlin the extent of her power. Of Igraine, being deceived, seduced by the wrong man. Of Yvain, falling into madness.

I don't want any of their fates. And I'm apprehensive of what they might tell me of Constance's. The only way to know is to go in, but I feel out of control, my heart racing, thoughts swooping in on me.

I can't do this when I feel like a love-struck, doomed teen-ager and I know that it is beyond ridiculous; I should be over it. My heart shouldn't soar the way it does when Maxime drops me crumbs: knowing smiles, allusions to something we've shared. Yet these crumbs have kept me going for years.

Have I just—not been *living*? Have I been hopping from memories to the residual emotions of others, all that time building nothing real for myself? I picture the trajectory of my life, looking for the handrails I can hold on to.

Like Lowen. He's always wanted to see me as someone who was capable of giving him as much as he gave me. He made me want to try to be that person. He mostly forgave me my failings, while holding me to account, with my best interests at heart. Is that unconditional love?

In the dark eaves, in the castle, stirring like a beast in its sleep, I'm overwhelmed by the need to call him. I need something real. I need him to remind me that I exist, that I can be seen. That I'm not just an abandoned, lost girl. I grab my phone.

"Cam?"

I wasn't expecting him to pick up straightaway. He's not someone who has his phone glued to him.

"Uh, hi, it's me," I mumble.

I can hear his smile. "So I hear. What's up?"

I was right—through every mishap, our friendship subsists. I can still call him and he'll speak to me like everything is normal, like it was just yesterday that we hung out on the seafront eating fish and chips and licking the salt off our fingers and guffawing at something or other.

"Not much. I just wanted to... How are you?"

"All right. Just packing."

A pang—*Where is he going?* Then I remember. "Are you off on your course soon?"

"Yeah. Tomorrow. Mum is fussing about—she's packed me some proper tea." A pause. "You sure you're all right?"

Even through the closed door, I hear the faint echo of *Lancelot*, the dark shape of a knight, face swallowed by shadows. Is he begging Guinevere, or threatening her? Their mechanical dance in Avalon, the hooded figure running away from me—nothing here is as I expected it to be. "This Breton job. I'm there right now. It's..." My voice trails off, but Lowen waits, like he used to. "It's really bloody hard, Lowen, and I'm so confused and I don't think I can do it..." I'm so close to crying.

When it becomes clear that I won't say more, Lowen says, "If it's too hard, you can quit."

"You know I can't do that."

"I think you can, but you won't. And I wish you would."

"I'm not a quitter."

He chuckles. "That you are not—true. You're too stubborn for your own good. But you need some rest. I knew it as soon as I saw you in London. You're all burnt out."

I want to spill it all out to him. The fact that I'm so scared I'm broken; that I can't stop thinking about Maman, Maxime, Constance, and being inadequate; that it is all going to swallow me in a big tsunami I can no longer contain, and it's affecting my gift—as if my own feelings are destroying what is right and real and authentic about it. I'm like a malfunctioning automaton.

"I can't quit," I repeat, finding my firm voice.

"All right. Well, can you at least take a break? Come to Rennes to see me, say, the day after tomorrow? We can grab a bite to eat. You can show me around."

I breathe. "I would love that. Thank you. I hope your journey goes well."

"Yeah, I'm sure it'll be fine." He sounds casual but I know he's not been out of the UK since his father's stroke. Lowen doesn't really like traveling anyway; he's always preferred to spend his holidays back home. I sometimes wonder if under his laid-back composure, that salt-of-the-earth, "if we're lost in the woods, I'll build a fire to keep us warm" kind of vibe, he is lacking the confidence to spread his wings. Him going on that course is a big deal.

"You've got this," I tell him. "It'll be worth it."

"Ah, thanks, Cam. You've got this too, whatever the hell you need to be doing. Just—try a small break. A step back, OK? That always helps me. Try and do something else you would be doing anyway—look at the problem from a new angle."

He's right. "That's very wise."

He chuckles. "I try my best. I'll see you soon. Will text you when I've got my head around the whole thing."

We hang up and I'm so excited to see him. Lowen always promises a place where everything is clear, calm, uncomplicated. Then I remember I haven't told him I'm working for Maxime.

I ignore my tightening stomach—why would Lowen care that I'm spending time with Maxime? It's not like he knew him anyway. And what he knew of him wasn't much. And it was years ago. I'm not silly enough to have continued betraying my infatuation beyond, say, three months after the V&A, when I finally got to Cornwall and told him and asked, *What does it mean? Do you think he could still like me? Will I ever see him again?* When I didn't get answers to any of these questions, I dropped it. So I'm in the clear. More importantly, there's nothing to hide.

You've got this too. Just take a step back. Full of the thought that I can always run to Lowen, hide in one of his giant bags of flour and disappear from the world as he feeds me cake, I decide he's right. For whatever reason, tapping into the sculptures here isn't working. I need to prepare myself for what Constance went through, try to get closer to the mystery of the end of her life, to calm my own apprehension and enable me to find her. There are only two other ways I can try to find out more about Constance's time at D'Arvor: ask Maxime, or go and see her other works. This includes *Viviane*, the sculpture that started everything, which I haven't seen since I was seven. And they all happen to be in the same place.

14

I SPEND THE next day avoiding the sculptures, poring over online archives, revising the little I know of Constance's time at D'Arvor. Then at dinner, I tell Marie-Laure that I have booked a taxi to take me to Rennes in the morning.

"What on earth for?" she asks.

"There's a collection of Sorel sculptures in the Museum of Fine Arts," I say. "It will help my research."

Her brow furrows as she tosses the salad. She's more tanned than she was when I arrived. I have hardly seen her inside.

"Surely you can access their collection online," she says.

"It's not the same." I look to Frédéric and Lila for support, but they're pretending to study the cutlery, like a pair of children caught in a parental row. The thought comes that Marie-Laure doesn't think I know what I'm doing. *You shouldn't have to justify yourself, Camille. You're the expert.*

"They have works from the same period of her life," I explain. "Yet they're very different. I'm hoping, by comparing and contrasting, to be able to make sense of a chronology. That will really help."

She seems absent, off in her thoughts. "How different?"

I'm about to answer vaguely, but Frédéric interrupts me, addressing his mother. "Didn't we used to have one of those? One of the fairies—the one Max got a bit obsessed with?"

Obsessed? I stare at him, but Marie-Laure shrugs. "We donated it years ago. And now I have been made to feel like we shouldn't have."

I didn't mean to criticize her—we're off on the wrong foot, and I can't quite understand why. Frédéric turns back to me. "I'm surprised you have to do so much, Ms. Leray. I mean it all sounds like rather hard work. I would have thought you'd merely take a quick look then slap a price tag on the things."

I burst out laughing.

"Frédéric, don't be so crude," Marie-Laure scolds him.

"I wish it were that simple," I tell him, thinking how it is often the people who grow up surrounded by priceless beauty who can't appreciate it at all. "I'll only be gone for the day," I turn back to Marie-Laure. "And I assure you it's an important part of my work."

"A whole day? Rennes is merely an hour away," she says, her lips pursed.

I can't hide my surprise at her tone. "These things take time," I say. I've had many a worse confrontation, but my hands under the table start to twitch. I don't need to justify my time to her. I don't need to ask her permission to meet up with Lowen in the evening. *Not you*, I plead with Marie-Laure silently, *please don't be like that.*

Then, she relaxes. "Of course you have to go. Sorry if I seemed a little taken aback." Her lipstick is so bright her other features disappear in it, as if absorbed. "We have been enjoying your company. It is quiet here, and you have been very welcome."

So she wasn't berating me—*she likes having me around.* My cheeks flush with this praise, the sustained attentions of her garden salads, and her quiet vigilance.

"Luckily," she continues, "Lila is going to Rennes tomorrow as well."

Both Lila and I move our gaze from Marie-Laure to each other. We've been avoiding each other since our confrontation that night on the stairs. And I'm to be strapped inside her car again? I imagine sinking into a pile of chewing gum wrappers, Lila standing outside, watching me disappear.

"I am?" she asks.

"Yes, dear. You were going to leave right after breakfast, weren't you?"

Lila's brow tenses. "Ah yes, I'm going because Maxime forgot his…" She trails off.

"…diary," Marie-Laure says. "He is under such stress at the gallery. But you're always so helpful." Then she turns to me: "She'll drive you. You can have a road trip, can't you, girls?"

Lila and I both nod, and through the tension I also feel our shared puzzlement at Marie-Laure's use of the word *girls*. Nobody ever called me that, not when I was nine, or fourteen. I was never a *girl*, always a mini-adult, functioning as such, and certainly not part of a collective bearing shiny hair and lacrosse sticks. I have to admire anyone who uses that word in reference to an adult woman wearing a black suit who has two master's degrees.

However, it feels nice to have someone like Marie-Laure talk to me like I could be her niece. It is also, I suppose, nice for her to assume Lila and I could become friends. I wonder if she'll give us pocket money for the trip. I smile to myself to try to stifle the growing ache of what a normal family the Foucaults are turning out to be, with their bickering and blunders. I suppose I'm not used to having someone look closely at what I'm doing *because they care.* I think of Maman and find a flash of anger where before there was only cold understanding.

Why could you not be part of this family, says a quiet voice, *in any way possible? What if you please the Foucaults with your outstanding work?*

What if you could even give them more—something nobody else could? Make yourself precious to them, unique and irreplaceable?

What if that's the reason Maxime never forgot you?

15

THE NEXT MORNING, I'm surprised to find Lila in a shiny black Audi, engine idling on the drive. It's a hot day; my fair skin is already burning where my hair parts. In the car Lila looks smaller, but cool and composed, wearing a leather jacker over a loose, uncreased linen shirt. We eye each other warily as I drop next to her.

"We're not taking your car this time?" I ask.

She shrugs. "I've got orders."

I sink into the leather of the seat, the air-con blowing coolness into my face. I have hardly clicked my seat belt in when Lila propels the car forward with a roar and no warning.

"Woah," I can't help but gasp.

"Yeah." She accelerates along the drive, gravel flying off in our wake. "Indeed."

"Surely this is nicer to drive than your Clio? No offense."

"Oh, definitely. It's also not mine."

I have an hour to spend with her, this charismatic and mysterious woman who gets to be with my dream man. Who speaks to me as if I am failing to grasp some kind of subtext. Her eyes are lined with smoke and tiredness, her gaze deep and clever. I'm not sure if she's wearing makeup or simply has phenomenal eyelashes—she is clearly blessed by either skills or nature. Whereas I have to touch up every single one of my features if I want to make myself presentable. The aircon, now that I've spent more than two seconds in the car, is clearly turned up too high and I start shivering in my short-sleeved top. From hot to cold, cold to hot, in the blink of an eyelid, I'm at her mercy.

But then her last words linger. *It's also not mine.* I wonder at the contrast between the brands she is wearing and the car she actually owns. How she implied she was told to drive the Audi today, her badly repressed surprise when Marie-Laure sent her with me. How worried she was about me telling Maxime she had picked me up late in her Clio. I realize I don't know anything about her life—about what in it she might consider hers, and what she doesn't. I'm weirdly elated to have a day out, escape the pressure of pleasing the castle and its inhabitants, and it makes me feel a bit more generous toward her.

"I think I get that," I say.

"What?"

"Wanting stuff that is yours, not just borrowed or imposed."

"Do you *really* get it?"

I'm too tired for jousting, and I need a clear head for the art, and for Lowen, whom I have arranged to meet in the evening after his course. I lean back and say, "Sometimes I'm not sure how much of my life is really mine."

The rural road dips in and out of villages with stretches through the countryside resembling single-track lanes. Lila's eyes dart to me, her left hand on the wheel, the right one poised on the clutch. I glance at the speedometer. 95 kph. 60 mph. Too fast, but the road is thankfully clear. "Your life sounds fine to me," she says.

"My life is great," I snap. "You're right. I'm so lucky."

Well, I tried. I don't know that I should open to her anyway. So far, she has been either freaked out by me or messing with me. Not a great baseline for a "girls" heart-to-heart.

Is my life great? After Lowen left London, I used to lie down every night and count my blessings on my fingers to remind me. *I own a flat in London. I am respected in my field. I have just sold a Rodin. I have been tipped for promotion.*

Now that it's all been derailed, I'm starting to feel I want more. Being in D'Arvor allows me to touch the lifestyle I've ever only dared to dream of. I want to *be* in love, not just borrow the feeling from someone who died a hundred years ago. I want to experience passion and take risks and become unashamedly myself and find where I belong so that existing stops feeling like work. I want to be the subject of my own art. Except that, after years of living vicariously through others' emotions, accumulating achievements and promotions, I'm not sure who I really am.

I shut my iPad, which I have been toying with while thinking. "How did you and Maxime meet?"

Lila seems surprised. "In Paris."

"Where? How?"

"I'll write it all up in a fifty-page report and email it to you."

"All right," I say. "I was just making conversation."

She accelerates further. 105 kph. I imagine it's Maxime at the wheel, that I can just let him steer, safe in the knowledge that he is in charge.

"When I drive, I often think how easy it would be to veer off the road. How little there is between staying on course and crashing." Lila spoke as if she was just thinking to herself.

Then she glances at me. I don't know if she wants to check if I'm scared, but I'm not.

I hold her gaze until she turns back to the road. "I think about it too, every time. How easy it would be, to just—" I flick my wrist as if holding an imaginary wheel. "It's not that I want to die. In those moments I just think about a radical change. Permission to derail and escape."

As I wait for her response, she brings the car back to legal speed, the numbers on the dial decreasing slowly. "I think that's the first time we've understood each other," she says quietly.

The mood in the car feels much more companionable

now, as if I've passed another secret test. We drive through more villages, dotted with boulangeries and roundabouts.

"To answer your question earlier," Lila says after a while, "about how Max and I met. He saved me."

"You don't seem like you need saving."

She doesn't smile. "I used to. And he likes saving people. It was a match made in heaven."

Jealousy is so physical: electrodes attached to my guts, that can activate without warning. I don't want to be that person pining after someone else's boyfriend, but my inner voice, the deepest part of myself, is shouting that I want him to save me too. I want someone to take me by the hand and fix up my life to be bigger, better. "Sounds lovely," I say.

"And that's why *everyone* idolizes him."

I catch her sideward glance—like a warning. I want to laugh it off, tell her, *That one time he tried to kiss me, I passed out, so you really don't have to worry about me,* but I still feel too embarrassed to laugh about it, and I don't want to admit out loud that I ever did fancy him. The next leap for her would be an easy one: me coming back here and finding myself neck-deep in my infatuation again.

And also...I know deep down that I could like Lila. There's something about her. A briskness, efficiency, watchfulness that is so close to my own, with a dose of hidden mischievousness that I might be able to enjoy if only I could relax around her.

"What did he save you from, then?" I ask. I think of

Guinevere and Lancelot, their dance frozen in D'Arvor's attic. Of Constance and Boisseau's affair, the giddiness of early infatuation.

"When I met Maxime, I had nothing. I was living in my car."

I'm shocked. I assumed so much about her. Because of the Chanel pumps, the grace, the charisma. Because I know rich people tend to associate with their own.

"And then he took you to D'Arvor," I say.

"Yes. And suddenly, everything was possible." Her hands tighten on the steering wheel. "I know what you're thinking. But it wasn't just about the money. He valued me more than I did myself. It was the first time in my life that I found myself in the right place. To him, I was golden, I had meaning. That was…dizzying."

I see a pond, the bristles of the gorse, a scattering of gold petals. In my mind's eye, it is now Lila who Maxime pulls by the hand beside the Miroir aux Fées, as she stumbles to follow him. He pulls her to him. *My love, what would I do without you?* Did Constance and Boisseau's love story match theirs? Is this why Lila was so spooked when she followed me and caught a glimpse of it?

Then she speaks quietly. "I haven't forgotten."

"About Maxime?"

Jealousy pulls at my heart's flesh with pincers as I wait for her to say something about their love. Yet I crave it; I want Lila to pour its effervescence straight into my veins.

"About the Miroir aux Fées, in the attic."

I think a long time before replying, then decide that the masks are off. "And I haven't forgotten that you seem to have been given the mission to chaperone me."

More silence.

"Is this really what art is like? I mean, for you? Walking around in other peoples' heads?" she asks.

I brace myself to deny it once more, to tell her she imagined things, but…is this really who I want to be? Someone who lies and gaslights people? The way Lila asked the question too—softly, matter-of-factly—disarms me. I feel we've been honest with each other today, in this car, and I want to honor that. I allow myself to own the guilt and discomfort I've been feeling.

"I'm so sorry. I didn't mean to take you in. I never mean to hurt anyone when I do it." My throat is tight. It's all bubbling back up. Lila's eyes, as she turned halfway down the stairs, flash back at me. The woman in the Hepburn dress, recoiling.

It takes an age for her to speak again.

"It didn't hurt."

I gasp with relief. "Jesus, Lila. I mean…how…how was it?"

She thinks for a little while as we speed along the motorway, the sky blue and mellow. I hold my breath. This is such unchartered territory, but having someone to talk about it with, someone to share…it's exhilarating.

"I don't know… It was quick, like a blink. A dip. But it

felt—terrifying. Exposing. Fascinating. Like that moment at the top of a roller coaster," she says.

I can't believe someone else is talking to me about Avalon. It was an intrusion, a glimpse, but Lila gets it.

"So you were really there," I say, because I need to hear myself confirm it.

She nods. Then, after another pause: "Are you not scared?"

"About what?"

"About losing yourself in there?"

I'm so tempted to open up completely to her, to let her know that the fact she didn't get hurt might have been sheer luck, a fluke, that I haven't felt in control of my gift at all since Courtenay, that I nearly died in *Wrong Night Swimming* and it may well happen to me again, but she still reports to the Foucaults. She didn't deny that she is my chaperone. I don't want them to know I'm struggling. "Ah, well. I suppose there are worse things than getting lost in some of humanity's greatest masterpieces."

She indicates a turn, and I realize the rural landscape has made way for the urban outskirts of Rennes.

"If you say so."

16

LILA PARKS IN the city center. The midday sun is hitting the pavement a bit too hard. I do my best to ignore the feeling that I would like a break from it all, telling myself that the museum is probably the coolest place to be.

"Have you texted Maxime?" I ask Lila as we approach the entrance, a wide stern door set in a neoclassical building flanked by the city's river.

"No. Why?" She sounds distracted.

"His forgotten diary?" Perhaps I'll get rid of her if I stick by the lie. Or it might conjure Maxime. Either way: win.

"Oh. Right. I'll do it after this."

"You know you really don't have to come with me."

As we approach the biggest public collection of Sorels, I'm excited in spite of everything. Constance will always have my heart. Not all the sculptures were visible when I last came for a temporary exhibit of local artists. The donated *Viviane* was kept hidden in storage; if I had known she was there, I would have played the "expert" card and requested to see it. The museum recently acquired a few other pieces when her life started to gather interest, and now she has her own small area for display.

Apart from *Viviane*, the real standout, the sculptures here are exquisite scenes of everyday life, typical of Sorel's D'Arvor period. No nymphs or knights to be seen, but instead servants, local girls, and farm boys. I had fully intended to come and visit, I realize—I thought her room opened a few months ago, but it must have been about five years. Five years of working constantly, of not making or having the time; I abandoned Constance. I feel like she's following me along the corridors, Lila in tow, through the rooms lined with deep red walls and arched windows, her apron grazing my legs as I hurry. I abandoned her while I got distracted selling other, more famous artifacts.

Perhaps Lowen had a point about me working so hard I lost sight of what was important.

She is sharing a charcoal-gray room with Boisseau. Lila and I have to tiptoe our way around his colossal *Narcissus* to find her. *Lovers and muses,* the sign says in her corner.

They should get it right here: she is a local artist climbing to international recognition. But this is no different from any other room she's in. She is tucked away, still, while the world wakes up to her talent too slowly. I should have come earlier. Made some noise about it, demanded better. She's still voiceless. I have failed her.

If I almost close my eyes, I can imagine it's *Night Swimming* in the middle, drawing all the attention. The story it would tell the world. The way it would reclaim her agency, be the final letter she would have chosen to share. Through me. If I found it, I could make sure they saw her, *heard* her.

What flicked you off the road and made you derail, Constance? What huge piece of your life am I missing?

I hear Lila's breath catch behind me as we enter the room, which softens me toward her. Now she is next to me, bent forward to decipher the small notice next to the works.

Constance Sorel's work owes a clear debt to Boisseau, her master and lover. The way she plays with strength and fragility in her figures here shows a charming attempt to ape his signature style.

"'A charming attempt,'" I hiss.

Lila turns to me. "I can see why you're angry."

"I'm not angry. I'm fuming. But I'm glad you see it."

I see her catch herself and relax her fists; she was staring the sign down.

"Still, you must be biased," she says.

"Excuse me?"

She weathers my outrage with a mischievous smile. "You're obsessed with her work. Of course you'll think the sign is wrong, that *she* was the genius. But all geniuses owe a debt to someone."

I roll my eyes, point to the closest sculpture, a marble bust called *Washerwoman*. "Wrong. Try again. Now, Lila, *really* look at her."

I should be annoyed, but there's something in the way Lila provokes me, jousts with me, all the while revealing, in spite of herself, our points of connection, that sharpens my wits too. The room is quiet as we approach *Washerwoman* together.

We keep catching glimpses of each other behind the bust, faces of flesh playing hide-and-seek with a face of marble, someone long gone. The light shines through the woman's plait, chiseled so thinly that it appears golden and fine, but I'm drawn to Lila's big dark eyes catching mine, while Boisseau's *Narcissus* ignores us.

"She's happy," she whispers. "I mean, Constance was happy when she made this."

"Yes." More flickers at me as Lila and I circle each other—droplets spinning around my ankles. Something I'd never seen in Constance's sculptures before. A new dimension I yearn to go in.

I look across to *Viviane* a few paces away. I came here for her, but this sculpture exudes the excitement of something new, of a fresh hit. Something much easier, purer than I recently felt at D'Arvor. I breathe deep the scent of my upside-down world where everything is in its right place. I have craved it like the dream of a perfect relationship.

"Who was this woman?" Lila asks, and I hear myself say, "Would you like to come with me to find out?"

The pond is there, waiting. It seems like everything is

back to normal, like I can control the process. The relief is immense. It feels safe here. With someone else.

Lila nods. My throat tightens. "It's unlikely to work," I warn her.

She smiles. "As you know, I'm good at sneaking into places I'm not invited."

It's the glimpse of mischievousness that does it. I take her hand as the water rises, bring my mind to what we both saw in the sculpture, that moment of connection. Lila gasps at the coldness of the pond, but I keep my focus. I gesture for her to follow me. "We need to swim through—down." The parquet of the museum sinks deep. Lila approaches it with that recklessness that I really admire in her.

The swim is easy, swift, as natural to me as breathing, and Lila keeps up with me. I feel the water her body is displacing, catch her determined expression as she pushes down to the rays of light signifying the world below. Doing this makes me feel dizzy, powerful, and somehow—alive. Lila chose to trust me.

We emerge from the lake on D'Arvor's grounds. The sun lands, soft, on my hair, and I bask in the peaceful quiet of the grass and water. A blue dragonfly skims past Lila's hand.

"What the hell?" she whispers.

"Can you hear me?"

"Yes." She looks like she's about to cry. "It's so beautiful."

I'm in Avalon, interacting with someone. I never thought it was possible.

"Come," I tell her. "Let's go meet Constance."

We both approach the woman by the pond, standing mid-thigh-high in water, washing her hair so it obscures her face. The sun shining through it makes it copper, almost white. But it's not Constance. She is tall, fair, her skin translucent, whereas Constance is shorter, with wiry dark hair. The woman startles, reveals her face, her eyebrows so pale they're almost invisible. She smiles widely.

It's you.

I thought she was addressing me, then Lila, before I realize that Constance has walked up behind us, her hands deep in the pocket of her working apron. I'm so happy to finally see her that I start to run to her, but Lila stops me.

Do that again. The way the water fell on your face.

Splashing my face, the woman snorts. *Elegant indeed…*

You've got something perfect. Will you pose for me?

She laughs, throwing a wet cloth in jest, which misses Constance. Lila tries to pick it up, but can't. I know this world is not for us to grasp—I observe; I don't change it. It welcomes me as a place of rest where I can do nothing but witness. But today, I'm burning with all the questions that I've never been able to ask her directly.

"Who is that?" Lila whispers at my side.

You mean I'm so good at standing still, doing nothing.

She grins, walks out of the pond, drying her hair with another cloth.

No. You, you are…

I see the way Constance jitters, how she is looking at her. At once some kind of openness takes hold, a sweet ache. I look at Lila's face, her widened eyes reflecting the sky, the light dancing on the pond.

And then, as the woman puts on her red dress, I recognize her finally.

The lady in red. Viviane. The same woman I met when I was nine, the first time I went to Avalon, in D'Arvor's attic. Why is she here when this sculpture isn't about her?

You, Anne...you are my friend.

Friendship is everywhere in the landscape of Constance's dreams, this memory of hers distilled into inspiration, trapped in a block of marble. This moment mattered enough for her to pay for the stone, spend hours designing, sketching, and chiseling. It was so important to her and took me totally by surprise.

Likewise.

I startle as a child runs past us, toward them, a head of wild blond curls, holding an armful of daisies, calling *Mama...* I feel dizzy. The cloth Viviane threw at my feet dissolves in a puddle of mud. I got it all wrong, all those years, I misinterpreted who Viviane was. I thought she was a fantasy, a metaphor, but she was real. What else about Constance's life did I get so utterly wrong? How else have I failed her?

"Camille." I turn to Lila. She's trembling. Where a minute ago, white butterflies were twirling around us, now they're a flurry of snowflakes, big like moths.

I'm cold too. Through the snow, the loop starts again, the hair being washed, Constance like a twitchy fawn, approaching…

"Camille! Take me back, please." Lila's eyes are half-shut, her face drained.

What if I keep her here for too long? What will happen to her? This spurs me to action and I take her hand to guide her back.

We are welcomed to the museum by hushed voices: a young couple, both with dreadlocks, and a group of ladies with short white hair and colorful scarves, holding maps of the museum, all absorbed in Boisseau's masterpiece at the center of the room.

The air is warm but Lila and I shiver while we look at each other, thoughts swirling in my head like the butterflies of Avalon. All this time, the lady in red, *Viviane*, was Anne Foucault.

"Camille…"

"It wasn't only peace that Constance found at D'Arvor, it was friendship. And it changed everything. I always thought she was a loner"—*like me*, I choose to leave out—"but then, she…" I start looking around, and sure enough, I see Anne's face in every sculpture, her portrait branding Constance's inspiration.

You are the key to unlocking it all.

I startle as Lila grabs my upper arms and shakes me. "Camille! Stop this. *You took me in*—you took me into Constance's sculpture! You actually did!"

Then her grip loosens and she nearly collapses. I catch her just in time, help her to the bench. That sobers me up, along with how cold her skin feels. "Shit. Lila, I'm so sorry." I rummage through my bag to find a light jumper, wrapping it around her shoulders. "Are you OK?"

She nods, her eyes shut tight. As the adrenaline recedes with the last of the sculpture's hit, it dawns on me, really dawns on me.

I took someone in with me, deliberately. Lila walked around in Avalon, seeing what I was seeing. She was in there for a long time.

When she opens her eyes, I swear there is some of that golden afternoon trapped in her irises.

"I'm fine," she says. She looks a little better and I'm relieved.

"Lila…" I need to know. "What exactly did you see? I need to know if I'm going mad."

"Two women, one in the lake. And the boy calling his mother. Then you got all weird and it started snowing. So if you're going mad, I guess I'm going mad too."

We sit like that, on a bench, watching the sculptures from afar, warming our bones in Rennes's August for a while. I know we're both replaying what just happened, both working our hardest to make sense of it.

"I can't believe you wanted to come with me," I say.

Lila's seriousness melts, and she mock scowls. "Does this mean *we* have to be friends now?"

Friends. Some of the warmth of Constance's emotions lingers in the air. We snigger at this, a little awkward, as the retired ladies examining *Narcissus* a few paces away whisper excitedly about his private parts.

Then Lila's serious again. "I didn't really believe it would happen. But then…here, when you—when I *really* looked at that sculpture, I wanted to *know* her so badly…"

She understands. My heart flutters in my chest. "Was it how you expected it?"

She shakes her head. She still looks quite shaken. "He wasn't there."

"Who?"

She points at the Boisseau in the middle of the room. I'm about to launch into another diatribe about the way Constance's story is presented on those damn labels, but she seems to decide to change the subject. "Was the snow normal? Is it always that cold?"

I shrug to mask the unease. It was warm and sunny, and then… *Then you got upset, Camille.* But that's impossible. I've never been able to move anything in Avalon, let alone change its fabric. "I suppose that's what the weather was like in that memory." I'm so happy to have seen Constance, to have found her intact and happy. The euphoria is strong. However, there's also the revelation of what I had managed to miss all those years ago.

"I'm not making it up, right?" I ask Lila. "Did you feel it too—how important Anne Foucault was to her?"

Lila nods. "Was this all new to you, then?"

"I'm afraid so. Now I think she was Constance's muse while she was at D'Arvor. Friend, inspiration, model certainly. I just can't believe I never noticed this before. It was like—hidden from me. Perhaps she *wanted* to hide it?"

"Do you think that an artist could deliberately hide things from you? Even with your gift?"

I think. "I guess they would have to know how the gift works to set out to deceive me. I usually see through regular forgeries immediately. But that's not Constance. I'm starting to think I've failed her. That all those years I just looked for what I expected to find in her sculptures and missed what really mattered to her." It pains me to admit that I might have been biased, looked for the tale of someone who needed nobody, who was stronger by herself. It hurts and puts me to shame. What else might I have missed?

"Sometimes we're not able to see what's right in front of us," Lila says.

But now something else is bothering me. How the sculptures in D'Arvor's attic are so completely different from these. How they're resisting, dark, deliberately playing games with me. Attractive, opaque. How unsettled they're making me feel. Not like *Wrong Night Swimming*, but also not like this. It's what Lila asked—*Do you think that an artist could deliberately hide things from you?*

"Lila," I start, "what do you know about the sculptures at D'Arvor? What did Maxime tell you?"

There's a sudden change in the air we are breathing, and the whole room turns toward him, as if caught red-handed. Maxime walks over to us briskly in his blue suit, the face of his watch catching a stray ray of spotlight, blinding me for a second. You shouldn't look straight at him for risk of being petrified, of course.

"Sorry I'm late." He seems irritated. Or has he been rushing?

"I wasn't aware you were joining us," I say.

I give him a smile, which I hope for him to reciprocate, but he seems on edge. "I fucking hate this room. How can it be of any help?"

I try to hide how taken aback I am by his tone. This is certainly not the moment to give away my doubts about D'Arvor's sculptures. I don't want to be responsible for France's most eligible bachelor's heart attack. And also…I realize I want more time to talk to Lila. "I think we can get some useful stylistic comparisons to locate your sculptures in her timeline."

At this, he seems to mellow. "Ah yes, very well." A pause. "I'm so sorry, Camille. It's just… Don't you think she isn't best served here?"

I'm relieved to know his mood was in fact based in some righteous anger we share. "There *are* a few things in this room I wish I could smash up, that's true."

"Well," he takes a step back and puts his hands into his pockets. "Surely that's enough hard work for now. I have some time before my evening engagement. Shall we all go for a drink?"

"Actually, Max, I'd like to stay here a bit longer if that's OK," Lila says.

"Are you sure? You hate these artsy places."

She nods. "Camille might have started to change my mind."

The look he gives her, then me, is peculiar. I can't make sense of it.

Does this mean we *have to be friends now?*

"I'm busy this evening, actually," I say.

Maxime turns back to me. "What?"

"I'm meeting a friend. In an hour."

"And what's her name?"

"His name is Lowen." I have to force it out of me, as if his name doesn't belong here, in this dimension of Maxime in his white shirt surrounded by sculptures stretching their arms out to him in lust. I would rather stay here. My head is ringing with Anne, with questions about Constance, this new side of her life. And Lila. All the people in this room seem to escape me, whatever they're made of.

"I see," Maxime says, and I turn back to him. "Where are you meeting?"

"He suggested a bar not far from his venue."

"Well, let me take you there. I want to be the first to buy you a drink today."

I glance at Lila but she's turned away. I nod.

"Splendid."

I follow him back through the museum, doing my best to shut all the works out. Maxime speeds to the exit like a man on a mission, his elastic step perfectly regular. Until he stops, just in front of Boisseau's *Anticipation* in the hallway, a life-size marble of two lovers frozen in the split second before their lips meet, with a throwaway comment over his shoulder:

"Reminds me of the last time we were together in a museum."

I blush, hastening my pace. In the V&A, he had bent toward me, his hand knotting my hair, time stopping between Constance's yearning and ours. Then I remember how I threw myself at Lowen in my flat, some weeks ago that feel both like years and yesterday. I cringe at both memories of missed kisses.

Maxime and Lowen, colliding in the same space. Well, this promises to be interesting.

17

WHEN WE ARRIVE at the bar Lowen suggested, a small local with plastic chairs and ashtrays on the tables, Maxime shakes his head.

"God, no, Camille. This won't do."

"It's perfectly fine," I laugh. "I'm sure even you can survive for an hour among us mortals."

He shakes his head again, with the hint of a smile. "That's not the problem."

"What is the problem?"

"I don't think it's worthy of you."

I'm knocked off-kilter that he is outright flirting with me. "But I'm meeting Lowen here," I say.

He sighs. "There's a place I know just up the road. A bit more interesting. Listen, I promise I'll walk you back here in time for *Lowen*."

The hint of jealousy in his tone gives me butterflies, and

once again I follow him, without any bearings of my own, to the unmarked entrance of a residential building in the old town. Maxime opens it and I follow him in.

The bar opening at my feet is a stunning space of curved pillars, mossy frescoes climbing the walls and ceiling. Spirit bottles are set like jewels against the deep windows, the soft furnishings absorbing an already hushed atmosphere. It's late afternoon, still bright outside, but here the lights are dim—this space exists out of time, a bijou universe hidden from the world.

Maxime nods to the waiter and leads me to a table in a quiet corner, all dark, gold velvet and suede.

"What do you think?" He's been watching me, I realize, drinking in my reaction. His white shirt stands out like the moon, the strands of his hair picked up by the gilded details of the murals; he is the centerpiece, something refined and priceless that I long to touch. As he leans back, his legs stretch under the table, his shoes nudging mine.

"This place is *you* distilled into a bar," I say.

It even smells like him. Leather, and something foresty, with brown sugar.

He laughs. "So if I ask you if you like it, the question becomes a tad more weighty." I smile, but I don't answer. The waiter has arrived to take our order. "Absinthe?" Maxime asks me.

"I'd rather have a coffee."

"Come on, Camille. It's *l'apéritif.* Happy hour. Tongues must be loosened."

I roll my eyes to mask my giddiness. "Absinthe it is, then."

He orders, and my mind latches onto what he said in the museum, about *Anticipation*. I indulge in watching him through my eyelashes, as I throw my head back and pretend to admire the faux frescoes on the ceiling, artfully faded (flashes of Beaux-Arts students bending backward like Michelangelo in the Sistine, small trembling paintbrushes in hand, flecks of paint in their eyebrows and hair, the crushes that ignited between them like little wildfires), of some kind of Roman garden and ivy and butterflies, flickering. Pomegranates. The underworld, reclaiming the skies.

"Stop that." Maxime's voice brings my eyes down.

"Stop what?"

"Studying that ceiling like you need to sell it. I need you here, with me."

There's nowhere I'd like to be more than here with him… But I force myself to carve out a bit more space, lean back into my chair. *Stay professional.* "What would you like to talk about, then?"

His teeth glow in his perfect mouth. "There was something going on when I came into the museum. I saw your face. I want you to fill me in."

I saw your great-grandmother, Constance's deep affection for her, and how it unlocked her art at D'Arvor, and her absence in the works you put in front of me is making me doubt them.

"There's nothing to fill you in on yet."

His eyes are searching mine. "Did you enjoy seeing *Viviane* again, after all these years?"

"Immensely. Why exactly did your parents decide to part with it?"

"They thought it was a piece of local history that would be better looked after in a public collection."

I know that's not the whole truth. "Frédéric said something about you being *obsessed* with it?"

My line of sight is broken while the waiter sets our glasses on the table, and an art nouveau water fountain, with its intricate tiny silver taps. The Absinthe glows green in our glasses.

"May I?"

I watch as Maxime sets a silver slotted spoon on top of my glass and slowly pours some ice-cold water through a cube of sugar. His hands are precise, the drip of the water so exquisitely slow that I shiver.

"The green hour," he says. "We're joining the artists and poets who sought visions in the Green Fairy." Still the water drips, seeping through the sugar, as it crumbles into the drink.

"Let's hope we don't catch their madness," I say, unable to take my eyes off the process. They all drank Absinthe in the nineteenth century, as can be seen in works by Degas, Manet, and Picasso. The drink was eventually banned for causing psychosis, even murder. It is safe nowadays, and one glass will not have such an effect, but still. As Maxime's eyes flash at me like emerald, I think he might be Merlin, pouring potion into my cup.

But I can't let him intoxicate me. I need answers.

"*Viviane*, Maxime?" I ask when we are set, and he has leaned back again.

"Right. I was seven, or thereabouts. After you and I looked at *Viviane* together, I—started to feel it. I took it down to my room, set it on my desk. I spent hours looking at it, studying it. To the point that my parents got concerned and my father decided to take it away."

"So you lost her too."

"She always escaped me." He brings his glass to his mouth, and I imagine swimming in it, my limbs tingling in the alcohol, the softness of Maxime's lips along the length of my body in the most delicious, green-tinged hallucination.

Cam, please *get a grip. Right now.*

"My father never got it," he continues. "Anything that goes beyond the *monetary* value is useless to him. He made me quit L'école des Beaux-Arts, you know. I hadn't told him I had enrolled—did a whole year before he realized—but still, he wouldn't have it. When he did turn up, the boot came down hard."

I feel his bitterness on my tongue as I sip my drink. It tastes of pine trees, medicinal herbs, masked by sweetness. "But you studied art history, still?"

He shakes his head. "That was the compromise. A year doing that, then off to Paris School of Economics. It wasn't just me. He made Fred study medicine but he couldn't cut it."

"I understand how you feel. My mother had loaded expectations too."

"I'm so sorry."

"And I'm sorry you lost *Viviane*. I can imagine you found comfort in it."

"It's more than that. It is hard to explain, but, Camille, I think everybody still gets it wrong. You too, if you don't mind me saying. The sculptures at D'Arvor—*Lancelot, Merlin, Viviane*—those *are* her most personal. Those are the way she told her love story."

"You mean Boisseau," I say, thinking of Anne, the golden pond, their laughter. I'm completely torn between what I found out today and what Maxime is telling me, what I sensed in the sculptures in the attic.

Perhaps Constance went back and forth, for inspiration, between her love for Boisseau and the friendship she found in Anne. Who knows which relationship had the biggest impact? Who was *Night Swimming* inspired by and dedicated to, and why were neither of them with Constance at the end?

"Surely you agree how important he was to her, even at the end of her working life," Maxime says. "The sculptures confirm it."

"I think that's impossible to really know unless we find *Night Swimming*."

"I thought *Night Swimming* had been found already," he says.

I take another sip to give myself courage. "Maxime, stop playing games with me. You were there at Courtenay; you know I don't believe that was it. If you agree with them, why would you invite me here?"

"Why do you think?" he asks, his voice low, his hand so close to mine that I feel his warmth. "I'm interested in your theory, Camille."

"I think you might have the real *Night Swimming*, and for whatever reason you have been concealing it from me."

Suspended in this semiaquatic world of ferns and soaring fish, waiters moving in slow motion, women dotted around in pink and beige like starfishes, we are two sharks in the fishbowl, Maxime and I. His eyes are darker than I thought, and I wonder if it is the room, my mistake, or the moment, but I know there is more to him than meets the eye. I know he has a plan he hasn't been sharing with me, but I can't make sense of the dissonance of the sculptures at D'Arvor with the ones here, or what he really wants. Finally, his mouth opens and he says, "And I think you have power, Camille, a true magical gift that you have, also, been concealing from me. So that makes two of us with secrets."

I swear the fishes and birds of the ceiling come alive then, swooping down on me. My mouth opens but I'm too stunned to speak.

"Maxime Foucault. Good evening."

Maxime's knee was pressing against mine; he pulls it back as we turn to the interruption, a short, closely shaven man who would be the most perfectly average person if he didn't sound inordinately posh, his clipped vowels erring on the side of scornful.

Maxime stands up to shake his hand. "Hello, Charles."

"I'm terribly sorry to interrupt." The man looks to me, but Maxime makes no move to introduce us. I see his knuckles tense on his glass as I try to recalibrate my mood to being able to pull off some small talk with a stranger, pushing aside what Maxime just told me.

"No, you're not."

"No need for prickliness. Just swinging by to say hi. I wasn't expecting to see you here. I thought you would have had...*work* to do." He emphasizes *work* as if it is a dirty secret. He turns to me again. "The poor chap never rests. He is an absolute trooper."

"And you are?" I ask.

"Oh. Terribly sorry. I assumed... Charles-Emmanuel, Duc de Lautrec."

"Camille Leray."

"*Enchanté.*" He gives me a deep nod. His name is clearly old French aristocracy, and everything in his demeanor suggests he belongs to a class that few of us even know exists.

"Did you want something, Charles?" Maxime asks.

"Ah yes. I came to inquire. Make friendly chitter-chatter. I hear you're cooking something, my boy, hoping to make some money at last. Always been the poor cousins—fate might turn—if anybody wants to buy crazy Connie's little fancies, that is."

I glance at Maxime. A tight smile is pasted on his face. "I take it this is you telling me you're not coming to the charity ball at D'Arvor, then? I'll make sure to cross you off the guest list—one of my many *jobs*."

Charles laughs. "Oh no, we *are* coming. Wouldn't miss it for the world. I might even bid on Connie's trinket. You know you can always count on me to sponsor a few tiles for D'Arvor's roof."

"Great," Maxime says. "See you there."

"Nice to meet you, Ms. Leray." With one more foxish smile, Charles is gone.

As soon as he's out of earshot, I turn to Maxime, my mouth open on a queue of questions. But I notice how fast his breathing is; he's repeatedly tearing his napkin into pieces.

"Are you OK?"

He nods, but he tears and tears and tears, avoiding my eyes. I'm struck to see him like this. Not knowing what to do, I put my hand on his. His skin is warm, smooth, and his hand stills. We stay like this for a few moments until a long sigh escapes him and he clears his throat.

"I'm quite all right, thank you," he says, sounding like his usual composed self. Then, as I go to take my hand away: "No. Stay here, please."

An electric pulse starts running along my arm. Our skin

touching is much more intoxicating than Absinthe could ever be.

I could stay like this for a whole night. We have so much to discuss. Then I remember Lowen.

"Oh no." I snatch my hand off to retrieve my phone and check the time. "I need to go."

"Do you really need to? I thought you wanted to talk."

"Yes and yes, on both counts. Sorry. I'm already late. I can't—I promised—"

"Of course." Maxime is on his feet, shaking his jacket on in one swift movement. That crack I've just seen in his perfect countenance—that vulnerability, I swear to God... I want to tear his suit off him right here and now. A new dimension of desire has opened: he knows my gift, and I too caught a glimpse of the man behind the mask—I crave to know all his imperfections and fears.

But I can't keep letting Lowen down. I promised myself.

"You should stay here, have another drink perhaps?" I suggest.

He shakes his head. "The last place I want to be is here alone right now. I'll walk you."

It is strange to be reminded that it is still early evening outside, the light bright, people hurrying out of offices or smoking cigarettes and drinking black-currant kirs on the pavements as we walk back to the other bar. I'm struggling to keep up with Maxime. In the end, I catch his elbow to attempt to slow him down.

"What was that, by the way?" I ask him.

"What was what?" He does slow but keeps looking straight ahead.

"It was uncomfortable," I say. "That Charles guy..."

"*Duke of Lautrec*," Maxime says, as if he is spitting. "He will never have any troubles in life and therefore is bored out of his mind and finds his entertainment in belittling those who have less."

"He was very disparaging," I say. "*Crazy Connie*. What is Constance to him anyway?"

"It's not really about her. It's about my family. We're rivals in a way, have always been, for power, for land, generations back. Except his lineage is... well, more straightforward than mine, and he loves reminding me of this."

I scoff and he gives me an irritated look. "I mean," I say, "*lineage*? This is the twenty-first century."

"Welcome to my world, Camille." He sounds so tired, so flat. "So, you think family does not matter?"

I stop. "I—"

"You would not celebrate your heritage? Protect it at all costs?"

"What does he think is wrong with your lineage then?" I ask to mask how uncomfortable I am that he is speaking alien to me right now. Yes I would love to think that I'm making my mother proud, finally, that if she were to walk toward us on this pavement, in her faded peach cardigan, hiding behind her sunglasses, she would do a double take and I would notice respect, admiration, perhaps envy. *Was that Maxime Foucault, Camille? You've been staying at D'Arvor?* But also I always wanted to better her, better what she left me with.

Maxime sighs. "The Foucaults came from trade."

"And what's wrong with that?"

"People like Charles can link their family tree back to the Crusades. We never stop hearing about it."

"Surely, it doesn't mat—"

"But that's fine," he says through gritted teeth. "That's fine, Camille; he can laugh now, he and his congenital micro-dick." I gasp, but he continues. "Soon they'll learn some respect and they'll all want a piece of what we have. They'll realize where we actually come from."

He suddenly looks up, as if noticing my presence. It was strange to see him smiling in a sort of trance. The same smile I sometimes feel creeping onto my lips when I think of him and imagine a completely fantasist version of my life, making my mind walk those steps that don't belong to me, yet. It is that very *yet* that fuels Maxime too. But what is in it, exactly?

We've arrived, and I can see Lowen sitting inside the almost empty neon-lit bar, the smell of chlorine bleach reaching us from the pavement.

I turn to Maxime. "We're here."

"Is that him?" Lowen hasn't spotted us yet. He's absorbed in his phone and I wonder if he's still texting his dad everyday when he's not around, like he used to when he lived in London. He looks tired, familiar in a way that makes my heart warm up, like buns fresh from the oven.

I nod.

"He is…a friend, you said?"

"Yes." I wait for Maxime to say his goodbyes and walk off, but he doesn't move.

"I've got time for one more drink," he says. "Let's go and meet your man."

Jesus.

18

I OPEN THE door to the bar as if the glass might implode at my touch. The place is mainly empty. Lowen looks up with a smile on his face, and my heart hangs in the couple of seconds it stays there for me, before he clocks Maxime.

"Cam, hey," he says, pulling me in for a hug.

He smells mildly of sweat, like someone who has spent the day working and hasn't had time to shower or change. It's not unpleasant, but when I pull away I'm acutely aware of the contrast between both men, of Lowen's crumpled black T-shirt and his battered trainers. Maxime doesn't wait for me to introduce him.

"Maxime Foucault," he says. "A friend of Camille's."

"I know who you are, mate," Lowen says as he shakes his hand. I catch myself staring at Lowen's big calloused hand and Maxime's smooth and elegant one, battling it out.

"I hope you don't mind if Camille invited me to join you for a bit."

Lowen looks to me, but I'm busy readjusting to a universe where they're in the same room. "Knock yourself out," he says. I wish he were a bit less colloquial.

Lowen drops back into his seat and Maxime sits next to me, opposite him. He orders another drink for us. I catch Lowen's eyes. I want to tell him... What do I want to tell him? That I don't want Maxime here? Is that the truth?

"I thought you were working," he finally tells me.

"She is," Maxime says. "She has been working for me."

I finally get my voice back. "I think that's a slightly reductive way of putting it." Then I see Lowen's worried face. "I just mean I don't work *for* anyone. The art might belong to you, but I'd like to think that I'm working for Sorel. On her behalf."

"So how is it going? You said you had trouble with it the other night."

Ignoring Maxime's curious glare, I spend a little time talking to Lowen about the sculptures, without saying too much. Maxime might not trust Lowen to keep it quiet, and I don't want any doubts of mine to be too obvious to Maxime. I know that Lowen doesn't care though, nor does he have any connections that would jeopardize any grand reveal Maxime might be planning.

"That's smashing," Lowen says, "Cam, I know how much you love her—you must be chuffed."

"I am," I say.

"You don't sound it." Maxime sounds put off. Is he on to me?

"Just tired, that's all."

If anything, being here around these two men is the most exhausting situation of all. I slide my finger along the glass I haven't touched, drawing erratic patterns on the condensation.

"Camille?"

I look up to see Lowen's concerned face, that wrinkle between his brows. His face is so familiar—with his big forehead and lovely, boyish features, his soft hair and eyes—that I can't help but smile.

"She said she is tired," Maxime says with an authority that makes us both turn to him, as if we are children and he is the tutor.

All I can do is nod. I finally pick up my gin and tonic and take a big swig. I know I'm already tipsy from the Absinthe, but I need something to take the edge off this situation.

"So, *mate*," Maxime says to Lowen, and I cringe at his tone, "what brings you here, if you don't mind me asking?"

Lowen shrugs, explains his pastry course.

"So you own a bakery in Cornwall? What is your turnover? How many people do you employ?"

Lowen is remarkably calm, but I know him well enough to catch a hint of irritation. "I work with my dad," he says. "It's a small business, but we do all right for ourselves."

"Just the one, then," Maxime continues. "Do you have plans for expansion? Is that why you're here? Thinking of diversifying?"

This is so painful—painful because while I want to tell Maxime to stop, I realize that I have also been that person asking Lowen the same questions.

"Lowen is incredibly talented," I say now, and I mean every word of it. "That's why he's here."

"Yes, it is a prestigious course," Maxime says. "Very over-subscribed. They train all the best pastry chefs—I attended an exclusive party with a caterer who had trained with them a few weeks back; the profiteroles were to die for. Well done for getting in."

He sounds so superior, so patronizing. Is that how he's sounded all along, and I failed to notice? It can't be. I think I'm overprotective of Lowen's feelings, and Maxime is doing some kind of peacocking. It's insufferable but also...a little voice in my head says, *He's trying to show off for you.* Is he? Is this all about me?

Lowen nods. I can tell it's been hard. I notice the deep lines around his eyes. I know he isn't someone who is com-fortable anywhere he goes; he is unused to traveling and adapting to new environments. He's always planted deep roots over time, relying on meaningful connections with a handful of lucky people. I suddenly realize that this drink was as much about him wanting to see me as him offering me a break when I was feeling down. And I let Maxime crash our safe place.

I want to ask Lowen how the first few days have gone, what he's learned, how he's been finding it, but in front of

Maxime, it might sound like I'm highlighting vulnerabilities. I turn to Maxime hoping to put the spotlight on him.

"Speaking of exclusive parties," I say, "what was that about a charity ball at D'Arvor?"

"Pardon?" He puts his glass down. He's drained it.

"What that—*duke* mentioned earlier." Lowen's eyebrows arch in mock admiration, and I cringe.

"Saturday, in two weeks' time. It's been planned for a while. We're fundraising for a charity that looks after retired racehorses."

I daren't look at Lowen anymore. "Not for D'Arvor's leaking roof, then?" I see immediately that it makes Maxime angry.

"We could do with an extra caterer, actually, if you fancy a job for that evening?" Maxime has turned to Lowen, and both Lowen and I stare at him in bewilderment. Was that a genuine offer or a way to punish me for trying to drag Maxime down to our level? But Maxime isn't mean-spirited, surely.

"No, I mean, he can't—" My eyes go from one to the other as they stare each other down. I'm tired of this. "Well," I say, "*I* will be back in London by then. So you sort it out among yourselves." I sound like a petulant child, or worse: I sound like I'm begging for an invitation, but I don't have a clue what's going on here.

The bar is deserted now. It must have started raining because the windows are steamy. I can't see outside, as if nothing exists but the three of us in this claustrophobic space. I look around for something else I can place my attention on—a cheap reproduction of Monet on the wall, perhaps, or a local artist's pictures of chickens—a fleeting thought comes, then grows into something more desperate that I could perhaps attempt to snatch Lowen and take him away with me, someplace where Maxime won't be able to follow.

But I find nothing of interest. Empty walls, empty floor, empty bar, and Maxime's eyes on me, burning.

Oh my God. He knows what I was trying to do.

The edges of my reality get blurry, the space shrinking like an accordion.

"That would be a great shame, Camille," Maxime finally says, and for a second I think he is telling me not to attempt to get out of here. For a second I mistake it for a threat, but then he adds: "I was really hoping you'd be at the ball. You have an important part to play."

"Oh?"

"Who do you think will be leading the auction?"

I scowl at him. He bears a half-amused smile, and it angers me that he's making plans without my consent, assuming complete commitment. I feel it all bubble up like a shaken fizzy drink.

"Ah," I snap. "I've been demoted to charity auctions. Selling scented candles to a bunch of inebriated penguins. Fine, then."

"An essential role," Maxime repeats, in a way that implies

here and now isn't the time for him to explain, but that he will. That it will be between us, something only he and I can understand. "I'll need you there."

And in his eyes I see a reminder of what he was like in the bar earlier, trying hard to contain some deep vulnerability he has hidden from the world. I see the child who took me by the hand to see *Viviane*, who pleaded with her for months to talk to him. I see that he might need me as much as I might need what he can promise me.

When Lowen speaks, I have almost forgotten that he is in the room.

"I'll come as a guest," he tells Maxime, "if you're happy to invite me."

19

MAXIME TOLD ME Lila had gone home, that he would drive me. I sit next to him in a sleek Bugatti I didn't know he possessed and put my life into his hands. The car is low to the ground; my seat leans far back; it's like being driven in a coffin. I feel wretched without knowing why, remembering Lowen's face as I hugged him goodbye. When he shook Maxime's hand, he didn't look at him—he was looking at me, and I felt the bubble I've been building over the past week burst with his scrutiny.

Maxime didn't go back to any of what happened earlier. As soon he started the car, he set to outlining his plans for the charity ball, which has been months in the making and which I have suddenly become instrumental to. A couple of weeks ago I was packing for a few days, and now it is assumed that I'm a cog in D'Arvor's machine. I both dislike and adore it, the thrill of Maxime writing me into his life, while I fight with the unease of not being in control.

But there is also the doubt about the sculptures, like the scratch of a forgotten pin in my jacket. The artworks at D'Arvor and the ones I saw today feel completely different. I know in my heart that the ones in Rennes, as well as *Viviane*, are by Constance. I know now that Anne Foucault was her muse, friend, and confidante throughout her time at D'Arvor. I think back to my experience in *Guinevere and Lancelot*, how everything felt staged, how the artist was hiding behind its subject. There was no trace of Anne, but there was a hooded figure scampering away from me… Lila asked if this was possible—clearly the artist of the sculptures in the attic was deliberately hiding something. I have to come to the conclusion that it's either Constance trying to conceal something that happened to her at D'Arvor, or that I'm dealing with an outstanding forger.

I can't throw myself completely into this, offering Maxime my assistance, striking deals with him (my help for a piece of D'Arvor—my devotion for a piece of him), pouring my brain and heart and soul into his life legacy, until I know for sure what I'm dealing with.

"Maxime," I start, noticing the inky darkness we are speeding through, realizing I'm completely at his mercy. I have no idea where we are. The night stretches into unknown wooden alleys, the fields threatening to smother us. I fancy I can hear the screech of a night bird, or perhaps one of the washerwomen catching an unwilling soul.

"Hmm?"

As we got to the car, he threw his jacket into the boot, rolled up his sleeves. The bright white of his shirt outlines his torso in the dark. His arms are covered in fine golden hairs, catching stray light as he handles the steering wheel, gently pulling and pushing to follow the curves of the road.

"Is there a—there isn't, I mean, any chance that your sculptures might...?" I'm hoping he might say something, help me out, but in his silence I have no choice but to stumble forward. "That someone might have tried to *emulate* her style...?"

His voice is cold with shock. "You think they might be fakes?"

It's fine. It's a natural question to ask, I tell myself, yet I know the violence of bringing this up when we're talking of family heirlooms. "No, not at all... I—it's just—they are so different from those in Rennes. It's—a bit difficult to make it all fit together. I was just wondering if there's something we haven't thought about, another explanation, maybe."

In the silence, I imagine what would happen if, at his push of a button, my seat fell through and I landed on the tarmac, bruised and hurt. I think he's going to speak, but, out of nowhere, he slams on the brakes.

"Merde," he hisses, in that painfully long moment when time stops and the car threatens to spin, frozen in the imbalance, gravity pushing it to the edge of an accident. I'm bashed forward against my seat belt, which, thankfully, locks, and the screech of the tires echo the ghosts and the night creatures and the ghouls and the malevolent fairies as the car struggles to stay on the road and Maxime and I both hang on.

We've stopped. We're still on asphalt. In the middle of the track, but motionless, facing forward. In the headlights, a fox stands for a moment, a copper shape of long limbs, his beady black eyes absorbing the light—then it scampers out of sight.

Maxime and I breathe out in unison. I am brought all at once so close to my parents' fate that I can feel them near, as if a portal has been opened, as if it is their ghosts awaiting me in the forest. This dangerous, magnificent desire to stay here, to make some kind of mark upon the world, to scream my name, comes upon me. I have the urge to pull Maxime to me then—tell him he saved my life, kiss the hell out of him, feel the warmth of his skin against mine.

Like the fox, it lasts the time of a blink, then it's just me, composed again, my hands snatching at the seat belt that is still cutting into my throat. Maxime switches the light on in the car as if to find his bearings. Its sharpness exposes me completely.

"Can fakes be that—*good?*" His voice is hoarse. He moves forward and I think that he's going to turn on the radio, but instead he brushes my hair from the side of my neck. "Are you hurt?" His fingers tenderly stroke the flesh the seat belt ate into.

"The answer is: *not likely,*" I whisper. I close my eyes at his touch, not daring to move.

"You're not hurt?"

"I'm not hurt. And you're right. Fakes can be great, but there's always a tell. Something that doesn't add up."

"But *you* would know, Camille, wouldn't you?"

He's still stroking, then with his other hand he cups my face, gently but firmly making me look him in the eye.

"You're right," I tell him.

"Why aren't you sure then?"

Is he going to kiss me? I'm losing my mind here.

"Because the sculptures you've shown me, Maxime, they're different… They're extraordinary."

"Like you," he says.

I take his fingers, to examine his hands in mine. I want to attach them to my heart, so he can feel how fast it's beating. *Wait.* What is that, under his nails? He snatches them away, clicks off the light, then bends forward, this time to punch some buttons on the radio.

"At the bar earlier," I start again. It feels like days ago. "You talked about my gift."

He is silent while a song fills the car. *Respire encore. Breathe, still.*

My eyes linger on his hands holding the wheel, and I wonder if the flecks of plaster I just saw on his fingers were real or a figment of my imagination. Am I making things up? Projecting my thoughts onto him?

We both have secrets.

"You're right," I continue. It feels a bit easier to say in the dark, when I don't have to look at him. When we just escaped a car crash. "I can tap into art. Physically transport into it. Into scenes of the artist's past, their inspiration to make the piece. I know it sounds mad, but—"

He interrupts me. "I know. But that's not all, is it?"

"What do you mean?"

"You can bring people in with you."

"How do you know?" Did Lila tell him? But they haven't been by themselves this afternoon. Unless she told him earlier, that night after the attic… I can't help feeling betrayed, but of course her loyalty would be to him. What did I expect? That Lila and I were really becoming friends, just because of what we shared this afternoon?

"I've always suspected, Camille. You put *Viviane* in my head. I knew something was happening then. Then at the V&A, surely you realized I caught glimpses of what you were seeing? The pond, the water, some sunlight. *Incredible* confidence." A pause, while the car's ventilation purrs, the radio blasts, and I'm staring at the night beyond the headlights, trying to reconsider my whole history with Maxime. "I saw the way the woman reacted at the Courtenay showcase. And today, I think Lila was lucky enough to get a proper *grand tour* in the museum and neither of you are telling me. The truth is, I think you're a coward."

"What?" I'm stunned. That's a lot to process. But—a *coward…?*

"You—*tap into things* (your words); you *observe*, you *watch*, when you could be using your power to a much greater extent.

Have you ever thought of where Constance's fame would be if you had been more *active*?"

I feel like he's punched me right in the heart. This space is too small; I'm too vulnerable, lying back in my seat, at the mercy of Maxime's words while they cut me open. My fingers grasp the door handle.

I thought I was safe here with him, that he was the only one who seemed not to judge me for my failures, and now this? I can't bear to stay here while he too is telling me how I failed Constance, and myself.

I rattle the door, but it's locked. "Let me out."

He sits very still, watching me struggle.

"Camille, I'm proposing that we work together. That I help you refine that power. Do you think it's a coincidence that *Viviane* unlocked it for you? That after a mere two weeks here you are stronger than you have ever been, able to take someone in with you willingly?"

"What do you mean?" I gasp.

"I think it's all linked to the estate, to D'Arvor. And I think that *there*, you and me, somehow...we can magnify each other."

I let go of the door. That part of my brain desperately trying to get to grips with our history kicks off again and I see it all: how Maxime held my hand in D'Arvor's attic the first time I went to Avalon. How I kept returning to the lake, the glimpses of the boy with golden locks. Maxime was there at Courtenay too, when I pulled the woman in. He was there

to receive Lila in his arms, my head full of my infatuation for
him, when she snuck in. Every time my gift has progressed,
it's been thanks to him and D'Arvor.

"What exactly are you hoping to gain from this?" I ask.

"I told you. I want the world to know the extent of
Constance's talent. I want them all to see her the way you
showed her to me, all these years ago."

"You want people to buy a sculpture at the ball," I say
slowly, putting the pieces together. *Crazy Connie's little fancies.* "Is it all about the money?"

"Ah, Camille, is this really what you think of me? After all
those years?" He rubs his eyes with his fingers.

I think of Duke Charles's amused contempt, of Maxime's
reaction. If it's not about money, it must be about prestige.
What's in it for me? Then I see, again, Rob marching me out,
the crowd in Courtenay staring in silence. Rob chose not to
believe me and fired me without a backward glance. All these
years I've had to hide my gift, make it a containable hidden
quirk, for fear that people would think me mad and discredit
me. I've worked so hard to mold myself into somebody who
stayed in her lane and strived to give them what they wanted
in a way that suited them.

Maxime was right. I was always watching the story pan
out, never an actor in it. I think I may have been a coward.

I think of Constance's unmarked grave, how she could have
gone from the elated, confident artist I saw in *Washerwoman*
to disappearing from the records. Have I done the same to

my own life by erasing my potential? What role did Anne Foucault play in Constance's fate? Then I think of Maxime's nails. Of his reaction when I questioned the sculptures. I have a lot of figuring out to do, and I do think only Maxime and D'Arvor hold the answers. Maxime didn't deny that he had *Night Swimming* earlier in the bar. Even if there's a tiny chance...

"I suppose I do want to see how far I can go," I say.

I hear his smile in the darkness.

"But there's one condition."

"*Anything.*"

"You give me *Night Swimming* after the ball. You let me be the one who shows it to the world."

"Of course," he says. "Dear Camille, that was the plan all along."

20

FOR THE NEXT two weeks, I spend most of my time in the attic with Maxime. He's adamant he wants me to take people into one of the sculptures during the ball's charity auction. I tried to take him in straightaway, to no avail. We came to the conclusion that what happened with Lila was a fluke and I have to practice, build up my ability. He watches me as I tap into and out of the sculptures, makes note of every detail of the mechanics of my power.

He cares so much about it that, for him, I push myself beyond my limits and exhaustion. These sculptures are tougher, more opaque, but at the same time more one-dimensional than the ones in Rennes. They pull me in like a magnet, and allowing myself to give in repeatedly is unpleasant, confronting me with emotions I would rather avoid for myself. The couples are not happy. They tell a sad story. I've renamed them secretly: *The Apprenticeship, The Devotion,*

The Deception, The Madness. But because Maxime is here, and because I need to find out once and for all who made them, I keep trying. The artist is still hiding themselves from me, a skittish hooded figure I sometimes catch a glimpse of behind a thick bush of gorse. The landscape still feels made-up, rather than real, like the decor of a theater. I think I know now that they're hiding deliberately, but I don't know still if it's Constance, or someone else.

Meanwhile the couples dance, argue, deceive each other, on a loop. Steadily, I become more in control when dealing with them. I harden to the emotional anguish, the tar-like pond. Maxime spurs me to go in, and out, until I feel in complete control of the pond opening and closing at my feet.

"Let's try again," Maxime says one evening. I've just come back; I'm shaking, and I realize I'm completely drained. For a while now I've spent more time in the sculptures, trying to make sense of them, than the real world. All the traveling in and out and the opaque mystery of them are starting to take hold.

"What if it all goes wrong?" I ask him. His presence in the tiny attic makes the space crackle with electricity. Around him, the sculptures seem more alive, pleading and recoiling.

"I trust you," he says.

"What if you get stuck and I can't get you out?"

"You got Lila out, didn't you?"

He's right; it's time. I can't continue on this loop; I need something to happen. I still think Maxime holds the key—what will happen when I introduce him to Avalon? Will anything become clearer? I also, deep down, know that it might work. I know my power well, and it's become more pliable to my will now.

"Which one?" I ask him.

He points to *Morgane and Merlin. The Apprenticeship.* "That's my favorite." He winks at me, and my heart soars as the water starts to spread, so black it looks like a void. Maxime gasps as it rises to his ankles. "There you go."

His widened eyes hit me. Anxiety fights his determination as we prepare to dive in, but I'm in charge now. I take his hand, press it against my heart. Our roles are reversed; he is fearful, and I'm confident. "Are you sure you trust me?" I ask him. He nods and, brazen, I grin at him. Then I pull him down with me.

The swim is unpleasant, but I've grown more resistant to the voices echoing in the pitch black, telling me I can't do it. I clearly *can* be extraordinary enough. Maxime's presence helps, because I know he's believed in me all along.

I step out of the pond into a stormy landscape of D'Arvor. Morgane and Merlin are here.

So is Maxime. Despite having taken extensive notes about my process, he is trying to fight his utter bewilderment with focus, and I feel pride that I've impressed him so.

Merlin is coaxing Morgane to try a magic spell.

You are extraordinary. Only you deserve to be my student. Together we can achieve anything. We'll show them.

"You've done it, Camille." I bask in the warmth of Maxime's

tone, but he's not looking at me. "So, this is Constance and Boisseau, right? When he was teaching her. It all makes perfect sense."

He starts walking around, trying to prod this and that, attempting to rectify things as if he is personally in charge of this theme park.

Meanwhile, like I have since the museum, I look for them: Anne and Constance. But I already know they're not here. There is no hope down here—only the ropes of disappointed, mistreated love, cutting through my neck.

"Can you—interact with things? Can you pick up this stone?" Maxime points at a pebble on the ground. I shake my head.

Not like this, like that. You can't do it. I invested so much in you. Was it all a lie?

I—just—can't.

Of course you can.

The air feels thicker suddenly, as Merlin shakes Morgane's hands while she attempts to trace a spell and fails. Maxime is watching them, and I see him bring his hand to his heart the way he did in the bar, his face—

It's too much. I'm dizzy, and I fear I might pass out. "Maxime!" I have to call him three times, like a spell, until he looks up. Green eyes. Merlin's green eyes. Morgane is withdrawn, small between the two men. The forest around us grows thick and spiky with thorns. "We need to go back."

"Why?" Maxime asks, seemingly over whatever has just

passed. "We've barely started. You need to show me what you can do."

We've barely started. Morgane whimpers. I can't see her face, obscured by the curtain of her thick hair.

"This *is* what I can do." My voice is strangled. "What more do you need? If we stay too long…"

"We need to see how you can *affect* things. Here. Try to pick up this stone."

Reluctantly, I do. And I can't, because I've never been able to. My breath is haggard, tears wobbling behind my eyelids. "Why? Why do you need me to change anything?"

He looks at me like a disappointed mentor, points at the cardboard-like landscape around us, the puppets replaying their scenes. "Because this is not sellable. We need it better, for when you bring others in. We need to make it extraordinary."

I try again, and growl in frustration. I can't even feel my feet on the ground. "*I can't.*"

"Camille." His arms wrap me suddenly. They're real, even in this universe of deception. Everything else recedes, as if the volume of malice has been turned down by two notches. I tremble against him, warm, held. "Let's do it together."

When I bend to pick up the stone again, my hand is cupped in his, his body hugging mine tightly. The stone feels lighter than it should, as if made of papier-mâché, but dusty, concrete.

"God, I've wanted to hold you for so long." His whisper

sends a shiver down the whole length of me. My knees buckle but he holds me up. "Now I want you to pour something of yourself into that stone, mold it into something so perfect people would kill each other to possess it."

I won't have a repeat of the V&A. But I'm on the point of collapse, between Maxime's breath caressing my neck, the stone burning in my palm as if absorbing all my desire for him, to please him. My energy is fading quickly. Surely he'll see this and will let me go before it's too late? What if I collapse here and we get stuck? "Maxime," I beg, "please…"

And then, Morgane moves. She has ripped herself from her stilted scene and is running at us. It takes me a second to register it's at Maxime, not me, and I think she's going to embrace him, but this is not love. She throws herself at him claws out like a cat—

"No!" I shout. Without thinking, I throw the stone at her. It makes contact with the earth, which rises all around her feet, a solid pedestal of rock holding her in place.

Look what you made of me, she whimpers.

She struggles to get out, but the ground has changed. *I* have changed it.

Maxime turns to me. "Well, this is promising."

I gather the last of my energy and I pull him after me, into and through the pond, like the little mermaid does to Prince Eric, in a desperate effort to reach the surface before I lose consciousness. The dry cold air of the attic smacks me as I collapse in a heap on the parquet.

I hear Maxime's voice, think he's kneeling by my side, but I can't open my eyes. He kisses my fingers, one by one, like precious stones. "With more practice," he mutters, "I think we'll be ready for the ball."

My eyes fling open. "So you don't just want me to take people into a sculpture at your auction, you want me to change what they see?"

He makes me feel, in his reaction, that I've been slow to catch on. "Of course. That's where your true power lies. You can make sure they see what we want them to see, in there."

"But that's lying," I say.

"No, Camille. That's no different from what you always did, presenting the artworks in a way that appeals to the buyers, revealing them to their best advantage."

"A charity ball isn't an auction house. You know this won't be the best place to rehabilitate Constance."

He sighs. Again, I feel I'm slowing him down with my questions. "The ball is a small taster. A trial, if you wish. If it works then, with those idiots, then we go to the press with the rest of the sculptures. We take on the art world. So, ready to try again?"

Exhaustion washes over me. My vision is blurry—I can't make out the lines of the furniture in our sparse office. I'm not sure I want to take on the art world. I'm not sure I want any of this. "I need a break."

He looks frustrated, but eventually he nods. "Very well. You know best."

He helps me down the stairs, to my bed, and I lie there fully clothed, my thoughts utterly scrambled, grasping for snippets of things that I know I should be able to put together, my body yearning for Maxime and for that world where I can stop furies in their tracks, where elements ply to my will, where he could be at my mercy. It all swirls and swirls in my head like a snow globe until, in the quieter hours of the dead of night, when the grip of Avalon loosens, it settles.

And I can finally, finally put it all together in a way that makes sense.

Merlin's green eyes.

I studied at the Beaux-Arts.

The plaster under his fingers.

The way he walked around, prodding and appraising, like a metteur en scène.

Look what you made of me. The concert of the night reaches me through the open window. Owls scratching branches with their claws, washerwomen of the night ambushing lost souls with heavy wet linen.

Of course Constance is nowhere to be found in D'Arvor's sculptures. Because the artist who made them is not only hiding behind their subject, but hiding, specifically, from me. They knew I would be visiting them.

It all makes sense. These sculptures *are* forgeries. And I think Maxime made them.

21

I LOOK FOR Maxime the next day, bewildered, but he's nowhere to be found. I need confirmation that he has forged the statues, but it feels mad in the clear light of day, impossible. It is such a wild accusation... I need more proof. I need to understand why he would want to do this, what exactly he would have to gain by taking the risk of forging some works of art that would be scrutinized so deeply.

If it's true, I should be furious to have been played. Furious at his arrogance, at the fact that he almost fooled me. Equally...his talent is dazzling. He hid himself from me, even with my gift. His mind is infuriating, dangerous, addictive, and I've just been given a key to it.

I imagine those hands at work, modeling me like they gave life to the clay. *Focus, Camille.* What is he bargaining to gain? Is it about the money he might make? It feels so wild a risk, so huge an effort, for someone already at the top of the food chain. Someone who could surely seduce their way into any pocket. I'm restless, grasping at strands that keep breaking.

I also think his training is working. I've become even more porous to the souls in the castle. The crying baby comes back on the regular, especially when I'm in the office, but I try to push his wails away. I'd rather be outside, surrounded by nature, where it's quieter. I'd rather occupy myself in the frenzy of ball preparations. I join Lila to help Marie-Laure make bouquets of flowers from the garden, trying out various color combinations. My hands, already burning and sore, keep catching on the thorns, drawing invisible but painful scratches that no rubbing can soothe. I'm lost in my thoughts until they become flies bothering me. I feel Maxime must be hiding something from me, a truth about his family, something linking him to Constance that would justify the pains he's taken to rehabilitate her. Has it got anything to do with Anne Foucault?

"Marie-Laure," I say, snipping off a tender rosebud—one bloodred, that she said she needed for the centerpiece. "Do you know anything about Anne Foucault?"

I can't see her face under the brim of her hat, but she brings her gloved hands down to her knees. She's a petite woman, even smaller than me. I wonder how the frequent gusts of wind here don't topple her over.

"I know who she was, of course. My husband's grandmother." She picks up her shears again; they hang around the thin stem of a rose, but she doesn't snip. She seems rather stressed today, jittery. I think the pressure of the ball might be getting to her. Now that I think about it, I've hardly seen her these past couple of weeks. Maxime and I were so absorbed in our mission that we forgot to have dinner most days.

"What about her child?" I think of the blond boy running in *Washerwoman*. He was in *Viviane* too. It was clear how much both women loved him.

"What child?"

I'm surprised at her puzzlement. "Maxime's grandfather."

"Ah. Of course. I never got to know him, sadly, but Anne adored him. She used to say Maxime was his spitting image. She said she pulled him out of the pond, that he had been left behind by a fairy. She was adamant she hadn't stolen him, that she was merely looking after him, waiting for the fairy to return and fetch him." She stops. "She was very old, you understand. Her life and stories got all mixed up."

"I think Anne and Constance were friends," I say, aware of Lila going to town on some kind of weed next to me with her bare fingers. She is digging, pulling hard, not managing to dislodge its roots.

"Constance Sorel was rather a loner."

"You really don't like her, do you?"

"Ms. Leray." Marie-Laure finally snips the rose, a sharp sound that makes me flinch. "Constance Sorel brought sadness and misery to D'Arvor. Like all artists, she was selfish; for her art she needed to create drama and anguish wherever she went. She tried to destroy our family. So I don't think she would have made *friends*, as you say. In fact, unlike my son, I think it would have been much better had she never come here."

"What do you mean, she tried to destroy your family?" I ask, despite Lila's eyes telling me that I shouldn't probe.

"She was unhinged. She nearly drowned him, you know that? The boy."

Marie-Laure throws her gardening gloves on the ground. They land with a quiet thump. She brings her hand up to attempt to undo the knot under her sun hat. The longer she tries and fails, the more her fingers tremble. Lila watches her—I think she's enjoying her struggle. I go to help, but Marie-Laure bats me away. She grows more and more agitated until Frédéric approaches from the house, carrying a pot of white paint, his T-shirt smeared with it—one look makes him hurry to her. Quietly, almost sadly, he pulls the hat off her head.

"We can undo the knot later, Mother." The features of her face are melting now, as if she doesn't have the strength to hold them in place any longer; her bright red mouth smeared, pulled downward. Frédéric wraps his arm around her shoulder to guide her back to the house.

"She's going to do it all over again," I hear her say. "Even dead, she will pull us apart."

"What does she mean?" I ask Frédéric. I don't care if it's not the right moment—I'm outraged on Constance's behalf.

He stares at me. "Not now, please. Can't you see she's unwell?" Marie-Laure gasps, and he turns back to her. "Let me give you something. You'll soon be right as rain again." As they walk away, he glances back at me among my cemetery of chopped roses.

—

In the evening, as I walk past the yellow salon's open doors, Frédéric calls out to me. He is hanging fairy lights in the garden. I approach him unwillingly, the gravel crunching under my brogues. I'm still shaken from my interaction with Marie-Laure, her vitriol about Constance, which felt only one step removed from ill feelings toward me. I could leave, I suppose. I could send Maxime the unsatisfactory dossier and an invoice, tell him I'm done and I have better to do back home, but that would be a lie. Even Lowen is here, in Rennes—although we've barely talked since that awkward drink. I forwarded him the invitation to the ball, at Maxime's request. Are you sure that's a good idea, Cam? I didn't reply because I wasn't sure at all.

Frédéric is perched precariously on the rim of one of the fountains. I imagine visitors being told not to touch, not to sit, and here is Frédéric, trampling and groping. He beckons me, holds out the end of the cable for me to wrap around Neptune and his putti. "Thank you."

We work in silence, then he says: "You must excuse my

mother. She gets a little stressed. We're not really used to hosting parties anymore. Certainly not on this scale."

"What did you give her?"

He smiles. "I seem to be my family's pharmacist. Just something to help her settle." Then: "Don't worry, Ms. Leray, it's all aboveboard."

When it's done, we take a few steps back to judge our work.

"I think it's going to look lovely," I say.

Frédéric shakes his head, unsure. "Shall we try it?"

He jogs back a few paces to press a switch. The whole garden illuminates. Garlands of blue, red, and green bulbs caught on hedges; rows and rows of tiny white fairy lights twinkling on topiary and statues, multiplied by their reflection on the water basins.

It must have been hours of work and I arrived for the final flourish. *Like any piece of art*, I think grimly. *I'm always there once it's all said and done, right at the very end. I never make anything.*

But you're the one pressing the switch. I feel like I can hear Maxime's voice in my ear.

"It's gorgeous," I whisper. "Just like Merlin's spell when he made Viviane's crystal palace." I always imagined it in floating balls of color, spinning around the lake faster and faster until the air solidified into crystal spires, turrets, and windows.

Frédéric smiles, resigned. "They will find flaws with it, but I tried my best. Thank you for your help."

"Who will find flaws with it? Your father?" I ask, remembering what Maxime told me in the bar.

He stares at me. His coloring is darker than Maxime's; he has straight ebony hair, kept a bit longer to hide that it's started to recede at the temples, heavy eyelids, and long eyelashes. He is shorter too. I wonder if everyone looks at him like I've done just now—to compare and contrast, highlight his shortcomings. "Sorry," I say, "I shouldn't have said that. None of my business."

"That's all right," he says, mildly. Then: "I'm going to check out the orangery. Care to walk with me?"

"Why not?" I don't really want to, but this is an opportunity to ask him about what Marie-Laure said earlier. The one in her confidence, Frédéric might also be the Foucault who is most likely to open up away from other ears.

The sun has completely disappeared now but the fairy lights guide us some way across the grounds. Our steps make damp thuds on the grass; we are walking on soft soil you could bury bodies in.

"Thank you for helping," he says again, and I know he's trying things out in his head. I know, because I feel that he and I connect on some deep level neither of us want to verbalize. In our families, we're the ones who scramble, who strive, whose trainers slip at the edges of monuments.

As we get deeper into the grounds, I lose my bearings. The air grows thick and cold, mixing dew and earth and, every so often, the faded pungency of rotting rose. I expect

Frédéric to use the light on his phone, but he clearly knows the park like the back of his hand, and I follow him, trying to trust that my feet will continue to meet solid ground.

"Why are we checking out the orangery?" I ask.

I can feel his proximity. It's a different warmth from Maxime's—this one is needy, urgent, quietly pulsing with frustration. I try to get a little more space but he keeps closing the gap, his elbow bumping into mine.

"I often walk over at night. Check that everything is OK. Gives me an excuse to leave the house."

"Why would you want to leave the house?"

The frustrated noise he makes startles me. "I thought you understood."

I'm getting annoyed with him now. But I'm also walking deep into huge grounds, at night, with this man I now realize I never properly looked at. There's something so...repressed about him. I just hope all his frustration won't come out right now, in a form I won't be able to contain.

"Frédéric...you must know I don't understand anything. There's so much concealed here. What did your mother mean earlier, about Constance? *Drowning* a boy?"

I can't see his face in the dark, but it takes a moment for him to respond. "Constance wasn't well, Ms. Leray. She became very poorly at D'Arvor. Some kind of madness. She lost track of reality. Family knowledge has it she thought my grandfather was an evil creature and she threw him into the lake. He was only a toddler. She was sent away shortly after that."

We must be coming to the lake now because I hear lapping water. We could be walking right into it for all I know. The shock of what Frédéric just said is overwhelming. All the dampness is starting to cling to my clothes like a shroud. "That can't be true," I say. "Constance wasn't mad." I know her mind. I know her so intimately, and yet...after the sculptures I saw in Rennes, she stopped. Is this the key piece of information I was missing about her fate? Her, what, *losing her mind*? It doesn't even mean anything. That's not a condition, not an illness. It sounds more like posthumous slander.

Frédéric laughs. "You have so many ideas about what is true, yet you have no bloody clue." He comes to a stop, and all I can do is the same, bracing myself for the violent push that might come, when he sends me headfirst into the murky water and I disappear, pulled down by ropes of algae and the claws of fairies that come alive at nighttime.

You're not supposed to know our secrets. Now you can't ever go back.

"Now you know, though. She was unwell, she was kicked out after she tried to hurt a child. She stopped working, fell into poverty, end of story. I'm sorry, but that's a truth even you and Maxime can't rewrite. So, when are you leaving?" His voice is so close to my ear. I can't even see him—I can't see anything.

I try to remain calm, to pretend this is a normal conversation in normal circumstances, while I try to process what he's just told me.

"I don't know, Frédéric."

"But you are planning to, though, aren't you?"

"Yes." My heart jumps into my throat as a screeching, terrifying noise erupts nearby. *It's an owl. It's a barn owl,* I tell myself, trying to picture their cute round faces, rather than their jet-black eyes. "Soon. After the ball. Maxime and I haven't really talked about it yet."

He crashes into me and I brace myself for the fall, but he wasn't pushing me; he grabs my upper arms and shakes me. It is a weak shake, and a weak grip; I could easily shrug him off, but I freeze.

"Camille"—his voice is urgent, lower than usual—"you must leave. He told me—he told me about what he thinks you can do. I think he's going mad. I think we'll all suffer if you—if he realizes you can't—that nobody can…"

That brings me back to life. "What?" I hiss, "Get your hands off me!"

But he is stronger than me, and the panic takes hold. Until there's a noise in the lake of something much bigger than a frog moving in the water. Frédéric lets me go, fumbling to turn on his flashlight. He keeps dropping it. A human form emerges and advances on us, dark algae dripping along their arms.

The lady of the lake. She's finally here to snatch me.

Frédéric finally manages to turn on the flashlight and points it right at her.

"Lila?"

"Leave her alone," she hisses.

"Do you mind? This is a private conversation—" Frédéric starts.

"*Fucking stop*, Fred." She turns to me.

Is it really her? A short dark wetsuit reveals the strength of her core, of her limbs. Her hair is loose, like a thick mass of algae, longer than I've known it to be, sticking to her arms. Her furious eyes catch the light, but she doesn't blink.

She's magnificent, terrifying. She *is* the lady of the lake.

"Are you OK?" she asks me.

"Yes, thank you." I just want to get away from Frédéric, from the unsettling darkness. I turn and start running back toward the castle.

"You'll get lost." Frédéric's voice echoes on the water.

Tears prickle out, and I struggle to retrieve my phone from my pocket. But eventually I do, and it illuminates grass and more grass, and a path through the shallow woods. Eventually D'Arvor comes into view, as if to say—*How could you think you could get lost when I'm this close? Did you think you could escape me?*

All the while, I hear Frédéric's voice. *Some kind of madness. You must leave.*

22

WHEN I GET to my room, it feels different. I question everything, walk around it for hours, picking up random objects, trying to find some evidence in them that Frédéric's story was all lies. There's unease for sure, but it might come only from me. I hardly sleep after that—I keep hearing the same owl, its bloodcurdling screech. I mistake it for Constance, screaming from the pond. When, eventually, morning comes, I catch a couple of hours' slumber, interrupted by a knock on the door.

I jump out of bed, heart thumping, throwing on my dressing gown. I want it to be Maxime, yet I'm not up to the confrontation we need to have.

"Yes?"

It's Lila. We've hardly exchanged a word since Rennes. Although we've been in the same space, we have remained two separate entities. I think it was through some kind of mutual understanding, even if the rules of this game still escape me. And I'm still spooked by last night, her supernatural emergence from the pond.

"You ready?"

Dizzy from ill sleep, I rock in my body as if on the deck of a boat. I stare at her, trying to remember what I'm supposed to be ready for.

She sighs. "Our shopping trip? To find you a dress."

"Right." Maxime was supposed to take me.

"Unless you'd rather wear one of your suits," Lila says now, and I'm suddenly aware of my hair sticking out at the sides, my cheap dressing gown with holes at the elbows and some permanent tea stains, versus how immaculately turned out she is. Her hair hangs over her right shoulder in a heavy, seemingly effortless mermaid braid. Her white shirt, tucked into her jeans, does not, unlike me when I try to pull this look off, make her look like she is wearing pajamas.

She's the last person I want to go and try on dresses with.

"Something wrong with my suits?" I ask, trying to gather my wits.

She scoffs. "See you at the car in ten minutes."

———

When Lila parks on the Quai Lamartine in Rennes, I can't really see any boutiques around. I expected Chanel or Dior or another big expensive name. I follow Lila, still resentful

of her comment about my suits, that kind of resentment that
burns hotter when you know the person has hit a nerve. In
my case, I know I've been hiding in my suits all my life, but
that's how I'm comfortable. Or was until my reliable rituals
started failing to bring about results.

I don't intend to let Lila use Maxime's credit card for me.
The boundaries are already so blurred—despite part of me
yearning to *Pretty Woman* the hell out of the occasion, it
wouldn't be appropriate. I therefore was ready to redirect us
to Zara, but the boutique she leads me to, tucked outside of
the main arteries, seems to hit the spot. The clothes are elegant, simple, well cut, and almost affordable; I relax as I stroll
between the holders, forgetting for a moment what I'm here
to buy, lovingly stroking silky blouses and summer dresses.

Now the chinos I'm wearing do feel coarse, and the shirt
too tight, too stiff. There are things in here that would do
for work, I think. A reinvented version of professional me.
A fresh start, something a bit more…playful, without trying
too hard.

We browse in silence for some time, until Lila takes a look
at the pieces I've thrown over my arm. A dark-blue tailored
dress, a gray shirt in a slightly different fabric from my other
inferior gray shirts. She shakes her head and I think she'll
scold me for not devoting my focus to the evening dress section at the back, where I can glimpse long silk numbers in
navies and greens.

The truth is, I'm out of my depth—I have attended a few

black tie and charity evenings in my life, but not in a castle. Not surrounded by fricking dukes and Maxime Foucault in black tie.

"Let me find you something."

"I thought you had strict instructions on what I should buy."

"Yes. But we can have some fun first, can't we? I promise you nobody's watching." I try to protest but Lila winks and darts about the rails I've just browsed like a cat, picking three pieces quickly.

"Oh my God." I hit my forehead with the back of my hand.

"What?" She peers at me over the clothes.

"Are you trying to give me a *makeover*?"

"Would that be such a bad thing?"

"It's patronizing." But I'm starting to feel better.

"Do you always feel that people who are trying to help you are looking down on you? Go try these."

I examine the clothes. A gorgeous summer dress, a top in silk that shimmers like the surface of water, to pair with some plain, yet incredibly soft, dark culottes.

I hadn't even spotted these pieces as I browsed. They're wonderful, different but not completely off, giving me a tantalizing glimpse of a sublimized me, and I'm suddenly very uneasy.

"That's not me…"

Lila nudges me gently to the changing rooms, hands the clothes over to the shop assistant, and I let myself be led. In a blink, the curtain is drawn shut, and I find myself stroking the blue dress.

"If you *are* planning a makeover, I'm warning you—don't think you can remove my glasses and I'll suddenly look super-hot. It's not going to be like that. Under my glasses I just look like me without glasses." I'm babbling to Lila through the curtain to ease the awkwardness and the weird excitement tingling my fingers as I take off my stiff clothes. The woman staring back at me in the mirror doesn't have a clue, I realize. She's been dressing like she wanted people to take her seriously, while she didn't really believe she deserved it.

"You don't wear glasses," Lila responds patiently.

"Precisely."

I shut up when I try the clothes on and they all fit like a skin. A skin that is much more me than anything else I've worn before. I *love* these clothes. If I buy them, I don't think I can ever wear anything else. They will change the way I am in the world. Am I ready for this? Plus I'm not sure I want to give Lila the satisfaction of being right.

I'll never see her again once I get back, though, and try to patch together my career and my life. Dressed like this, I could do anything. As I waver, wondering whether I have the courage, I give myself a stern, silent talking-to in the mirror. "I'll take them all," I call out to Lila, not knowing whether she's wandered off.

"Hang on, one more thing..." Her voice is startlingly

close, and she drops a T-shirt to me over the rail. I startle at the look of it: so young, so out of place.

Je donne ma langue au chat—I give my tongue to the cat— is written across the chest.

"I don't know what the words mean," I tell Lila, assuming she's still out there. I understand every individual word, I know it must be an idiom, but as a French speaker who never lived in France, idioms aren't my forte.

"But you can still put it on, no?"

I shrug, and only the mirror sees. When it's on, twenty-one-year-old Camille is looking back at me. I remember that girl, the one at the V&A. I wish I could go back and tell her how beautiful she was. Perhaps tell her to stop wearing other people's lives and expectations like a badge of honor.

"Can I see?"

"Yes."

The curtain draws back and Lila appears behind me in the mirror. She's wearing the plain navy dress I selected before. She looks stunning, but muted next to my cheeky print. Suddenly I fear that it's all been another one of her tricks. As we stare at each other in the mirror, a flash of embarrassment I haven't felt for a long time rips through me so hard I have to shut my eyes.

I'm at home, in Reading. In my bedroom. Maman is appraising me. The look on her face. *What are you playing at, Camille? You're not wearing this to go to work. You're already going to struggle to be taken seriously. And I told you that short hair doesn't suit you.* Points to my newly cut hair. Points to the dress I had chosen especially, with its lovely bright pattern of ink stains I thought perfect for my first day in the art world. Points to the whole of me. She is close to me, her breath against my cheek, sour with wine.

"You look great," Lila says. "Younger."

My breathing grows faster, louder. Maman never gave me the key. She only ever told me what I did wrong. I remember not having anything else to wear, going to my first day at work in the dress she had just criticized, fighting back tears. Running to H&M that evening and spending hours not knowing what to pick, second-guessing what would be right. I was always straining to make myself acceptable to her, but she just wanted me invisible. Is this what I've been doing in the art world, and with my power? The feeling is so stark, and this changing room feels so small, I am so big in it, touching all the sides with my wide hips, and growing and growing until I will surely spill out. I can't—

"Wait," Lila says, suddenly alert, "are you OK?"

I turn away from the mirror, pressing both my hands below my ears.

"I need to get out of here," I pant. She's already stepped out and pulled the curtain shut for me. I tear the T-shirt off and re-dress, a race against the walls closing in on me, and as my armor meets my skin, the shock starts to ease. I stand still a little longer, pressing my forehead against the mirror. I'm appalled at the impact Maman has had on me that I never questioned. At the lengths I have gone to erase myself.

"What happened?" Lila asks when I emerge. She looks genuinely mortified, and it softens me.

"Just—I don't know. Ignore me. Sorry."

"Was it a man?"

"Pardon?"

"Your bad memories."

"No," I say. I'm gripping the clothes Lila had me try on originally. I left the T-shirt in the changing room. "My mother."

There. It feels good to say it. The bad memories don't come from me; they come from Maman. *She* made them.

"We should go back to D'Arvor," I say, trying to straighten my back, avoiding looking in Lila's direction.

"Camille." When I feel the warmth of her shoulder against mine, I want her to take me in her arms and rock me like a little girl who has grazed her knee. "You still need a dress."

I know I'm in no state to make rational decisions. "Can you choose for me?"

Her eyes search mine. "Fine. Wait here."

When she comes back, she hands me two dresses. One is simply cut in black velvet, with long cuffed sleeves and a fuller skirt, coming down to my knees. The other is a long satin green number with a cowl and a slit that comes up to the thigh.

"Which one would Maxime want me to wear?" I hear myself ask.

She shrugs. "Why don't we take both? He's paying anyway. I'll return the one you're not wearing on the day. Deal?"

I can't afford both at once, so I nod, promising myself I'll pay him back.

Lila watches over the shop assistant as she folds both dresses in silk paper. "You look like a mother who's about to send her child to school for the first time," I tell her.

"There's something in it, yes."

"Lila…" She looks sad, but I don't know how to comfort her.

The young woman at the till returns Maxime's credit card. Both Lila and I stare at it. She doesn't move. I pick it up, feel the sharpness of its corners against my fingers. Lila's hand finds my wrist and I think for a minute she's going to restrain me, but she just touches it. Her hand is cold. "I think I might know what we need," she says with a kind of urgency, and though the mood is thick, the prospect of being taken care of leaves a fizzing dust of sherbet at the tip of my tongue.

23

WE WALK A little way from the center of town and I'm almost hoping Lila might be planning some kind of heist—something dangerous and fierce. I'm brimming with misplaced destructive energy. The sun is less kind here, the breeze not quite reaching us, my body pressed into the tarmac. We walk down streets of residential buildings and, every so often, like an island, a café-bar whose tables have spilt onto the pavement, people smoking cigarettes and reading newspapers, tiny coffee cups in front of them. I'm carrying my bag too, the two dresses competing with each other. Lila and I don't talk much, keep glancing at each other sideways. What is our relationship now, and how much longer will we have to walk like this, in this painful state of in-between?

Then, eventually, she stops in front of an old patisserie, a plain shopfront in white with faded gold lettering.

"Here?" I can't hide the disbelief from my voice.

"Yes. You need some sugar."

"Not what I was expecting." But a grin spreads on my face.

"What were you expecting?" Lila asks, as we step in, and are shown past a counter of perfectly aligned *religieuses*, lemon tartlets, gleaming bavarois and glazed chocolates, piles of macarons arranged by color like a sugar-frenzied painter's palette, into a tearoom at the back. The decor is simple, but the atmosphere is hushed, as if people instinctively understand the respect owed to the culinary miracle of choux pastry. I nod at a family of tourists as we walk to our table, excitedly whispering in English, each of them sitting in front of a different mirror-glazed square of happiness.

"I don't know what I was expecting. Something like those aquariums you dip your toes in and the fish come and eat your dead skin—"

Lila laughs, disgusted. "Oh please, it takes a lot to put me off my food, but—"

"Sorry, a *spa day*, or a personal shopper experience?"

"Is this how you see me, then?"

I tear my gaze from the icing and fresh raspberries to meet hers. Her face is calm, not exactly amused, but thoughtful.

"A car chase?" I ask, to break the tension. She laughs.

"That's more like it," she says. "I'd be up for *that*."

We place our order—when I hear Lila choose two pastries, I do the same. She goes for lemon and pistachio, I for chocolate and strawberry.

Her phone beeps as we wait. She seems to hesitate before typing something. I can see she's trying to hide the screen from me.

"Everything going according to plan?" I can't help but ask, bitterness on my tongue.

"What plan?"

"Come on, Lila." I can't believe I keep almost falling for her being my friend, for some kind of connection. "I bet that was you reporting to Maxime. *Dress acquired. Don't worry, I'll make sure she won't embarrass us.*"

She holds out her hand, but doesn't touch me. It hangs there across the table, against the backdrop of waiters carrying single macarons displayed on porcelain plates like jewels. "All right. Yes, Maxime asked me to keep an eye on you."

I don't know why, but it hurts. I thought she had come with me willingly at the museum, that we had shared something that was just ours. "So you were a spy."

She shrugs. "The worst one, apparently."

"You told him all about the museum?"

I can't read her eyes. "Yes," she says. "Eventually, he got it out of me."

Our pastries arrive. Lila waits for the waiter to leave; then she says: "I think you and he are playing a dangerous game."

"I'm the one playing a game? This is no game to me. This is my life. I didn't ask either of you to—barge in."

"Your gift..."

"What about it?"

"It's beautiful, Camille. I think you should use it much better."

"Not you as well! You said you don't care for art."

"I just find it tricky to relate to," she says. "To you, and Maxime's, version of what 'art' is. What it is for, I guess."

"What do you mean?"

"You work in an auction house, selling things for millions. He hides in his gallery with top security systems and petits fours. Why should people who are poor not be allowed beautiful things? Why keep them behind bars, like a private joke for rich people? And now you're organizing some kind of private, exclusive entertainment party, where the wealthy get to tap into an artist's soul? Sounds rather exploitative to me."

"I think everyone should be allowed beautiful things," I say.

"I'm sure you do. Yet people like you and Maxime ensure art stays in the private hands of wealthy wankers."

"I'm sorry, but aren't you dating such a wanker?" It feels easier for both of us to say these things away from the castle. Maxime was wrong—it isn't Absinthe that loosens up tongues, but cake. I like this with Lila, knowing where I stand. Having, for the first time, access to her unfiltered opinions.

"I'm well aware of that fact. But I'm tired of the argument that the less you have, the more your preoccupations should narrow. Art isn't proof of status. It's universal, a reminder of all the iterations of our collective human souls. Take this pastry, for example." She taps at her lemon tart with her fork. "Could you read it? Someone made this. Someone who cared. Isn't it art in the same way a Boisseau might be?"

Defiantly, I slide my fork through my bavarois, and time stops as the silky mousse parts. This is not the kind of pastry you gobble up in a few strikes; rather you must explore the different textures, then let them merge on your tongue. The strawberry is the best possible version of itself: zinging with sun and summer and lime. I take my time, then move on to the dark chocolate, coating my palate with velvet and smoke.

Lowen used to make the most intricate cakes for me when he lived in London. He was never one for talking about feelings, and those cakes were the gateway for me to understand how he felt. If I'm honest with myself, I knew he was in love with me long before the opera cake he made for my birthday, but I refused to acknowledge it or do anything about it. I simply continued to eat the cakes, tapping into the leftovers long after he left, to visit the memory of him standing in his tiny shared kitchen, a piping bag in hand, singing "Best of You."

This stopped when he joined his dad's bakery and had to stick to fifty-year-old recipes—they were good, but I know his life became safe, predictable, uncreative. Just the way mine did. I think I've been too harsh on Lowen, too dismissive of him. I'm so pleased he's doing something about his passion now, yet I've never felt more at risk of losing him completely.

"There," Lila's voice brings me back to reality. She's watching me, as she scrapes off remnants of lemon curd. "You do know exactly what I mean."

I do. But this world of cakes and children's drawings is so small. With Maxime I know I can be so much more. I have a taste for greater things now, and I want to know how far I can go. I could make important people take me seriously, listen to me. I could finally make them see that what I know matters. It's tantalizing.

"Speaking of a dangerous game," I say, to change the subject. "You spooked *me* when you came out of that pond last night."

"Yeah, I enjoyed that." That smile again. Mischievous. Then she becomes more serious. "I struggle with insomnia. I often go swimming at night. Sometimes cold water is the best cure."

"Isn't it a bit...scary? The murkiness. Not seeing the bottom. Not *knowing*."

"You can't see the bottom of the sea."

"I know it's irrational. Fears are, most of the time."

"I think mine are pretty rational."

She tips the last drops of her coffee into her mouth, throwing her head back far.

"Surely there's not much to fear at D'Arvor?" I ask her.

She doesn't smile. "When Maxime brought me here, I was blown away. I couldn't believe he had this life. And he was ready to make a space for me in it. For a week, all we

did was drive around. Brocéliande, Saint Malo, the Val Sans
Retour. the Miroir aux Fées. I don't think I'd ever been hap-
pier. But I think I might have lost myself a bit." As she
speaks I see something familiar in her eyes, the smoke of
romance, of heartache, curling up in her dark irises.

You are my better half; you are the key to unlocking it all.

A sprig of heather, the flash of green eyes. The delights
of a prison of air, something dangerous lurking under the
surface of the pond.

Of course: Maxime poured their love story into his sculptures and Lila saw herself in them. It was all in *Guinevere
and Lancelot*—their infatuation, the giddiness of early days.
Even the places they visited together. And I invaded it. No
wonder she was angry with me. Or with him, most likely.
Was this a kind of exploitation? Is this where the unease I
felt came from?

I shake my head. I need to ask her. "But you *are* happy
with him?"

Her answer takes a while to come. "You're the first person
who's asked me that. Everybody else assumes it goes without saying that I'm the lucky one. I know you think it too,
Camille. You've been pining for him."

I feel my cheeks ignite, but I try to hold her gaze. "What?
That's not—"

"Don't protest. When you're around him, you're different.
On a high, perhaps."

This is so messed up, but I decide she deserves my honesty.

"I'm sorry," I say. "Young crushes run deep. It makes sense you've been uncomfortable with me being here."

She shrugs. "I'm best placed to understand this. He is really very charming."

"Lila, I'm not here to steal anyone's boyfriend."

"Well, time will tell. Who knows what choices we might make further along the line." She looks sad. I want to interject, but she doesn't let me, skimming over the topic like it was nothing. "Being here in Brittany wasn't my choice. D'Arvor wasn't my home. It came with Maxime as a package."

"Why not leave?" I ask. "I say this with no ulterior motive, Lila. Why not?"

Her eyes tell me her barriers have come down again. "Could Viviane leave? Could Constance?"

"No. Viviane's deal was that, should she venture out of Brocéliande, she would lose her powers. But Constance?"

"Constance lost her powers too when she left. You said she stopped creating." It strikes me as a peculiar comparison, another one of her riddles.

"Lila…what exactly do you know about Constance? About what happened to her after D'Arvor? Where did she go?"

Instead of answering, she leans forward again, looking left and right, rummaging in the internal pocket of her coat. "I did mean it, Camille. Your gift. It's meant to be a transcendental experience. Something authentic, real. When I was in there with you, I…I think I really understood what Constance Sorel's art was about for the first time. I know you're obsessed. I know you're looking for what happened to her. I don't think you'll find it in the sculptures Maxime gave you. You should take a look at this."

I stare at the delicate old piece of paper she's handed over. Constance's handwriting is on it. *I should be wearing gloves* is my immediate thought, fighting with the drumming of my heart.

"Did Maxime give you this?" I whisper, as if the police are going to barge on us any minute.

She scoffs. "I found it when they asked me to sort old family papers. They must have thought it was all rubbish if they trusted me with them."

I'm not sure she's telling the truth, but I run my eyes over the note as quickly as possible. It is Constance's handwriting; there is no doubt about it. Her energy jumps off the page, crackling with her spirit. Adrenaline runs through me—a kick much more powerful than chocolate.

Perhaps you too think I'm mad—everybody seems to think I'm mad, but I know they're going to take him from me. That's what fairies do, don't they? They snatch, preferably what a poor woman like me holds dearest. Then they'll take me away so I can't have him back.

I don't want to go to Sainte-Vilaine.

There is no more. She clearly didn't finish, either got interrupted or thought better of it. Her fingers held the pen that wrote this. I stare, mesmerized, at the letters she formed, trying to connect them with her soul.

"*Take him from me*. What did she mean?" I ask Lila.

"Max said he thought she was talking about Boisseau. That she was jealous of the other women in his life."

"No, that doesn't feel right." I try to let the note take me. Not the words so much as the hand that wrote them, shaking so much she blotched her ink. But ink is lighter than plaster, and Constance's words were always less confident than her modeling. I can't tap into it like I would art, but I'm hit with dread at a man's empty face, a lady with long red hair, sobbing, holding a toddler's hand. Flashes, impossible to hold in my mind.

Constance and Anne. The same toddler? Anne's son?

"Lila, why did you give me this?"

I think she wasn't supposed to. This isn't a trap.

"I've met them now. I suppose I'm committed. I want to know what happened to them too. And you're the only one who can find out."

We look at each other, the note splayed out on the table between us.

"You know what Saint-Vilaine was at the time don't you?" I ask.

She nods. I know, because I looked for Constance everywhere. I checked every place. But I want to hear Lila say it.

"A mental hospital."

We both keep quiet for a while, until I throw my napkin

on the table with some force. It makes Lila flinch. "Sorry,"
I say. "But I've done all the research. I looked everywhere.
Constance's death was recorded by a private doctor. And
there are no records of her being at Sainte-Vilaine."

"I give up; please give me the solution," Lila muses.

"Pardon?" I'm dying to keep the note, but she puts it back
in her pocket. She pats her lips with her napkin, puts it down
carefully. Then she leans back into her chair, places her hands
on her belly as if to say, *At least we have cake.*

"*Je donne ma langue au chat.* What was on the T-shirt. It
also implies that somebody knows the solution of the riddle
and can share it with you. Put you out of your misery."

24

IN MY DREAM, I'm in Avalon, and the baby cries in Viviane's arms. She rocks and coos at him with an intensity that makes me uncomfortable. Behind her, the forest is burning. Huge flames that turn the trees red and gold. *Give him to me*, I say, knowing it's a boy, for his mane of golden locks, his eyes. I try to snatch him, but with one flick of her hand, I am turned into stone. I scream, but all it does is echo in my head. My body has become my own prison.

The baby. I wake up, alone. No—I'm not alone—heart skipping, I jump out of bed, ready to defend myself with whatever I can find. A copy of Boisseau's biography, battered, over-read—a poor weapon, with its dulled corners. Eventually, I realize that what I thought was a hooded figure stooped over my bed is the combination of both ball dresses hanging on the wardrobe's door, flapping gently in the breeze of the open window. I collapse back onto the bed, wrapped tight around myself under the bedsheet, waiting for my eyes to stop playing tricks on me.

When I was a child, I used to set boundaries for my safety. *If nothing touches the floor, you'll be all right. If you can't be seen, not even a strand of hair outside of the duvet, she won't get you.* I guess it was a way to make sure I felt I had some control, when in fact, my mother held all the power. She could decide to come in and scream at me for sleeping in the wrong position. She could pull me out of my bed in the middle of the night because I was a pig for not changing my bedsheets. I tried to find rules, explanations, safety protocols, but there was none. The bedsheets needed changing weekly, or daily, or on odd days, or when it rained, depending on her whim.

D'Arvor brings her back so strongly, as if its walls hold her spirit. She's the one I wish I had been able to lock in a prison of air, far from me, and from here. Her dying didn't solve anything, didn't make me feel any better or freer. Who would I be had I had a better, healthier childhood? Would my gift be different? Can I allow Maxime to help me heal and finally believe in myself?

Marie-Laure's words about Constance haunt me: *She nearly drowned the boy.* I refuse to think Constance would have been like my mother, that she could have abused a child. I felt her affection for the toddler; I have visited her head extensively through her works, for goodness' sake. And now I'm questioning everything, doubting what I have believed for years.

Later, I wake up in the fetal position, a hand stroking my shoulder. I can see through the faded peach sheet that morning has arrived, but I can't see who the hand belongs to.

Lila? I emerge on my guard, but less spooked now that I can see the room in the light of day.

It's Maxime. My eyes adjust to the incongruity of having him sitting on my bed early in the morning. He is in a fresh white shirt and his hair is damp and he smells like expensive shower gel.

"Morning. Time to get up."

I sit up, wishing he hadn't found me at my most vulnerable, curled up like a little girl hiding from the world, with hair sticking in her mouth.

"Maybe knock next time you want to come into my room?" I ask, instinctively crossing my arms over my chest.

"Last time I checked this room still belonged to me," he says, and I think he's trying to joke. When I stare at him, deadpan, he adds, with a smile: "We have work to do. You're late."

"You mean the sculptures? I'm not doing that today. We need to talk."

"What about? You already missed yesterday." I feel him tense.

I wish we didn't have to have this conversation here. Ideally, I would have been standing over him in a heavy silk dress with drooping sleeves, holding a sword, and he would be kneeling, head drooped in his knightly armor.

But I have to say it. I need him to be honest with me, and

he hasn't been. "I know the sculptures in the attic are forgeries. And I know you made them."

So much happens in those few seconds he registers what I've said, some that I understand, much that I don't. Then he says, slowly: "So we do need to talk. But not here."

"Where then? You keep running away from conversations. Enough now." I'm aware my chin is trembling. I won't allow him to escape to Rennes or the gallery or wherever he disappears to. *The workshop*, a voice whispers in my head. *Making his mesmerizing, dangerous creations.* It makes me want to pull him to myself, skin against skin, to drink him in right here in the bed Constance might have slept in.

God, get a grip, Camille.

He smiles, perfect white teeth, his hair catching the early-morning light, his eyes hinting at shared lust, and I wonder if he's seen it all pan out on my face. "I think we should take a little trip."

———

The drive to the Val Sans Retour takes us along the narrow roads of Brocéliande, past villages of simple houses, made striking by the use of dark-red shale in their facades, the local building stone ran through with iron oxide. Everything else is so quiet, so green. Lush fields of maize and wheat stretch between patches of the forest; brown cows watch the world go by.

"Do you know that of the twelve thousand five hundred hectares of the forest today, ninety percent is privately owned?" Maxime asks. "So we're always trespassing. It's outrageous."

"Well, you own part of it too," I say.

He seems irritated at my comment. "Only the very edge. Hardly anything. Most of it is split between a dozen or so big owners."

He is a focused tourist guide, pointing as we drive to the bridge where Lancelot and Guinevere met in secret, Merlin's tomb, the Fountain of Barenton, which, he explains, is always cold, yet boiling, and is reputed to cure people of madness. Yvain, the Knight of the Lion, was one of them, and I think about that sculpture in the attic. I have dreamt of returning to these places since visiting them as a child, but I quietly listen to Maxime as I wait for the moment to resume our conversation.

Eventually, he parks just off the road in the village of Tréhorenteuc, and I follow him. It is early, and quiet, and I'm grateful for it. The many signs seem to indicate that this is quite the tourist motorway. We walk for a short while on a tarmac track between golden fields to the edge of Brocéliande.

"Morgane put a spell on this place," I tell Maxime, knowing full well that he, like me, grew up on these stories. That these woods were the playground of his youth. But his silence and the looming presence of the forest, like an entity we're about to beg for forgiveness, is unnerving, and I need to hear my own voice, the litany of the familiar legends. "She was a loner, socially awkward at the court—I guess they knew her magic had the potential to hurt, that she was conflicted, dangerous. Yet she met someone, literally a knight in shining armor, and they fell in love. When he went off to adventure, he promised to come back, and she waited. Surprise surprise, he forgot about her and, when she used her powers to locate him, which she hadn't before because she trusted him, she found him here, making sweet bucolic love to another woman in the valley. Morgane didn't want anybody else to feel like she did—as if someone had torn her heart out of her chest and stamped on it. She turned the cheating lovers into stones and cast a spell on the place, and made it so that anyone who is unfaithful in action or thought will remain trapped here."

I realize I've stopped at the edge. It's ridiculous—I hesitate, as if I don't know what's real anymore, what is a fable, which world I inhabit.

Maxime has walked in and is now standing over the threshold. "You know it was all party-party in here, though, jousts and banquets, hardly a hardship."

"Until you tried to leave and either the dragon or the giant came for you." I'm still not moving. "I fight with archives and gallery receipts, Maxime; I'm not so sure I'd be good against a club made of a whole freaking pine tree."

I think about my lust for him, the urge to have him, to devour him and his whole universe. *Anyone unfaithful in action or thought.*

"But you've got nothing to worry about, right?" He gives me a knowing smile.

I shake my head and step over the threshold, telling myself that my love for him has been pure for almost thirty years. The stuff of courtly love. Unrequited. Unconsumed, from afar.

The forest is a rich embroidered universe of ferns, with bushes of broom and holly growing under the canopy of ancient beech and oak trees. Every so often, a fluttering magpie or robin crosses our path. A small stream runs through its heart, its stones stained with blood. It's the iron oxide again, I tell myself, but it's easy to imagine wounded lovers seeking rest here, their hearts quietly bleeding.

We stop to take in the sight of the Miroir aux Fées, a calm silver pond, mirror to the alder trees dipping their roots into its water.

"My mother used to tell us that blue dragonflies were fairies," Maxime says.

"Or white butterflies," I add.

And you're the bridge, Camille.

We continue on the narrow path along the stream, which is hardly anything at this time of year, and soon we have to start climbing up the rock face, jagged like dragon scales. We emerge from the dense forest into a landscape of pine trees, yellow gorse, and purple heather, displacing pine needles as we walk. They wouldn't have been there in Constance's time, I remember, knowing they were planted after a great fire destroyed most of this area of the forest in the '90s. Another reminder that her world isn't my world. I'm here and she isn't. She is deep underground in an unmarked mass grave. The world I'm walking through now has since been sculpted by time and fire and erosion.

Finally, we're at the top, overlooking the valley and the forest, dense and deep green at our feet.

"Breathtaking." It's easier to forget my conflicts when the place seeps with so much beauty.

"Yes. It's not bad." Maxime stops next to me, his hands in his pockets. Standing at the edge of the rocky outcrop, I'm even more aware of how unsuitable my shoes are—the soles of my faithful brogues are so smoothed by use, they offer no grip whatsoever.

I turn to him, trying to find a better place to plant my feet. "So, what's the deal?"

He laughs. "What a question. What *deal*, Camille? I deal in many things."

"I gather. So here's what I want to know: why you keep messing me about, *when* and *how* you started making the most beautiful, amazing, incredible sculptures I've ever seen. And most importantly, what your plan is for them. And exactly what part you're expecting me to play. No more lying, Maxime."

I'm too hot and bothered to be looking at him. Next to me, he opens a bottle of water with a great crack as the seal breaks. The thought comes—a quiet alarm—that there's only a very low, innocuous cord separating me from the edge and a plunge into the valley. If I were to fall or, say, be pushed, my body would bounce on the sharp rocks like one of those crash test dummies, pierced and bruised in all the wrong places. I would land in the river below, a corpse joining all the other doomed lovers.

"Let's sit down." I try to keep my voice businesslike.

We drop down next to each other on the rocks. The path we followed to get here is invisible, drowned in thick trees.

Then Maxime says: "I was hoping you'd figure it out."

"You could have told me straight."

"I needed to trust you first. And…if I could fool you, with your gift, I knew I could fool anyone. I worked very, *very* hard to cover my tracks."

"Thanks," I say. "You very nearly did. But not quite."

He nods. "So, to answer your questions. I'm not messing about. I've never been more serious about anything, Camille. Firstly, I want all those fuckers who will be at the ball to fall over themselves to buy one of our sculptures. I want the word to spread, then to go public with the rest of them. I want them to sell for millions, to make the headlines of the art world."

"Why?"

"I told you. I want the world to finally acknowledge Constance's worth. I want justice for her."

"So…it's all a noble endeavor? Nothing to do with the money?" I can't help but let my sarcasm drip.

"All right," he sighs. "You're right. We also desperately need the money."

"Is this what it's all been about then? D'Arvor's leaky roof?"

He looks at me like I've disappointed him. "You make it sound so crass. But yes, in case you haven't noticed, rich people need money too. Especially when they're broke."

"Broke?"

"My father spent it all, and continues to do so. We're in debt, about to lose everything. D'Arvor is a money pit. Whatever we throw at it, it hardly makes a difference. If it all weren't so personal, we should have put it on the market a long time ago."

"What? No—"

"You wanted the truth," he says, and I see in his eyes how vulnerable he has made himself just now.

"Okay. Well, I don't think the sculptures you made, even as brilliant as they are, will make enough money. There are only four, and you know Sorels aren't selling as well as Boisseaus, and—"

"There are only four *for now*. And *Night Swimming* would sell for much more. It is the key to getting the whole business going. You're the first to know that, after that near-miss at Courtenay. I'm so glad that random fluke came to light, by the way, that you were so vocal about it; it enabled me to work out what I had to do."

I stare at his profile, stunned, as he brings the bottle to his lips. "You're—you're making a fake *Night Swimming*?"

He seems shocked at my use of *fake*. "Well, yes. You asked for one, didn't you? They've already got it wrong once, so...there's clearly an appetite for it, and together we can give them something better than they ever bargained for. Something there really can't be any doubt about."

I'm unable to speak for a few seconds, so I turn my eyes to the valley, the sparrow hawks circling and swooping. Reality is shifting, boulders threatening to topple, tree roots losing their grip, and I need time to adjust. Was this the *Night Swimming* I was meant to find all along? Not Constance's, but Maxime's? Will it hold the key to something about *me*, finally? About *my* future, how I should live this life, what place I can find in this world whose gates I have pressed my nose against for so long?

"Can I see it?" I ask finally.

"It's not ready yet. But yes, of course. Moreover, I'll need your input." Then, seeing the doubts on my face, all my internal turmoil, he says: "Camille, nothing has changed. The plan is still the same. You will simply help me make the sculptures perfect, from the inside."

"Jesus, Maxime. No, it's not. We're talking about a whole bloody forgery business. Cheating the world about the work of my most beloved artist."

"*You'll* always know, though. It won't change who she is for you. It's only those—sheep, those cretins, that will come and eat from the palms of our hands. Camille, you and I know the art market doesn't exist for love's sake. It is power, privilege. The art is a commodity like any other. Wouldn't it be amazing if it played in our favor? Plus Constance's reputation would soar. The value of her real pieces would soar with it. She would be in pride of place in all the best museums of the world. Further along the line, we could build her a museum at D'Arvor if you wish. In the orangery, perhaps. A place she deserved a long time ago." He pauses, his hand relaxes, finds my chin, tenderly lifting it so I am forced to look at him. "You and I want the same thing. We are two sides of the same coin. If you were to work with me at the gallery to sell the sculptures we can make, we'd own the art world."

"And what if you—*we're* found out? Forgery is a crime. We could go to prison."

"We won't be found out. Not with your gift. Plus the sculptures are good, aren't they?"

"They're extraordinary," I concede, dizzy.

"*You're* extraordinary, Camille. And I very nearly fooled you."

"You're making *Night Swimming*," I repeat, unable to compute what is happening. I stand up, thinking I should walk away. I'm literally poised at the edge of the cliff, about to fall. Or fly. Then I think of Lila's note. "Was Constance really sectioned at the end of her life? Is it all true?"

He hesitates; then I see him opt for the truth. "Yes. She was sent to an asylum near Rennes."

"I checked all their records," I say. "I conducted such thorough research. She wasn't there."

He looks sad now. "Sadly, she was. We—well, my family at the time—had the power to make it unofficial, let's say."

"You locked her up? Left her there to die?" The thought is so horrible I can't bear it. My heart splinters like Morgane's.

I go to storm away, but my foot slips, and I stumble, losing my balance. In a flash, Maxime's hand catches me, holds me securely on the ground, and I regain my composure. We are standing centimeters away from each other, staring into each other's eyes. His hand keeps hold of my wrist.

"No. Whatever my family did—I'm *not* them, Camille. Didn't you listen? I love her too. Unlike the rest of them, I reel from that injustice."

"But why did they lock her up? What happened?"

"I don't know." He seems genuinely bereft. "I always assumed she was suffering, perhaps a mental health condition that nobody would have known how to treat at the time. Frédéric told you about my grandfather nearly drowning…" I nod. "But I want to repair what they did. I want the same thing you do."

"By making a *Night Swimming* that isn't hers?"

"*Night Swimming* is the key. You said so yourself, in your articles: it was her last letter to the world. Together we can make sure that it makes an impression. That the world remembers her, celebrates her like we both do."

"There must be another way," I say.

He shakes his head. "That's what you've looked for all your life, isn't it? It's only right if you are the one bringing it out into the world. Those bastards I saw at Courtenay, watching and judging your every move. Waiting for you to fall. You deserve to show them you were right. They should fear you, queue to eat from your hand. Camille, you are the key to it all."

Then he pulls me to him and kisses me. The birds quiet, the wind stops, the river stills. His lips burn on mine like a spell that can't be broken.

When I pull away, both of us panting, he says, "Ever since I met you, I knew. There are no limits to what we can do together. We can protect, create, influence, even rip this reality apart. It's together that we're the most powerful."

I take a moment to let his words sink in, turning my head away as I feel I might melt under the intensity of his gaze, the intensity of this moment I didn't even dare to dream up quietly. Maxime offering me, what—to be with him? Live at D'Arvor, as his partner?

"What about Lila?" I ask.

His eyes. "Lila and I have been over for a long time. We broke up officially last night. She broke up with me, to be honest. I was only staying with her out of obligation. I knew she had nowhere else to go; I couldn't do that to her. So now, as you see, I'm all yours. If you'll have me."

Another sparrow hawk soars from the valley, in his claws a wriggling mouse, fighting for her life.

"Are you in, Camille? Can I trust you?"

Suddenly I am the hawk, seeing us from above, in the

Val Sans Retour, two lovers of stone: Maxime, the Arthurian knight kneeling at my feet, and me—I am a different Camille, long dark-red hair floating in the breeze, and my features are hard like the dagger in my boot, my fingers bony and strong and ready to strangle small birds and squirrels. My heart is bleeding into his, and his into mine.

"Yes," I say.

25

THE NIGHT OF the ball, D'Arvor opens its wings like a dragon allowing strangers into its lair. It breathes out gusts of wind as cars line up on its lawn, chauffeurs dropping off guests in black sedans. The night is starting to fall and the clouds grow heavier, soon to be burst open by the towers' spires. From my room I hear music and the rising clamor of a building crowd.

The ball will take place in the older part of the castle, formerly defensive and medieval. The vast downstairs dining room is impossible to heat up and not in regular use by the family today, Maxime said—but the space, with its two-meter-thick walls and original granite floor is perfect for summer balls. I love that this part of the castle was spared mock-medieval nineteenth-century decoration and the walls have been kept bare—it is austere, but grand. Having gotten used to living in the "modern" eighteenth-century part of the castle, it does feel like a different place entirely. A harsh, unforgiving, and awe-inspiring space. I don't think Maxime or any of his family like it very much—I heard him call it "my father's dark wing."

Upstairs, I have both dresses, the black and green one, laid out on my bed. I'm late. I should be welcoming guests, teasing out their interest for the auction. Instead, I'm standing in my underwear, unable to make up my mind.

My mind is a puzzling thing at the moment; I'm going too fast on the conveyor belt of Maxime's plan to be able to catch my thoughts. I miss the handrails I used to find in my head that led me somewhere safe, reliable.

"Would you go through with it?" I ask the room. *This is only a teaser, a rehearsal, Camille. The press conference, once we have* Night Swimming, *will be much bigger. Relax*, Maxime said, as we went over what should happen. The window is open and the murmur of the guests who have spilled into Frédéric's enchanted garden rises along the peculiar breeze announcing a storm. I'm trying to conjure Constance. In this castle, she used to be the only person I felt I truly knew, but now even she escapes me. I stroke the headboard. There are scratches in the wood I never noticed before. A flash of her nails, digging, her screams. They're trying to pull her away. Did this really happen or is it all in my head?

You could leave. That's what the wind says. Unless—I spin around, but nothing. Then I turn again and she's here, lying on my bed—

No. It's the green dress I've laid out. But now my choice has been made, because I imagined I saw Constance in it, and it suited her.

I'm sorry I neglected you, I tell her as I put it on, the silk like scales and fairy skin merging with mine. *We're trying to right the wrongs you've been dealt.*

The laughter is faint in the distance as I tiptoe into the bathroom to give myself a final check-over in the mirror. I struggle to recognize the woman walking toward me—I swear my features are thinner, sharpened. I don't think I've done too bad a job with my makeup, or maybe it's the dress. Lila does have an eye.

I take a breath, supporting myself on the sink. The bathroom's door slams—the wind. Rumbling thunder in the distance, coming from the sea to wipe us all out.

—

When I venture downstairs, it is silent—the guests are in the other part of the castle. In the vestibule, there's a man with thick dark-gray hair combed back, who looks up at me as I descend.

We lock eyes on the stairs—well, until he slides his eyes down the entirety of my body and smiles, showing perfect teeth. He isn't that tall, but his presence fills the room, the way his bow tie hangs undone, his eyes ice blue, one hand in his pocket and the other on his phone. I've seen that posture before, in his son.

"Hello," he says.

"Camille Leray." I introduce myself, approaching him with an extended hand. He comes to life and shakes it, surprisingly animated, radiating warmth. A man of contrasts—the kind who would pull me into a snowstorm only to immediately wrap me up in a blanket.

"*Enchanté*, Ms. Leray. Guests aren't allowed in this part of the castle, but I think I'll choose to forgive you." I note that Dominique Foucault, the elusive father and *maître des lieux*, doesn't think it necessary to introduce himself back.

"That's very kind of you. Except I've been staying here for a while now," I explain.

"Ah, really. And which of my boys are you a *friend* of?"

"Maxime." I don't like the way he said *friend*, as if he meant something demeaning and irrelevant reserved for women.

"I see."

The vestibule is dark and I remember Lila throwing herself into Maxime's arms. I haven't seen her around, nor her car, since Maxime said they broke up. I wonder if it all stemmed from our conversation in the patisserie, if I played a role in this. I would have wanted to say goodbye. I feel Viviane is watching us from the garden.

"I don't think you do. Allow me to explain. I'm a sculpture specialist; Maxime asked me to take a look at the Sorels that recently resurfaced."

"A rather long look, by the sounds of it."

"And to help with the auction tonight."

A sudden draft rattles the stained-glass panels above the entrance.

You should leave.

"Well, it sounds like Maxime, as usual, has underestimated your talents. Leading his little auction sounds beneath you. I think it will go down slightly better with some champagne, don't you?"

He holds his hand out to invite me to follow him. There's something in his manner that mesmerizes, hooks me by the throat. I feel that I want to follow him even if he's going to hurt me.

I'm about to slide my hand into the crook of his elbow when Maxime rushes in.

"Camille. There you are." The way he doesn't acknowledge his father, or even look at him, cools the room by a few degrees.

"Maximilien, you're interrupting." Dominique's amused smirk does not attempt to hide the warning.

"You're needed," Maxime continues, speaking directly to me.

I nod, stepping toward him.

"And what is she needed for? You're going to give her a pot of paint and a brush and send her to touch up the damp moldings? I thought your brother had taken care of that." That's his natural voice when speaking to his son. I shudder because I know it well.

"And that's more than you've ever done for this place."

Outside thunder rumbles, or it could be a rogue helicopter

surveying the coast. I feel like we are under siege, preparing to duck behind the furniture when the delicate stained-glass passage is blown to smithereens.

"Behave yourself, boy."

I wince and so does Maxime, and I'm struck with how much of a boy he does look like right now. As if he is under some kind of spell, reverting him to the seven-year-old who took me by the hand and showed me his fairy in the attic. That boy, was he damaged? Were the bruises on the outside or the inside?

No wonder we formed a pair then. Me, beset by near-misses and emotional neglect, and him, forged by *this*. No wonder Constance's kindness marked us more than hands or teeth ever could.

"I think I'll go in search of that champagne," I say, looking from one to the other, offering a smile as if this atmosphere has any chance in hell of warming up. "If you'll excuse me."

I slip out into the covered walkway that was installed as a link between the ancient and "modern" parts of the castle, but I can't move on. I stop, listening for raised voices behind me. I can't hear any, and it is worse. I know, intimately, within the fibers of my skin and nerves and blood vessels, that silence. Those hushed, violent words that can be worse than slaps. The wall of disdain you slam into repeatedly, blocking your every exit. My heart is drumming, my ears humming with blood. I want to break the glass keeping us apart and pull Maxime out of his father's claws.

Very soon, perhaps after a minute or two, the door opens and Maxime, only Maxime, comes to join me.

"Are you all right?" I rush to him, before realizing that my question was silly—he is holding his chest, breathing fast and shallow. He presses both hands against the stone of the decorative pillars, his head hanging low as he shakes.

"Come sit down," I tell him, gesturing, though he doesn't see, to a stone bench in the passage, unsure as to whether I should touch him, then thinking better of it. What he's projecting hits me like stray shards of glass: distress, aggression, despair. It hurts with every strike, embedding into my cheeks, under my eyes, in the soft parts of my exposed arms.

"Every fucking time," he mutters. "I should know better. I'm thirty-fucking-five years old and I still can't deal with him."

All the swearing doesn't seem to help, and his breathing is out of control. I crouch down as much as my dress allows so I can be at eye level with him. He brings a shaking hand to the bridge of his nose.

"You don't need to deal with him. All you need to do right now is breathe. Can you do that for me, Max? Breathe with me."

After a while, his eyes open, a flash of green. His breathing isn't perfect, but it's calmer. When he looks up and starts straightening his back until he is standing right over me, I become acutely aware of both of us standing in our finest in the soft multicolored light of the stained glass. I put my hand on his arm to anchor him and he catches it, presses it onto his chest. His heart is still drumming, his hard chest rising and falling still a tad too fast. He holds my hand there for a few minutes while our breathing and hearts sync through the bridge between our bodies.

"Camille, my father is a bad man. He's a gambler, a selfish narcissist. As far as I remember, he always left us to fend for ourselves—and by that I mean for the castle, for our family's reputation, everything. When he was around, he was worse with me. He did things that he said would ensure I'd grow up...*tough* enough. That I wouldn't need anyone. That I'd be able to take on the work that should have been his. I grew up conflicted between how he showed me one could be, and how I thought, from my mother and great-grandmother, that I ought to be, to be good. I thought I had to choose, and I tried to choose to be good." His voice reaches me through water, the light of a lazy late-afternoon flickering on the surface of a pond. "He used to make me sleep in the turret room, far from anybody else. With no heating. He would lock the door at nine p.m. every night. You understand, don't you? What that does to you?"

He doesn't need to tell me about the fabric of their relationship. I don't need the sordid details. I know them by heart, and he knows it. "Yes."

He nods, more like a deep bow. Then he lets my hand go, straightens his collar.

"That's why I need tonight to go well. I need to know that

we control the narrative now. Also, I need you to change your clothes," he says.

I look at him, aghast. One minute he's holding me, the next telling me—what?

He shakes his head, a frustrated, low growl escaping him. "Camille. I really need to see what you can do. You're going to distract them like this. Like—like you're distracting me. It might not work." He waves to the green dress—to me. I flush.

"All right, then." I make to go away, back to where I came from, up the stairs to my room, to sulk there like a teenager.

Leave.

His hand catches me, holds me back. His other hand wipes my hair off my shoulder, starts tracing maddening patterns on my bare skin. "*Way* too distracting," he whispers. I feel like my dress has turned to water, is running off my skin like a shower, goose bumps all over. "Camille, when we're in there...please—"

We're interrupted by the door to the passage opening. Maxime's hand retreats hastily. It's not his father, but Lila, accompanied by Lowen. They stroll into the place thick as thieves, in stitches.

The laughter dies on their faces when they see us.

I don't understand. I thought Lila had gone. Maxime told me he'd have someone pick Lowen up, but I didn't think in a million years that it would be her. I look to them, then to Maxime, but don't register any surprise.

"Sorry we interrupted," Lila says. She's stunning in a

floor-length dark-blue dress cut so high on her neck it looks like her head is detached from her body, floating in shadows. Her hair is tied back in a low bun. All the mischievousness in her deep eyes when she was, for a second, oblivious to our presence fizzes away.

"You're not interrupting anything," Maxime says. "We were waiting for you. You've been ages. Let's go," he says, and she follows him.

Then: "You too, Camille. Like I said, I need you."

He doesn't wait for my answer as they disappear.

It's Lowen and me now, where just before it was me and Maxime. I feel dizzy with what has just passed, lightheaded, and now it is a different landscape, as if Lowen's presence makes the room more solid. I feel a great fatigue and the evening hasn't even started yet. I drop down on the stone bench, gesture to him. "You look..."

"Like a penguin?" he asks.

He very much does not look like a penguin, and I wonder if he too has somehow been at the receiving end of a Lila makeover. His suit is loose enough to bring out his broad shoulders in a kind of classy way. I notice he's refused to go for a tuxedo—he's in deep blue.

"You're wearing a tie," I say dumbly.

"Yeah, I guess penguins don't. That's one difference you spotted. Can you spot the other nine?" He smiles and that makes me smile too. It's impossible to resist.

I grin. "It really suits you."

He seems to relax, comes to sit next to me. "Cam, you look smashing."

It's so nice to feel that he's in my corner, so to speak. That no matter what I wear or what I do, he'll always be telling me I am, like Goldilocks's porridge, just right. But Lowen doesn't know this world. He doesn't understand any of its rules, that there are games you must play to win. He takes everything at face value.

"Thanks."

"This place is unreal." He rakes his hand through his messy hair, looking up and around. I smile because this is literally a corridor. He hasn't seen anything yet.

Lowen's eyes are kind. He knows me well, but I have changed so much in these past few weeks. I hope he can't see into my soul anymore, as he always has. I know he would disapprove of what he would find there. He continues, "It's impressive what money and an unfair political system can achieve."

"Oh, Lowen," I huff, half-irritated, half-amused.

"What? You brought in the enemy, a socialist peasant, to the Beast's castle. Does your Maxime know about your treason?"

"He's not my..." But I stop. Is he? I don't know, and I don't want to lie to him.

"Cam. Seriously, you are being careful, aren't you? With these people. I just can't imagine their intentions are straight-forward. Not when a place like this is at stake."

It's my turn to stare at him. "What else do you know?"

He holds his hands up, giving me a reassuring smile. "Nothing I can't second-guess having spent ten minutes in this craziness and half an hour with that posh twat."

"You know why I can't—why I can't leave it behind."

His hand pats my knee. "I know. It was your mother's dream. It's been your dream too, since you were tiny. And Constance Sorel lived here. But Cam, if you really think about it, that's all in the past. Do you really need it? Or is it holding you back?"

I can't do this now. Not here. "How has your course been going?"

He smiles, defeated, relaxing against the wall, before leaning forward again as if it is burning, and trying to brush off his suit. "It's been hard work. I don't know what I was expecting. Well, maybe having worked in a bakery for five years, I was a bit complacent. They tore all my processes to pieces, but I'm learning. Tell you what—I'm excited about cakes again. And that feels great."

"I'm so pleased to hear that." My heart swells for him now, and I think: *We're connecting, when you're like that, Lowen. When you understand, and I understand, how much creating, learning, pushing yourself matters.*

That's what Maxime has always understood, I think. That's how we're akin, have been since forever. *Camille, you are the key to it all.*

Somewhere, at the party, or perhaps in the kitchen, a glass crashes.

"We should go," I say.

"Should we?" He arches an eyebrow. "Can we not just grab a case of champagne and leg it?"

I laugh. "You didn't come all this way for that."

"I came all this way to see you."

I smile. "I'm glad. But there are petits fours to be enjoyed. Though I bet they're not as good as the ones you can make now, you pastry genius."

He shrugs, but is smiling as well, and I love making him smile. "You're coming?"

I quickly kiss his cheek. He smells delicious today— caramel and something spicier, more grown-up. It flashes before my eyes: I take his hand, we run out, stealing Maxime's Audi in the process, and drive far away, and I never know what I could be. How much power I can have. What my influence really can be and how much I can rewrite of the past if I wish to. And I abandon Constance once and for all, screaming in her straitjacket.

I shake my head. "I need to go change first."

"Why?" He's confused. "You look incredible."

I laugh. "It was nice while it lasted, but this isn't me, Lowen."

"Well, then. I'll see you by the famed petits fours."

"I expect a full-fledged review so I can get straight to the best ones."

"You got it."

26

THE FIRST FEW drops of rain fall like a clatter of bullets on the terrace overlooking the *jardins à la française*, forcing the guests to retreat early into the dining room, where they continue to mingle among the waitstaff desperately trying to set up jugs of water and bread rolls. I count about fifty guests. Perhaps it's ironic, but the fact they're all in their finest makes them look more ordinary. They are middle-aged men with balding heads, shaking each other's hands with enthusiasm, accompanied by women with tanned skin and dyed shoulder-length hair and chunky jewelry.

Lila and Lowen are the only guests who stand out. Him, because of the unruly hair and the hint of a tattoo under his sleeves. And also because of the blue of his suit and the absence of a bow tie. Her, because she is the most beautiful woman in the room.

I'm about to go to them, try to find out from Lila what

is happening between her and Maxime, when I get hailed. I blame the black dress, which might have had me confused with the waitstaff, and turn to point out the error. It takes me a second to recognize Charles-Emmanuel, Duc de Lautrec.

"Sorry, you'll have to ask somebody else to bring you champagne," I say.

"Ms. Leray, is it?"

"Yes. Good evening." I don't know if he expects me to address him in a certain way.

There are no pleasantries. "So what do you make of this?" he asks.

"What, a charity ball? Is this your first time?"

He laughs. What is it with these men and their phosphorescent teeth? "I hear you are selling us a special sculpture tonight."

I nod, not knowing what to say. He continues. "Come on. I'm sure you secretly agree with me that the man is deluded. Selling a poor relative's fancy from his attic."

"Not an art connoisseur, then?" I ask him. "Don't worry. I'll ask my dentist to lend you the lithograph of *Nympheas* hanging in his waiting room, if you wish. Alternatively I'm sure you can purchase some perfectly nice wine here tonight."

I leave him there. Those men, those ordinary faces, are wolves. They're not better than the washerwomen, cackling together while weaving the shroud of the world through their bony fingers. As I walk, Maxime, who is busy talking to a group of them, gives the black dress an approving nod.

I'm still a ways from Lila and Lowen when I stop. They're snorting in unison, attempting to hide their smirks in their drinks. My heart goes from fondness to intense doubt. I've committed to being here, in the midst of things. Not to look at everything ironically. I've committed to belonging. Could I step out now? Choose to recognize this for what it is—a masquerade, where everybody around me wears the same face, the same outlook? And then there's Marie-Laure and her crimson mouth, smeared lipstick on her pearly chin, Frédéric's wringing hands, and Lowen and Lila, alive. They're outsiders, laughing while we all struggle at the border of the uncanny, the zombielike land of appearances.

For a second, I don't know which way I'm going to tip.

Then I remember Maxime's father, my mother, and my hand pressed to Maxime's heart. The force of both our beats, drumming through everyone's contempt. He's right—together, we can dominate this world. Tell them what to believe, force their respect, rewrite history—ours, and Constance's. I throw Lowen and Lila an apologetic glance, but they don't notice me. So I change course and join Maxime again.

———

After dinner, when the stage is set and the last empty dessert plates have been cleared, I stand on a makeshift stage in front of a bored but polite audience. All prizes have been sold, bar one; most guests have lost interest and are playing with their phones or engrossed in conversation.

"I don't know if this is right," I whisper to Maxime, as I know we've lost their attention. I catch the Duke's sarcastic grin; Lowen gives me a thumbs-up; Lila is nowhere to be seen.

"Camille," Maxime whispers back, "we have to know if it can work." He steps onto the stage, gives them a short brief about Constance, which does elicit some interest, but not much. It's true this sculpture doesn't look like much, especially from a distance. It's *Uther and Igraine*, my least favorite. It pictures the moment Uther deceives Igraine, making her believe he is her husband, whose appearance Merlin gave him. Together, they conceive Arthur. Maxime did an exquisite job of showing Igraine's trust, abandon, and lust for him, and hinting at Uther's duplicity by giving him two different profiles: one turned to her, and the other his true face, hidden from her. It's unsettling.

I can see, on the side, a door ajar at the lobby of one of the medieval towers. There are cracks in the walls, evidence of water damage, as if the tower has been weeping. I wonder if this is where Maxime's father made him sleep, if part of his soul is caught there, just like mine in my family's tiny bathroom.

I think again about our parents, the nastiness they refused to acknowledge in themselves. I think about all the broken, deceived, and abused children walking the earth as adults

bearing the chains that were made for them. I think about
Constance, screaming in her cell. Was she the abuser or the
abused?

Maxime's words echo in my brain: *I thought I had to choose,
and I tried to choose to be good.*

Perhaps good isn't always deserved. Maxime is waiting;
his eyes are still soft from earlier, looking at me expectantly.

I give him a brief nod. He moves on to explaining that
we are offering a rare chance to step into the sculpture itself.
"We hope, this way, if you are brave enough, you might truly
appreciate its value." There are looks of confusion, some
snigger at the exaggeration of his metaphor. Then all turn
into gasps and expletives when I step forward and the pond
creeps in, red at our feet.

I'm alone in the water at first, but I focus on Maxime's
presence across the room and the confidence of our practice,
of his convictions to open the path. *Come with me. Don't be
afraid.* It takes a while for the sound to start of someone else
wading through water, but then, one by one, they join me.
Maxime was right; I feel all eyes on me, like wolves in the
forest. Turns out it's not so different bringing in a crowd once
I've opened the passage. At my command, they're swimming
down after me, through the wine-like darkness to Avalon
below.

Perhaps I am Viviane, drawing knots of air around their
ankles and their minds.

They emerge from the pond after me, in stunned silence,

shortly followed by frantic whispers. Now I am a tour guide; I know my role is to *make* this world attractive, present them with a story they'll want to keep going back to, while helping the artist to hide from them. I draw them away from the river that runs red through the Val Sans Retour, where Maxime used to sit as a child, dreaming of Merlin and Merlin's mother and the devil that was his father. I conjure my love for Maxime, how his story touched my heart, to imbue the landscape he drew, give it glitter and relief. I lead the group to a clearing where Uther and Igraine are performing their dance of treachery and seduction.

You're always away, always far.

And yet I keep returning to you.

Don't think I'm going to make this easy.

And yet you're mine.

All those powerful, enthralled guests watch this as if it is the best play they've ever seen. The loop goes on and on, Uther pulling down Igraine's gown, revealing her pearly shoulder. He kisses it. She is both resisting and relenting. I find it uncomfortable to watch them watch it, to know how they lust for her, in a way art has never before reached them. I know some of it comes from Maxime, and some from me: glancing at him, a bit removed from the group, his hair glowing in the supernatural light, his eyes briefly catching mine, I paint the sky peach and gold. It is a scene of perfection, poised between danger and yearning, and I know its addictive properties are working.

They're so enraptured, they don't see the hooded figure bent over the river, making small figurines out of its bank's clay. Shaping expressive, pleading small human shapes, their hands stretched out in supplication.

Just waiting for you to want me, to think I'm enough.

"Do you also feel strange?" The guests are starting to ask each other. Some are pressing their foreheads as if to stifle a headache, or deal with the wrong air pressure. What would happen if we stayed here too long? When I turn, Maxime has appeared at my side.

"You've done it," he says.

"I think we need to go back."

"Wait, Camille. Please come with me." I protest, but he grabs my hand. He walks us straight to his father, who is by himself, looking at the hooded figure, smirking.

"So?" Maxime addresses him. It pains me to see, through the layers of detachment and control he's built over the years, that little boy craving praise.

"So what?"

"Are you impressed? Not bad for an evening's entertainment."

Dominique doesn't answer. He doesn't even look at him.

"Can't you see what this will do for our legacy? The potential this has? They all want it," Maxime continues, but when his father's mouth opens, it is for a scornful rictus.

"This is all show. No substance. You've been wasting your time, boy. But you said it yourself. It's mere entertainment."

I see it hit Maxime in the chest like a bullet. His face falls.

"Shit." Maxime turns to me. "I can't believe I'm still playing his games."

"Let's go back." I put my hand on his arm. "Maxime, leave him be. You don't need him."

"No. You're right. You go and leave me here with him."

But I have to watch everyone. Like a schoolteacher, I will have to be the last one to leave, or they won't be able to.

Maxime's green eyes light up. I'm aware of the others looking for me now, gravitating toward me, expecting the tour to end soon. "My husband is not feeling well," someone says. Some get hold of my sleeve and pull. "Please take us back."

I stroke the side of Maxime's face, trying to make him look at me. He seems possessed, and I'm afraid of what is going to happen.

"I don't think that's a good idea," I tell him.

A cackle of laughter next to us makes us startle. Dominique, pointing to me. "So she's something more than the help, then? Another one of your women who wear the trousers?"

My fists tighten. I remember the way I half buried Morgane when she went for Maxime. I could open the ground, entomb Dominique here forever. I feel the power tingle in my fingers.

"Camille. Just. Go." Maxime's voice does it; I hold back, but the earth still moves, enough to trap Dominique ankle-deep in mud.

"He's all yours," I tell Maxime as I turn away.

I round the others up like children, walk them through the maze of beech trees to the pond. Blackbirds and magpies can be heard, never seen, in Avalon. It is devoid of what makes our world ours, but I thrill to think I can ply the environment to my will. I open the path. It starts from the surface of crimson water and delves deep toward the dimmed electric lights of reality, of D'Arvor's dining room.

"You need to swim back. Just straight down, to the light of the surface." And one after the other, they leave. I go last and, when I emerge, I close the path. I shut it, like you shut a moving airplane's door, struggling against the force of the wind that should be greater than you. But it is not greater than me.

It is eerily quiet in the room. The tables and chairs look vain and ridiculous. I'm used to this sensation of being back to a disappointing, less sparkling world. I look at the crowd of disheveled people at my feet, their eyes shiny with exhilaration. My heart beats in my chest like a fist that is trying to break out.

Anytime now, when the shock has passed, they're all going to run out, or call for me to be sectioned, for witches to be hunted. But I need to save this, for Maxime. I need to ensure this goes well so I can go back to get him.

Words come out of me, slow and steady. "There was a time when all creatures lived in harmony. There was a time when we believed in the magic within. There was no separation between the world of fairies and the world of men. Then we stopped believing, and we started building walls…"

I don't try to sell the sculpture. Instead I tell them the

story of Merlin, the biblical-inspired conflict of good vs. evil. Then, the story of Uther, of someone who demanded Merlin's help and got exactly what he wanted. Nobody tries to interrupt. No phones come out.

When I finish, the bids for the sculpture start tumbling in. Tens of thousands, turning into hundreds. I lead it all, eventually having to break up a fight erupting between two couples over who won the auction. Meanwhile, half of my soul is still in that world, counting the minutes that Maxime is spending there. His body is in the room, next to his father's, on their chairs, their heads hanging low. To someone who doesn't know, they appear to be resting. Marie-Laure is trying to shake them, her mouth opening and closing in horror, ignored by everyone.

I know that time doesn't flow the same in Avalon. I need to go back for him.

I nod to Frédéric to deal with the check and tell everyone that it is time to go and dance the night away. They get up from their seats with some kind of appetite for life they certainly did not exude before. I watch them go, wondering how far I could take this. How much suffering we could deal them in Avalon if they refuse to cooperate. I stand watching the room empty quickly, as if a tap has been opened, my hands poised on the sculpture, swearing I can feel Igraine's heartbeat.

"Camille, that was—I'm not sure—that was wild." Lowen comes to stand next to me.

"Not now," I say. I know I sound hard, hurried.

"We need to talk about it."

"Not now, I said." His smile drops. I mellow. "I have to go back in. I'll find you in a bit," I promise, shutting the doors, seeing Lila's dark eyes flash with anxiety behind him. *You knew he made the forgeries*, I think, *and you never told me.* Betrayal for betrayal.

I go to Maxime's body.

"You silly girl—what have you done?" Marie-Laure hisses at me. She wasn't in Avalon; she must have been told to stay away, but Frédéric was. He looks at me with a fear I have never seen on someone's face, and I think, *You will never try to intimidate me ever again.*

"Take her away," I command him, and he nods.

———

I find Maxime where I left him. I can't see his father. My God, what has he done? He takes his time before turning to face me, and I'm scared that he's lost his face, his mind.

But when he does, he smiles, a relaxed smile I've never seen on him.

"You're back."

"Where's your father?"

He nods to the river where Dominique is crouching. He glances over at us, and I think he is afraid.

"What have you done to him?" I ask.

"Let's say we had words." Then, seeing my face: "You can take him back now if you want."

"What about you?"

"I'll wait for you here."

I don't try to argue. I nod to Dominique, who scrambles to follow me like a puppy. I open the path for him, watch at the edge as he returns to his body, Marie-Laure's sobs filling the space between.

Everything tingles because of the way Maxime said, *I'll wait for you*. Because of the way he smiled, like he was free for the first time in his life, and it was thanks to me.

"You did it, Camille. Do you realize how fucking powerful you are?"

When I reach him again, he is different. A magnified version of himself. In a linen tunic Arthurian knights might have worn on a day off. He is as I imagined him in all those feverish nights I have had since St. Andrews. I had so much time to build on my memories of him, to fill in all his gaps with Lancelot and Yvain and Percival. The intensity of his glare scares me for an instant.

We're alone in Avalon. Now the silence starts crackling, flecks of dust igniting all around like embers. I glance at Igraine as she abandons herself to Uther.

"Have you found the sword, gotten it out of the stone?" I joke, but he pulls me to him. So tight, so hard, as if he wants to merge us together like the stone lovers we saw in Brocéliande.

"You're a fairy, a creature of below, at the frontier of the two worlds," he says. "Coming and going as you please. Able to trap us all here at your mercy. Able to hurt us, to sublimize us."

"You made this world," I whisper.

"You definitely added the final touches."

Following his eyes down the length of my body, I realize I've walked straight out of the lake, in a white tunic, gorged with water, that is clinging to me.

I'm in charge. Making my wildest imagination real.

"I'm just me, still me," I say.

He ignores me, his eyes like green flames. "Alone, finally."

"We need to get you back... I think it's dangerous to stay too long."

He peels my wet hair from my neck, and his lips are hot, soft against my pond skin. "I feel fine. Extremely fine, in fact."

"Max," I say, swallowing down the moan pressing inside my throat.

"Not just yet. There's something I need to ask you."

More homework? is my first thought. But instead of asking me to do more and more, he says: "Camille, I'm offering you my life. My partnership. Come live in D'Arvor with me. Work with me. Sleep with me. God knows I've wanted you for years."

I'm stunned. "Really?" is all I manage to say.

He sighs with mock exasperation. "I even found what uni you were going to, followed you all the way to Scotland, for goodness' sake. Is that not commitment enough?"

He what? "But—you hardly spoke to me there."

"You walked away from me," he says. "That night, outside the bar. I thought you weren't interested."

"And the V&A?"

"I spent the whole summer in London, haunting the museums, thinking I had a chance of finding you there. Now I finally have you, and I want to give you everything. But... do you want it?" He whispers against my neck, his fingers cupping it like a choker.

In this moment I know everything makes sense. I'm the heroine of a story. Everything I've done has led me here. All the sacrifices were worth it. And I'm going to allow myself, for once, to grab exactly what I want. "Yes."

His eyes, as he pulls away from me, make my knees buckle. "Come." He leads me away from the river. I think for a second the hooded figure is going to turn, watch us go, take off their hood, and I will be faced with two Maximes, but that would be a bit much even for me. They continue building.

I follow my Maxime, thinking that any second I might dissolve like solid sand poured on with water, feeling the strong pull not only of his hand but of his body. The magnetism that has finally been set free. *We're not in the real world. Reality doesn't matter here. It doesn't have a say. Nobody but you, Camille, has a say.*

I will the forest to open on a clearing of moss and ferns. There he stands right in the middle, under the red sky

that the trees are not quite reaching, and kisses me until I
can't stand up on my own. Everything is glowing, his locks,
the threads of his beard, his skin, the setting sun falling in
golden bubbles between the oak branches. And I think the
glow is coming from me, because of how he is making me
feel right now.

I let him lay me down on the ground, then I come to
life. Finally, I am me, grabbing what I want. I *am* a fairy, the
queen of both worlds, coming and going as I please, with
the power to hurt and the power to heal, and the power
to sadden and the power to spread happiness and lust and
joy. I reach for him with all my being, pulling his tunic off,
revealing a muscular golden chest that is still adorned with
droplets. He must have tried to swim back, tried to find the
surface without me, and failed. Here, he is entirely mine. His
skin quivers against my fingers as I trace a spell against his
neck, his pectorals, then lower.

I—want—you.

He is too slow, we must hurry, so I peel off my dress,
pulling him instead on top of me as a blanket, as a source
of warmth. When the length of his naked body aligns with
mine, a noise escapes me that has been nesting in me for
fifteen years.

"Camille, finally."

"Finally," I echo, as the river soars.

27

I WATCH THEM dance in the ballroom, stunning. Well, Maxime is restrained, tired, and I swear his mane is now run through with a few threads of silver. Lila is mad, over-the-top, electric, and fuming, throwing long ropes of hair about as she shakes. People around them are in a similar kind of frenzy, as if needing to dance away a spell. The castle's solid, bare stone walls contain them. *Boom, boom,* the bass goes, echoing cannons of battles past and present.

When Maxime and I got back earlier, we looked at each other, unsure how long we had spent away, until our ears caught the music of the ball. Our watches displayed 1 a.m. Time had gone faster in the real world for sure, but not by much. My head was spinning, my body was sore, high on power, on the verge of imploding. I turned to him.

"Max—"

I wanted reassurance, but he cut me off. "Camille, I just

need a moment alone." He didn't say, as I had hoped, "I'll come and find you," or "We *will* talk." I didn't dare ask more as I could see how dull his eyes looked, the bags of tiredness under them. He had spent too long there; the magic had seeped out of him, and I felt depleted too. As I turned back to look at him before leaving the dining room, he was cradling his head in his hands. I tried to conjure the memory of his body and how we connected in Avalon. What we had had there was still real, wasn't it?

I went to my room and did the same—I sat, trying to anchor to this reality, my heart beating too fast for my breath. Why did I feel that I had done wrong when everything had felt so...*right* there, as right as a luminous, violent bead of light? I tried to tend to the hope that what had happened would mean something in this world too.

When I went back to the ball, in my sober black dress, having combed my hair into submission, Maxime and Lila were the first people I saw. In the middle of the room, dancing like their life depended on it. I've been watching them since, clutching a glass of champagne and hoping the bubbles would take the edge off the dread.

Did I just dream what had happened in Avalon? Maxime offering to share his life with me? I'm losing my sanity—I can't bear this. I shut my eyes tight, knock my head back to gulp the rest of my champagne.

When I open my eyes again, something has happened, like an abrupt freeze-frame change, and Maxime is standing by the bar, talking to Charles the Duke. Lila is nowhere to be seen.

I'm done sitting in the shadows. *You only ever watch. You're a coward.* I must learn to be who I am in Avalon, to act, to grab. I walk up to them.

"Ah, Camille." Maxime's arm immediately wraps around my waist and everything in me relaxes. "Charles was telling me how impressed he's been. By your talent." He pulls me closer, and I remember his body under his clothes, the surprising broadness of his chest, the way I had him exactly as I wanted him, as if I had sculpted him. The music and his proximity still fill me with electric current, the tips of my fingers tingling on the cuff of his shirt.

Charles tries to speak, but I ignore him. "I think we need to talk about what happened," I tell Maxime.

His grip tightens. "Must we? Can we not just enjoy this?"

Is he drunk? There's a looseness to him, the way his pupils are dilated, eating up the green of his irises with black, that makes me shiver. Then he seems to compose himself, and his arm falls away from me. "I have things to deal with first. I promise I'll see you in your room when this madness is over."

"Where's Lila?" I ask him, because I'm worried she's the one he needs to deal with, without quite knowing what it means.

"Stormed off," he says. "She's angry with me."

"Why?"

He smirks. "Apart from the obvious…Lila's always angry."

That's not my experience. Unless her containment is anger. "Perhaps you should just... Why is she still here?"

"Because I can't afford for her to *stay* angry with me. You don't know what she's capable of. Just enjoy your evening and I'll see you later. Carriages were supposed to be at midnight, but I don't think anyone wants the dancing to end. Suddenly, this is the place to be. Thanks to you. My love, what would I do without you?" He smiles, nodding to the room, the medieval tapestries trembling with the music, the crowd of bodies wriggling in satin and mohair. I spot several couples making out in corners, some piled onto priceless medieval chairs that threaten to break. One drunken man in his fifties wolf-howls, *"I'm the king of the world!"* I cringe, but I guess we weren't the only ones taken by some kind of lust for life. I shake my head to dispel the thought. Maxime and I are different. What we have was—*is*—a real, deep connection.

"Another champagne?" Charles asks, but I glare, and he practically runs away from me.

I could follow Maxime, spy on him, but I want to trust him. On the other hand...he is Merlin, conflicted, and I feel he's still hiding things from me. Will I find out something I'd rather ignore? *Damn it, Camille. The truth matters. You need to know.* I slip out of the room, aiming for the corridor he has disappeared into. My head is spinning with drum and bass and thoughts coming so fast I haven't got the capacity to organize and digest them. I turn the corner, and bump right into Lowen.

"Cam, thank fuck you're here."

I laugh. "Hardly the language of a gentleman suited to this grand occasion." But he's looking at me, his face falling. "What?"

"You said you would find me."

Irritation flares up in me. "I just did."

"Were you going to explain to me what the heck happened back there? That insane Technicolor theme park, fun family adventure, with added jeopardy and nefariousness? I mean, was it real, or did *he* slip something in all our drinks?"

I'm tired. So tired. "You've always known I could get into her sculptures," I say. "You were the only one who knew, for the longest time."

"But you never took me with you. That was *wild*."

"I didn't think you cared. Plus I didn't know I could. Until recently."

"Until him." He doesn't even try to hide his contempt.

I'm done with this, I realize. I'm done with Lowen trying to pull me away from where I belong, stamping on my ambitions. "He pushes me, Lowen. He believes in what I can do."

"But you know it's messed up, right? Nothing good can come out of it. That place, Cam, it was…" He stops. "Am I the only one who noticed the… deception? Coercion?"

"Are you quite done?"

"No, I'm not done. Lila told me the money"—he lowers his voice, a bar of worry appearing on his brow—"that he—that *you* made him tonight, isn't going to go to a charity. He has a

scheme to invest it back into the castle. The bloody horses—
it's all a sham. Don't you see it? Those guys are ruthless. He
thinks he owns all of us, including you. I don't know how he's
planning on using this, on using *you*, but it can't be good."

He stops to take a breath, and in this moment, I remember us when he taught me to swim. The waves crashing up
onto us, the salty water getting up my nose, and him, standing strong, immovable, never letting me go, not even to push
his hair out of his eyes. He felt and saw and handled the
world with his hands, his feet planted in the sand, his body
strong in the rockiness of the sea. He was my compass.

"Yes, Lowen. We're going to build a museum. For
Constance. Here. That's where the money is going to go."
But I hesitated, and he saw.

"Are you sure?"

"What do you want?"

"I want you to come back to England with me. I'm begging you to leave this place and find a normal, good life to
live. Something that makes you happy. Please come back to
me, Cam."

"A normal, nice life, like the one you have?"

"You know I love you," he says. It sounds like a warning,
not like a declaration. Nothing like what he said that night
in my flat a million years ago, when my life was walled up
in all directions. This is something you tell a sibling who is
about to overstep the mark.

"You don't think I'm up to this? You worry that I'm

something special, that I might—I might be extraordinary,"
I say. "Would you know how to handle it? To handle *me*?"

"I know you *are* extraordinary. I've always known it. But
extraordinary doesn't have to be mean. It doesn't have to be
exploitative. I don't like his influence on you."

"If you think I can be led that easily, it's me you don't
trust. The truth is you think very little of me. You always
have. All my life you've told me I was working too hard;
you've always watched me and judged me like the bloody
guardian of What Is Good for Camille. But all you wanted
was to make me into some kind of perfect companion for
you. News flash—that's not enough for me. I can, and want,
to be more." Tears are running down my face now. I hastily
swipe them off my cheeks.

When I look up, I see his dejection. And I see Lila too,
standing next to him.

"I need to get out of here," she says, to Lowen. Her cheeks
match mine in wetness, and she, like me, is working hard to
contain herself, bottle up whatever has passed. We stare at
each other like two sides of the mirror, sirens in dark dresses,
storms in our eyes and hearts. I wonder if he told her about
us. If he kicked her out. I wonder if this is the time, this
precise point, when our lives tip over. When we all make our
choices. In the real world this time.

Lowen nods, and I notice how small Lila's luggage is.
Some kind of sagging gym bag that she's dropped at her
feet. Are these really all her possessions?

Lowen turns to me. "Last chance, Cam. Are you coming with us?"

I see Maxime in the clearing. I hear his heart synchronizing with mine. *There are no limits to what we can do. It's together that we're the most powerful.*

I shake my head, feet firmly planted here, in D'Arvor, and with a last glance over their shoulders, they go.

28

THE NEXT DAY, and the next day, and the next, I wait for the change to catch up with me. I'm going to wake up a new person, fling open the window to survey the vast, perfect expanse of my life with a new kind of purpose and internal peace. Maxime will take my hand; together, dressed in yellow waterproofs, we'll amble through the grounds in the drizzle, arguing gently over what place would be best to build Constance's museum. The orangery? The old barn? Or perhaps nearer the lake, so visitors don't cross the threshold between public and private, and leave us forever, him the king and me the queen, to reign in peace over our estate.

But Maxime seldom appears, apart from giving instructions. "Back to work," he tells me at breakfast the day after the ball. He looks like he hasn't slept, yet he exudes freshness, athletic purpose, his locks wet, a white towel around his neck. Has he gone back to Avalon? Has he swum through without me? Then I remember that this is how I saw him the first day: back from his morning swim in the lake, a god of mist. I yearn for him to stop bristling about work and really talk to me. I yearn for the knight with emerald eyes who wrapped me in his attention.

But he tells me, as if we've agreed on this, that we must prepare for the press conference, during which the sculptures will be unveiled publicly. That I must continue to practice, polish the world he created and make sure everything in there is as attractive and convincing as possible. That I must work on the press kit, package Constance's story around the sculptures to make it scrutiny-proof, dazzlingly convincing.

"Will that include *Night Swimming*?" I ask him.

He nods. He's on his phone, distracted. I wish I could catch his attention. I wish he came to meet me in my room, after the ball, like he promised. But he's stressed, and perhaps I need to accept that I can't only have the parts of him that I crave.

Someone is crying. I stiffen, strain to hear if it's real, Marie-Laure at the stove, pressing her hands on her mouth, but the cries creep up the edge of my consciousness, vanishing as soon as I try to catch them. It's raining now, big drops slapping against the single-glazed windows. There's a patch of mildew on the wall, just behind the curtain. How did I never notice it before? Maybe I should ask Frédéric to paint over it.

"Will you show me?" I ask. Breakfast feels quiet. Marie-Laure doesn't lay the table anymore like she did at the beginning of my stay. Perhaps the emptiness is Lila's absence, I realize. Perhaps she was the only one, in her quiet watchfulness, who really saw me.

"Show you what?"

"*Night Swimming*. Your workshop. Where you've been making the sculptures. I want to see them and I want to watch you work. You said you would need my input."

Maybe it'll feel real then. It might help me anchor myself a bit more firmly in this reality that right now is made of sliding tectonic plates and gaping holes.

The cries, again…a baby? Here? But it can't be.

Maxime doesn't look up from his phone. "Sorry, Camille. I need my creative space to remain personal and private. Please understand that. I'll show you *Night Swimming* when it's ready."

When he leaves, I step out of the French doors in the yellow salon. Even the lemon walls look dirty in the grayness of today. I stand in the rain, as if it can change the nature of me forever. *I could leave*, but maybe Maxime will have time for me tomorrow. I take a deep breath, and go back in.

———

One evening, when Maxime misses another dinner, I'm surprised to find Dominique in his seat. It's the first time he's attended a family meal since I arrived. The atmosphere is heavier, and I would love to know for sure that it is entirely due to his presence, but Frédéric's eyes keep darting my way then off again. He hasn't said a word to me since the ball.

Dominique is a loud diner. The room fills with his chewing and the scraping of his knife on his plate, the long gulps he takes of his wine. He sighs; he coughs. The noisier he gets, the quieter and smaller Marie-Laure and Frédéric become. Yet he seems in a good mood. I'm conflicted, hating him with every fiber of me, but also relieved to see that, after I trapped him with Maxime in Avalon, he seems fine.

"I'm rather impressed by your *skills*, Ms. Leray," he says.

"Thank you."

His eyes hurt, like putting your hand on a block of ice. They stick as well, following my every movement.

"So you'll be staying awhile? We must make time to talk."

I hesitate, and Frédéric jumps in. "So you and Max are together now?" His tone certainly doesn't scream approval.

I look to Marie-Laure for some support, remembering how warm and motherly she used to be to me. She adores Maxime; surely she'll approve of his choices? Is this what I have become in this sphere now—Maxime's *choice*? His gamble? I remember the way she used to be toward Lila and I feel sick. I hate that I ever felt jealousy toward Lila, or wanted to take her place. That I might, in my mind, have sided with Marie-Laure against her.

Dominique pushes his glass toward me, and it takes me a few seconds to realize he expects me to top it up. Marie-Laure isn't looking at me; she's fussing with a small stain on the white tablecloth, scratching it with the nail of her index finger with no success. The stain must have been washed in.

Silently, I fill Dominique's glass. Now that Maxime wants me here, that I might be a partner to him, romantic and beyond, that I have a legitimate reason to be at this table, why is everything feeling so uncomfortable?

"I guess so," I tell Frédéric, trying not to sound apologetic.

"Then I can sort you out with some pills too," he says, dripping with sardonic bitterness. "Sleeping pills? Sertraline?"

What? My mouth hangs open, trying to find an appropriate response, but then, the cries. The baby is back for a couple of wails, then silence. I've been dismissing him all along, but could he be real? I don't know anymore. It sounded like it was coming from the attic.

"This is random, but there isn't, by any chance…a baby in the house? Do you have any visitors?" I ask, trying to sound lighthearted.

They all stare at me. They don't even need to answer. I shudder, the wine spills.

"I'm so sorry." I jump to my feet, trying to wipe off the mess, but the cloth is stained, and it is much worse than whatever Marie-Laure was worrying at earlier. Five perfect dark-red dots, linking Dominique's glass to my fingers. I blink, seeing the glass broken, shards embedded in my wrist. Blink again, the glass is intact, full to the brim with blood— *wine*. They're still staring at me, and I don't want to wait for the first one to scream, for their faces to start melting and their appearances to distort; I don't want to find out that none of them are the people I've met before but are instead some malevolent beings, demons, or fairies—the kind who slit people's throats.

Am I still in Avalon, a kind of messed-up version? Did I never make it back since the ball—has it all been a simulacrum of horror, a sliding version of reality, like clay becoming too wet?

My napkin falls on the floor as I jump to my feet. I don't even wait for them to show any concern as I run out of the room, my feet tripping on the edge of the Persian rug.

I need to confront this, finally. I need that baby out of my head. I run up to the attic in one panting stride, struggling to breathe and to retrieve my phone from my pocket. The door to my office is closed. I try it; locked. Is Maxime controlling my access to his sculptures now? Or is he worried I'll take a hammer to them? All my certitudes are slipping through my fingers. These sculptures are meant to be very valuable, I tell myself. It's only natural that Maxime would keep them safe. All part of his plan to keep up appearances, until lies become truth.

There's no baby, Camille. You're going mad just like she did.

A long piercing wail brings my focus back to the attic. The door is ajar; I push it open and it clatters against the wall. I pat about for the light switch, but nothing happens. I have to try three times until I manage to turn on the light on my phone.

Then I follow the cries, picking my way through the clut-
tered, stifling room. The mugginess of the day is sitting right
here under the eaves. Sticky cobwebs catch on my forehead; I
bump into a big trunk, an old hatstand lashes at my shoulder
as if alive. Every time I move my hand to brush dust off my
face, the jerking flashlight startles me, creating alien shapes
in the dark, glimpses of long-lost lives attached to the objects
that remain, crying out for me to let them take me.

Until I get to the source of the cries. A hard shape,
coming up to my hips, covered in a dust sheet. They are
so loud now that they can't just be in my head, surely? It's
the first time I've felt that kind of motherly instinct they
talk about, that a baby's cries have been designed to tap
into repeatedly; that button of urgency, infatuation, madness. *Feed me, save me, take me.* My index finger and thumb
worry at the corner of the dust sheet, my eyes closed in the
searing pain of knowing that this baby is distressed, needs
me to pick him up, and...

It's a bed. The most beautiful child bed, hand-carved in
solid oak, adorned with motifs of the forest, small animals
and streams and gorse and, at its head, a woman holding a
baby.

It is empty, but I know immediately that she made it. I
place my hand on it and, with relief, throw myself into the
darkened pond.

The forest is a happy place here. It is teeming with life,
rabbit cubs, fawns, nests visible on the high branches of the

trees. She's walking with the baby on her hip, talking to him, pointing to things of interest.

I feel her pride. I feel her love. How she marveled at him. It's everywhere.

You're the most precious thing I have. The best sculpture he's ever made.

I tap into the fabric of this love, absorb it like it's made of stars and galaxies.

Constance, carrying the boy with the curly golden hair. She coos at him.

My Erwan.

Everything is permeable here, and the whole of this landscape is what she wanted to make for him, her own child, when she lovingly carved the bed. It smells of roasting chestnuts and pureed carrots and fresh soap and joy, and love.

The baby was hers. And Erwan looks exactly like Maxime. I look up, and the lady in red, Anne Foucault, is strolling alongside them. Everything is so clear in this dimension. She leans over the baby, tickling his pudgy hands.

He looks like you, she tells Constance.

Hold him for a moment.

Their friendship radiates. Constance's trust, and the love Anne feels for both of them, the little unit they form, as she holds the baby on her hip, pointing butterflies out to him.

Are you sure you want to go through with it? I know how much he hurt you.

If I can sell Night Swimming, *Anne, the only way is through him. He has the connections. The influence. Then we'll be free. We can leave D'Arvor and set up something of our own, together.*

Except…darkness falls like a veil on this scene. The fear that spreads like ink on tear-strewn paper comes from me, because I know we don't have a record of Constance ever having a child, of the baby reaching adulthood, and Constance Sorel's line stopped with her. She didn't have any family. She died alone, unloved. So what happened to him?

Ms. Leray.

A male voice reaches me faintly, no more than the wind in the oak trees. I could shut it out, but I don't. As the scene starts again and the loop of Constance's most cherished memories plays over, I know I've seen what I could in the wonders of the bed she made, into which she poured all of her love for a baby who was erased by history.

When I return to the attic, I'm crouching on the floor. Frédéric is towering over me.

"What are you doing here?" It's an accusation.

"I heard—I thought…" I try hard to focus, to dispel the remnants of the heartbreaking happiness, clinging to my soul like cobwebs.

"These are our family memories. None of your business."

"The door was open."

"So that made it acceptable, did it? My mother doesn't lock her bedroom, so should I expect to find you rummaging through her underwear at any point?"

"Of course not. I heard a baby."

"The mystery baby?" He rakes his fingers through his hair, reminding me of Lowen, all those men at a loss for what to do with me—infuriated, concerned. It makes me sick.

"The baby was crying; he needed—and I found Constance."

It takes a few seconds until he understands what I mean. He is new to this, after all.

"You were *there*, weren't you? In that messed-up place... It's unnatural; it's so wrong. Did Maxime not—"

"What? Did Maxime not tell me where I'm allowed to go, what I'm allowed to do? Did he not manage to keep me in line?"

"It would be much better for all of us if he did." His hands are fists at his sides. I spy the elegant dark lines of some hunting rifles behind him, propped up against the wall as if they've been used just yesterday. Then I gather myself. Of course he wouldn't shoot me cold in this attic while his parents are downstairs eating brie.

I take a deep breath. "Listen," I say, as conciliatorily as I can sound in this moment. The baby is silent now, and this is just an attic in the early night, full of objects nobody wanted and nobody had the heart to throw out. Wood, screws, moldy papers. "Constance had a baby. I never found a record of him anywhere."

Silence. I need to read his reaction, so in a highly impulsive move, I flash my light right into his face, as if I am a detective in a film noir.

"Bloody hell," he hisses. "Stop."

"You *knew*."

"Of course we're aware. Now move this thing away from my face."

"Enlighten me."

"If I do, will you leave?" I choose to interpret this as *leave the attic* and not *leave our lives forever*. I nod.

He sighs, looking around, then goes to sit on a chair, covered too in a dust sheet. It creaks under him. He gestures to another one opposite, but I shake my head. I glance at the door, mentally planning an exit route around the obstacles in my way.

"That's why Constance came to D'Arvor. She was pregnant with Boisseau's child. She broke up with him and came here to have the baby secretly. Then she decided to stay."

"That's huge," I say. "How long have you known?"

He shrugs. "Max did some digging, in his twenties. He took way too much interest in Constance Sorel. Frankly, I wish he hadn't cared so much."

The clouds. The sadness. I can feel it on the crib. Not when it was made, but there's a layer on it, like a varnish, scratched by nails.

Just like the headboard in my room. I see her cling to it. I feel her bleed from its shards as she screams.

Jesus.

"What happened to him? Constance's baby? Frédéric?" I ask again. "Oh my God, did he die?" I swear I can sense the mark of some maddening loss. I'm in its grip, its claws running through my flesh and into my heart, like an embedded object it is safer to keep in than to pull out.

"Don't worry, that baby who lived a century ago and has nothing to do with you at all was completely fine."

The urgency of my heart and the spikiness of my nerves recede. I follow Frédéric's gaze to a framed picture leaning between the cradle and the wall.

It's a family tree. One of those that families make either to display their strength and status to the world, or to establish prestige they worry escapes them.

"My grandfather took it down when he married a commoner," Frédéric says. "His own father had opposed the marriage and they waited until he died. I guess he didn't want to be reminded that the love of his life was a disappointment."

I follow the lines with my fingers on the dusty glass, brightening up the names as I go. Here they are—*Raymond Foucault 1871–1942, married to Anne 1885–1991.*

"Anne lived a very long life," I say, cogs churning in the background.

"Yes. Max and I were lucky to have known our great-grandmother. She was an incredible lady, outlived her own son and his wife. I swear you wouldn't have known her age; she looked much younger with that fiery dyed-red hair. My main memory of her was her giving us caramels when Maman wasn't looking."

The caramels. Child-Maxime saying: *You won't tell on*

us, Annie? So the kindly, old lady who gave me sweets in the yellow salon…wasn't Maxime's grandmother, but Anne, Constance's friend? She couldn't have been that old, surely? I remember her hand looking every bit as young as a twenty-year-old's, her kindly blue eyes. How thrilling to think I've been in the same room as her, who knew Constance; her beloved muse and friend whom she jokingly called Viviane.

Fairies live a long time. Perhaps eternally.

I shake my head. Absurd. But there's something else…

Erwan, born 1909, Raymond and Anne's son, is where the tree stops.

Erwan.

"He… They adopted him? Constance's son?"

"How do you know?"

"That's his name, right there."

The air thickens. I feel a bead of sweat running down my back, my hair weighing heavy and hot on my neck.

I remember what Anne said, when Maxime and I left the yellow salon: *Just so long as you don't go too far. She might come back, you know. She might come back for you.*

And Marie-Laure said Maxime looked just like his grandfather. That Anne got confused.

"Oh my God," I continue, "they took him from her, didn't they? They took her baby as their own and sent her to an asylum."

As I realize this, the culmination of my life's research, the answer to the mystery of Constance Sorel's disappearance, something dark takes hold. Anger, deep sorrow, like a well I might never climb out of. That's not what I expected to feel when I finally found out the truth of her fate.

The family tree and cradle vanish as Frédéric pulls a dust sheet over them. "She was *insane*. She was a danger to others and to herself. She tried to drown her own son; my grandfather nearly died because of her. What choice did they have? Adopting him was the kind thing to do. Yes, as Maxime found out and he keeps reminding us, we are the descendants of Crazy Connie. For some reason he's still obsessed with that, but we have already suffered enough from our not-so-aristocratic heritage. So please, keep that to yourself and stop enabling his madness. Go pack your bags, and I'll take you to the station first thing tomorrow."

I don't know that child. I don't know that child, I repeat myself like a mantra, to try and keep my countenance. Except I do. I do because I know Constance, and I know how she felt for him. I know how loved he was. I wonder how well Maxime does know her, how wrong he got her work in the end, having left her love for her child out of it. And her affection for Anne. Her dreams of a simple life, narrowed down to love. Two women as a support unit, and a baby.

What Constance told Anne in Avalon echoes Boisseau's famous letter, the one where he mentions *Night Swimming*. She went to him to try and sell it; she wanted to buy a life with Anne and Erwan away from D'Arvor.

So how did Anne end up taking the baby? *That's what fairies do*, the note said that Lila showed me. *They snatch.* Did Anne really turn on her? Or are the Foucaults right: was she really unstable, a danger to those around her? I can see the gaps now, where my old knowledge and certainties have crumbled like big chunks of plaster.

I make for the exit, throw myself down the stairs with such chaos I almost miss a step. I don't stop by my bedroom but make for the front door. I can't stay here, I need air—

Lila is just coming in through the door. With Maxime, and her bag.

I can't even speak. More pieces of the masonry of my mind come crashing to the ground, although it's a relief to see her. I'd like to take her hand and run away from D'Arvor. I want to tell her what I've managed to find out, thanks to the note she stole. I smile and she smiles back and—

"Camille, you're not right." Maxime's voice. He puts his car keys in his pocket, but I'm watching Lila, standing among the rubble.

"You didn't drive?" I ask her. She shakes her head. "Maxime insisted I leave my car in Rennes." I look at her with horror, knowing that she's speaking in code, and what this means to her. Complete and utter lack of freedom.

"I hope you had a nice journey."

Maxime seems unsettled that we're having a casual chat. That's all I can do—my default position—my mouth uttering polite words when I want to scream.

"Very nice, thank you," while her eyes are telling me, *Are you OK?*

"Good. Welcome back," and I respond, *No, I'm not. Are you? No.*

We both catch the giggles and Maxime stares at us before asking Lila, "Can you give us a moment?" Wordlessly, she picks up her bag and climbs the stairs. *Don't abandon me*, I shout after her in my mind.

"Camille. *Camille.*" Maxime shakes me by the shoulders. I'm still laughing.

"I'm sorry," I manage to say, "I don't know what's come over me, stress maybe…"

He is looking at me with concern. "Perhaps I should ask Frédéric if he can give you something." That starts the giggles all over again. "Camille, I can't be fucking dealing with this right now," he hisses finally, and that does it. I'm sober again, as sober as the last soldier standing in a battlefield.

"I'll get some fresh air. Then I'll be right as rain," I promise, as if to apologize for ruining his evening, cramping his style, whatever. He nods, and I go to open the heavy door, when I remember. "Why is Lila here again?"

"It's complicated. Let's not get into this now that you're in such a state," he sighs. I'm starting to get rather fed up with the propensity the Foucaults have for sighing. I can think of better family traits, like a sense of humor. Freckles. Or integrity.

"I don't see what could be that complicated."

"Of course you don't. You've been here five minutes and you think you know everything about our lives."

"All right," I say, "then I'll go upstairs, pack my bag, and take up Frédéric's rather strong offer to take me to the station first thing tomorrow?"

Maxime's jaw tenses. "He said what? The fucker." Then he seems to calm down. "Listen, when I met Lila, she wasn't exactly in a good place. She was homeless, you know that? To be honest, Camille, she needs me. I can't just send her back to the street. It's just temporary, until she can get back on her feet."

Lila's voice, in my head. *He likes saving people.*

"All right," I say. "Of course you can't let her sleep under a bridge tonight." I don't ask if she will have her own room now. For all I know, the castle is crumbling and there are no rooms left, no rules. "Now I think I'll go and take that refreshing tour of the gardens, thank you."

My voice is breezy, I sound like an annoying Jane Austen aunt, and I slip out before Maxime can hold me back.

29

I DON'T KNOW this garden—is it hers or mine? Is this Avalon? The tail end of the setting sun gives all the plants, every bead of glass, an eerie glow. The birds are silent; the wind has fallen. I progress in a universe that is coming apart in and around me.

I'm a child, trapped in liquid plaster. The boy's green eyes dart at me through woods of thorns. Bodies decay, yet sometimes the worst is left behind.

I didn't find *Night Swimming*. I didn't find Constance, only remnants of her abuse. The loneliness, betrayal, the utter abandonment. It's finally *gotten to me*, like they all warned me. Rob, Maxime, Frédéric, even Lowen. They are all watching me choke on Constance's despair and mine.

I trip on a stone, fall knees first into the dirt. It hurts more than I remember when I was a child, perhaps because I was forced to be more careful, more controlled back then. I'm certain Marie-Laure's work in the garden was to lay traps in the grass. I know this whole estate is out to get me, that I can never leave now that I know too much and not enough at the same time.

You're losing your mind, Camille. Just like her. I cry and laugh in raspy sounds that I take to be boars in the forest, torn apart by a party of knights. I don't know what lurks inside or outside of me anymore, what I'm observing and what I'm living. What I'm tapping into or creating. Am I this chaos? Did it all come from me?

Fire. Perhaps it's fever; perhaps it's all those emotions raging in me. My fingers itch and tingle; I rub them, splitting the skin open on my knuckles. It burns stronger.

Night Swimming. The lake. What did Maxime say? The magic water had the ability to cure madness. Yvain was dipped in the fountain and he regained his senses. Perhaps that's what I need. *Sometimes cold water is the best cure.*

The lake is quiet, but the water is quivering even in the absence of wind. In the last remains of light, I watch bubbles rise to the surface. It can't be boiling, can it? Like a big cauldron, ready to cook me. I dip my fingers in. It is pure cold, zipping to my nerves. Soothing, actually. Then the light dies and everything is plunged into darkness, until my eyes get used to the obscurity. It's scary, not knowing the boundaries of earth and water, but needs must. I take my jumper off and drop it in the grass. My trousers are next, but I keep my shirt on. I need some protection from what I could find down below.

Entering the water is akin to the lake grabbing my ankles with freezing hands and pulling. But there's also relief to it as I progress, the silkiness of the mud enveloping my feet. The water fights the fire in my body and mind. I stop and stand still, trying to muster the courage to throw myself wholly into it.

"You're not doing an Ophelia, are you?"

A smile cracks my lips. "You know, Lila, you sure know a lot about art and literature for someone who said they weren't interested."

She snorts. At the ruffle of clothes being pulled off, I turn around. I can just about catch the edges of her. She's wearing her wetsuit, black and long-sleeved. When she told me she swam at night, I imagined loops of gold and delicate knots behind her neck, perhaps Chanel's golden double *C*.

I'm shaking with cold but it's comforting to have her here. It helps me sober up, regain my senses and some bearings. "Are there pikes here?" I ask. I'm still not immersed, not properly, standing on tippy-toes with water up to the middle of my thighs. When I was little, Maman told me that pikes had inward-bent teeth, that if you tried to pull them off, you would only dig them deeper into your flesh.

Just like her. Just like this place.

"I don't know. But I've seen frogs and dragonflies."

"The fairies," I say.

"Maybe. But also, maybe just dragonflies."

"I wanted to be alone," I say, but we both hear the doubt in my voice.

"We're always alone. Both of us. I'm tired of it," she says. "I thought you needed me. So I'm here."

"Okay." I take a deep breath, and I launch myself forward into the dark. For a second I float, and everything is fine, until my body registers the cold. "Fuck!"

She giggles. She set off with much more elegance than I did and is gliding past me.

We swim for a while, in a circle. It's so peaceful. I feel the ripples coming from her, and I reckon she feels the ones coming from me. I really appreciate her presence. Night has settled like a dark feather on top of the trees. The volume of the birdcalls has gone up, nature preparing to take over as we retreat. Or should retreat. But we stay.

It does help: swimming in the darkness, nothing to focus my eyes on, my body wrapped in this cold embrace. Alive.

"I understand why you enjoy doing this," I tell Lila.

"Do you?" I can't see her, but her voice sounds close, as our arms and legs displace water in circles. I imagine us from above, two human frogs not going anywhere, just being. She continues, "Did I tell you I nearly drowned in here once? I didn't want to leave and I waited until I couldn't feel my legs. Then I couldn't get myself to the shore. I thought about letting it happen. But then, at the last possible second… something kicked in—I fought and got myself out. Every time I get in my car, I fool myself into thinking I could drive away and never come back. That's why I was late picking you up at the station the day you arrived. This time, I mean— yesterday, I thought that was finally it."

"Why wasn't it?"

"Because I'm trapped," she says simply.

"How?"

"If I could tell you, I wouldn't be trapped."

"What do you need to be free?"

"I don't know," she says, after a moment. "I just don't see it. Everywhere I look—there's only walls."

"I used to feel like that. When I was younger. Do you not have…anyone you can go to? Any family?"

"I have four brothers. But we haven't been in touch for a long while. My parents—they always waited for me to become the daughter they wanted, not the one they had. It's not a bad thing to have those expectations removed. I miss my younger brother Samir though. He always had my back…"

She trails off and she must mean *until something happened*. Was she really homeless? Unless she means *until Maxime*.

"I think my mother didn't want me at all," I say. I hear Lila stop herself from protesting, and I'm grateful for it. "Then I discovered art and it helped." Did she just scoff? "Swallowed some water?" I ask sarcastically.

"Camille, as you know I've been watching you closely these past weeks. Art doesn't seem to have helped you. More the opposite."

I can't see her face. I don't know how close she is, her voice bouncing on the water like skipping stones. As I swim, a fight rages in me between exhaustion and exhilaration. It strips away some of the complications, some of the over-thinking. I wait until I'm sure I want to say it. "You know the sculptures here are not by Sorel, don't you?"

"Of course."

It infuriates me that she knew. That she was complicit in the whole thing from the start. The pond gets a few degrees colder, but I realize it's because I'm burning hotter. "You made a fool of me. You could have told me. You could have helped."

"Camille, what part of *trapped* makes you think I had any power to do that? I tried to help—with the note. Now that you figured it out..."

"I told Maxime I knew it was him, but he still won't show me his work. I need to see the workshop. I need to figure out how his craft is so bloody brilliant that I nearly thought it was her, that he makes me stronger every time I tap into it... I hate that I can only seem to be capable when he's around."

There's a silence. "You think it's Maxime who gives you access to it?"

"It all started with him," I say. "Then he was the one who helped me figure out my power. That I can start writing my own story. That I might be special."

"Ditto," she says.

"Lila...you know I'll help you," I say. I'm pretty sure my

lips and nails are blue. But I don't want to get out and feel my body weighted by gravity just yet. "If you really want to leave. Anything you need. If you need a place to stay, or—I know a few women in my field who'd understand; they could help you find a job."

Her hand catches my forearm out of nowhere. She was so close, all along. "Wait. Can you see this? Below."

Under us, there's a glow. Cold white crystal, the shape of turrets. As I stare down, it's like looking through panes of thick ice.

"I can see it," I say. We're both like crows surveying the castle, the reverse of D'Arvor, from the sky, squinting into the dark depths of the lake.

At once, my mind opens and I can feel them. Their minds join mine and Lila's. Anne and Constance swam here, and their memories are still here, trapped in the molecules of water, embedded in the moment. They made this vision of the sunken castle with their imagination and wished it into reality, and I let them join us.

Look at the stars—below they tell a different story.

I'll sculpt us a world, Anne. A world upside-down, where we can make our own rules.

Where we can make our own freedom.

Our world beneath the lake.

A castle with our own rules—you, me, and Erwan.

"They swam here. This is the sunken palace they dreamt of," I tell Lila. "Constance and Anne."

A silence. "I feel them too."

I tell her what I found out earlier. How it doesn't feel right that Constance would have tried to hurt her own baby, or that Anne would have taken him.

"Perhaps it was her husband's doing?" Lila muses.

"Raymond? He's nowhere. I haven't seen him, found him in any of her work."

"Sometimes that can be worse. Sometimes it's the person who kept quiet that holds the truth. The one we didn't even pay attention to."

"I think I need to accept her life will always escape me. Maybe I need to let it go," I say. "Let her be."

A pause. "For what it's worth, I think they really were friends. I think they loved each other very much, Anne and Constance. We felt it in her sculptures at the museum— that was real. And I feel it here. This was their place. Their Avalon."

"I agree."

"Maybe we should dive down and go live there. Maybe *that's* our escape," Lila says.

"We shall be ladies of the lake, together, making our own rules." As we whisper to each other, our voices echo theirs, and I don't know if we are still Camille and Lila, or Constance and Anne.

"I would love that."

"Lila… you know I could make this happen. I mean…we could escape to Avalon. We could go back to the museum, pick one of her sculptures. A happy one. Stay there forever. See what happens."

A beat, then the spell breaks for both of us, and I'm relieved when she says: "Tempting, but I think I'm still too committed to this reality. And I think you are too."

Then a cramp takes hold, and I realize my body is getting dangerously numb. "Better go back."

I remember what Lila said. *I nearly drowned in here.* Something we have in common. I wonder if Viviane spoke to her too.

And there's that other soul, who was nearly taken. The wind brings me snippets of him.

I want to swim like you, Mummy. And Auntie Annie.

Erwan! Erwan, oh my God…

I try to catch it, but it is fleeting, like a dragonfly. The moment, the print of that tipping incident, and the sunken castle, have gone. Silently we return to the heaviness of our earth. Hearing Lila's movements, I wonder if she, like me, is struggling to pull on clothes over her wet skin. They keep catching as if my body is now covered in scales.

30

MY STUDY IS unlocked for me every morning. I don't even question it anymore; I wordlessly follow Maxime upstairs, my laptop under my arm, brogues echoing where servants used to hurry down, or drag their aching bones up the steps. Every morning I hope for some kind of tenderness from him, a gesture that would feed into the promises he made me of a life together. But every time I approach him, he reminds me of our great task at hand. Soon we will reveal the sculptures. Soon we'll be in the eye of the art world. He doesn't really promise anything for us after the *soon*.

In the small room, with nothing but the sky visible from the tiny bull's-eye window, Maxime looking over my shoulder, I write the story of the great genius Constance Sorel, mixing truth and make-believe to the point that I might fool myself. I find a home for D'Arvor's sculptures in her life's story, tie them tightly into her tragic fate. I don't know if I'm doing this for Maxime, the public, or for me. Trying to convince myself that it is acceptable. That it all fits. That it *could* have been true, if only she had had more time. That's why I accepted to play a role in this in the first place, isn't it? So that justice could be done to her. I've stopped hearing the baby—the silence is eerie. It doesn't bring peace, merely more space for my doubts.

Still, in the way I know best, I construct the armature of Constance's life, try to rebuild a polished version that will suit everyone. And what a life it is, what a dossier—it is quite magnificent. I should really be proud of myself.

Texts from Lowen appear on my phone at greater and greater intervals. I leave them unread. He exists in a different universe now. I know he can't reach me, and I certainly don't want him to save me. Shouldn't it all be my own choice, through to the bitter end? I hear Maxime's voice: *At the end of the day, it's only stuff. Matter. Plaster with fingerprints on it. If we give people what their hearts desire, we're not responsible for what they will read into it. If it makes them feel inspired, who are we to decide what is right or wrong?*

"I think we're nearly ready. I've called the press conference," Maxime tells me one morning as the key rattles in the lock. "They're coming to hear about the huge discovery of the real *Night Swimming* and more sculptures by Sorel. So we need to make sure they get what they'll be looking for."

"I can't do that until I've seen *Night Swimming*," I tell

him. "You need to show it to me. You told me you'd need my input. We have to make sure that it's good enough."

"It will be, Camille, if you *make* it hers."

"But I'll need to practice."

"You'll see it closer to the time. You have already proven you can do it. I'd rather you spent the next two weeks recovering and preparing. We need everything to be perfect on the day, and, frankly, you've not been yourself."

I ignore that last remark because it's true. I feel like I did just after the fallout at Courtenay, even worse, because here I share my space with the rest of the Foucaults. When I skip breakfast and pass them on the landing, and I know my hair is a mess, and my face a ghost of what it ought to be, they look right through me. Sometimes I close my eyes in this claustrophobic study, and Viviane's palace is the only place I can summon to make me feel better. I can't imagine a world outside this castle, and the pond is the only escape from its stifling walls.

You can't leave.

"What's your plan for the press conference?" I ask as I sit down mechanically, flipping open my laptop like I do every morning.

He sighs. "We will show them the sculptures; I'll do the 'rediscovered in the attic' spiel; you'll authenticate them, sell their importance for female art, Constance's genius, her aptitude to tap into the supernatural, her feminine mystique, et cetera"—I wince—"then you'll take them in. Give them a magical mystery tour that will knock their socks off. Show them that all along *Night Swimming* was the key to unlocking another dimension of the human experience."

I flinch at the sudden contact of his arms around my shoulders. *Like a straitjacket.* "What happens after that?" I ask as I force myself to relax against him, inhaling the heady pine-tree scent of his skin.

"They'll be amazed by it, by *you*, as amazed as I am. Then as they spread the word, we prepare for the sale."

"What if they don't like it?"

"You just need to make sure they do. Just do your—take them there, dazzle them, just like you did last time. They ate it up. And then, when they're back, we hit them with *Night Swimming*." He pauses. "I suppose it would be a shame if, say...we left some of them behind. Only if they cause us any trouble."

Sometime soon, he'll realize how far this is going and will snap out of it. But the casualness with which he suggests we could hurt others reminds me of his father's look when I returned to them in Avalon. What if I told him I won't go through with it?

I'm scared, I realize. Fear has been the undercurrent of everything I've been doing since the ball. Perhaps even before. I'm scared of how far Maxime will make me go. I'm scared of disappointing him if I refuse to play along. I'm also worried about what will happen to me if I go in and pour that amount of energy into masking things, tweaking the story, influencing all those people who have been trained to get at the truth. I remember Courtenay, the state I was in, the close calls we've had when Maxime trained me too hard. I'm still suffering from what I did at the ball, feeling like I'm losing my mind and can't find a grip on reality or make-believe.

But I'm still angrier about Constance's fate. Maxime is the only one who the world will listen to, who has firsthand authority on what happened to her. Constance deserves to be revered. She deserves to be known, no matter how. This will bring people to her sculptures, toss them back into the spotlight she's always deserved. Everyone will believe it, and everything will be fine. Maxime doesn't really mean what he said. And I'm still the one in control, aren't I? I can make sure nobody gets hurt in there.

"Maxime, how much of this has to do with the fact that you're Constance's direct descendant?" I ask.

His eyebrow cocks. "Everything."

"So this is all about prestige? Family reputation?"

"It's to do with justice. We're descended from a genius, the best sculptor of the late nineteenth century. If that was your history, would you not claim it?"

Of course I would. I would die for the world to know who I am, where I came from, if I came from her. And now I'm starting to wonder how much my obsession with Maxime was a way to bring myself closer to her.

I know he can feel my heart thump against his skin. I

peel his arms off me and swivel so I can look at him. Is he a knight, of the modern kind? His eyes shine, ready for battle. He says he's fighting for justice, taking down enemies blocking his way. He says we have those enemies in common, that we're both fighting the same faceless trolls. His jaw is set strong under his stubble, his hand clenching his phone like the pommel of a sword.

—

Every morning at about ten, there's a knock on the office door. When I open it, I find a plate of snacks left on an old chair in the corridor. I know it's Lila's sweet gestures of half éclairs and blackberries, but she is never seen and never comes in during the day. We only talk at night, as if we can't be overheard or our friendship can't be spied on under cloak of darkness. Nobody ever told us that we couldn't be friends, but we know Maxime would disapprove.

In secret, we meet at the lake, every night at ten, and I tell her about the sculptures. It's become a friendship language of sorts—she fuels me with sugar during the day; I fuel her with stories at night. We talk about Constance; I trace her life sculpture by sculpture, reminding myself of what is true, and where I connected with her real self. Then we both talk about our families, what we were like as children, our dreams to become a dancer (her) or a professor (me)—always the past, never the present, nor the future. We swim until we become numb, but we don't see the underwater castle again.

When we share, our pasts merge into other people's pasts. We talk about our parents, how her father emigrated to France after the Algerian independence with his best mates and met a young student in Paris. I tell her about my mother and all the things I inherited from her that I realize are still sticking to me like some kind of pollution. She tells me our parents have this in common (for her, her father—forever chasing the life he thought he would find in France, dissatisfied), about her closest brother who made her feel safe and loved, and I tell her about Constance. How her sculptures gave me shelter, taught me love and the hope for bigger, better things. The reassurance of being special when I was constantly told I wasn't good enough.

"I thought the only way to show everyone I deserved to be here, in this world, was to find *Night Swimming*."

"That's why it's been so important to you."

"Yes. But honestly, Lila, I don't know if it's out there anymore. I think she might well have destroyed it in the end. I don't even know if it still matters. Soon the world will be given a *Night Swimming* by Constance Sorel—and only very few people will know it's a fake."

"Do you really think everyone will buy it?" Her voice, tentative and quiet, travels across the ripples of the pond.

"The sculptures are incredible. They're so—they're so *good*. I don't think anyone will know they're not hers. Heck, they're even better than some of hers I've seen."

And as soon as Maxime's *Night Swimming* makes an appearance in the world, and we sell it as such, that will be it. The provenance is too good—the quality, the style, the strong link to this place and to Constance—it will be undeniable. I think everyone will be fooled, and the story will be rewritten in a way that suits him.

And that suits me. I will be fully complicit in this. The lies spread will be wholly mine. I will be rewriting the history of art, the Foucaults' lives, and mine.

"Do you think he would have a chance as an independent artist?" I hear pride in Lila's voice, mixed with sorrow. She cares for him still. Cares despite all the complications. Another thing we have in common.

"I really think so. I understand he was turned away from that career by his father, but he really is hugely talented. And God, Lila, the way he got under Constance's skin... understood her so intimately that his Avalon was so close to hers...I would love to see what he could do that would be completely his. If he stopped hiding behind her, I think the world would be all the richer for it."

There's a long silence.

"Could you help him find his way?"

"I guess I could try. Maybe, yes." I hadn't really thought about that. How I could help emerging artists reach wider audiences, be seen and understood. For as long as I remember, I've been set on one path and one path only, never thinking of branching out. I feel a flutter of something, like a tiny door that has opened, letting in some breeze. Courtenay might well want me back after this, but even if I could overlook my own lack of integrity as an expert, I'm not sure I want to be part of that world again. I remember the ball, the rich and powerful ambling in Avalon, Igraine undressed by their eyes, as their entertainment. Do I really want to keep feeding them? Maybe my *meaningful* is smaller and more authentic, more direct and under my control. Helping struggling artists to be discovered? It feels so liberating to be shown that there might be something else, a third way for my life to go.

"I don't think Maxime would be up for it," I say, my doubts reflected back by the long cry of an owl somewhere in the forest.

"Maxime? Maybe not."

"What if you *are* good enough, though, in yourself?" Lila asks after a while, as we come out of the water, the cold night air immediately spurring goose bumps all over. Our teeth clatter as we wrap ourselves in towels and psych ourselves up for the return to the castle. "What if your worth isn't in Constance, or in proving anything to anyone?"

"If the world were upside-down, maybe," I say, and we both laugh.

31

THE NEXT DAY, Maxime is sitting at breakfast, his long legs stretched out under the table. I can see his teenage self in this pose and it makes me feel softer toward him, protective. Just like when he was having a panic attack and I was holding him. It all feels like a dream now, rippled with illusion.

We haven't touched in days. I haven't seen him interact with Lila or even his own family. I fear Frédéric might be right: he's Yvain, dipping into madness, ambling alone in the woods of his ambitions.

Conversely, my night swimming with Lila is sobering me up, dip by dip.

I survey the breakfast spread that, today, reappeared out of nowhere. The basket of croissants and pains au chocolat, the homemade apple and blackberry jams, opaque in the absence of morning sun. Today is cloudy, a first taste of autumn. I've been living on oversugared black coffee since the ball.

My body has become taut, hungry, dissatisfied. I imagine sweeping everything off the table, glass jars crashing on the parquet, trampling the remains with my bare feet, pressing Maxime's face between my hands. *Will you look at me? I won't be a specimen to you. My life won't be another antique for your attic. Please come back to me as you were.*

Instead, I pat my lips with my napkin. There's nobody else around anymore. Marie-Laure disappears into the garden, frantically trimming bushes until there's nothing left of them, and Frédéric and Lila... I'm not sure. The castle is vast enough to lose someone here for good.

"We're not going to work today?" I ask Maxime.

He doesn't look up from the newspaper. "I told you, you need to rest. Make sure you've got your head screwed on for the press conference. Why don't you eat something?"

I look up, and ghosts have joined us in the room. It isn't Constance and Anne, but Maxime and me, years in the future. He is sitting as he is, and I'm fussing, wearing one of Marie-Laure's peach mohair cardigans, as expensive and soft on me as hers is frayed, with smeared lipstick, the evidence of anxious face-rubbing. He is saying, *I hear you've been having another one of your episodes.* I spill coffee on the table as I try to serve him. His eyes linger on me, irritated, disgusted.

I can't allow this to happen. We're not that; I'm not her—yet. A quieter, more subdued version of my mother, her prison made from different air.

"I have thought about something else," I say.

"Hmm."

"What if we didn't sell the sculptures as Sorels? What if, instead, they were a tribute, by an exciting new contemporary artist. We could hold an exhibition here, really put the spotlight on Constance as well as launching your creative career. We would just need some original pieces as well, some that really show your voice…"

"And what exactly would that achieve?"

"Well, you're incredibly talented, Max. You don't have to lie about your sculptures. Together we can use my gift to make people see how important and meaningful *your* art is. We can still go public about the fact that you're descended from Constance. It would really help sell the story. But that's all the truth. There is no lying, no crime involved in this. Really, I think it's a no-brainer—"

"No."

I look at him over the steam of my coffee, stunned. "Just *no*? Is that all the consideration my brilliant plan is going to receive?"

"I think you overestimate your influence."

"Oh, right." After everything he's said, I'm lost. Am I powerful, am I extraordinary, or not so much? He keeps changing his tune—it's baffling.

He sighs again. I wish he would stop talking to me like I'm an irritating child, and him my tutor. Unfortunately, I'm starting to realize, there is no open, straight-talking version of Maxime Foucault. Everything has to be controlled, packaged, twisted in a way that makes him the only guardian of the truth, the great dragon we all have to bow to and plead with. "I didn't say anything about your power. As to your influence in the world of art—shall I remind you that you, not long ago, completely discredited yourself?"

I try to look hard at him, but I feel like he's stabbed me, even though he is right. "This applies to the press conference too, then," I say. "If you think they won't trust me, won't listen, why am I here?"

"Camille, the press conference is precisely the point. Don't you see? That is the key. If you are the one showing the world the actual *Night Swimming*, that means you were right all along. That the big show you made at Courtenay was you calling for the truth. I made *Night Swimming* for Constance *and* for you, it will save her legacy and your career. I wish you were more grateful and stopped arguing with me constantly."

"I'm not arguing. I just—I've been wrestling with this, Max. I'm not sure I want a career at the expense of the truth. And I'm not sure that's what Constance would have wanted."

"She would have wanted the world to know how much she loved him."

He folds the newspaper slowly, looking for the right creases to do it neatly. The top of the Arts page reads:

BOISSEAU'S SMALL BRONZE OF NARCISSUS SELLS FOR 2.4 MILLION DOLLARS TO A PRIVATE COLLECTION IN BOSTON

Maxime's nails are impeccably clean, his hands soft and moisturized. I think of Constance's hands, red and sore and cut, breaking ice on water jugs, her honest and fearless exploration of her feelings. I think of how being at D'Arvor stopped her speaking in metaphors, how she pursued a more direct approach in all the sculptures in Rennes, of Anne and Erwan, their lives together. How she marveled, in the *Tide*, at the precarious balance she had found. How she was happy, and how Maxime, with his plans, and with my help, will upturn her narrative. Now it will become all about the couples in the attic, the tortured metaphors of Arthurian legends—all about her doomed love story.

It's to do with justice. We're descended from a genius, the best sculptor of the late nineteenth century. If that was your history, would you not claim it?

It's like a veil has lifted in my brain. How could I have been so gullible? So blind?

Boisseau. It's *him* Maxime wants to claim. The most expensive sculptor of the late nineteenth and early twentieth centuries. He is the genius Maxime was talking about, not Constance. The man whose works, when they come on the market, can sell for tens of millions of dollars.

That's the story of her life he wants me to tell—how devastatingly in love she was with him, how he was the inspiration for every single one of her sculptures. Boisseau is the prestige Maxime wants to reclaim, through her. Her work is only valuable to him when they're read in the light of their love story. She's a gateway to establishing himself as the descendant of Boisseau, to harvest his prestige.

If his family can't be descendants of St. Louis, if the dukes can sneer at their commoner grandmother, surely that's the next best thing.

Realization flows over me like scalding-hot coffee spilt on my chest. It burns. But for the first time, it feels like I've hit on a truth with no other truth hidden behind it. This is Maxime's brain in its barest form. Nefarious, narcissistic, self-obsessed. Did he make me fall in love with him to fill my mind with echoes of their love story in ours, to ensure I'd be prepped to sell it in the right way?

And then...surely not. But it does make sense—if the Sorels are a gateway, a means to get all his ducks in a row, surely the Boisseaus are next. *That's* the big forgery he's planning. The one where the money is. As for me...I will be trapped in his crime forever, incapable of coming clean, because of being complicit in the sale of the first batch of forgeries. It will never end. He will own me.

I try to steady myself, flattening my palms on the table, but everything is on fire, the floor lava, the wallpaper melting. I can't tell Maxime what I'm thinking. If I'm right, I might be in danger. Surely not? But I can't be certain of anything. Better not confront him right now.

"This is what you need them to see? In *Night Swimming*? How much she—pined after him, or something?" I croak.

"Are you saying she never loved him? Are *you* rewriting

her life now? Camille, I worry about you. You were the first one to say that *Night Swimming* was the last love letter she wrote. It can't be anyone else but Boisseau, can it?"

But it can. Friendship can be as powerful, safer, and more fulfilling than romantic love. Yet Anne has been erased from Constance's life like everything else—and I've allowed it to happen.

"I don't want in. Not for *that* story." I make to stand up. The tablecloth catches in my hand, making the fine crockery rattle.

"Very well." I look at Maxime, wary of what he is going to say next. "You're free to leave. Just go."

"Really?"

He laughs. I can't believe those are the eyes I found the world in. The mouth I kissed so passionately. The soul I longed for, that I thought I met in Avalon. It's distorted, a cracked mask. "I don't keep prisoners, Camille."

Doesn't he? Why does it feel like it, though? He and D'Arvor, complicit.

"I could tell the world what you did, what the sculptures really are." I need to see him confronted with that possibility, so it becomes real. So that I regain some kind of agency. But I already feel, terribly, that I have lost all power in this.

He looks at me with tender pity. "Listen, I didn't want to show you. But I think you need to know." He grabs his phone from the table, brings up an email, and slides it toward me.

The message is from Rob, dated a couple of weeks back. I scan it quickly.

Dear Mr. Foucault,

I hope this finds you well. It's come to my attention that you are working with Ms. Leray on some sculptures of great interest and value... I thought it my duty to alert you to the fact that she has proven somewhat unreliable lately, refusing the psychological support she clearly needs... We parted ways with her... I would strongly advise that you consider using our services... would be happy to come to France to offer you advice and valuation... reliable, dependable, and highly respected in our field, unlike Ms. Leray at present... Highly unlikely a sale would go through on the sole recommendation and expertise of Ms. Leray or that your priceless works would reach anywhere near what they are worth under her name as the expert... Sincerely yours...

"I'm afraid nobody is going to believe you. They have seen you literally go insane. And they have somebody claiming that you abused them until they broke down." In a shiver, I remember the woman in the Hepburn dress. "As far as experts go, you have completely discredited yourself. Without my help, nobody will ever take you seriously again."

There's a roar, and I wonder if it's the dragon finally waking up from under our feet. An empty fine porcelain cup is flung hard against the wall, smashing against the fireplace. I flinch...then realize I've done this. I study my extended hand, then the shards, sharp like baby teeth, while trying to grasp that the world outside these walls thinks I'm insane. That I'm not to be trusted. I'm unstable, destructive. And it might be right.

What Maxime does next surprises me. He isn't angry; all tension seems to have left his body with the crash of the porcelain. He bundles me up in his arms. I let myself be held, hating my body and soul for being so lost and craving this— craving him.

"*Or* you could stay. And we could go ahead with the plan. You can have the career you've always deserved. You'll be rehabilitated; you'll be the one who has been right all along. A superstar. You know I think you deserve it. I'm the only person who truly knows your potential and I'd like you to let me help you."

I nod numbly, and he kisses my forehead. When we part, I catch Marie-Laure's eyes—she is standing on the threshold, a brush and dustpan in hand, her face a scowl of contempt, and understanding.

Max likes saving people.

But for that, they have to get in trouble first. Lila's voice rings in my head like a wisp of clarity that wakes me up.

I smile at him.

"Are you going to be all right?" he asks. "I'm going to the gallery today, but I could stay, if you need me?"

I shake my head, pulling my cardigan tight around my body. "I'm all right. Thank you. And sorry"—I turn to Marie-Laure who is clearing up—"about that. It just—flew out."

Where was Constance's workshop? I dig deep into my brain to find the knowledge I painstakingly accumulated over years of research, that a few weeks with the Foucaults were enough to make me question. *In the old barns.* Didn't Maxime deny it, in one of our very first conversations here? I mentally review the map of the grounds, highlighting the location at the edge of the estate. If there's evidence that Maxime is planning forgeries of Boisseau, it might be there. I need to know his plans for sure, and what better way than through his sculptures? There, if I find them, he won't be able to hide from me.

A muffled cry, and I see Marie-Laure has cut her finger. A drop of blood falls on the white porcelain. "Frédéric can sort you out with plasters," I tell her.

Extraordinary doesn't have to be mean.

I think we're past that, I silently reply to Lowen as I hop past her.

32

PERHAPS IT WOULD be better to snoop around at
night, but I have no time to waste. I can't believe I've waited
this long—that so many barriers had sprouted in my mind
to keep me away. The morning is gray, a cold edge to the air,
wind bringing in salt from the sea beyond. Dew creeps into
my skin; I am forever permeable to this place, absorbing its
moods, unable to protect myself against it. I'm walking with
purpose away from the castle, to a remote, neglected part of
the grounds. The barns were built when some of the estate
was used as agricultural land after the Revolution.

The cluster of buildings does look derelict, like Maxime
said, apart from one of them. I spot it immediately—walls
intact, roof clearly only a few years old, double-glazed windows. If you weren't looking, though, it would disappear from
view, merge into the clutter of rusty farming implements,
wheelbarrows full of stagnant rainwater and splintered

pallets. The courtyard looks as if it has served as a landfill for a couple of generations but, to me, the mess is immediately intentional. It feels like art, and I think I could read it. Somebody has set up this space as neglected, forgotten, off-putting. But I don't have time to waste; it reeks of secrets within, which is what I'm here for. *Focus, Camille.*

I find the door, secured with a thick padlock, then quickly survey the windows, pressing my face against one of them. Blinds are drawn from the inside. I'm trying the door again, rattling it desperately, when I hear the shuffle of feet in the grass around the corner.

Damn. I quickly squeeze between the wall and a big dumpster, offering me a partial view of the courtyard and the door. Frédéric appears, his hair flopping back high on his head, his forehead glistening.

"Somebody here?" he asks, as if he is unconvinced of his role as a security guard. He gives the courtyard a quick glance around, tries the door, finds it locked, then shrugs. Before he leaves, he picks up a plant pot. What is he doing? Is he looking in my direction? I hold my breath, resisting the urge to move, knowing the gravel and general fragments under my feet might give me away if I do.

Crash. I flinch. He has smashed the pot against the skip, so close to me. Is he trying to coax me out, to make me betray my presence? I wait, hearing him move the shards around with the tip of his boot; then he takes a few steps back and surveys the scene. Satisfied with his input, he finally leaves.

Today is a day for smashing things. For breaking in, and out.

I remember Frédéric mentioning the plays he and Maxime put up as children. I bet he was in charge of the decor, of making Maxime's vision happen. He is still the guy running around with a pot of paint, masking damp patches and cracks. The thought comes, a doubt, suddenly. What exactly is Frédéric's involvement with the forgeries? Why was he so adamant he wanted me gone? He makes things. He is handy. Could he...?

Only one way to find out.

I take out my tape measure. I had hours of practice at this when I was young and Maman would lock me in the bathroom whenever she wanted some peace. I was a peaceful child anyway; I had learned to mold myself to her moods, so I guess it wasn't so much peace as distance she wanted, not having me around as a reminder of God knows what. Or she wanted to take it out on someone, and I was the only one there. I became quite good at finding inventive ways of forcing the door open, resisting her that way. My messed-up teenage rebellion. Until she finally realized there was no point in locking me in.

I'm not thankful for what Maman taught me anymore. I don't feel gratitude, but tenderness: for little Camille's resilience and determination, her ability to teach herself, to fight, which helps sharpen me and steady my hands. It's taken a while, and many conversations with Lila, but I'm finally feeling compassion for myself, for all the mistakes and bad decisions that stemmed from being abused. That compassion strengthens me. Looking around, I find an old rusty pair of garden shears, use them to cut out a thin strip of the measuring tape. Then it's steady, patient work: I insert the strip into the lock, work to depress the catch, and after a few minutes, I'm able to pull open the shackle, and I step in.

It's exactly how I imagined Constance's workshop and, to some extent, I think she's still here. I feel her energy, her memory, and something else, some kind of lingering of her vision, like wisps of magic in the air. Like broken shards of her soul cracking under my feet as I close the door behind me, holding my breath.

But there's also someone else. Someone whose presence is much stronger. Their aura lives in the astonishment of the sculpture at the heart of the space.

Night Swimming.

I know full well it's not Constance's, yet it's everything I wanted to find. I forget where I am, forget the precarious snooping I'm doing, and just stand in front of it, like a mirror.

Because it's me. It is my own face looking back at me, beyond me. I don't think anybody else would notice, but I know—the sculpture tells me, shows me, pleads with me.

And it's her. *We meet at last. See me, at last.*

My heart swells as I start walking around it. I'm stunned by knowing that this will always be a defining moment. A chef d'oeuvre on such a personal level that nothing after it will make the same sense again.

The two women are swimming, their ankles caught in the swirls of waves. One looking up to the stars, the other one down at the spires of a palace emerging from the mud. Both have the same face. The sculpture is so light, so alive with movement, as if a whirlpool is dragging them to the other world, their feet pointing downward. As I move around, I find their hands, reaching out to help propel each other. Their mood changes depending on the angle, at times happy and excited, then melting into anxiety, reluctance.

I study and marvel as I start catching whispers of the truth that this piece has been imbued with. Voices, impressions. The water is building, bulging at reality like a balloon. I brace myself for something strong and pierce it.

The darkness takes me—a coldness, an overbearing presence—and my heart grows louder. My mouth opens to try to breathe, not finding any air.

Not like that.

He needs to be there.

Her love for him. His influence.

Make sure you do as I say.

The dread is in this too, but this time, I expected it. Just like the sculpture at Courtenay. It comes from a different artist, yet it's the same story.

It's always been the same story. The same sublime contradiction—when a piece radiates gentleness, pure friendship, and hope, like a hand reaching out to the world, looking at it straight in the eye to say, *Connection exists; love is worth it,* and at the very same time—this horror? When it screams existential angst, entrapment, coercion, the slow and unstoppable erasure of the self?

That's why this is a masterpiece—a masterpiece with the power to shatter my mind in many contradictory fragments. And this time, despite my lungs burning, tears streaming and mixing with the water, despite knowing myself to be caught at once in the depths of my own angst, and hers, I don't try to resist. I embrace its whirlpool to swim down, down, toward the even darker world of the truth.

It is shattered. This Avalon is built on contradictions. The pond is quiet, peppered with blue dragonflies. Its surface is copper and gold in the last remnants of the setting sun. The two women are swimming. I'm there, floating on my back, looking at the sky. And this time she doesn't try to hide from me.

Look at the stars—below they tell a different story.

A world upside-down, where we can make our own rules.

We could escape to Avalon, Lila—together.

But I know we're not alone. There is a chasm in this world. A great rip in it, and as I turn slowly to the couple arguing, a little ways away, I trip on sharp shards of clay. This is the cemetery of her broken dreams.

Two sets of hands have made this Avalon. One making, one destroying.

He is cold, on edge, not screaming at her, but it is worse.

What are you doing? That's not what we discussed.

A mug of coffee—he didn't even use his own hand— slammed hard against the sculpture's limb, shattering on the floor. The break, her face—*You might as well have broken my own arm. It* was *what we discussed. You said two people swimming, at night. I know that's what she would have made.*

He rakes his hand through his hair. He is shaking with rage. *Because you know her so well now, do you? You've been spending too much time with Camille. He was supposed to be in this. He was supposed to be the key. You did this deliberately. And now there's no time. Fuck, Lila.*

He—can't you see?—the two women, they're both her, thinking of him. He's everything to her. The castle is him, her dream of a world they could be together... I'm sorry. I thought it would work, but I can remake this, of course I can, as you wish.

She's lying to him, heart hammering under her calm demeanor, as pieces of clay fall around them like rain, her intelligent dark eyes darting between her eyelashes. Under that humble small persona, she has learned to develop around him, she is vanishing into a whisper.

Now his arms wrap around her. He asks, *Why didn't you explain earlier? Sorry I broke it. I've been under a lot of pressure, lately. Can you fix this?*

It was supposed to be broken anyway, to fit the story. She smashed her work, remember? You've given it an authentic edge.

He pulls her to him; it is violent, mock-tender, and I see her freeze. I hear what he says, against her neck, as he abandons himself. *You always make me do things I regret. But,*

*Lila...no more swimming. Stay away from Camille. I don't
think your little night excursions have been good for either of you.*

She nods, rigid in his arms, then she looks over his shoulder, right at me. She is pleading with me.

Camille. Help me.

She saved the sculpture from his wrath, repaired it, and this is her message to me. She didn't try to hide from me this time. I can imagine her as she worked, remembering the scene, twisting her memories to pour her message into the clay, just for me. Knowing he could control her time, her output, but not what she would leave in the sculpture for me to find.

The true artist, all this time. She is the extraordinary talent, the hands behind it all. Lila.

When I step out of the water, I'm shaking. I'm shaking with the fear she repressed when he hit the sculpture, the tension when she thought he would turn on her.

I'm overwhelmed with my utter failure to see the truth all this time. The rage I feel toward myself is almost unbearable. How I so desperately wanted it all to be about Maxime that I was incapable of seeing through the veils Lila had hung, the way that she, like any good forger, worked to hide herself within her own art. The way he coached her to hide from my gift.

Of course she was the true genius. He kept her close, talking about her like she could destroy him. And yet he owned her. And when I got it so utterly wrong, he was only too happy to take all the credit. He must have known that I would figure it out—did he care? Or was he so certain of both Lila and me being so utterly under his thumb that it wouldn't really matter?

I feel sick at the way I've treated her, refusing to see her. I shudder at the way I responded when she asked me if I thought the artist was good.

But also this, this—*dissonance*, like two scenes mixed in one, competing to take over the landscape, is so familiar. I still feel the unease, but also, something is dawning on me. Something becoming clear so slowly I can't catch it yet.

I calm myself, examine the physicality of the piece more closely. There's a crack in it. One of the arms of one of the women has been patched into place.

That's the dissonance I can feel. His input, his rage when he broke it—her love and hope when she made it, the memories she poured in for me when she repaired it. Their voices are entwined, contradictory, making this piece complex to entangle. They both made it what it is.

Then it dawns on me: this is so similar to *Wrong Night Swimming*. All those sleepless nights I have struggled to get to grips with it, its reality crumbling under my feet like moving sand, the distortion of the voices and feelings so contradictory, so personal, so desperate that it nearly broke me.

That sculpture was broken, then repaired, too.

This opens a whole new realm of possibilities, but right now I need to help Lila. I know she made this for me to find.

I know she wanted me to see her and see what their relationship is really like. I think she wanted to tell me she sees me
too, that the only way we'll get out is by joining forces.

As I look around the workshop, I notice it's full of
other clay sketches that confirm Maxime's plans. They're
of Boisseau's *Anticipation*, clearly an attempt to repro-
duce it, already stunningly accurate. Lila is a chameleon, a
stunning forger, someone whose sight goes straight to the
heart of other artists' visions. She borrows their hands, like
Constance did in Boisseau's workshop. I remember Maxime
flirting with me under the shadow of *Anticipation* in Rennes,
how I swooned, and I feel sick. Lila's forgeries are almost
better than the originals, but they're also desperate, alone.
She's been trapped for so long, like a bird of paradise hitting
and hitting and hitting the window of a room it's fallen into
through the roof.

No wonder I found her sculptures in the attic difficult.
No wonder she was hooded, eluding me. She is the only one
who has the talent to be able to ply Avalon to her will, to
give me a run for my money. *I'm good at sneaking into places
I'm not invited.* She even snuck into Avalon that night in the
attic. Then she came in with me so naturally at the museum.
That I had even considered Maxime to be the key seems so
laughable now.

As I amble among the bodies, the strong muscles and
artful poses in a simulacrum of love, transfixed by Lila's
talent, I realize two things. One: I'm disposable. Once I have

authenticated the sculptures, sold the story and anchored Boisseau in D'Arvor, with the Foucaults, there will be no more Sorels. And Boisseaus sell themselves; of this quality, with the provenance firmly established, I doubt any expert will refuse the authentication. Maxime will sell them the story of his family secretly collecting them to honor their legacy—I won't be needed anymore. And I don't know what Maxime's plan is for me. Does he really think I will follow him through all of this? A huge business of forgery, spewing multimillion-dollar fakes into the world?

Yes, he does. Because you've been nothing but obsessed with him and his estate, and he knows it only too well. His madness feeds on your own.

Two: Lila is the one he needs. He won't ever set her free, unless I'm able to show everyone the truth.

Lila took a risk with this sculpture: she trusted me to find it, laid bare her soul and story for me to find, exposed herself to Maxime's wrath by deviating from his design. And I feel our kinship in my bones, having spent so long in her work, chasing her soul. Having felt awe, jealousy, sorrow, admiration, rivalry, companionship, connection to her. Having swum in complete darkness and faced the ravenous pikes and the stifling dining room of the Foucaults together. She watched me fall for the same man she did, for the illusions he spun. She watched me willingly break my wings and crash into the pit she was already in. She tried to warn me, as best as she could. I ignored her, envied her, and she forgave me.

Every night, we healed some of the madness in a cold, boiling pond.

We either get out of here together, or we don't. *This* is my choice, I think, as I feel her presence in the walls, an exhausted Lila, working through the day, before sneaking out and seeking the release of water. And the companionship I managed to offer her. This is where I regain my agency.

And then, there's Constance here too, smashing her work with a hammer. I know some of her story is here, trapped in the dust, perhaps even traces of her *Night Swimming*. But I think I know now what happened to it.

However, it doesn't feel so important anymore. That was the past, and I know I'll have to let it go in favor of what I have in my life that is real. Right now, I know I'm going to set Lila free. And for this, I will need to take Maxime down in a spectacular fashion.

33

RAIN IS POURING on the afternoon of the press conference. D'Arvor's austere medieval dining room has been set up with neat rows of simple wooden chairs, to command respect within the bareness of ancestral walls. Frédéric put up some kind of stage on which a trestle table showcases the sculptures, as well as a screen and laptop for my presentation. No need for a mic, he assured me, as sound travels well in the space.

I didn't ask for a mic. I didn't make any request. I'm sitting quietly in the tower room to the side, in the black dress I wore at the ball, wishing I could rip all this decor off my life in one confident gesture, like a tablecloth in those magic tricks. The rain is battering on the deep windowsill, not reaching the glass. The whole place hums with the voices of journalists, art experts, and academics. They're waiting for us.

"Remember, Camille, just as we discussed. Bring their

love story to life. Build the hype. Do whatever it takes in there to make them all yearn for her as much as you have. They must want to possess her, get under her skin."

"I know."

"You seem very calm," Maxime says. My hands are steady on the notes he's made me rehearse constantly this past week. He sounds troubled, like an overbearing parent coaching their child before their first performance. "I'm so happy we're in this together."

"Me too."

In my sleeve, I feel the edges of my other set of notes. The exposure of the truth. In my head, I go over my argument. I will tell them what happened calmly, step by step. I am an expert, respected in my field. Maxime is wrong— they'll have to believe me, like they believed the hundreds of authentications I have made in my career. When I lay this out rationally, they will hear me. I'm brimming with determination and fear.

—

The trick is to walk in and present yourself externally as if you belong, as if you are a step ahead of everyone else. More than the research, the hard work, the hours poring over dusty books and clicking through archives, that is how they believe you are an expert. It is all about the stories and a packaging that sells. I psych myself up, standing quietly next to Maxime as he takes the stage to talk about his family's history and spins a smooth, romantic lie about finding the sculptures in his attic, about his great-grandmother Anne, who had known Constance and preserved her in to this pristine state. He is doing the greatest job with the provenance, anchoring the story until it is so tight the sculptures might as well be bolted to the castle. I can tell the crowd is sold. The excitement runs through the room like a frisson.

Then, as planned, he steps aside for me. "What if we could show you, really show you, what Constance Sorel's life at D'Arvor has really been about? The truth about her inspiration. Over to you, Ms. Leray."

I take a couple of seconds to survey the room. I recognize some British and French journalists, people who have covered stories about juicy finds in the past. Those who were falling over themselves to report on the failed sale at Courtenay. Drama is rare, and good stories are worth their weight in gold. Rob is there too, in the first row, a giant with his arms crossed, right next to Dominique Foucault, who is looking paler than usual, an arm hugging the back of an empty chair next to him. My eyes meet Rob's, and he raises his iPad, as if to toast me. I remember his email, and my determination falters for a second.

Frédéric and Marie-Laure are at the back, like an afterthought. She's wearing a dark-red dress with pearls, he an impeccable gray suit, the perfect photo for *Paris Match*, looking the part of a benevolent noble family, just about tolerating all the fuss, avoiding the spotlight but willing to share their riches with the world. Benevolent enough to give us all a glimpse into the glamour of the other side.

The most imposing audience member is the castle itself. Marie-Laure and Frédéric are part of its furniture, trapped in its walls like ghosts of flesh and breath. This is the fate I'm forsaking, if I take my stand. In this moment before I speak, the headlines in a few years' time could still read: *Maxime and Camille Foucault decide to put another Boisseau up for sale, a true masterpiece, estimated at $4.5 million.*

This is what I'm about to give up. If I go ahead and speak with integrity, I will instead find myself having to deal with *me*—with no place to hide, no protection, staring at the blank canvas of my future. This upside-down world of deception that I have been obsessed with for so long was a distraction, a fantasy that prevented me from dealing with what I truly needed.

Then I see Lila, leaning against the back wall in her white shirt and dark pinafore, nervously knitting her fingers, who most people would mistake for an assistant, like I did that lifetime ago, and my heart soars. In this room of masks and mirrors, she is the only thing that is real. I know her truth, and she knows mine. She allowed me to see her authenticity, her vulnerabilities, she forgave me my failings and I know the friendship we have found for each other is better than the prestige of an orangery Louis XV flirted in. Better than the respect and admiration and envy of all of those influential people in front of me. Showing up for her is also finally showing up for myself.

I haven't seen her since I found her *Night Swimming*, and this time I'm so relieved she's back. It gives me the courage I need to start.

"Good afternoon. Thank you for coming. What we have here is very exciting indeed…" The room is hushed, iPads and phones drawn out in anticipation. I click on my laptop, to the title of my PowerPoint, vetted by Maxime of course. He nods to me, as if to encourage me to speak through my shyness. *I will save you. Just do exactly as I say; it will be all right.*

He can't even imagine that I might speak against him.

I breathe deep and dive in. "What we have here, ladies and gentlemen, despite what Mr. Foucault has just explained, are outstanding fakes."

The gasp bounces against the walls a few times until it hits me. I glance at Maxime, as my voice fills the stunned, thrilled silence.

"When Constance Sorel stayed in D'Arvor, she brought with her clay and heartache. Not only this—she was pregnant with Boisseau's child. But she didn't love him anymore. Here she found a simpler life and a greater relationship: her friendship with Anne Foucault, which quickly became the inspiration for her greatest sculptures. You can see these in the Musée des Beaux-Arts in Rennes. These sculptures in front of you are an attempt to ignore this friendship and, once again, tie Sorel to Boisseau. When actually, it was all about the women, their dreams of independence and autonomy."

I don't tell them Lila is the forger—I'm careful not to detract attention, the blame, from Maxime. I explain that he coerced a talented young artist into making these outstanding forgeries.

"The Foucaults are descended from Constance Sorel and Edmond Boisseau. And they would very much like you to forget how they treated her. In fact they'll do anything to twist her story to fit their needs. None of the sculptures you see here are by Sorel. They're masterpieces, forged to make you believe that she was nothing more than her love for Boisseau. They're extraordinary, but they're not hers."

When I finish, Maxime's smile is much more terrifying than the silence in the room. "Well, *that* was certainly a twist. Are you quite done, Ms. Leray?"

I glance at Lila, who is very still, her arms crossed on her chest. Then I look to the room, trying to read their faces, gauging how my bombshell has been received. They must believe me. These are my people. I was one of them only a few months ago. They should be my comfort zone, my support group, my cheerleaders.

I can see they're considering whether to laugh, with Maxime, at my intervention. The castle presses its walls on them, and Maxime is its commander. Surely what I did before, how I proved myself to them again and again, with every sale, every piece whose truth I brought to life, must have counted for something.

Maxime turns to the room again. "I'm extremely sorry. It seems that we too have fallen victim to Ms. Leray's delusions, or should I say *self-deception?*" He turns to me, his eyes brimming with mock concern.

He nods at Frédéric, who starts making his way toward the stage. He has to be kidding me—Fred Foucault is the least believable bouncer in the world. I think I could easily slap him out of my way, swat him away like a pesky fly. I feel strong, because I made a decision, and my core is hard like iron. I will not let him take me down.

"That's the truth. I know what you did. I'm the leading expert on Sorel, and I'm telling *you*"—I'm addressing the room more than Maxime, but I can tell it's not quite landing with them—"that these are not by her."

"This is a repeat of what happened in London, isn't it?" Maxime's voice. "You are so...*obsessed* with her, Ms. Leray. You can't accept there are parts of her you don't know. You are no longer able to accept when her narrative doesn't fit what you wanted her to be. *A strong woman who didn't need anyone.* All these sculptures, these couples are proving that she was broken by her doomed love affair with Boisseau, that his influence never left her, and you just hate it, don't you? That's feminism gone mad, ladies and gentlemen. Obsessed with feeding its own narrative at the expense of the truth." He shakes his head as I try to interject. "I believed you when you said you had recovered your mental health, that I could trust you to be objective with this. But alas, I was wrong." His hand falls on my elbow, his grip strong like a vise. "I can't believe I've trusted you enough to allow you to sneak into my family's affairs and poison them with your delusions. You need to leave now. We'll make sure you get the help you need."

"She's telling the truth." They all turn at once, to the back of the room. Lila's back has straightened, her hands in tight fists against her sides. She speaks before everyone, magnificent and brave. "I made the sculptures. First because he asked me to, then because he forced me. They're not Sorels. They're mine."

"And who are you?" They ask in concert, fingers furiously tapping in their notes apps.

"I'm Lila Madani," she says. Her chin is trembling.

I try to smile at her; I don't know if she can see me. There are so many people between us now, half standing up to scrutinize her. "You can't make me leave. They know the truth now," I tell Maxime.

"Camille…" How can they believe his eyes are genuinely saddened? I see the violence in them now, the cold, self-assured threat of someone who owns the narrative. "They don't believe you. Why would they? All you have done in the past few months is discredit yourself. I gave you a chance to go back to the truth, regain your prestige, but you're clearly past that. As for you." His gaze turns to Lila, and a frisson of excitement runs across all the gray heads like the top of a lake, and in this moment I *hate* them all. "I knew you craved the attention you never received in your childhood, but it has gone to your head. Do you really think they would buy that anyone is capable of copying Constance Sorel to this degree of precision? Furthermore, that *you* could have done it? There are lots of forgers in the world. But to be this good, it takes talent, and it takes guts. If you had either of those, people would have heard of you by now. All you have to your name is one failed exhibition at the back of a kebab shop where nobody bar me bought a single piece." He turns to the room again, addressing his kin. "I'm afraid there seems to be some kind of plot against me tonight. By all means, do your duty to investigate. I'm sure you'll find nothing untoward, and I would be grateful if you could put an end to these ridiculous claims and the relentless campaign to discredit my family's heritage."

I see on Lila's face that she realizes we've lost. We spoke the truth, together, as firsthand witnesses in this, and yet we weren't believed.

Rob has stood up, and for a split second, I think he's going to help us, but he addresses Maxime directly. "I'll take Camille back to London. Make sure she gets the right support."

He's been invited as some kind of guarantee, I realize now. As someone who's witnessed my downfall, he can vouch that there's a pattern to my madness.

My gaze goes from Frédéric, who has seized my upper arm, to Maxime on the other side, to Rob's embarrassed gaze. Not a single person in this room believes us. They're all willing to go along with Maxime Foucault, happily caught in his web of lies. Worse: they're enjoying the moment, like we all slow down on the motorway to catch a glimpse of an accident. Nausea takes hold of me when I realize Lila and I are the casualties they're fascinated by. What is going to happen next? Frédéric plying us with Xanax to ensure we slip away quietly or worse?

It must have been the same for Constance. Perhaps in this very room. I have flashes of her being wrestled away too—taken away *for her own good*. I'm not surprised she took a hammer to everything she could break. Her art had failed to speak for her, to be believed.

It's over. They think you're deluded. And it's all your fault. I don't know if that was Maman's voice, or Maxime's, bending to whisper quietly in my ear as I fight to keep my feet on the stage, to force them to acknowledge me for longer.

"I haven't tried everything I can yet," I tell him. My voice is not mine, low, cavernous, coming through water, and I know I'm gone already as I open my mind to Lila's sculptures behind me, and start welcoming the water into the room.

"You won't dare." *That's* him. He hisses it, peppering my skin all over with spikes of disdain. Rob and Frédéric manage to pull me away, and my feet leave the floor as they drag me, then land again, their faces registering fear as the black water rises to their knees, the muffled shouts of the assembled crowd, the door handle rattling.

It isn't a nice school outing this time. I don't give them a choice. The fabric of its violence comes from the rage I've repressed for most of the years I have been alive. It is coming from Lila too as I draw it all out of her sculptures, all containing the story of her ordeal, my past, her past, everything we have strained to push down and ignore, as we smiled and carried on topping up others' glasses.

Maxime's eyes meet mine. Unlike the others, he's not freaking out as water climbs up his legs, his waist, at a high rate. He and I are the only ones standing strong against the flow. "Remember you can only do this with me, Camille. Only if I'm here, allowing you. Without me, you're nothing. All you'll end up showing them is how insane and unstable you are."

"Fucking watch me, then," I hiss; then I open the gates and the flood takes all of them in with me.

—

This isn't a swim; it's allowing yourself to be sucked in by the most hectic whirlpool, thrown out of a shipwreck by a storm. I think this is how I end. Not only can I not breathe, the air knocked out of my lungs, but my soul is imploding. Convinced I'm going to die, I swim through every way in which Lila and I have been undermined, diminished, told we weren't good enough, encouraged to make ourselves smaller, better, quieter, to please. It's all here in this murky water and I can't find the light and it lasts for all the ages of the earth, my story mixing with hers. The people who let us down: Maman, Maxime, Rob, everyone Lila showed a piece of her art to before, who sneered at it; everyone who told us we didn't have the right background to make it, the right clothes, the right connections, the right approach, grabbing my feet to pull me down under, all their voices slashing at the core of me. Telling us we are impostors and are only too lucky they're willing to keep us around.

But, this time, I keep going and I stay strong, my rage the protective shield saving that small part of me that said, *Fucking watch me.* Fucking watch *her*—what *we* can do. I am so angry that I continue swimming because they told me I should give up and die.

After an eternity, I'm spat out of the pond into darkness, the eye of the storm. They're here with me, castaways trying to stand on wobbly legs. Storms make great noises, the ominous cracks of branches, the rain slashing against the earth like a whip. Rivulets of blood pool at our feet. They're all here—Frédéric, Marie-Laure, Dominique, Rob; everyone who was in that room, I've taken with me. They're small and terrified, lost children trying to find something to hang on to, some hugging the trunk of an old alder tree.

This is a world whose rules they don't know. This is her world, and mine.

"What's happening? Make it stop." Rob is on his knees, forehead smeared with blood, or mud, I don't know. I don't care. We're at the heart of Lila's art. All those sculptures on the trestle table, her blood and tears. They're alive here; they made the stone, the air, every part of this landscape. This Avalon is one big open wound.

"Watch," my voice repeats, hard. "Really pay attention, for once."

The hooded figure of the artist, whom I met in *Guinevere and Lancelot*, in *Morgane and Merlin*, *Uther and Ygraine*, in *Yvain and Laudine* is here, and gingerly the crowd makes space for her. A memory of Maxime is holding her, they're dancing.

You have an unbearable talent. You are extraordinary.

She laughs. *Careful. I might start to believe you.*

You stole my heart, and my eyes. What else do you want?

Your soul.

What will you give me in exchange?

With our eyes we follow them, watching as she tries to get away and climb the steep path, hitting a wall of air.

Not like that, like this. *You need to study better. You need to understand her. I'm disappointed in you. But I know you can do it, if you try harder.*

She bangs on the emptiness that restrains her.

My love—what would I do without you?

Never have tender words sounded so ominous.

You could be so much, and you settle for so little.

Don't make me do things I'll regret.

I know they see it too. Their story of love and coercion is entirely here, how she fell for him, how he "saved" her to trap her in a web of lies and deception and promises, until it was too late. It is all caught in the empty air, hanging like garlands in the soundless forest, the thorns of the gorse catching her ankles as she, repeatedly, tries to escape. I turn around, and he's gone. She is sobbing, down by the river, making small figures out of clay. Modeling, modeling, modeling, trying to channel someone who isn't her, to please him.

"Who is that?" voices ask behind me. "Who is the woman with Maxime Foucault?"

She told them, and they still don't believe it. I go to her. My hand on her arm doesn't make her flinch. I don't know if she feels it.

May I? She nods. She already spoke up and it changed nothing. *Thank you for showing it all to me. For putting all of this in here, trusting I would find it.* I remove her hood, and to my surprise I feel the soft fabric move with my fingers, until her face, haunted, beautiful, is revealed.

The silence is uncomfortable. *You were told. She told you.* This is not so much seeing with one's eyes; above all I make sure they *feel* it, are living it, images taking hold in their heads, inhabiting the nightmare of a love that turned so hard against her that she had to erase herself to survive. And she trusted me to tell her story.

I look into this Lila's tearful eyes and I think I'll die of a broken heart. Every stone, every molecule of this Avalon is imbued with her trauma. It is electric, painful, cutting my fingers and toes, fizzing under my skin like an infection. Every bit of this landscape reveals what she has been through, and the unfairness of it multiplies my rage until I can't contain it.

I fall on my knees in the river. My eyes are streaming, my heart bleeding, and I scream. The floor cracks open. The water runs red. Boulders tumble down from the steep slopes of the valley, some spiky like dragon scales, huge arrowheads narrowly missing Frédéric and two journalists trying to keep their footing on the shore. I don't say anything— they don't deserve a big moralizing speech about believing the underdog. About not seizing the most convenient, most sellable version of events. About siding with the power and the prestige. I want them to live her truth, and mine. Finally. More rocks fall; screams rise to the dark skies; the great crack of a bolt of lightning hits the surface of the pond. We might all get trapped here, die here, and I don't care. Now they know the sadness, the waste, the cruelty they've all been complicit in.

"Camille."

Her hand is on my shoulder, the only thing that can be warm here. I'm drenched in tears, in rain, in sorrow and frustration.

"Lila. Is it you? Or—*you*? Which you is it?" I ask. I'm drifting. Going too far, too big. My rage is running away from me, taking Avalon down. Taking everybody down.

Yet Lila stands next to me, and she smiles. "Come with me."

There's a lull in the disaster as I follow her into the storm, moving boulders out of our way, tree branches flattening. Everything is plying to our will, and together we make a path. I can still hear the others scream. Maxime is nowhere to be seen. Lila takes me to a quiet clearing, a few wisps of moonlight catching on the pond.

"What do you want to show me?" I ask, then I see the two women, swimming. Us. Another version of Lila and another version of me, circling each other under the stars, laughing at some nonsense, breathing the night, numbing their limbs.

"That's here too," she says. "Our *Night Swimming*."

The eye of the storm, the inception of the piece. Under us, the promise of authenticity, of freedom. Of friendship. In the upside-down world that we could go back to.

"The crystal castle was an illusion. We can't just make up a world with our own rules," I tell her. "It's always going to be theirs."

"But we can leave *this* messed-up place. Together, Camille."

I understand that she is offering her friendship to me. I understand that, with her help, I've already achieved what I needed to set her free. Now she's helping to set me free from becoming like him. From allowing him to guide my actions and taint me forever with cruelty and control.

"Got you," I say.

"And I got you."

The sound of thunder recedes as we walk hand in hand,

back to the Miroir aux Fées, welcomed back by terrified, exhausted white faces.

"Now you've seen what you needed to see to believe me," I tell them. "You better remember it when we get back."

I'm so tired, I could curl up here in the prospect of the end of the world and just sleep. But I open the gateway, guiding them back to the pond, the light twinkling at the bottom.

"Lila goes first," I tell them, and they follow her. I wait on the shore, ensuring nobody is left behind.

"Camille."

"Maxime."

We face each other at the edge of the water. His linen shirt, his messy curls of gold, his eyes. Everything I wanted for more than half of my existence on earth. As if my worth could only come from something so out of reach that it had to be created by my own mind. The solution to all my yearnings. Something completely and utterly fictional.

"I underestimated you," he says.

"So I *do* prefer the version of you you are here."

"And you ruined everything."

"On reflection, you're both equally unbearable."

"You know what's funny?"

"All the time and energy you've invested into a scam that has just come quite literally crashing down in your face?"

I realize he's breathing hard. He takes my hand and places it on his heart, just the way he did before the ball, during his panic attack. The contact of his skin still makes me fizz a bit.

Old habits die hard, but I know I won't need fifteen more years to get over him.

"Your career is ruined too. They'll never trust you again. That was too horrible, too scary, too inexplicable. You've made yourself a pariah. They'll turn away from you at parties. They won't give you the good commissions. You've ruined both of us, Camille. You and me. And you ruined Lila too, when you swooped in to rescue her. With me, she had purpose. She could have seen her art in all the biggest museums of the world. When she was trying to make it as an artist, she was sleeping in her car. We all needed each other to be something and you've broken us apart."

I could trap him here. He'll never be a threat here. Except...as he said, we've all lost most of what we spent years building. He doesn't even think that Lila and I could have found each other, which shows that he, after all, doesn't understand anything. He is holding me, I notice, quite a bit more tenderly than his words would imply. I consider kissing him, as a way of saying goodbye, then I realize I really don't want to. Oh—I guess I *am* free of him. That feels strange, after all these years.

"I don't *want* that career," I tell him, turning away, starting to wade through water. "Unlike you, I've gotten over caring about prestige. Unlike you, I have nothing to lose, and I will build the rest from scratch. I don't want D'Arvor, and I don't want you. And neither does Lila. Sort out your mess, and we'll sort out ours."

I feel him hesitate. This could be the Val Sans Retour for him. A way of avoiding his crumbling real world, and the way they're all going to look at him when we return.

The water is nice and cooling on my skin, and I realize there is no more fear in my heart. I know Lila is waiting for me on the other side, and that we'll leave D'Arvor together. I call to Maxime over my shoulder, "Come on. Let's go back."

Epilogue

I DIDN'T THINK I'd be downsizing in my thirties. But I have, so that my life suits me better, like a baggy dress I've had tailored. I sold my London flat for a small cottage along the Devon South coast, a perfectly ordinary white dot among the sea and sand and the dots of the other cottages. This landscape shines bright, as if applied in thick, rich paints by a palette knife: ochres, cerulean blue, pearl white. From my front porch, I can wave to Brittany. I like to keep it like this: at arm's length, or a seabird's voyage.

After what went down at D'Arvor, I crashed. It was different this time; I burnt out in a way that felt like purification. Lila and I retreated to my flat for a few weeks, living off macarons from the small French patisserie around the corner, laughing and crying and, for long periods of time, lying on our backs, staring at the ceiling. I think we were both painting on its surface, sketching what life could now look like. We got temporary jobs in cafés, in a bookshop, in a museum, life modeling (her, of course—are you mad?). I enjoyed those few months very much, being her housemate, figuring stuff out. Once she had saved up a bit, and when I bought the cottage, she returned to France and crashed with her brother in Paris. She was soon able to settle there properly: the articles that exploited Maxime's demise gave her the notoriety that helped launch her career as an artist. So, ironically, I guess he *did* help her. At first, people turned up to see the work of the woman who had nearly conned the art world out of millions but came clean. Soon they bought her work outright because she is a genius.

I might have visited every one of her exhibitions, and I might have made sure people *really* understood her. "Helped" them connect to her. She never asked me if I used my power. I think she knows, like I do, that her work is strong enough to speak for itself. I just had to make sure people saw it. I didn't spend my life honing and growing this power never to use it—but from now on, I will make sure I use it only for truth.

For myself, I wanted a project. I was itching to make something from scratch that was mine. For all my life, I knew now, I had plied myself to other people's projections and expectations; I had put them on like cloaks to beg them to see me. I was appalled at how far I had gone chasing those dreams. I had to stop and tap into myself. It was hard, confusing, allowing all the layers of others to fade away first. It took a while to settle. I didn't know who I was, what I liked, when I had not been given a task or a set of expectations. I fell in love with the cottage because the previous owners had gutted it bare, then changed their mind and put it up for sale. The first thing I did was whitewash its internal walls, creating the empty canvas of my life. I knew there was so much to do and I might have to paint all over again further down the line, but it brought me joy.

It still brings me joy, as I sit at the little table in the main living space and drink my tea and watch the sea. It is a camping table, and the chairs are mismatched, scratched wood and rusty legs. The only other piece of furniture in the living room is a battered leather sofa by a gaping hole that used to be the fireplace. I like to curl up there and read.

There are no walls upstairs; the space just about passes as a bedroom, if you squint and ignore the paint marks on the bare floor. A big window opening onto the sea, a double bed, which was left behind, and a free-standing bathtub looking out. The only toilet is in a pokey room under the stairs. It's a mess of bareness, of absence, and I love the potential of it. I love the silence now, because it is filled with *my* thoughts, the beats of *my* heart, *my* breathing. The clink of my mug of tea on the table. I am here. I deserve to exist. From now on, I am choosing to try to be good.

I found a job in a gallery in a town along the coast. It was run-down, struggling, and I fell in love with it and its owner, a gorgeous, clever activist woman, past retirement age, called

Moira. I started as an unpaid helper; I think, given my credentials, she must have wondered what the catch was. But my heart knew that this was the right place, for now. Like a fairy godmother, I adopted it, sprinkled some magic on it—magic, or love? Passion? Hope? Now, two years later, we attract visitors from all over England. We mostly show deserving, underappreciated young artists from underprivileged backgrounds. There's nothing "under" about their work, and somehow, *somehow*, people give them a chance. Then, with a little help, they quickly gain the confidence to speak for themselves. We help them, and they help us. They come back and see us, they send us their progress, they treat this place like home.

I have a home.

The knock on the door today comes when I'm just putting the finishing touches on the dossier of our next exhibition. The work is so colorful, so full of hope and joy and sherbet, laced with Afrobeat, it is making my heart sing and dance as I type. I slap my laptop shut, tackle the uneven stairs cautiously on my way down. The work is still ongoing; little by little, I'm building my own castle.

"Hello!"

Lila drops her travel duffel bag on the doorstep. We hug tightly.

She takes in her surroundings. "Still very much a work in progress since I last came."

"What? *This* wasn't here. And *that* wasn't finished. *Loads* has happened."

She cocks her eyebrow at me.

"Well, *you* have changed. Is that a new haircut?" I ask.

"I've had it a month now."

"It suits you."

In the past couple of years, the internal Lila I got to know has been reclaiming the external Lila that had been washed off by D'Arvor and its inhabitants. There are no more navies or grays in her wardrobe. She kept the Chanel pumps and matches them with her outfits in a way that feels irreverent, cheeky—utterly her. Today she is a mermaid in teal, her hair fading into pink highlights. I have loved seeing her grow into herself, healing all over like a garden after the apocalypse.

She grins; then in a flash she's running upstairs; I follow to find her splayed out on my bed, giggling. I remember her on Constance's bed at D'Arvor, transfixed—a shadow of what she is today. Yet, that cheekiness was there. That spark that now runs free, setting fires all around the world. I'm so grateful she's allowing me to fuel some of my energy on it.

I lie down next to her, she finds my hand, and we both look up at the ceiling.

"You know you're staying in the guest studio, right?" I say after some contented silence. "This is my bed. You're not having it."

"*You* should move to the studio. I can't believe you finished doing it up before your actual house."

"I wanted you to know you'll always have a place to stay."

"And I love you for it. But you know I'm quite comfortable now. Financially."

"I guessed as much. I've seen all the press about your latest exhibition."

"Still. It helps to know about the studio. It really does," she says.

Turns out she was indeed living in her car when she met Maxime; he stumbled upon a struggling exhibition of her works, immediately identified her gift, bought her coffee, and proceeded to convince her that she would never make it without his help. Sound familiar? We don't talk about him or what happened in D'Arvor anymore. It feels like a different age, a different life. But it bonds us. We both know we wouldn't have gotten out and through without each other. Except there's one last thing we need to do.

"Have you heard from Lowen?" Lila asks, apropos of nothing. She always asks me, and the answer is always the same.

"No."

"He still doesn't know you live a mere hour away from him?"

"Have *you* heard from him?" I ask, as I always do. Of course I've thought about him, over these past two years. Every day, when I watch the sea, I remember him teaching me to swim. That trust Lila and I now have, I used to have with him. I also remember how badly I treated him; how he always tried to convince me to take the safer path, never understood what drove me, either. It didn't feel right to jump right back into our friendship, or more, when I was still so raw that I ran the risk of letting myself be molded by someone else's expectations. I had to grow into myself first, before seeing if we still fit, and on what grounds. Turns out it's a long process.

She shrugs. "We still text occasionally. I follow him on Instagram. The bakery's doing so well."

"Ah, is it?" I feign detachment. Obviously I stalk him on Instagram too. The social media account popped up after his course, and soon fine pastries started sharing the spotlight with his father's traditional scones and iced buns. Lowen has built up quite the following, and he's become more experimental. I love that bravery for him, wondering whether that might be the bridge we need to start moving toward each other again.

I know Lila isn't fooled. She smiles at me with acceptance, and impatience. I shoo her off. "Are you ready for tomorrow?" She asks, propping her head up with her hand.

"I think so. I know it sounds silly, but I need to say goodbye."

"I understand. Me too, to be honest."

"Thank you for coming with me."

———

Last month, I found out that the sculpture that started everything, the one I had labeled *Wrong Night Swimming*, was to be loaned to a small museum in Exeter for its exhibit on *Women and the Sea*. I drive Lila there the next morning and we play Clara Luciani in the car, windows open to the Cornish drizzle, our hair frizzing and our voices singing in unison. *Respire encore. Breathe again.* Or *breathe, still.* A perfect girly road trip, Marie-Laure would say. I remember her slicing carrots, snipping roses, blood prickling at the tips of her fingers, and I am so grateful for the life I have chosen for myself.

I know the curator and I've managed to obtain permission for a private viewing an hour before it opens to the public. The exhibition has been quite successful, with a couple of big pieces on loan, Lichtenstein's *Drowning Girl*, and a sketch by Monet. Lila and I greet the staff who are setting up for the day, then slip through the corridors into the temporary exhibition. The sculpture is on a pedestal in the corner, easy to forget, even in a small showcase.

We sit side by side on the bench in the middle of the room, watching it.

"So, it was the real *Night Swimming* all along," Lila says after a while.

I nod. "Back where it all started. I just couldn't see it back then. It's your work that made me understand it."

It was finding Lila's *Night Swimming* and realizing that the dissonance I found in it came from the fact it had been broken. Maxime's rage, his own emotions had imbued the piece. I realized that Constance's *Night Swimming* had been so hard to read, that it was so traumatic, because it had been broken too. She had taken a hammer through her piece when they threatened to section her. She had been afraid, devastated, thought herself betrayed by her friend. Then it had been tampered with, someone repairing it, pouring their own sorrows into it.

"You don't have to go in if you don't want to," Lila says.

"And you don't have to come with me."

She bumps her elbow against mine. "You're not the only one who needs closure. I need to say goodbye to her too."

I bump her back. "Let's go, then."

We close our eyes as we welcome the water into the room; then we swim into Avalon.

———

When we come back, we smile at each other through the tears. We sit for a bit longer as the exhibition opens, people start wandering into the room, mothers with babies in prams and a gaggle of art students who settle to make some sketches. Everyone seems to ignore Constance's great lost masterpiece. It sits quiet, isolated, mislabeled.

I sit quietly too, knowing it was my last time getting into her mind. I had been right all along; *Night Swimming* was her last work, and it finished her story. In its contradictions, its many layers, it managed to be a story of love, or friendship, a story of betrayal and madness and being lost, of great sorrow and grief, all at once in the different hands that tampered with it. Constance made it as an ode to her friendship with

Anne, destroyed it when she thought Raymond had taken her baby and Anne was complicit in her internment; then Anne repaired it. In her repairs I felt her sorrow, loss, and panic. I felt her empathy for her friend's state, her own feelings of entrapment in a life Constance had help her dream of leaving. Her plan to bring *Night Swimming* to Boisseau and get it cast in bronze, sold. With the money, she thought she would be able to get Constance out of the asylum. She thought she could put it all right.

That's where her thoughts left. I knew, because I had traced it back myself, that Boisseau sold it from his workshop years later. He never helped. Even after Constance's death, even after her child's, Anne kept waiting for her to return.

"That was tough," Lila says, "but so worth it."

"Yes." Together, we found both of them in there. Constance, and Anne, or Viviane. They had wandered in fragmented universes of misconceptions and poisoned stories. I tried to repair as much as I could, make it nicer for them there. A place they could rest together. Then Lila and I laid flowers on the lake to say goodbye. Daisies, bright blue hydrangeas.

"Are you going to let people know that this is actually it?" Lila asks, as we watch people walk in, straight to *Drowning Girl*.

"I don't think so. I think I'm done with it. Someone else can figure it out."

We sit a bit longer, and I think about the crossroads of

our lives. The times we decide what matters. When we take a stand. I'm so glad I stood for Lila, and she stood for me.

"So, what now?" Lila asks me.

"Do you fancy a swim?"

She shakes her head. "Later, maybe." She's getting fidgety, and I know what this means. Sugar.

"I think we need some pastries," I tell her, and her eyes light up. "And I know just the place, if you're up for a girly road trip to St. Ives?"

Lila chuckles, but also in anticipation of the lemon curd and apple-cinnamon donuts. I smile in anticipation of Lowen's stunned face when we come in. I'm hoping he has been waiting, like he always has. If he has…we have a lot to figure out. It might be forgiveness, or friendship; it might be love, or only nostalgia. One small step at a time, I guess. There's no pressure to figure it out all at once.

As we drive to him across the narrow leg of Cornwall, and Lila and I fall silent, I know I'm leaving it all behind for good now. D'Arvor, Constance, Anne and Raymond, the Foucaults, my old narrow definition of art. Now I know there's art everywhere, open to everyone. It is where the golden line of a beach meets the deep gray of the sea. It is how Lila ties up her hair. It is a simple perfect chocolate éclair. It is in the way we connect, thrive off each other. Without art we are empty shells. It is a portal into what makes us human, that push and pull between our beautiful and tragic lives, and our ability to make them more beautiful and more tragic with our minds, our eyes, and hands. Art is the tide of humanity. We advance, and we recede, and we are alive.

My job is to open that portal. I do this in a small whitewashed gallery in a little town on the coast. I open my eyes and heart to what they have to say, those beautiful, deserving artists who have taken the bravest step: putting their hearts out there, creating a bridge, a connection to others. Shouting, *We are here. Can you see us?* I strengthen that bridge; then it is up to them, all of them, the makers and the receivers, to do the rest.

I didn't use to think I could ever be enough. I strove to be accepted in cold, inhospitable spaces. And now, I am here. Camille Leray—no more, no less. And everything I need is within my reach.

Reading Group Guide

1. At the start of the story, our main character, Camille, is not only facing a problem with her magic but is also experiencing intense burnout from work. Have you ever experienced this feeling in your professional or personal life, and if so, what did you do to overcome it?

2. Camille has the power to enter artwork and see the worlds, feelings, stories, and truths imbued within them. If you had this ability, what artist or artwork would you want to enter the most and why?

3. D'Arvor is an old French estate that the Foucault family inhabits. What does the estate, and the Foucaults, symbolize for Camille, and how does her vision of D'Arvor change throughout the novel? Do you have anything in your life that symbolizes your desires?

4. Camille's powers reveal that something is wrong with the statues found at D'Arvor. What did you think was happening when the mystery was first introduced? Were you surprised by the truth revealed at the end?

5. Why is Camille so drawn to Constance's work, and how has her obsession influenced her career? Then, think about your own relationship with art. Have you ever connected with an artist (whether it is a musician, writer, painter, etc.) or an artwork in the way Camille connects with Constance?

6. Camille doesn't always make decisions based on what is right but is often driven by her own desire for success. What did you think about this, and in what ways did she change as the novel progressed? Did you find her to be a relatable character?

7. One of the central themes that course through the novel is obsession. How does obsession manifest in all the characters? Do you think obsession is a good or bad thing? Why or why not?

8. In the end, we find out the truth about *Night Swimming*. Why did Camille have such a visceral reaction to it the first time, and how does that change when she sees it in the end? What does this ending reveal about the fate of Constance, and how did the truth make you feel?

9. At the end of the novel, Camille says, "Without art we are empty shells." What did she mean by this? Do you agree? Why or why not?

A Conversation
with the Author

In this book, you have not only woven in a beautiful speculative element but also created an incredibly detailed world of art and history. What inspired you to write this story?

As a writer, I love exploring the places in our lives where magic *could* happen. The boundaries where, if things were only a tiny bit different, reality and fantasy might start to mix and blur. I need to see that sense of magic spurred on by something real that I have felt or experienced. My first novel, *Five First Chances*, explored time travel linked to mental health. For *The Estate*, the idea of exploring the way art can act as a window into the artists' lives and can make us feel other people's feelings and transport us into their world came naturally. I have always loved art and studied history of art at university as part of my degree, but even before that, in my teens, I discovered the tragic and fascinating life of Camille Claudel, a French sculptor whose works and fate stayed with me all those years. Every time I go to Paris, I make sure to pop into the Rodin Museum to visit her sculptures! Once I decided that I wanted to write about art and obsession, the character of Constance Sorel grew from that inspiration. There are many differences between Claudel and Sorel, but this is where it all started.

If you were to enter any artist's work, who would it be and why?

I would have to say Claudel now, wouldn't I? However, given that she struggled with her mental health at various points of her life, that might not be a very enjoyable experience. That said, I adore her sculpture called *The Waltz*, and I would love to visit her moment of inspiration for this. It is such a beautiful composition, with both lovers dancing tenderly at the edge of losing their balance. I wonder if she poured some of her love for Rodin in there, but I don't want to be like Maxime and assume everything she did was about her lover! Otherwise, I would love to have the ability to "visit" arts and crafts, some of the anonymous creations that can be found in museums around the world. Pottery, jewelry…I would love to be able to find out about the lives of the craftspeople who made those and have access to a slice of life in all those cultures and civilizations.

Camille is a complex character, one who you want to root for until the very end. What was it like writing her?

She was easy to write but less easy to like at times. Her drive and ambition, her deep emotional burnout, and her need for external validation all came together—I gathered quite quickly how everything she does comes from the fact that she never got that validation from her mother or her peers. Her struggles were painful to write at times, and throughout the drafting process, I understood how far she had to go as an antihero to realize how powerful she can be so that she can stop relying on others by the end and let go of her obsession with Maxime and his world. I knew some of her decisions, particularly the way she is with Lila and Lowen at the ball, would make it perhaps more difficult for readers to like her, but I really hope they can accept that she had to make mistakes in order to realize what she truly wanted to stand for in the end. I wanted to create a character that had to work out where her integrity lay and what she would sacrifice to be her authentic self, and that came with challenges.

Where do you find your creative inspiration?

Ideas for novels tend to come to me once I have just finished a project, but I would say that my process doesn't really rely on inspiration... I wish I could sit and wait for the muse to sing to me! Generally, it's by showing up at my desk and starting to type the things that come to me or by discussing kernels of ideas with my long-suffering husband (who is the absolute king of plotting!). That said, fishing for ideas and inspiration comes when I'm in a particular mood, which I need to consciously activate: some kind of openness to the world, a willingness to *really* look at what is going on around me, on television, in strangers' lives and conversations around me...

The process is like rooting around in sand for little nuggets of gold and thinking, *I could use this!* Art is very inspiring—I could stand for a long time in front of a painting or sculpture and wonder who those people are, what happened before and after the snapshot of the picture... And that's the same for older stories: there are lots of nods to Arthurian legends in this book, and as someone who studied classics and medieval French at various points and who loves listening to history podcasts, I'm spoiled for choice!

What's your writing process like? Do you have any tips for new writers who don't know where to start?

I don't think I know what my process is like yet. Or rather, I'm hoping it won't turn out to be what my process for my first two books has been, which has been to write and rewrite and rewrite and throw lots of words out while trying to figure out the story... I always tend to start with a situation, not a story, and this makes plotting difficult. So my advice to new writers would be: Don't be afraid of conflict. Ask yourself what your characters want, and put many obstacles, internal and external, in their way. Give them agency. Allow them to make mistakes and have to scramble to make it up to their loved ones. As per the act of writing itself...I don't think there's a secret to it, apart from showing up and doing it. I love writing, and yet most of the time, I would much rather sit and watch a cooking show instead of opening my computer. You have to be really disciplined, but the key to doing this is to set yourself up for success by keeping your goals realistic. Writing five hundred words a week is better than not writing at all!

What are you reading these days?

I work full-time as well as being a writer, so I honestly find it difficult to find much time to read. Recently, I have enjoyed some romances by Ali Hazelwood and Mhairi McFarlane, and I am currently reading *Tomorrow, and Tomorrow, and Tomorrow*, which I am loving. My tastes are quite varied, but I love stories about complex relationships, whether on the more romance-y or literary side. I really like books that surprise me by busting their genre bubble too or not quite fitting anywhere! *Isaac and the Egg* by Bobby Palmer was a perfect example of something really different and moving that I enjoyed recently.

Acknowledgments

This book (the dreaded second novel!) would not have been written if it wasn't for the support and encouragement of many. Therefore, many thank-yous go to my agent, Olivia Maidment, who believed in the story enough to allow me to go a bit rogue and who kept me going through times of self-doubt and near creative burnout. Knowing I can always fall back on your support and wisdom is priceless. To my editors at Sourcebooks, the fabulous MJ Johnston and Liv Turner, whose insightful notes brought the final novel much closer to my initial vision! Thank you, as well, to the wider teams at Sourcebooks and at Madeleine Milburn Literary, TV and Film Agency for their help shaping and promoting this story. To name but a few: Jessica Thelander, Gianni Washington, Anna Venckus, and Cristina Arreola at Sourcebooks; Valentina Paulmichl, Hannah Kettles, Hannah Ladds, and Casey Dexter at Madeleine Milburn Agency.

I have taken much creative license with Camille's job in an art auction house, as well as the places mentioned in this book. I am extremely grateful to Francesca Whitham for sharing her experience and insight as a picture specialist at Dreweatts. Her enthusiasm and passion for her job really shone through, and Camille's personal experiences bear no resemblance to what came from our discussions—thank you so much, Francesca, for so patiently answering all my basic questions and letting me know about the measuring tape you always carry in your bag! Thank you to Fanny Goujon from Bretagne Buissonnière who arranged the best research trip in and around Rennes, Brocéliande, and the castles in the area. D'Arvor is made up, but if the area has caught your imagination (as I hope it will!), I would highly recommend the Château des Rochers and Château de Combourg, both residences of prominent French writers, as well as one of Fanny's guided visits of Brocéliande. Thank you too to Belinda, chauffeur-guide extraordinaire, who drove me around and provided me with many Breton culinary delights.

The eagle-eyed of you might have noticed that a quote from Camille Claudel opens the book and that aspects of Constance Sorel's life and art bear some resemblance to Claudel's, especially her relationship with Rodin. Although most of Sorel's life is entirely invented, I would encourage readers with an interest in sculpture to check out Claudel's work. Since I discovered her in my teenage years, I have felt she deserved better recognition beyond France, and her

Soy

complex, sometimes controversial story is certainly worth exploring.

It is a while since I completed my master's in medieval French studies, and I hope the poetic license I took with Arthurian legends and characters will be forgiven. What is the point of these stories if not their tweaking to fit our own narratives? They have been constantly reinvented since their inception, and I wanted to pay homage to them here, as they have played an important part in my imagination.

A special thank-you to my mother, Barbara Jost, to whom this novel is dedicated and who bears no resemblance to the Maman in this book. Having lived the first few years of her life in Brittany, she's always felt a connection with it in heart and spirit, and she and Dad brought us moody teenage girls along to explore it on a few summer holidays. I'm grateful to you for introducing us to that beautiful region and its rich heritage and legends. I hope I've done it justice in this book. Thank you for loving us much better than the fictional parents I wrote here.

Finally, thank you, Luke, for keeping me going through doubts and meltdowns and patiently helping me make sense of my plot. Without you I'd still be trying to untangle myself from this story. I'm so grateful for your patience, honesty, and love.

About the Author

Sarah Jost was born and grew up in Switzerland in small yet stunning Montreux against the backdrop of Lake Geneva and the Alps. She studied medieval French, modern French, and history of art at the Université de Lausanne and worked part-time as a publishing assistant alongside her studies. She has been living in the UK since 2008 and works as a French teacher at a girls' school, which she considers an immersive course in character study. Sarah lives in Buckinghamshire with her husband, Luke, and their adorable and goofy golden shepherd, Winnie.

Five First Chances

What would you do if you had one more chance to get things right?

Lou feels like she is stuck on the wrong path: alone, in a city far from home, watching other people be happy. When the man she's in love with announces his engagement to someone else, Lou is consumed by "what ifs."

That's when she finds herself slipping back in time to a night two years ago, where one small decision changed everything…

Suddenly, Lou has a chance to fix her mistakes. But as her choices lead her down roads she never could have imagined, she finds herself stuck in a time loop of her own making. And with each slip, Lou notices her life intersecting with one person again and again. A friend of a friend who once lived on the periphery, who is slowly becoming the one person who makes her feel like she might finally be on the right track.

Lou is about to realize that our greatest love stories aren't always the ones we expected, but are the ones we choose to fight for.

"Anyone who has ever wished for a do-over will see themselves in Jost's poignant tale of love lost and found." —*Publishers Weekly*

For more Sarah Jost, visit:
sourcebooks.com